The Holy Grail

Also, by Sarah Delamere Hurding

StarScope

StarScope with Psychic to the Stars Sarah Delamere Hurding

Sarah correctly predicted the final line up of the pop band Six.
Bono called her in when he was setting up his Kitchen nightclub at
The Clarence, and according to Louis Walsh, she's
"the woman who knows everything."
Now Ireland's top psychic has decided to share her gift in probably
the only horoscope guide, you will ever need to buy.
For the inside track on where your love, life, career, and health
are heading, keep this by your bedside.
Which celebrity shares your birthday? What lies ahead for you this year?
Are you in the right relationship or are you and your partner completely
compatible? Are you in the right career?
Where should you go on holiday?

Get your life in balance with Sarah and *StarScope*
Published by *Poolbeg Ireland.*

The Holy Grail

A Love Story

by
Sarah Delamere Hurding

Published by
Rainbow Wisdom
Ireland

ISBN: 978-0-578-77989-8

CONTENTS

CONTENTS

CONTENTS

PART ONE

1242

CHAPTER ONE
The Cabin

Sari could hardly compose herself as the tears threatened to stream down her face. She could feel the damp heat pricking behind her eyes. She was conflicted between putting on a brave face and giving into the well of grief that threatened to overwhelm her. For the sake of composure and a serene atmosphere she decided to err on the side of caution. She knew that her father Frederick might be dying. His vibrant life force, usually steady and tangible, was fast diminishing, no longer emanating that visible glow she so happily bathed in as a child.

Frederick's body was weak and his spirit frail. Usually his ailments responded to the healing energy pulsating through her veins. But this time she felt things were different. Nothing was guaranteed. The heat from her hands was not reaching through the growing resistance within him. She knew he was on the brink of giving up. The Eternal Father seemed to be calling, or this would be what he thought, if he objectified himself in this moment.

Sari was also struggling and exhausted. Daily, she grappled with forces she did not fully understand. She appreciated that she had contracts which sometimes required her to act, and at other times required her to let go. Usually it was clear which option was required. She was generally efficient and detached and not personally invested.

This time, her whole world was threatening to crumble. Frederick was everything to her. Her life, her reason for living and her support system. The rock on which she secured herself, or the rock on which she floundered. She really did not know what to do. This unfolding tragedy was beyond her remit. She pondered the consequences of that ominous, reluctant inner shift of surrender she knew may be immanent. She baulked at her own resistance. She was vulnerable and human with no pretence of coping. She found herself trembling from deep within at the prospective shock.

Sari had powers that could normally intervene. She could often at least try to make a difference to ease someone's suffering or exit from this world. But she was all too painfully aware that sometimes she had to step back and let the Divine Will prevail. In this moment she did not know who she was, nor who she should pretend to be. She had reached the boundary of her experience. She was a suddenly floored child sitting before a resilient, all conquering beloved father, not knowing what to do.

Did he have the answers this time?

She thought not.

Tuning into the elements raging outside the primitive wood and stone hut they sheltered in, she checked her energy levels, gaining comfort from the intense thunder, as it ripped through her substance, to the core of her being. From deep in the night, mighty Thor empowered her and countered her fear. She allowed this charge-up safe in the knowledge it would prime her for what might happen next.

Sari had always loved the thunder. She was a full moon thunder child. Born in the light and shade of an eerie Scorpio eclipse. The thunder always spoke to her. She was a child of the air with powers of transformation and transmutation. People did not understand her. She understood this. Her frequency was beyond the world in many ways.

Things were always clearer by dawn.

She reassured herself, as she lay down beside her father listening to his short shallow breath. The slightly rasping sound was unsettling, and she wondered if it would simply just stop. She knew he would be okay with this, having long ago given up his soul in generous servitude for the greater good. But she, as loyal daughter, and stoic warrior, was a determined protector of his interests, or what she thought them to be at least.

Deep within she had resolved to fight the forces that threatened to take her father out for as long as she could remember. She had always done so, and she owed him the same commitment this time surely.

Or did she?

Her father perhaps did not at this point have the strength to decide or have an opinion. She could fight his fight and take the energy on. But if he really was resigning to the inevitable there was not much more she should do.

Frederick loved life, and although he was always ready to surrender to the ethers in theory, she felt if he were fully in his rational mind, he would choose to stay put. For now. They had so much planned and so much they still wanted to achieve; not least this major journey to France they had just embarked upon.

Others had wanted them gone. It was true. This was ever apparent in their daily struggle, and for once they were trying to oblige. If they could suit themselves, as well as the burdensome "others" they could facilitate a new dynamic that might benefit everyone.

As a duo Frederick and Sari were formidable. They knew things. He was a village elder. The wise one. The counsellor. She was his sage and muse. He would not always listen, but he always asked. Even though he looked to her for confirmation, she found that he always knew best. Except in those rare moments when he did not. This was when Sari came into her power. When her ability to see beyond the obvious was appreciated. When her insights and perspective and healing were asked for. As with her father, so with all people. Situations presented only when she was meant to do something. Folk came to her when they were at the end of their tether. When their own knowledge, experience, or comprehension had failed them. Otherwise, she had to let it be.

Sari had learned long ago that she should not impose her energy, nor indeed any information on those who did not seek it. Although she wished to help anyone that she could, she had to learn the discipline of leaving things alone. For some, it was their destiny to flounder. She had to accept this. It was not her position to decide for them. She must not to try to override their fate in any way. She was not The Almighty. She knew this. Nor was she a performance act.

Besides, there was always a price to pay when she engaged her energies. Despite her natural impulse to assist, she had to be selective. Although the temptation was to intervene where she should not, even to show off if baited in some way. She remained humble. In her rightful place as maid servant of The Divine. Always attentive. Always primed. Always listening. Always watching for what came next. Her next instruction.

No one understood Sari and Frederick. But they were inevitably called upon when the community was stuck, in flux, or sinking amidst division. There were suspicious factions and agendas always lurking in the background. Hovering, and blocking their best intentions. The forces of darkness monitored their ministry, and there was at times a sense of confinement and constriction, which felt bigger than their best endeavours. Sari knew it was ultimately not possible for them to thwart

Divine Intention. But she knew also that is was best to allow the toxic elements and shadowy figures to think they were all-conquering and all-powerful.

People would turn on them without a moment's notice, while in the next breath expecting them to deliver a definitive prophecy, a lifesaving piece of advice, or a miraculous healing. None of this made any sense. None of it ever would.

Things would be clearer by dawn.

Sari soothed herself again with the thought, as the storm descended, and enveloped the rugged Scottish landscape that elevated her spirits most of the time. She loved her native lands: the brooding damp fogginess of twilight. The smells of heather and wild deer on the breeze. The rustic colours, and vivid intensity of the sodden elements. The Highlands were her inspiration and backdrop. She was not sure she would even have her powers if she were removed from its rhythmic seasonal sounds and senses. She was amplified in all ways by her environment. The Scottish habitat inspired her life force, keeping it vibrant and engaged. The blood of the cattle coursed through her veins, and the unrelenting rain pulsated the beating of her heart. She was nature: nature was she. Sari knew nothing beyond the music of the mountains, the sparkling streams, the squawk of the hawk, and the bleating of the lambs.

"Pappa! Pappa!"

Sari urgently stirred her father as he coughed and spluttered in his sleep. Some disquieting dream disturbed what had become quite a peaceful countenance. She had been watching him sleep, unable to rest herself with the elements swirling outside. Her head filled with the impressions of all that had gone before, and all that she sensed was yet to come.

At points during the witching hours she thought he might be drifting off, and she became the detached observer of his process. She was not disengaged or without emotion. But she had come to realise a few hours into his fever that he would survive this part of the challenge. The prickling tears which had threatened to fall had subsided as she took solace in his deeper more resonant breathing.

Frederick half opened his eyes for a minute to flicker his vision around the room and scan his senses through their surroundings. Seemingly satisfied, he vaguely smiled, and drifted off into a more profound, restful, healing sleep. Sari dared to consider sleep herself when she saw that he had surmounted the fever. She was at least assured he would slumber more easily and less dangerously until the morning light, when she would have to make the decision to continue their journey or retreat home.

She was full of the awareness that it was now or never with their plans. If they doubled back, she would surely have to go it alone, leave her father behind, and travel to the place where she knew her destiny awaited. She was the living breathing oracle of a sacred lineage. She had no choice but to be the vessel she was called to be. Her adventure of deliverance beckoned. Possibly no one could help her really. Perhaps this rehearsal of her father's demise was due warning that he could not carry her or accompany her any longer. That she needed to take the hint and not drag him along on a treacherous journey he was clearly not able to achieve.

CHAPTER TWO

The Contract

O n the days that the crystal waters of the still lake were
particularly luminous, Sari could see herself reflected. She
could never quite comprehend or identify with the mirrored
beauty staring back at her. Sari felt far removed from the watery image.
Did not relate to it or connect with it. Indeed, it left her puzzled. She
did not understand how or why her mere presence stirred such intense
emotions in those she encountered. That she could engage complex
reactions without even opening her rosebud mouth to speak was truly
beyond her ken.

The perceived combinations of strength and beauty, wisdom, and
enchantment, for which she was renowned, were to her unrelatable.
She was aware of her power certainly. But she had not fully grasped
how much of it was conjured through her physical presence. In short,
she did not have to do much to make an impact. Her intentions, focus,
and being were enough to make waves. Her very existence stirred

ripples and created results. She ensured the magic. Fancy rituals, spells and incantations were not required. She was more than enough.

Sari's tangible covenant with The Divine was the edge she had over others that disarmed people. But it was also the mysterious means by which she could help them. She did not always understand the complete picture or the extensive mission to which she had been called. But she knew in any given moment what was required. She had an obligation to address those who crossed her path who requested or needed help. To those that actively sought her out, she must be available and open.

Sometimes her ability to protect herself from energy vampires who would suck her life force became compromised. But these were the lessons and challenges that ultimately strengthened her, enabling her to work at even more impressive levels of alchemical expertise. Sari concentrated on her inner world. Her unspoken worries and concerns. She did not see what she had going for her in worldly terms. Really, she had nothing going on in worldly terms, despite what anybody may have thought. She did not have the type of character that could trade-off her appearance. She certainly did not see herself or her skills as a currency. It was quite the contrary. Sari felt burdened by her gifts and supposed blessings. None of them seemed to bring her goodness, peace, nor quiet.

Deep within, Sari longed for a settlement and fulfilment she knew she would never quite achieve in this lifetime. Her other-worldly qualities and appearance opened doors, but only to facilitate her task in the service of others. True, she never went hungry. But when Sari was not monitoring her father and all his needs, she was looking after those who came to seek her countenance. Those in search of healing, solace, and information.

Her 'contracts' – they could hardly be called customers - may have liked to gaze upon her. Male and female alike seemed to be beguiled, bewitched, and quickly engaged with her beauty, energy, and charisma.

She was immediately trusted for her confidences and soothing healing demeanour. Miraculous outcomes, deliverance, and guidance were a given.

Sari was somewhat taken for granted. For her, the attention was oftentimes tiresome. But at other times, it was a pure joy to help someone back from the brink. Whatever abyss they were teetering over was hers to diminish and control. Sari knew what she had to do. What she was obliged to do. But, the intensity of the clambering, clawing energies were sometimes invasive and unwelcome.

As her magical powers progressed, Sari had to find ever more sophisticated ways to protect herself and her loved ones. Sometimes a rogue energy might bypass her resonant energy field yet impact a beloved horse who became lame for a time, or worse. Her familiars and accompanying creatures had a contract to protect her. When she got distracted, lax or even complacent, one of her spirit helpers was obliged to provide a buffer. This had led to the passing of several beloved animals, who knew what was required to ensure the continuing incarnation of their mistress. They had willingly absorbed the harm and so bypassed the live threat to their keeper. Sari's mission was not what you might call assured or safe. At times it was aggressively dangerous.

In the terms of her contract the veil was always thin. Sari could appreciate that she had to follow her instructions from behind the veil. The Spirit World did not dictate to her. But it could cause problems as well as facilitate deliverance. You had to know what you were dealing with. Her powers of discernment did not usually fail her. But sometimes there was something bigger than the remit of her life experience. She was always open to learning more. She had to be. It was made clear to her that it would not be worth her while to veer off the strict time-worn path destiny had set for her. Indeed, she would doubtless be punished horribly if she did so. There was no veering from The Way. She was stuck.

Any time Sari had entertained thoughts of escape or the modification of her mission into more comfortable form, there had been a severe lesson and reprimand. She needed to understand that her destiny was also her privilege. It did not always feel like it. The price she had to pay at times was beyond comprehension. She had no means to be privately, peaceably herself. No time to follow her loves, preferences, or personal pursuits. Spirit metaphorically led her along treacherous cliff top paths, across parched, sandy deserts, and up slippery, rocky canyons. There were no calm valleys or tranquil pastures in the rounds of this "Spirit Witch." Yet others felt she had all the power, freedom, and beauty any soul could wish for.

From the outside looking in, it appeared that Sari had everything landing at her feet. She had nice well-made clothes, food in her belly, and many a hearth that would welcome her on a cold night without question. Grateful though she was for her blessings, for Sari, the deeper reality was completely different. Sometimes it felt as if she had nothing at all. That her soul was a void, lost in service to others who wanted a piece of her at any given opportunity. Every time she helped someone, it felt as if she had a little bit less of herself for herself. In bleak moments she felt exploited. She was a vessel used randomly and completely in the name of a fate over which she had no apparent control. There was only a compelling obligation to deliver. At times it felt like no life at all.

She had an unusual and special mission. Sari told herself this in times of disquiet in a bid to quell any resentment or bewilderment at her predicament. There were adventures to come that might stir her in ways that she had not yet been privileged to experience. She hoped for and anticipated a Grand Amour in her future. She longed for the day when her womanly emotions would be properly stirred. Sometimes it felt like she would never find her true love. In other moments of reverie, it felt like he was just around the corner. She could sense his raw powerful energy in the ethers and knew that he would fulfil her in all the ways she needed. Whoever he was, he was her completion.

Sari knew it would soon be time for her to leave her beloved Scotland to journey to the land of The Cathars in the Languedoc region of France. For a long time, she had been getting impressions and flashes of future events. This adventure was imperative. Love beckoned, along with much suffering and a grave obligation. The depicted destiny was not sugar-coated. But it was intense and life enforcing, delivering the passion she desired and longed for. Her father was aware he could play a significant role in the preordained adventure. But he needed to be well enough to accompany her, and it was on his recovery they awaited.

CHAPTER THREE

The Oracle

S ari had a head start on the Universe most of the time. But this did not mean things ran according to plan. Quite the opposite. This tendency she had of advanced knowing, meant that the riddles and challenges became ever more complex and intense. Nothing was for free. Sari could help others, often quite simply and swiftly. But as for herself? At times it became nigh on impossible. The powers that be could always spring surprises, misrepresenting her visions for quite some time before flipping them into rectification at the last minute. When she knew something, she surely knew it. But it left no room for complacency.

Some might think it a privilege to be so blessed with such wisdom and knowledge. But Sari did not take anything for granted. Mostly it felt like a burden, even a curse. It was completely painful and apparent to her that it was not simply a gift, if she thought about it in any depth. She knew that she knew things, but that did not seem to come with any guarantee of their manifestation, at least not to the rest of the world who watched. Rather than feted, she was often questioned. Vilified, challenged, and disparaged. Yet rulers, kings, and princes sent for her visions. Their emissaries on horseback riding into the village unannounced, heralding the affectations, airs and graces that come along with privilege. The sense of entitlement and presumption that travelled along with her visitors frequently offended her to the core, and she was often tempted to send by return, messages of hardship, war, pestilence, and illness, even in peacetime.

Her unwritten ethical codes did not allow for such mischief in truth. Her reputation preceded her. Sari was paid in cloth, jewellery, and exotic herbs from The Holy Land, to which she felt so connected. Though sometimes the most obnoxious strangers assumed she would also like to generate further income between the sheets. Unsolicitous offers to attend the chambers of bewigged judges with bushy eyebrows and twirling moustaches were not uncommon.

NO Thank You!

How they even flattered themselves that this might be an appealing proposition was beyond her. But it was something akin to avuncular protection in their pea-sized brains. Or at least that is how they justified it to themselves. That along with the assumption that rare gemstones would be enough enticement for Sari to indulge their predilections.

She always said a resounding "NO!"

More-often-than-not, she acquired the glittery objects anyway, so pleased had the 'client' been with the comprehensive information or healing. Unbeknownst to the jurisdictions involved, Sari had solved many a crime, contretemps, and domestic dispute. She did not need to attend the hearing she asked for the merest sketch of information and then advised the prosecutor or defence – whoever was attending – how to proceed.

Victory was guaranteed once The Moidart Oracle was consulted. It was no wonder that emissaries, noblemen, politicians, and lawyers, travelled from far and wide to speak with her. Even the medical profession, or the loved one's family, would make the journey if a patient had been baffling them for long enough. Murderers and thieves would have indeed been nervous if they got wind of the energy and information steering their case.

Sari was able to pinpoint crucial concealed evidence that would either lead to an innocent's reprieve or would convict the most devious and corrupt. She had saved quite a few pure souls from the gallows. Souls who had been scapegoated to spare the truly guilty. No wonder she was paid handsomely. But the extracurricular bedroom-orientated suggestions were nothing short of insulting. She brushed them off with a heavy-hearted sigh.

Thankfully, the shroud of mystery surrounding her gifts did not put Sari in direct danger. She was always one step ahead of the dark forces that sought to undo her. Even if someone had tried to find her to reap their own form of revenge or justice, she would have been forewarned and forearmed. So long as she was doing the work of 'Spirit' as it arrived on her doorstep, she was honouring her contract. The trade-off was that she was looked after and protected. It made sense. She was too useful and willing to the powers that be, both etheric and human. Her faculties of listening and hearing the messages were exceptional. No one matched her. Not the travelling gypsies, most of whom were simply creative. Nor the cloistered clerical mystics who occasionally gleaned a prophesy from the heavens and scripted it in luminous manuscripts.

Sari had no time for either approach. She was too honest and scrupulous to make things up to flatter her attendees. She had a reputation to uphold. Equally she had no time to paint and indulge a wonderful vision from the angelic realms which may have taken weeks and months to translate and depict. The Monks of Lindisfarne did beautiful intricate work. But she did not have the discipline, inclination, or the time to dawdle with gold leaf. She preferred the direct approach. The Spirit World was hers to access. The information she was given was direct, accurate and useful. No one had to worry and fret if they were being misled. No one had to doubt that if they needed healing, some miracle was assured to happen; even if that involved a peaceful resolved passing over to the next world.

A huge part of Sari's work was helping people to experience a "good death." Birth and death were so connected in the people's psyche. In the blink of an eye a vibrant life could be struck down by the sword, in childbirth or with an indiscriminate disease. Sometimes the country folk did not feel the need for a priest with the rituals of baptism, handfasting, or the last rites. They were content to embrace their transition and the cycles of life in the peaceful calming energy of someone like Sari. Often these ceremonies were carried out by spiritual leaders not under the remit of The Pope. Sacrilegious although it was to the Catholic way, THE Way, held more sway in the wilds of Scotland. Sari was nature priestess of the people, and the trust they showed in her ministry was rewarded by the results.

Sari liked to travel down roads in her mind. She did this for clients all the time. Using her skills of projection and telepathy she could see far ahead. Able to jump forward, thereby understanding why something was not meant to be; she could explore the options this way, giving detailed accounts of what would happen if this route were taken, and what would happen if it were not. This dancing with destiny she indulged in would imply there was some choice involved. She did not really think there was. But it was fun to explore the terrain of a fantasy. It was also a useful tool she used to pinpoint the facts and the true reality. She would explain the complexities to the listening ear, knowing full well what she was saying was not truly grasped. She issued warnings about wrong roads, even as she knew the headstrong seeker would stroll down them in confidence, assuming they had the control and stamina to cope.

Men especially were guilty of this. A lot. She felt much of the time they consulted her as a kind of curiosity, and God forbid a form of entertainment. She was right. They did. But what they did not bargain for was that in one moment she would blow their minds, if not their hearts with information she could not possibly know, which in turn made them sober up a bit and consider the other breadths of her wisdom. Many a life was enhanced if not spared this way.

Sari did not really think we could ultimately choose our fate. She did feel there was free will which meant we could run quickly away from what we were called to do if our spirit baulked at the task. She felt too that we could idle through life. Just being, existing, functioning for as long as the elements and external forces would allow. But she and her ilk were interested in more than mere survival. She chose to live at a pitch of intensity which meant she dared to entertain her passions, as well as her mission.

CHAPTER FOUR

The Woman

Sari's youth, her pale skin and golden countenance, belied her. She carried the weight of centuries' old knowledge upon her shoulders. To look at her slight form, deep blue eyes, and corn-coloured wavy hair, you would think she was a painter's muse or a musician's inspiration. Scroll forward aeons later, and you would find her likeness prolifically gracing the Renaissance ceilings of Europe, or the paintings of Botticelli. She was an incarnated goddess, etherical, beautiful yet dangerously wise, guaranteed to stir jealousy, obsession, and compulsion in equal measure.

Despite her beauty, Sari was self-depreciating. It was the face she presented to the world. Her incarnated countenance for the benefit of others. Beyond her control. Though she did incline to downplay her natural luminosity where she could with plain adornment and raiment. She enjoyed walking and living in her body. But she did not feel totally at ease in it either. Her visual impact she was aware of. She could sense the projected reactions in her observers. But she did not see with their eyes. Nor could she really objectify herself in that way. Occasionally if the overhead moon light shone from the correct angle, it would hit the bottom of the well, and she could gather a glimpse of how she was received. But she did not indulge any aspect of her physical manifestation, preferring to meet people on merit. Soul to soul and heart to heart.

Sari did not really care about someone's physical appeal, unless of course her romantic inclinations were involved. With these she was as relatable, analytical, and human as any buxom, country lass who hovers outside the tavern hoping to snatch a kiss and a starry night companion. Her natural affections were as warm and real as the next lass. Some things never change. The problem was, Sari was not received in the same straightforward simplicity as the next lass. The wrong man was intimidated, even afraid of her.

She had tried to be normal, considering lusty connections when they presented. But something within made her feel compromised. She had caught the eye of some of the most handsome men in the region, and she was quite fascinated by the variable energies behind the gazes that met hers. Her quizzical research was entertaining at least. I mean at *some* point she would hopefully have time for all this!

In the interests of her heart, Sari indulged the moments when they arose. She tested the connections; only to find them disintegrating into fear, panic, arrogance, or a lusty hunger that she did not at this point know what to do with. At the tender age of twenty-two, she did not know much of the ways of the world or how they pertained to her. She had to experiment somehow without compromising her integrity and true mission. One thing she did know. She *had* to have a child. So, at some point one of these contenders was going to have to conquer, despite her resistance and their perceived flaws. One man would have to prove worthy of siring a special legacy. That much she knew.

Some men were timid. Some youthful and too keen. Some were kind and gentle but too elderly with a low life force. Some were cruel with odious hints of violence and lechery flickering behind their eyes; and some were simply predatory, working their way around as many of the fair maids of The Highlands and Islands as they could lay their hands upon.

Disconcertingly, some were blinded by her light. They bathed in it, were overwhelmed by it, and somehow became less than men in the face of it. She could see that these men felt they needed to do something different with her. That was their mistake. They did not. The last thing she wanted was to be deified and put upon a pedestal. She needed someone handsome, strong, gallant, kind, and passionate. She thought she needed someone interesting, wise, and funny too. But she had tempered her expectations somewhat, reasoning that all these ingredients in one definitive package might just be a bit too much for the love gods to deliver. She knew she would never work it out or solve the riddles by herself. So, she had begun to trust that the Universe probably had a plan that she would not be privy to until it happened.

Sari had toyed with impulsive, heated, and flippant affairs on two occasions, without compromising her purity. But even suitors with a wicked humour, knowing smile and a gentle twinkle in the eye did not resonate completely. She got increasingly frustrated. She did not want to objectify the men just as they were objectifying her. Each potential encounter was subjected to the weighing scales of judgement and analysis. Hardly romantic.

Because of her mission, Sari could not afford mistakes. She needed it all to just magically and organically unfold. She was not willing to find a husband for the sake of security alone. She had all she required to get through life under her own steam using her God given talents and resources. But she desired love and passion in her life. An intense sensual connection with a man. That really was everything to her, even though thus far it had eluded her. She needed, depth and understanding along with tangible intimacy. She needed to be fully *seen* and taken!

Sari apparently desired the impossible. She had even been told this by her father, who wanted her to marry a 'man;' not 'money,' bounty, status, adventure, or trouble. There had been one particularly keen suitor, William, who became desperately enraptured and captivated. Wanting her to marry him within days of his arrival in Moidart. Passing through the village with his men on rite-of-passage travels, his horse had needed attention and healing. William was transfixed watching Sari work as she soothed the animal and made a poultice of her herbs for his wounded, inflamed fetlock. He practically proposed on the spot. He and his clansmen resolved to stay a few days more, on the pretext of sourcing trade links with the community. It would be a great opportunity for the village and surrounding hamlets. But it was clearly partly a ruse contrived for William's personal benefit. His agenda was to win the hand of The Moidart Healer, and it did not look like he would rest until he sealed the deal. He had found what he thought he was looking for.

Sari pondered the option. William was not ugly. He was handsome, witty, kind, and attentive with a pale blue somewhat distant gaze. This made him captivating and mysterious on a good day. Overall though he was a bit tame and predictable. Sari could read him effortlessly, and she found this to be ultimately dull if she projected this union too far into the future.

William was certainly man enough to sire a beautiful child. But as Sari spent time with him wandering the mountains and moors of Ardnamurchan Peninsula, she found there was something a bit insipid, distracted, and less than dynamic about his countenance. Deep within his soul he was apparently driven by a force which required the delivery of something tangible and useful within an agreed time frame. He seemed to have hidden agendas, and Sari could not initially pinpoint what those were. He was too excited and exuberant. She could have found it flattering but instead it sounded her inner alarm bells. He was just too pushy. Not with his words, but with his energy. She could tell he was up to something.

Sari was not enamoured enough with William to ignore her intuitions. Her extra sensory perceptions did not usually let her down. Although rationally and logically this union made a lot of sense, she would have been compromising her heart and natural inclinations if she followed through blindly. It was with some relief, that she stumbled upon the information she needed to justify backing out of what was fast becoming an "expected" arrangement.

A loose-tongued stable hand, clearly in awe of his master, and more importantly, nurturing a soft spot for Sari, confided that William was set to inherit wealth and lands far away. Thinking he was furthering his master's concerns the poor boy confided the full background story. William would soon be obliged to return home to the distant lands of his forefathers' in the far north. He was expected to end his journey as the leaves fell from the sky and autumn descended. His elders were expecting heroic tales, bounty, and most importantly a wife to help perpetuate the ancestral line. William had been given the freedom of the summer to sew his wild oats and reap a harvest to benefit the whole community. The eldest, and only male of three siblings, William was obligated to, find a female to help amplify the ongoing prospects of *Clann Gunn*, an obscure lineage with complex roots and connections. One of the oldest clans in Scotland, *Clann Gunn*, descendants of the Norse Jarls of Orkney and Picts of Caithness, were at risk of extinction.

This whole tale was useful to Sari, for the information conflicted her emotionally. It affronted her inner sense of knowing and it felt all kinds of wrong. He could not possibly be representative of her future. Neither William's maternal nor paternal lines were truly Scottish. Where were the French elements she knew were to play such a strong part in her destiny? True, William and Sari seemed to have the same impulse to bring new life into the world. But his reasons and environment directly conflicted with hers, and the mission she knew was preordained for her child. He was of Nordic descent, not truly

Scottish, and therefore not resonant with her soul even on a human level. She had found the missing piece of the puzzle. This was the source of the niggle that had been driving her doubts. This prospective union would lead only to her unhappiness, the shrivelling of her soul and her physical demise. She knew a similarly challenging fate awaited her in France. But it had a grander purpose and she would be serving a spiritual lineage not a mercenary one. If she went ahead with this, she would have to bow to The *Clann Gunn* ways, and would be expected to be the loving wife and visual trophy of their beloved leader.

Marrying William would take Sari away from all that she knew and loved on The Peninsular. She simply did not love him enough. She was only vaguely attracted at the best of times. At the worst she found him irritating and rather selfish. A young pup full of notions and ideas for a marvellous future that was simply not destined to be. There is no doubt that William was engaging, convincing, and *almost* shaping towards what she *thought* she wanted. But it was all too indefinite and contrived. All too convenient. For *him*. Sari was not about to settle any time soon. She had not pursued the calling of her heart and soul in her dalliance with William. She owed it both to The Divine and to herself to honour the messages and long held beliefs, she knew in her heart to be true.

Frederick, her father, only too aware of his failing health wanted her to make the commitment for sureties' sake, even though he knew she would not. He tried. They both tried. In fact, they all tried. It was just. Not. Going. To. Happen. Sari had a primary purpose and although it was sometimes tedious, it was also preordained and divinely decreed. She could not afford dubious moves. She was *in* the world but not fully *of* it. She could not marry for the sake of security. Nor could she indulge a fleeting feeling. She needed a pure, lasting, passionate connection, and until it materialised before her without a shadow of a doubt, she might as well take her vows. The sensation of being romantically short-changed left her feeling ultimately isolated and alone. It further emphasised her father's importance in her psyche, heart, and soul. Some. Things. Never. Change.

CHAPTER FIVE

Moidart

For some time, Sari had been sensing a change in the climate and energies of their work in the scattered environs of her homeland. Frederick was aware of it too. The lands they both loved so well merged with their alchemy artfully. The one served the other. They could achieve what they did, only through the background support of the nurturing landscape. The elements empowered and sustained their purpose.

An Fhadail Dubh, Newton of Ardtoe, formed the nucleus of a thinly inhabited crofting community. The small hamlet merged with the surrounding landscape sustaining strong roots and energy threads between mountains, waterways, islands, and beaches. Nestling alongside the inner reaches of the Ardnamurchan Peninsula to the west, with the bulk of the Moirdart landmass to the north and east, Ardtoe and its adjacent districts were wild, inaccessible, and daunting.

Renowned for its natural beauty, the area was sparsely populated, isolated, and flanked by water on all sides. Only a comparatively skinny area of land, with a reach of about three miles at its thickest point, gave the traveller dry land access from the mainland of Scotland to the peninsula. Loch Horun, Loch Shiel and Loch Moidart formed a trio of lengthy, deep water borders surrounding Moidart, rendering it virtually marooned. Accessible from the north, west and east only by boat, unless you wanted a long arduous trek south and then west to Ardnamurchan via Glenfinnan. To reach it from the mainland, you had to travel onto The Peninsula itself. A journey attempted only by the most intrepid. This was a place you visited with specific purpose and intention. Beautiful though it was, it was not a land to 'happen upon,' or saunter through, unless you lived there.

Loch Horun in the north ran inland from the Sound of Sleat to Glenelg, where it formed a short but choppy passage to the Isle of Skye, giving spiritual pilgrims swift access to the famed Fairy Pools, sparing them a long circuitous route north to the alternative crossing at The Kyle of Lochalsh. Loch Shiel a fresh-water loch nearly eighteen miles long blocked access to Moidart from the east and made would-be travellers from Inverlochy some twenty miles away, rather less inclined to visit. This expanse of water, one of the largest in Scotland, seemed to be specifically designed to make Sari's homelands nicely secure, and self-contained. Locals thought twice about leaving, and strangers thought more than twice about visiting. Any risk of invasion came from the sea, not so much the land.

The final link in the chain of districts connected by these waterways was Loch Moidart itself. Running about five miles eastwards inland from the sea. Moidart was a sea loch with narrow channels divided by the large island of *Eilean Shona*, which at its vortex created further divisions in the slip stream. These subsequent smaller tributaries were joined at source by the River Moidart, where the fresh water merged with the sea, causing turbulence and massive confusion with tidal current and flow. Loch Moidart at low tide, was a congealing soup displaying a curious mix of fresh and salt water combined with mud, rock, silt, sand, and miscellaneous debris.

The lochs Horun, Sheil and Moidart formed a formidable triad of waters, containing the rugged landscapes of Knoydart, North Morar, Arisaig and Moidart. These lands were renowned for their harsh terrain and inhospitable environments. Knoydart was yet another uninhabitable, unfriendly peninsula, even more inaccessible than Ardnamurchan. Its entry points involved either a torturous undulating hike just shy of twenty miles over sodden windswept bogs, or an obscure boat ride to nowhere which docked at a rocky promontory revealing a track that trailed off into the distance and connected with the hike from hell.

Ardnamurchan itself was spectacular and blissfully remote, uninhabitable in theory. But over the centuries people had learned to carve out a living on the barren lands. Jutting out due west into the Atlantic like some massive mountainous landfilled pier, it sheltered the northern shores of The Isle of Mull, and strongly resembled an island, so tenuous was its link to the landmass of Scotland. The Peninsular was a chunky spur of land which was neither one thing nor the other. In some seasons it was surprisingly green, even pastoral looking, and several of its beaches were sandy and spectacular. But it was too inaccessible to feel part of the mainland, even though it did just about connect with it. This tenuous somewhat disjointed dynamic was reflected in much of Ardnamurchan's history. Vying diverse factions with individualistic interests, parried for ownership of what was essentially a strange synthesis of bog, hill, and rock.

Moidart at least pretended to be part of the mainland. But it too had a slippery identity, revealed when further investigation showed that it was essentially boxed-in by lengthy inconvenient strips of water. Moidart was aspiring to be an island, whilst still maintaining one solid, entrenched strip of land attached to the rest of Lochaber, that may or may not be flooded at any moment. Moidart was not about to be marooned. But, monitored by a remote, disinterested sheriff based far north in Inverness, doubtless its heart and soul yearned for a connection to the surrounding islands, which beckoned hauntingly in the shimmering distance. The Inner and Outer Hebrides displayed an unreachable mystical grandeur, tantalising with a tenuous promise of escape. Somehow the energy of the Hebrides did not feel as stark or as inhospitable as the Moidart lands.

Moidart was aspiring to be magical, and indeed it *was*. But it was rudely blocked by the penile intrusion of The Ardnamurchan Peninsula to the south, and had a brutal, stark reality draining its energy field. There was not the lightness and airiness of the islands to be found in this terrain. But there was a murky depth and substance that was compelling to those who could see past the mud.

For those like Sari whose vision could pierce the gloom, this was a land of deliverance. So primitive and primeval was Moidart, that it could not but speak to the soul. The primal urges and impulses of primordial man were still ingrained deep in its mud aeons later. Since time immemorial nothing had changed in these lands. This was quite possibly Moidart's main appeal. The dense energy had a grounding aspect, which the sparkling, luminescent islands in the distance lacked. The faery folk may well have been dancing around the sacred stones on the Isle of Lewis. But in Moidart the mud offered a bleak deliverance. A transmutation which comes through the deep purging of the soul, offering transformation of the Spirit. This profound healing potential sprung from the depths of these lands. Moidart offered a strange consolation.

CHAPTER SIX

The Sea Priestess

Known as The Rough Bounds, *Na Garbh Chriochan*, the West Coast remote areas of Scotland were steeped in shadowy whispered tradition and a deeply ingrained Gaelic heritage. Staunchly Catholic on the face of it, they were heretically superstitious if you scratched beneath the surface.

Named *Loch of Mud* by the marauding Vikings who had invaded its shores a couple of centuries previously, Loch Moidart had a mixed destiny. A complex sense of belonging. It was not always clear to whom it *did* belong. Was the tautologous '*Loch of Loch Mud*,' named by the Norwegians, Scottish? Or was it not?

Malcom III had secured Moidart for Scotland in the eleventh century. But in the twelfth it fell back into alien hands, and for many decades its rightful ownership remained unclear. The lands danced between the Norsemen and the Celts. David I of Scotland lost a grip on his Scottish inheritance during his exile in England, and The Kingdom became divided. Part of it landed back in Norwegian hands on Somerled's demise. Whilst the remaining Garmoran lands, which included Moidart, remained in the hands of the MacRory, *Clann Ruaidhri,* direct descendants of Somerled.

In 1124, David 1 of Scotland had regained his claim to much of his Scottish heritage with the backing of King Henry I; his partner in crime whilst temporarily exiled. The Davidian Revolution established land order, monasteries, and feudalism in Scotland. Scottish destiny was thereby forever linked with the French and the Anglo–French knights in shining armour, who bargained the lands in exchange for services of 'protection'. Usually imposed. In these times of apparent progression, self-proclaimed authorities, ear-marked desirable plots to exploit and vulnerable peoples to commandeer.

The Somerled coup lost King David his sway in Moidart and on the Ardnamurchan Penninsula. Somerled, with his Norse-Gaelic origins and mighty connections, married correctly. What he did not achieve between the sheets he managed to engineer through military means and subversive political manoeuvring. Although he was not Scottish, he had good intentions for the area ecclesiastically and economically. But it was all on his own terms. A Catholic warrior who unified the islands and created a huge kingdom, Somerled was to come unstuck because he was from Ireland with Nordic connections, and *not* in fact a rightful son of Scotland.

Somerled's power was renowned and inevitable throughout the Argyll area, until he was unceremoniously struck down in the Battle of Renfrew in 1164. Those whose agenda was *truly* Scottish finally got to him. Sari sensed the lands would ultimately be Scottish for the duration. But she knew she would not be privileged to see the complete squashing of the Somerled legacy. It was not until 1266 that Moidart became officially and permanently 'Scottish' under Crown rule. In the meantime, the MacRory contingent of Somerled's ancestry remained a force to be reckoned with in the region. Their *Clann Ruaidhri* stronghold at Castle Tiroum holding a dark, mythical grip on the hearts and souls of those who crossed the threshold.

The chequered rulership of Moidart and its surrounding areas, did not undo the established way of doing things. The haphazard, interchangeable leaders of The Kingdom had their agendas, and it meant that the locals never felt secure. They were on the defensive about any rogue element or external imposition invading their modus operandi. If the grander elements of society could not work out who owned what, then the country folk who worked the land would simply stake their claim by not kowtowing to anyone imposing rules and regulations on their lifestyle.

True, they had to work the crofting way. The marketing systems established by King David were useful, bringing some prosperity and material settlement to the region. But politically this is where it stopped in the minds and hearts of those who haunted and occupied *An Fhadail Dubh*. The ancestors had earned their right to freedom. The inhabitants of Moidart were not about to allow the church or the landlords to impose their authority or throw their weight around. Yes, The Church of Saint Finnan and Saint Nicolas was always full and well attended on Sundays, and the rents were paid. But out of hours, under the radar, the old ways held sway.

Frederick and Sari were respected in the area. But they were also challenged subversively and taken for granted. Church scouts from the East coast were able to effectively monitor much of what went on with their spies on the ground. Spies who feted Sari and her father to their faces, calling on them at a moment's notice when needed. But who were blinded by the intermittent flashes of authority and power, which heralded from The Lothians; distant lands which every now and again made their presence felt, usually in the guise of emissaries scouting the region in pursuit of Atlantic fish, seasonal grouse, and highland deer.

There were signs of an increasing agenda and undertones of religious suspicion emanating from the east. An inherent clash was brewing between the increasingly pastoral cultured lands of The Burgh, and the wild untamed, unforgiving terrain of The Rough Bounds. They were worlds apart in truth. A person might be forgiven for wondering how one could even have an impact on the other. But such is the greed of men. Where the pastoral men in the east tilled the land, sewed their seeds, and predictably raised a bountiful harvest; the stoic folk in the north-west read the skies and scavenged for the meagre pickings that were able to break through the rocky ground, or defy the mud. When they could not raise a morsel on the land, they turned to the sea with small inadequate fishing boats that could tip over at the whim of a random rogue wave looming over the bow.

The wild lands of the north were not about to be secure from the curious invasive eye of those who would access the region's riches. Despite its dark, foreboding, and brooding backdrop, The Rough Bounds held an intrigue and a mystical pull which emanated for miles around. It was no accident of fate that this was the home of Sari and Frederick. The landscape consumed and inspired them. It enabled Sari to perform her miracles and Frederick to serve the community in a pastoral capacity. They understood the history, their legacy, and their mission in this context. Moidart was a place out-of-time. A place to be at one with nature. A place to be untroubled by humanity and its machinations. All that was required was engagement in the game of survival that the environment demanded.

In a bid to scratch a living from the land and the sea, crofters made their mark. They were not about to be dictated to by politics or religion. Nor indeed anything which threatened the basic job of survival. The stuff which filled and preoccupied the minds of privileged men seemed largely irrelevant. Although they were somewhat God-fearing, the agendas of religion were perceived with suspicion by the locals. Their overriding respect was for the elements and the environmental forces which dictated their fate.

Was God in control of these oftentimes destructive energies? At times it did not seem like it. Or if he or she was? Well then, perhaps the rage of The Divine was randomly inflicted upon them to appease their sin and guilt. To keep them in their place. Acknowledgement of a loving God who specifically cared for them and in whom they could trust for deliverance, was most of the time not their inclination. What the Pope decreed from Rome was also beyond their ken and remit to understand.

The hardy simple folk of Moidart were canny survivors. But they were at the mercy of the elements and on the brink of disaster at the best of times. In the worst of times, everything was up for grabs. One bad harvest, one boat not returning from sea, one hunter lost on the moors, and the whole enterprise was in jeopardy.

This water-bound people enjoyed the freedom afforded by their settlements and close-knit community. Their joy of living was found in interaction with those who shared the common goals of food, fire, and camaraderie. If the fermented honey mead was good, there was food on the table, and the conversation was flowing; they were content, if not happy. Outsiders brought trade, goods, and blessings they would never otherwise have seen. But they were also somewhat unwelcome and treated with suspicion. In this area, you just did not know which invader or marauder from a strange land might tip the balance of power in a perilous direction. Even seemingly innocuous visitors or passers-by were treated with caution until they proved themselves friendly and of good intention.

Who exactly *owned* this land bound by sea and mud? The people themselves. That was their mutual understanding. They did not want to be dictated to by royalty, Anglo-French knights, or some random Viking renegade from Norway. Scotland was *theirs*. Theirs in its purist form. Theirs to nurture. Theirs to enjoy.

Acharcle, the main settlement Sari and Frederick attended, was a centre for the hunting, fishing, and farming of the area. Here they could service their people, and they were fed, housed, and cared for in return. Sari's gifts were indeed a currency in these circumstances,

41

though she was never able to come to terms with seeing it this way. Her energy and aura flagged her as an item of curiosity as well as a source of deliverance. An infamous fireside tale grew its own sea legs becoming ever more fantastical every time she and Frederick heard it.

As the story goes. One of their small fishing boats was struggling offshore, unable to steer its way past the various obstacles on the approach to home. It was able to navigate the treacherous seas, in blinding fog and rain, only because a gaggle of witches posing as crows intervened and chartered it smooth passage through the turbulent waters. Where had these atypical imposters come from? They were not the rare but dreadful albatross, harbinger of doom and certain destruction. Nor were they swallows indicating good luck for intrepid sailors chalking up their nautical miles. Nor were they the customary squawking seagulls that heralded the return of a laden boat. No, this was a swarm of crows that was somehow able to calm the waters and pull the boat around the hazardous rocks and wrecks by using the small rope which dangled from the mainmast.

Black crows were an atypical signifier of miraculous deliverance. This surely bore the hallmark of witchy intervention! Sari smiled to herself when she heard this tale recanted. Never mind a gaggle of witches. It was basically *one* witch, well, one *Sea Priestess*, who had helped to manifest this strength in numbers from the shamanic depths of her repertoire. Sari had appealed to the heavens to bring her uncle and his son, safely home from their monthly deep-sea fishing trip. She had sensed trouble as they approached the shoreline. But sensed too their potential deliverance. All was not lost even as the violent storm whipped up from nowhere. They were nearly home. But the turbulent waters lashing against the rocks of the shoreline made it impossible for the boat to steer a steady course through the narrow inlets to the beach. Safe steerage into port was required, and it was duly provided by the supernatural realms.

Finton the local harbour master had seen the boat limp home

surrounded by a blackening flock of crows instead of the usual hyperactive plaintive gulls. In the early hours of the morning, following the storm which had ripped fencing from its post, and mercilessly flattened seedlings ripening for the summer harvest, the sea worn vessel docked. Sari breathed a deep inner sigh of relief. She had successfully intervened. The subsequent fantastical stories gave her a wry smile with their every amplification.

As they say, "all's well, that ends well." There was subsequently much cause for celebration, as this near catastrophe turned into an abundant success. The bounty returned by the boat fed the peripheral community for months to come, thanks to the pickling and preserving techniques Sari had mastered using her foraging herbs. Her nephew Finneas had winked at her shortly after landing. She knew that he knew, and *that* was enough for her. She did not have to prove herself or shout a victory from the hill tops. Besides, it could not be easily explained. It was enough to know that she was *seen* by those who were *meant* to understand.

CHAPTER SEVEN
De Montfort

S ari and Frederick frequently heard about the Gnostic community at *Le Chateaux de Montségur* and had long felt a calling to attend and share with what sounded like a kindred clan of souls. Spiritual pilgrims on the way to Skye or the Isle of Lewis regaled them with tales of these simple peace-loving *'perfecti'* who chose a pious scaled-back life to earn their salvation and redemption from life's arduous challenges. Far removed from their beloved Highlands, but clearly resonant and connected to their borderline heretical beliefs, Sari felt a destiny linked to The Cathars that she could not put into words. It seemed like a calling she would not understand fully until she made the journey. The trip was illogical in many ways, but she felt compelled to embark upon the adventure, with or without her father.

It had been a long time coming. Sari's connection with France stemmed back to childhood dreams where she would randomly wake in the night speaking the Franco language she could not possibly have known cognitively. Sari was not intentionally bilingual, but somehow the language of the Languedoc was in her blood. She found that she could understand French when she heard snippets from travellers, and she channelled it in her sleep state, according to anyone who lay alongside her at night.

When a high-born French family once passed through Moidart on the way to Castle *Eilean Donan* in the north, Sari could instinctively communicate with them without flinching. Telepathically and linguistically France was in her bones. She knew it. Perhaps she had experienced other lives there. But in this lifetime, she knew she had to complete her journey. This was one pilgrimage she needed to make. Not only for her own understanding and destiny fulfilment. But for the benefit of her brothers and sisters who protected The Holy Grail Line.

In the night as a child she used to jolt upright with visions of screaming and mounting flames. She could hear the curdling screams and feel the heat coursing through her veins threatening to overwhelm her. She would wake with the sweat drenching her brow. The salty droplets of water dripped from her forehead onto her tongue. Her nightgown sodden, and damp from the ordeal.

You would have thought such experiences and their association with France would have forced her unconscious to block out the lyrical lilt of the soft French tones she so adored. But not a bit of it. She found the gorgeous vernacular soothing and reassuring. Something familiar, and akin to the safety a baby feels in its mother's womb. France owned her in some way.

Perhaps something dreadful had happened in another time and she had to go back to balance the karma. Or maybe she was getting flashes of what was to come. Flashbacks or prophetic visions? She was not sure. But what she felt was the obligation to explore what this meant to her personally and spiritually. She was not afraid. She was fascinated with an inexplicable internal pressure and drive to understand. To have been shaken awake so many times in her youth by this associated energy must mean something. She had to follow through. Not only to make sense of the visions. But to make sense of the inner knowing she had about her spiritual role in this current lifetime. She had to find out who she *really* was.

The delay in setting off with her father simply reflected uncertainly about whether Frederick was supposed to accompany her. In "Spirit" he wanted to. But, in the material realm it had become less and less sure his faculties would allow him to deliver on a long-held promise. As more time passed, they were both unsure Frederick's legs would enable him to fulfil his intentions.

Both Sari and her father were aware they walked a tightrope in their perception of reality and understanding of the world. The church watched their every move and sent spies to test their ministry and challenge their prophesies. They were never caught out, as they always proved to be correct and frustratingly useful. But it was becoming increasingly testing for them to work and function in such a hostile environment that took freely with one hand yet begrudged, poked, and monitored with the other. There was a sinister background feeling that one mistake or false move, and they would be purged from the community and exiled, or worse. Sari increasingly felt that a pre-emptive strike would be most effective. They would leave before they were pushed. Besides, the ante-forces were playing a contributory part nudging them forwards, towards what she knew she needed to do.

Word had reached them of a lot of unrest on the continent. Factions of the Catholic Church had been intermittently persecuting extremists and those that challenged their autonomy. The victimisation of the Cathar adherents, The *Perfecti,* was not news. The City of Albi in Southern France had hatched this good Christian movement, sometimes called the Albigensians in recognition. The Catholic Church did not approve the Cathar ritual of *Consolamentum,* which purified its partaker of original sin, and enabled an elevated plane of spirituality and understanding. The individual Cathar *'Perfecti'* was put in direct contact with God and did not need an ordained priest to intercede on their behalf. The Catholic hierarchy denounced this as heresy. Whereas Sari and her father found it completely compelling. From the snippets she had heard and the energy she could perceive, Sari resonated instinctually with this soul group. This felt like her blood line and her spiritual family. She felt seen by them without ever having met them. The persecutions were an affront to her heart and soul, and she felt she had an inexplicable protective role to play. No, she could not wield a sword and strike down the errant misguided knights. But she could launch her own crusade and assist with the internal deliverance required as the soul exited the body. Perhaps her ministry lay in helping the wounded or comforting the bereaved. She just knew she had to get there, and that time was running out.

Despite the 1229 Treaty of Meaux, Raymond VII, Count of Toulouse, had continued in his bid to impress the authorities. The Albigensian Crusade had run from 1209 to 1229, and its determined mission was to quash Catharism in France. This twenty-year religious persecution was originally commissioned by Pope Not-So Innocent III. The Pope had become increasingly alarmed by the strength of commitment and the numbers aligning with Cathar Gnosticism. These were a people, who followed a peaceable path admittedly. But they were essentially heretics who believed that the world was created and run by The Devil. Of course, the Pope and his cohorts simplified, misunderstood, and misrepresented the outrageous aspects of the Cathar doctrine to feed and justify their plans. This threat to Catholic supremacy must be squashed at all costs.

According to The Cathars – a purist group with probable roots in the hidden Gnostic elements which gestated during the Romanic Byzantian Empire - it was The Devil who held man in bondage on the earth plane. Redemption could come through the worship of Christ and through adherence to a harsh aestheticism which recommended poverty, celibacy, and humility as the best routes to salvation. The Cathars were required through living a good life to recompense for their sins. If they fulfilled the task, they were released back into heaven, to The Light, to experience true peace and freedom. If they succumbed to temptation on the earth plane, and engaged in wrongdoing, they would incarnate once again for another round of 'hell.'

It was no wonder the leaders of Rome were disquieted by such a distortion of Biblical Truth. The Pope had no tolerance for alternative belief system, however peaceable the adherents might be in their daily lives. It was the job of The Catholic Church and the Crusades to ensure all were following the dictates of the established religion. No consideration or reprimand was given to the blood thirsty methods of the knights who led the campaigns against The Cathars. All was justified in the maintenance of law and order. Religion was political. A means to control the masses. Independent thought and alternative lifestyles were not tolerated, especially not where they gained power and might in a rich, productive, and desirable region. The Languedoc needed to be purged of its heresy.

The Cathar Crusades were especially brutal at the beginning of the thirteenth century. The French Crown had a political agenda and jumped on the knights' mission to realign the area in its favour, at the expense of Raymond VII Count of Toulouse. The culture and percolating flavour of the region was of no concern to royalty, and the persecutions led to a weakening of the Cathar populace. No doubt some of their practice continued underground. But these were dangerous times to be linked to an exploratory religious group that had its own ethos.

Trouble deep was brewing amongst factions that dared to think for themselves, thereby affronting the dictates of increasingly unreasonable religious leaders. Actions or signs of independent thinking were being stamped on by knighted warriors under the leadership of the notorious Simon De Montfort, Lord of Monfort L'Amaury and Fifth Earl of Leicester.

Involved in the initial stages of the Albigensian Crusades, De Monfort was instrumental in the fall of Carcassonne in 1209. Even though the lineage of the powerful De Monfort family heralded from the north, Simon subsequently presided over the confiscated lands of Raymond of Toulouse, and the Trencavel family. To say he was hated from all sides was an understatement. By May 2016, when Raymond set off from Marseilles to join the Crusades himself, he was still fighting to resolve the vendetta in a bid to re coup his lands from the De Montforts. Simon's son Amaury was no less well disposed towards him. The Cathars might have had an unlikely ally in Raymond, if only they had known of his gripe against the unscrupulous De Monforts.

In the name of zeal and religion De Monfort was responsible for what was fast becoming the systematic genocide of dozens of Cathars. His power clearly went to his head. One fateful day in 1210 in the village of *Minerve* Simon ordered the execution of one hundred and forty peaceable men and women for not recanting their faith. Those who did recant were spared the flames. Those who did not were burned on a mass funeral pyre as a warning to all. Another good day's work for De Montfort involved the ransacking and attempted levelling of numerous scattered villages and Cathar strongholds. Lastours witnessed a grime ordeal as brave knight Simon ordered the defacing of his prisoners from Bram. If the poor souls did not recant their beliefs, their eyes were gouged out and their ears, noses and lips cut off. This barbaric man ruled under a reign of terror. Suppression and dominance were the order of the day. Word was that this mighty solider was leading by the sword, indulging in gratuitous acts and random bloody murder to impose his power and make his mark. This odious man was rampaging his blood lust and political ambition across Europe, taking free rein with his notions during the day, before retiring to his tents to enjoy the bragging rights with his gluttonous, whoring comrades.

No chances were being taken. The unrest stirred insidiously and covertly by The Cathars had to be controlled and squashed. Fear was monopolised and a gruesome divide-and-rule campaign left ordinary folk without recourse to appeal. No counter moves were possible. This was dictatorship and terrorism at its worst, and it was undertaken in the name of religion. In this climate you kept your head down, nodded to passers-by, sheepishly without looking them in the eye, and only went out to complete essential tasks. Murder, theft, and extortion were the order of the day. No one not clad in metallic armour had the right to speak their mind, nor display an independent means of survival. The people had to know their place, which was beholden to the Holy Catholic Church, the religious voice of God himself on the earth plane. Anyone questioning this with counter words, deeds and actions faced scrutiny, lynching, hanging or being burned unceremoniously as an example. Women had to cover their heads and hide their shame. Anyone expressing notions of leadership outside of the Catholic edicts and remit were doomed if discovered. The atmosphere was one of suspicion, gossip, and hatred. This was a climate where people who had a vendetta to fulfil could thrive. Moral decency had given into lawlessness and victimisation. It was dangerous to express an opinion politically, especially if it countered the narrow impositions of The Catholic Church. Clearly a noose was tightening its grip around a group such as The Cathars who practised a scaled back form of worship minus the trappings and paraphernalia of Catholic ritual. True most of the group were holed up and protected behind the castellations of the impenetrable Castle of *Montségur*. But it could only be a matter of time before those ramparts were scaled and their contents purged. Well if De Montfort had his wicked way. This would certainly be the case.

CHAPTER EIGHT

The Calling

By seeking to connect with The Cathars of the Languedoc, Sari was aware that she and Frederick were probably walking out of the frying pan into the fire. But her spiritual antennae knew that she at least, had an essential role to play. A large fraction of her soul family, and the secrets they protected were under threat. Sari sensed this in her bones. She, as an embodiment of The Magdalene Lineage, had to make her physical presence known. Also, she had a sneaking suspicion that her romantic life would not kick start effectively until she got the hell away from the gene pool she had exhausted. There was nothing in The Highlands for her by way of personal reprieve. Well, the one promising element she had connected with, namely Ronan, was preordained to play a part.

Sari sensed an energy lurking in the background which had the agenda of replacing her father with Ronan. She assumed it might be that he took over Frederick's tasks when they embarked on their journey. But more and more, Sari suspected their roles might be more interchangeable regarding France. It had been somewhat of a puzzle to her therefore that Ronan did not accompany them, at least part of the way as they set off on their journey.

Her father had begun to delegate the practical aspects of his ministry to Ronan, a young vibrant leader of fair complexion and glistening blue eyes. Between them Sari and Frederick helped and attended the sick of the village and the surrounding communities. They were often called quite far afield onto the islands or further north. They possessed acknowledged skills of comfort and healing and Sari was a wizard with her herbs and potions. Ronan, a caring compassionate man had started to accompany them on their rounds. Sari felt she had to teach him some of what would help the villagers, yet she was unsure what gifts beyond mere concern and humanity her had.

Sari was loyal to her father and watched Ronan closely. But she was also fascinated by his quizzical smile and mischievous grin in the moments when he was not gazing upon her bewitching countenance. Ronan was transfixed by Sari. But was just as fascinated with her spirituality, though bordered on questioning her methods at points. Being traditional and of a more religious mindset, Ronan's background had not helped him develop his sensitivities in favour of the mystical ways. Critical he was not. But underneath it all he was stoic and cautious, possibly having inherited a touch of his father's love of power and control. Well concealed as this might be, Sari sensed his tendency to flip loyalties and was monitoring Ronan for signs of treachery and betrayal. She was sincerely hoping he was no spy or turncoat. She rather liked him.

Ronan heralded from Castle Tioram but had been sent out to the villagers to connect with Frederick and Sari. He had been commissioned by his father to discretely learn about their ways. All the better if he could also minister to the common folk and report back to The Castle with any tales of unrest or discontent. His brief was to be alert for rumours and any gathering factions that threatened to overthrow his father Reginald's pre-eminence in the region.

Sari had visited Ronan with Frederick to ascertain Ronan's suitability to work alongside them in their ministry. Although they too were common folk, they were also seen as powerful and commandeering of respect. Their magic was feared and respected if truth be told. Reginald was keen to know more of how they may be used to serve him, and the interests of *Clann Ruaidhri*.

Reginald was nothing if not ambitious, and any information he could gain at grassroots level would surely be helpful. He knew he could rely on the loyalty of his favoured son Ronan, and it seemed that a mutually agreeable arrangement was poised to develop between the mysterious Sari and her sage father Frederick. This duo had access to what he had not. A ground level voice and command when the locals were at their most vulnerable. Reginald wished to harness this power and perhaps feign magnanimous compassion to serve his purpose. Sari and Frederick were fully aware of his potential agenda. But they knew also that their time was coming to an end in the area. Before too long, and for some time to come, they would not be available to serve their beloved community. They intended to return but they could not guarantee that they would. What they were planning put them in jeopardy, in the way of robbery, captivity, and even death. The open roads down through France were not exactly safe, and pirates also patrolled the channel threatening any sea crossing they needed to make; the most likely route being across to Bruges, heart of the commercial trade centre in Europe.

Overall, Sari was not complaining. She knew an extra young, fit companion served a purpose in more ways than one. She really was rather taken with Ronan. She had not felt the stirrings in her soul that he conjured for as long as she could remember. Possibly she had never felt them. Ever.

There had been twilight expeditions to catch frogs and watch moon bugs with Charles a local village boy at the age of six. But that really did not count, and certainly could not be compared to the passion and heat she had begun to feel. Ronan spoke to the woman within. Something was happening on a level she had not experienced, except perhaps in other lifetimes. She was understandably cautious with the background presence of Reginald's agenda ever present in her consciousness. Also, she had not yet ascertained if Ronan was her soul mate reappearing to settle some karmic debt. She hoped not, as distant memories of a hellish marriage and abusive domestic imprisonment still haunted her whenever she got flashes of her time in France many centuries ago.

The mystical energies and etheric atmosphere of Castle Tioram, and its environs spoke to her also. Ronan's home was evocative, familiar, and darkly disturbing in equal measure. It conjured a potent, otherworldly, out-of-time atmosphere she could almost taste in the air. This dank dark castle sitting on Loch Moidart's tidally compromised island had tales to tell, and she was not sure she liked everything she sensed there. The Castle may have been recently renovated, but it stood in an area full of ghosts, and on land that had been witness to much suffering.

Ronan could be presenting as some form of comfort and consolation, or he could be an adversary in beguiling disguise, returned to inflict torture and punishment once again. She was not sure which it was and so she remained on guard and cautious, even as his spirit beguiled and enticed her. Something deep and ancient was stirring and she was not sure she liked it. What she *did* know was that she was compelled by it. Was she lost in a haze between times, or sensing a familiarity that felt like home, a home that would not be ruinous as before, but loving and conducive and everything in her heart she wished for?

She was primed to this mysterious longing, yet aware that her mission did not really allow for it. She had to be in her full feminine power ready to serve and acknowledge the bigger reasons she had incarnated on the earth plane. The mystery, depth and evocative measure of the castle and Ronan its representative, could prove to be nothing more than a lair or trap. She hated to be thinking like this, as everything she ever wanted seemed to be standing right before her with this developing feeling. Ronan was stirring something deep within. She relished it all with anticipation.

Visions of life in the castle with beautiful giggling babies, a wonderful wealthy, extended family, a vibrant lover in the attentive form of the handsome Ronan who clearly adored her, were the stuff of her waking reveries. Not only did she shamelessly indulge these. She knew they were highly possible, if not likely. She was becoming fully prepared to willingly manifest this vision. But in her darker moments when 'reality' descended, she knew she may have to deny herself this future to honour the gravity of the rescue mission it was in her destiny to perform. If only Ronan could ride alongside her, she would know she had met her match. But if he chose to stay and gain power and regional wealth at the expense of both their fathers, she could not afford to be so impressed. It seemed like a complex maze of possibilities and agendas was unfolding. Sari had no choice but to reserve judgement for a time, finding that being the observer of her heart, when every impulse within prompted her to leap into Ronan's arms, was not the easiest task she ever set herself.

Anyway, needs must. It was essential her father had help, and it was important with his failing health that he could rely on someone local and courageous to carry the mantle. Sari knew all things considered Ronan should probably stay. But increasingly she felt that bringing an accompanying knight in shining armour as a guide and leader on their journey might be beneficial. Her father certainly had needs beyond being responsible for the lands and area they were leaving behind. True, there were family members who could shoulder some of the burdens. But Ronan also had potential as someone to protect their interests if his loyalty was proven.

Sari could not work out the conflicts that started to present. There were so many variable scenarios whirling around her head as Ronan spent more and more time alongside her. Despite her raging hormones and romantic inclinations, she found that reserving judgement was everything she needed to do in this moment. These things had a habit of being revealed in the right timing. It was all she could do to stop herself leaping ahead with her own wants and needs, until she reminded herself that she was not really supposed to have these in the first place.

Sari was on a path which did not allow for personal happiness, indulgence, or too much daydreaming. These were luxuries she apparently could not afford. She was required to be an independent woman and could not assume at any point that Ronan's duties and inclinations might involve walking her up the aisle. He was certainly handsome enough. Aesthetically pleasing with his strong handsome build, broad shoulders, and manly gait, he was everything she found attractive. She would certainly be the envy of the local girls on Ronan's arm. But he had yet to fully reveal his character and intentions.

The glimpses of Ronan's soul visible through those ocean-coloured eyes passed her test of preferences. He was attentive, kind to her father, and apparently not arrogant. She was beginning to wonder what could possibly go wrong, so beautifully set up did this all seem to be. However, she could not ignore the rumbling unease and turbulence she sensed on the ethers which was calling her to lands overseas, far from Scotland, her refuge and treasure. Sari had a mission to serve, and she did not know if Ronan was part of it, or an irresistible force designed to prevent it. She was ever aware of the tricks of the ante forces working against her and her father, and Ronan seemed to be a particularly tantalizing temptation threatening to throw her off track. Her destiny was in another place. Could he ride alongside them? It remained to be seen.

CHAPTER NINE

Ronan

Ronan knew he could love Sari. He was already transfixed and captivated by her beauty. But he knew he had to tread carefully. Within *Clann Ruaidhri* there were rigid structures in place. There were expectations, and as the eldest son he had to be very circumspect with his life choices. Did one of these involve a commitment to a magical woman walking a mystical path? A Highland witch? He did not think so. Yet he thought of her often. She even came to him in his dreams. Something was already stirring his interest beyond what he anticipated, and he was not complaining. He found her charming and beguiling, but he could not equate the pursuit of Sari with his daily life and what he knew was expected of him.

The more time Ronan spent with Sari and Frederick, the more his feelings grew. His curiosity was piqued in other ways too, as he witnessed Sari work her magic, and he adored the meaningful edifying mentorship of Frederick. He felt he had found kindred spirits and a potential partner for life in Sari. If only he could get past some of the judgement and prejudice about who she appeared to be. Sari was a unique mystery. He had never met anyone like her before, and he suspected he never would again. Ronan liked the challenge of not knowing her, as well as the accompanying sensation that perhaps he never would. She was inaccessible and unpalatable to many of the upper echelons of society. He could see past her chosen path. But he was not sure the Catholic leaders who were cohorts of his father would.

Ronan knew Sari was well-loved and adored amongst those who needed her services. But he also that knew she and Frederick were sometimes the brunt of gossip, and criticism. He also gathered that they were becoming increasingly prone to investigation. Ronan could not be part of that. He had to be upright, and beyond reproach. Not guilty by association.

The Catholic Church had shared commercial interests with his father and 'The Clann.' This potential union with The Sea Priestess was not likely to be perceived as conducive and helpful. Ronan was expected to further political and familial agendas with the alliances he made. To marry someone controversial, solely for love, not considering how it would impact upon *Clann Ruaidhri* interests, was something he could not entertain.

Ronan was quite a traditionalist at heart, and fully expected an arranged marriage to be imposed upon him by his father. He knew growing up that his love life was likely to fall foul of some convenient trade exchange that would enhance The Clann's power in The Highlands. He was a pawn in a chess game over which he had no control. Not much consideration was likely to be given to what would make him happy. Ronan dared not indulge too many flights of fancy about a possible future with The Moidart Healer.

Despite himself, Ronan's yearning for Sari and her company grew. He loved the tone of her voice, her smile, and the way she effortlessly conversed and passed the time of day. She was a joy to him. So easy to be with. Wholesome and grounded as well as desirable and intriguing. He loved to gaze into her deep blue eyes. They seemed to hold a world of wisdom as well as a delicious twinkle.

His pale blue eyes enjoyed indulging lingering gazes over her pale, luminescent complexion and rose bud lips, when she was otherwise distracted. Sometimes he dared to wander his attention further to include her frame. He found himself drawn to her curvaceous but slender physique. He liked what he could see. The teasing contours of her body as they made tantalizing impressions on the plain clothing she wore. She had no airs and graces. But her corsets were well filled, and sumptuously presented.

Sari did not exploit her womanly charms deliberately he noted. It seemed she was usually too distracted with the task in hand. But Ronan also noticed that the moments when her guard dropped were increasing. In those alluring interchanges she caught his eye, held his gaze, and smiled as if he were the only person in the world. She made him feel that way. One such look could render him quite agitated to pursue her without hesitation. To consummate what was at the very least a beguiling lust and magnetic attraction. But he held back, knowing she was worth more than a fleeting encounter. This passion could last a lifetime if it were correctly ignited. One thing he also knew. He was ready to blow a fuse at the slightest invitation!

Sari truly was the ultimate woman - he often caught himself musing.

If only her trade and lifestyle were not quite so removed from my reality.

As the planned time of Sari's and Frederick's departure for France approached, Ronan became conflicted about where his loyalties lay. Unquestionably he had to prioritize his father's agendas in the region. He had accompanied this amazing father and daughter duo on their rounds of the area. He was suitably impressed by their commitment to the people, and their ability to help them in all sorts of ways that *Clann Ruaidhri* never could. He had made his reports to The Clann leaders glowing and pertinent. He did not feed any controversy about Sari and her role. He explained her work as a healer. She was someone using the old ways, her instincts, and a knowledge of herbs as medicine to heal and help the people. Nothing more. This was surely useful to the community as the nearest medical doctors were often unavailable and several days ride away.

Ronan figured he could divert a more extensive investigation of Sari and Frederick by defending them in this way. He diffused any drama and controversy when he could, and subtly protected them at the dinner table. Ronan's father Reginald could not argue with his presentations, so decided to be cautious about over-indulging the concerns of the Catholic Church. He would hold back on aggressive action and would reserve judgment. He would not enforce demands and terms on Sari and her father. Reginald could see for himself that the two were harmless and likeable. He had entertained them at The Castle a couple of times to ascertain the extent of the threat they represented. He could not fault their demeanour or intentions. He could appreciate that the concerns of The Church were largely unfounded, and that the miraculous results of their ministry belied any benefit in shutting them down.

But theologically, there was still a problem. Reginald instructed Ronan to keep Sari and Frederick discretely at arms-length whenever there were church dignitaries in attendance at Tioram. The Church claimed to have a monopoly on miracles and did not like the spectacular stories circulating about this woman who could heal the sick, with herbs, potions, and sometimes her bare hands. Wariness of witchcraft was beginning to creep into local consciousness. Pious judgmental priests would not want to meet her in the corridors of The Castle.

Although wise women had been consulted for centuries, even secretly by clerics. Suspicion was becoming increasingly rife as The Pope felt threatened by any alternative ways of living and operating that were not approved by him. Various sects and individuals proclaiming stripped-back worship options had sprung up across Europe and were also being monitored. The wise women of the villages were spied upon and tested for slip ups and false claims.

Witches were not tolerated. The problem is, they did not quite know how to categorize Sari. She was a wise woman certainly. That technically was not illegal, even from the Church's standpoint. But the fact that she could perform verifiable miracles with reliable witnesses was not supposed to happen. This skill was the exclusive remit of Saint's, usually male Saints too.

Queen Margaret of Scotland was a notable exception. But she was not canonized by Pope Innocent VI until 1250. A pious Roman Catholic, Margaret of Wessex, aka Queen Margaret, had fled to Scotland following the Norman Conquest of 1066. Within a few years she had married the Scottish King Malcom III and proceeded to do many charitable works, the most useful of which was the establishment of a ferry across the Firth of Forth for pilgrims heading to Saint Andrews, the main ecclesiastical center in Scotland. The Queen's Ferry enabled many a devout Catholic easy access to the hub of Christendom in Fife, shortening journeys by days and weeks.

Even though she arguably displayed some saintly skills, Sari was not a powerful queen, nor was she a pious Catholic. She remained in jeopardy because she could not be understood or categorized. She may have been a queen of hearts, but she was not The Queen of Scotland. Saint Margaret was pragmatically useful; Sari was inexplicably useful. Their contributions as women were worlds apart. Perhaps Sari was a Saint-in-waiting. But it was doubtful she would ever be perceived as such. Her Catholic leanings were not apparent. She presented more as a pagan or nature sprite.

The Catholic Church was obviously active in the deliberate quashing of the female voice down the years. Mother Mary was feted and worshipped as the Mother of Christ. But the *Mary Magdalene*

Gospels, were a threat to all The Church stood for. Male control had been imposed on the interpretation of doctrine and theology centuries before, and various uncomfortable accounts including those allegedly written by the self-proclaimed wife of Christ had mysteriously disappeared. That Jesus may have married and had children was considered heresy and blasphemy. It did not correlate with Christian theology or the doctrines of Salvation. A powerful female like the wife of Jesus, and her fictitious "Blood Line" could destabilize the whole system. If, The Catholic Church got wind that Sari was in fact a claimed descendent and embodiment of this Magdalene legacy, she would surely be lynched or burned at the stake; or at the least locked up for insanity.

There were rumours that the Gnostic heresies had been recorded in multiple copies and distributed across the ancient world. The church had not managed to get its hands on all the mass reproduced manuscripts and scrolls that threatened to undermine papal authority. Something subversive could emerge at any time eroding the precepts that Catholics held dear. This made The Church extremely jumpy. Wherever they saw threats to their power and authority they were determined to act.

No wonder Sari and Frederick felt increasingly uneasy. They even wondered initially if Ronan could be playing both sides. They were not aware of his heroics on their behalf in The Castle. He kept those quiet for his own reasons. In truth Ronan *was* playing both sides gently and subtly. Not with bad intentions, but in a bid to keep the peace and protect all agendas. He reasoned that all factions could live side by side, and neither was a threat to the other. The problem for him was of a personal nature. As his passion grew deeper for Sari, so his frustration grew at not being able to act upon them. The stakes got higher. He felt stuck and doomed. Destined to keep these powerful emotions secret and under wraps.

Sari had no choice but to sit on her feelings, even as Ronan sat on his. This left the two of them dancing around each other; knowing very well that there was an attraction. But profoundly doubting that it could ever be acted upon.

Ronan was not yet privy to the secret information about Sari. She could only confide in Frederick about it. Even they did not fully understand it. They could not possibly risk sharing it with Ronan until his loyalty to them was fully proven. Their departure time came without resolution. Sari and Ronan were at an impasse. He did not truly know her or who she was; and he could not reveal his feelings without more surety. It looked as if they were destined to part company. Ronan had been willing to travel alongside them to France. But in the end his father intervened citing "clan business."

Ronan has reasoned he would find out more on the journey and would only be away for a few months. But his father was fully aware that a few months could turn into a year maybe more. He was not convinced Sari and Frederick even intended to return to Moidart. This along with the chemistry he could sense between Sari and his eldest son, made him nervous to encourage them to spend any more time together.

Reginald was not ready to kiss Ronan goodbye. There was too much on the table and he had obligations to fulfil. He did not wish to encourage Ronan to woo Sari, as he was not fully satisfied, she was of the right ilk for his beloved son. The infamous *Clann Ruaidhri* interests had to come first. He was satisfied that a paternal intervention was required. He acted quickly to prevent Ronan's departure for France, offering a diversionary recce up north with some young clansmen to retrieve stolen goods that had been recovered and were being held in Glenelg. The younger men needed Ronan's leadership and good sense on the journey Reginald reasoned. Besides, he could not allow him to leave for such an indefinite period.

This direct intervention threw Ronan. He had been all set and willing to align his destiny with the travel plan. He had always wanted to journey further afield and the trip to France offered so much, not least more time with Sari in even closer quarters. His father's interference made things clear. Ronan was not allowed to plan for himself. He had to cut ties with Sari, and accept his fate as dictated by The Clann. He had been a fool to think he could pursue any other path. His heart sunk into its chest and he felt wounded in a way he could not describe. But at least he now knew the terms. There was some peace in this clarity. He would park his unresolved passion and content himself with some gentle, inoffensive Highland lass who would bear his children and ensure the family line.

It was with trepidation and sorrow that Sari set off without Ronan. She had come to love his presence by her side. She had just about admitted to herself that she had deep feelings for him. The attraction kept her vibrant and interested in her daily rounds, and she was full of warm anticipation at the possibility of Ronan accompanying them to France. She dared not hope for it. But right up until the last minute it looked like it could happen. Frederick was happy about the arrangement too. Indeed, his own paternal instinct rather liked the prospect of Ronan as a son in law. He could not fault him or his gentlemanly good humoured countenance. He was a good match for Sari in Frederick's eyes. The two of them together made him smile, and he could see how happy they made each other. If only they would admit it to themselves. But he knew there were background agendas at play. He had been surprised that it looked like Ronan would be able to come with them to France. And he was not surprised when it fell through.

It was Sari and Frederick against the world.

Condition normal.

CHAPTER TEN
The Return

On walking the next morning at dawn, Sari knew she must get her father back to Moidart and the safety of The Peninsula. Even if he had to rest up for several more weeks, that was okay. They had waited so long anyway.

What was a month or so longer?

She could not justify pressing on, at the risk of him dying on the road with her, or at sea in the small Cog boat that would likely be their means of transport across The Channel. She was not strong enough to dig a grave for him on some random roadside verge in France, and she could not bear the pain of seeing him flung overboard in a sea burial, which was what she was sensing would happen if she proceeded at this point.

Frederick seemed to be complicit with her decision. He was not speaking much, still weak from his ordeal the night before. He had felt his Spirit threaten to leave his body several times in the night. A luminous bright light had been beckoning, and he was quite content to move towards it. But something pulled him back every time he gave into the temptation. An energy was holding him in the earth plane. Probably for good reason. He was stuck between two strong agendas and forces vying for his Soul. At times it was not clear which was the lesser of two evils. The lack of resolution tired him further. He was accepting and resigned within, though did not honestly feel fully desirous of the exit either. He was physically done. Had been for years. But the strength of his purpose and love of life kept his Soul within his body, and he defied the odds that sought to defeat him on many occasions. Truly a cat with nine lives. A magnificent human being determined to indulge every drop of life. To help whomever he could. To savour every last smile, conversation, and view.

The presence of his daughter was a roadblock in his release into the other world. He did not want to burden her with the responsibility of having to deal with the dead weight of his body. He would be fine at the timing, whatever that might be. But she would not be. He had been ready to die at so many points in his life, he had lost count of the opportunities. His bond with his daughter was always a compelling reason to stay. He adored Scotland and loved to spend time with his family, ministering to the community at large. He took a lot of pride in his ability to help people. But in profound private moments he was tired. His Soul was tired and craved eternal rest.

"The peace which passeth all understanding," was really an enticing prospect to Frederick. Not that he had a destructive death wish. Quite the opposite. He loved life and all its simple pleasures. He relished them, appreciating them all in minute detail. But he also had such resonance of faith and belief in the welcoming loving arms of The Saviour.

Frederick had seen The Godhead waiting right at the end of the tunnel of bright light, one other time before. The synergy of 'The Father, Son, and Holy Ghost' felt so warm, vibrant, and ironically life-filled, that he willingly moved towards the exit point; only to hear the

66

words,

"Back you go Frederick. It is not your time yet. There are more people who need your help."

Reluctantly he sunk back into his body, feeling again the dripping sweat, the laboured breathing, and that familiar shakiness indicating an urgent need for something sweet. The nectar of life. Frederick needed it regularly. It was a puzzling metaphor bestowed upon him by the gods. For he was more than sweet enough in his nature already. For some inexplicable reason, his destiny was inextricably linked with the minutia of his daily routine. The challenge was to monitor minute by minute food, drink, and sugar intake.

Frederick suffered from what was labelled the "sugar disease." This unkind scourge affected everything. His bodily functions were permanently bowed at the altar of 'sugar.' He had to discern when to lie down, when to eat, when to walk, when to get up. All his bodily needs had to be meticulously noted. There was no room for much variation or spontaneity. If Frederick were not near fortifying food when he needed it, he would suffer immensely. Missing a meal would knock his system off for the whole of the next day, sometimes longer. It was crucial to get the balance right. This persistent 'search for sweetness' became a metaphor for everything. His Spirit was blessed with an overload of sweetness; whereas his body craved it in random undulating moments that were difficult to predict.

Frederick's problem with the balance of his energy levels had haunted him since his seventeenth year. He had been a healthy child, with a propensity to wet the bed and feel the cold. But as he matured into a young man, he was suddenly afflicted. He succumbed to a craving thirst, weight loss, and extreme lethargy. No one knew what to do about this. But by instinct Frederick found relief thanks to the bees he tended on the family farm. The fodder of the pollen-rich Scottish heather proved to be a life saver. His portable magic pot of honey become his saving grace. Without it his years would have been short and grim.

The sugar sickness was the thorn in Frederick's side. He learned to manage it. He had ways of making sure the crisis points did not occur too often. Eating regularly, sleeping long and well, and avoiding major doses of the lethal Highland mead were his main methods. The pot of local honey hidden in the lining of his thick coat was a shared secret, staving off many a crisis.

Truly the elixir of life!

As they worked, Sari knew how to tend to Frederick's needs in terms of managing their time. Whether they stayed too long in a dark, damp abode ministering to a woman who had just given birth to a still born; or they had a crowd gathered around them listening to one of Frederick's stories, hanging on his every word, Sari always knew how to beat a retreat and protect her father. Willing to serve though he was, he also had his own needs which needed to be carefully respected, or he would of course be of no use to anybody.

Frederick knew a heavenly reception awaited him when he finally succumbed to the alluring light at the end of the tunnel. It was all becoming too familiar, and predictable. He was resigned to the process and was content to leave whenever The Almighty required it. He did not want to leave Sari, or other members of their close-knit family. But in recent months he had become more convinced of her independence and strength. He knew she did not really need him quite as much as she used to. She had blossomed into a fine young woman of whom he could be proud. She took no prisoners and could stand up for herself. But he understood her where others did not and knew this was important to her. *That* part was still a worry. Frederick was concerned that she had no partner with whom to share her life, and ideally, he would like to see such a union established before he departed the earth plane. Like Sari he knew The Divine may have another plan. But he hoped and wished for his daughter's happiness, as all good earthly fathers do.

"Let us go Pappa! Let us get you home."

"We can rest you up and then assess things. God knows we waited a long time. We can wait a few weeks more."

"Yes love." Her father responded with the soft gentle lilt she knew and loved so well.

"No one lives forever you know!" He added with a wry smile.

Sari sensed he was trying to comfort her and bring a bit of humour to the grim situation he intuited she had faced the night before. It was typical of Frederick to always lighten the tone and keep spirits up whenever something difficult was looming. His ease and grace in the face of life's difficulties always inspired her beyond words. She did not understand how her father was able to put up with such relentless physical suffering and yet minister to the whole community with such magnificent selfless compassion, and patience. His wisdom was unbounded and his countenance always generous, attentive, and engaged. Folk gravitated to Frederick like moths to a flame. His charisma and aura radiated for miles around. He did not impose his presence, and yet he was not someone you could ignore. His words were soothing and reassuring and there was a healing quality to his insight and tone. The warmth of his touch as he took your hand in his was indescribably magical, causing anxiety to melt away effortlessly.

He truly was a Saint amongst men.

She mused to herself for what felt like the millionth time.

CHAPTER ELEVEN

The Lineage

There was a horrible chill in the air as Sari and Frederick approached Inverlochy. They had got as far as the mountain hut on the flanks of Beinn Nevis. The *bothag* used by Shepherds, when they were not inclined to make the journey home, always served its purpose. But as a family they seemed destined not to pass beyond it, either to scale the magnificent mountain above, nor to proceed with journeys further afield.

Sari remembered the accommodations from childhood, when she had made the journey with her parents to Inverlochy. The Pictish duns and early Celtic settlements had been almost destroyed by The Vikings. The wider community hobbled along after the massacres, rebuilding their crofts and duns while nurturing plans to build a grand castle in defiance of invading marauders. The damaged largest dun, which was still inhabited, had stayed in her consciousness as a place of intrigue and compelling darkness. She smelled damp and murder within its walls. She was right, not many in the area survived the Nordic raiders.

70

Those who retreated up The Beinn were the ones who effectively hid themselves out of reach, and as a result there were a number of shelters in various states of repair on the lower flanks of the mountain, hidden in the trees.

Their intention had been to climb The Beinn. But her mother Magda, who was in the early stages of pregnancy with her younger brother Friel, did not feel she could risk scrambling higher. Sari's mother had lost several pregnancies after giving birth to Sari, including a stillborn child when Sari was four. They could not afford to take any chances.

Sari knew that her mother had the same divine obligation to produce the extension of The Mary Magdalene Lineage as she did. Magda had already achieved this on her first attempt with Sari. So, it did not seem certain that another child would be viable, or even "allowed."

The family had learned through their ancestral line that they were the likely descendants of Jesus and Mary Magdalene. Hidden stories and preserved secrets verified that Jesus had married Mary and had children with her. The Gnostic teachings discarded by The Catholic Church, claimed that Jesus "kissed her often."

The references to Mary as Jesus' companion and "favoured" disciple were frequent, inspiring questioning and jealousy amongst his male compatriots. These inconvenient truths were dismissed as unreliable gossip by The Church. But the Cathars knew differently. They guarded physical evidence of the secrets and perpetuated the stories orally to ensure their maintenance amongst the '*Perfecti.*' A privileged few were the guardians of these documents. But the spoken accounts were also necessary in case the physical scrolls were ever destroyed. The Cathars knew The Catholic Church had sniffed out the existence of these documents that threatened to hurl their ecclesiastical structures into oblivion. The oral history was confined to the relevant descendants as much as possible, who usually felt the truth in their bones anyway. Such was their legacy.

Sari at the age of four already knew inexplicable things, and she was able to reassure her mother as Magda held the dead bloodied stillborn boy in her arms.

"Don't worry mamma! He will come back next time."

"He wants to be here."

"Next time he will stay with us."

Sari's mother Magda was moved by Sari's certainty. Though of course she mourned the baby. The expectations she had had; the lovely pregnancy she had this time enjoyed, and its' terrible ending. All had to be processed. Magda had been full of wonderful hope for this child. Having lost three early gestations prior to this, she had felt this child, who she sensed was a boy, would go the distance.

Magda wanted to give Frederick a son. Although her husband's devotion to Sari was guaranteed. She could see they were close, almost at times to her exclusion. But the continuation of the family line for the male side of things still had to be fulfilled.

This family sometimes seems to be too much about the girls!

Magda often thought to herself.

"It's a girl!"

Frederick had exclaimed when Sari popped out with the greatest of ease. He was not disappointed and adored the new child. But it took him some time to adjust. Magda could see that. She herself wanted to birth a son or two for their dotage. There was some hard work on the land that needed to be done, and the community always celebrated the birth of boys with true delight.

Sari had been expected. Magda *knew*. Her own honed senses required her to carry a special girl, who had a unique destiny unbeknownst to many. She did not know exactly what this would be. But she had been told of The Magdalene Legacy in whispers by her own mother Mary, and she knew the female line was in this family, just as important as the male. More important she reluctantly conceded.

Others looking on would not have known this. But Frederick appreciated the gravity of their mission in these ways. He had been told of the heritage as all spouses of the spiritual line were. He had just expected his first born to be a son! Magda had warned him repeatedly, it might be otherwise. As the pregnancy developed, she could sense the powerful but gentle energy of a wise female soul. She knew in her bones, the first born would fulfil the 'requirements.'

Magda's own special mission was to bring Sari into the world. Frederick understood this, and once his initial shock had abated, he delighted in Sari's rich chuckle, sparkling blue eyes and rosebud shaped mouth.

Never was there a more beautiful child!

He reflected everyday as he gazed upon her.

His beautiful baby girl brought Frederick endless joy, and as she grew, so did their connection.

Every time thereafter that Magda lost a child he was devastated. He still hoped for a son in the back of his mind. But he became more and more resigned that this may never happen. He became more and more invested in Sari. Frederick could see that she may need his full attention and that too many siblings might hold her back. It became increasingly apparent too that their mission might be merged. As a single child Sari gave him a lot of scope for his paternal energy. He began to think he may not cope with anymore "little blessings" anyway.

Sari's nurturing and development were crucial. She had a lot that she would take on in later life. They all knew this. Both Magda and Frederick began to accept that Sari was all they needed. A true blessing to enjoy. An exceptional if 'only' child. More than enough for them in any case. Naturally as soon as they had resigned themselves to this decision, Magda fell pregnant again. And again. And again. Each time, the premature loss led to the same conclusions. Either they were going to be a powerful trio, or there was a persistent fourth element trying to join them, that kept changing its mind at the last minute.

Magda took heart at Sari's prediction. As she held the dead stillborn baby boy in her arms. She believed her young daughter, and resolved to try one more time, before she took the herbs that would ensure she never could bear a child again. She still wanted to honour Frederick's heartfelt wish as a man, and she also wanted some company herself. She could already sense that Sari and Frederick would be as "thick as thieves" throughout their lifetime together. She did not feel left out. But she had started to feel a bit emotionally isolated. There was much more time alone these days. This was part of her own devastation at the loss of this baby boy. She had carried him full term sensing the soft life within. But if she were being honest, she sensed again that he was lacking in enthusiasm and movement as the birthday fast approached. She had had her concerns but did not voice them.

The small family named the dead baby Frederick as they buried him in deep dense ground by the river. They wanted to do a natural burial and their own baptism and ceremony. Sari's confidence that this little boy would be back within the next year or so gave Magda and Frederick hope and heart. They had begun to listen increasingly to their little oracle. When they first noticed her comments and predictions they smiled. Even her expressions and pointing little finger before she could speak indicated her legacy.

They knew who she was. But did not expect her to be at work, so quickly at such a tender age. Most of the initial hints had been in the form of how Sari responded to people as a baby and young child. Even by the age of two Sari would quickly cower in the face of shady characters and would cry at a moment's notice if the energies were off in any place that she was taken. Magda with her own sensory perception, was always able to validate what her baby was meaning.

Sari was taken seriously right from the start. She even spotted things her mother missed and was proving to be increasingly useful in their decisions and the way they planned their day. Life started to revolve around their wonder child. Perhaps a little too much. But they adored her and were happy to give her the priority she deserved. This also served their own needs, even at times the needs of the community.

It already looked as if Sari was progressing beyond expectations. She was fast becoming a self-reliant self-contained autonomous Spirit Healer in a league of her own. A couple more years and she would have left them all behind. Her intuition was magical. Her ability to read the signs on the horizon did not have to be taught. It all came to her without any apparent thought. She was young to be channelling such comprehensive information. But that is exactly what she was doing. At this rate she would not even need an education. Everything she needed to know was at her fingertips. Magda was introducing her to all the herbs and techniques that *she* knew. But already found that Sari was concocting her own effective potions using foraging skills beyond reproach. Magda would test Sari for what might be required in any given situation. But was never surprised that she already knew the answer. She superseded her expectations repeatedly with new observations and perspectives.

Sari's spirit was intrepid. Her anticipation and eagerness for life was remarkable. She absorbed everything like a sponge and did not miss a trick. She was strong and canny and could run rings around the best of them. At the age of six, Sari was keen for adventure. Already she was older than her tender years in so many ways. Her eloquence had been apparent from as early as the ages of two and three. Clearly an old soul in a young delicate frame, her spirit was stronger than her physical capabilities. Her energy was obviously going to propel her through life, even at the times when her body disagreed with her.

Magda was fourth months into the last pregnancy and everything was looking promising. Even though she felt assured that this child would be born alive and thrive, she was alarmed at the slight bleed that had happened during the night. She did not have the same feeling of unease that she did with the other pregnancies, but the horse riding over rougher ground had obviously disagreed with her.

Magda, Frederick, and Sari aborted their plans to scale the heights above them. The disgruntled horses who had been due a longer rest at the *bothag* reluctantly turned about, retracing their steps from the day before. The small convoy proceeded cautiously, reversing their outward journey along the shores of Loch Eil, and Loch Shiel to Acharacle, where they rested another couple of days at Magda's sister's house.

Sheena was Sari's aunt, another of the sisters of The Holy Grail lineage. Less important than Magda who was her elder by a couple of years. It was always the firstborn daughter who bore the burdens. Now Sari was incarnated, Sheena was not even the oracle-in-waiting any longer. So long as Magda kept in good health whilst Sari was young, it looked as if Sheena was destined for a blessed life of contentment, happiness, and joyous motherhood, overseeing the development of the winking Finneas and his brother Finton.

It was disappointing to have to return home without climbing the Beinn. Sari had admired its peak from afar in her mind's eye and sensed its magnificent brooding energy. She instinctively wanted a "charge-up" from mother nature at its peak.

Already Sari was consciously learning the ways of communing with energies. It was second nature and she was teaching herself. She noticed how she felt near rivers, by the sea, climbing hills. The deer on the moors and the birds in the sky would view her curiously. They were drawn to her calm disposition, and the community noticed that from an early age she had a special connection with animals. Some of them even wanted to double check Magda's suggestions with Sari's. A phenomenon that was a little difficult for Magda to adjust to. But Adjust she did. Each blessing of mother nature affected Sari differently. Already she was starting to play with the "molecules." If only she had known that was what they would come to be called.

Stories of Beinn Nevis reached them frequently, and Sari was fascinated by the mountain's ability to be friendly one minute, menacing and threatening the next. Climbers spoke of clear days where the ascent had been clear and glorious and the views spectacular, only for the descent to turn into a slippery treacherous slog from hell, with no visibility, and no surety of safety. Sari was unperturbed. So was Frederick. They likely would have continued if not for their obligation to Magda, the sibling and probable son growing in her belly.

CHAPTER TWELVE

The Reunion

S ari could not describe the relief she felt deep inside as she saw Ronan riding towards her. As she stood in the doorway of Sheena's small stone croft, Sari's heart fluttered with delight. The reunion she had sensed with increasing anticipation as she and Frederick neared The Penninsula, was here, riding towards her at breakneck speed.

She had not been sure how to instigate seeing Ronan. But she knew she had to. Now, it was clear. No action on her part was needed. Except to respond to his lead. She needed to be primed to not hold back. Willing to go wherever this may lead. She really had had enough of dancing around the possibilities. Now was the time for some engagement. Something real. Something not curtailed by doubt, fear, or interference.

She recognized Merlin from some distance away, and sensed Ronan's energy on his back, though she could not be quite sure until they drew closer. She would know him anywhere, even from a distance. But she needed her eyes to fully *see* him before she dared believe.

He had come to find her!

This was a wonderfully delicious moment and gave her much hope for their developing connection. Who could have known that her father's ill health in the cabin would intervene to bring Ronan back to her in what seemed like the blink of an eye! She did not want to indulge thoughts of destiny and "meant to be." She did not want to tempt fate. But the signs were good. She noted a flickering in her psyche. An acknowledgement that the stars might be finally aligning.

Sari needed to hear what Ronan had to say. Perhaps he was just bringing news of Castle Tioram or an instruction to his father's tenants. Sari was good at arguing herself down from premature excitement, such her disappointment been. She had little choice but to keep her emotions in check. But her heart and spirit were full of magical expectation as she saw him fast approach. She could hardly take it all in. A few days ago, she had left Moidart thinking she may never see him again. Now here he was, admittedly bedraggled and exhausted looking, galloping towards her.

Ronan had heard news of Sari and Frederick's return and that they were resting with Sheena and her sons. Desperate to see Sari he was concerned about Frederick too. He had not really wanted him to go on the long journey, and if not for Reginald's intervention Ronan himself would have surely accompanied Sari all the way to France.

Anything could have happened!

Ronan had felt acutely bereft when Sari left. Much more than he expected. His half-hearted resolution to settle with an innocuous highland lass lasted for about half of the journey to *Eilean Donan*. As he approached the fortified islet, he resolved to follow Sari and Frederick to France despite his father's wishes. He would complete this stupid mission and then be on his way. He knew the two of them could use his company. It was a dangerous route and he knew he could catch up with them within a day or two. He felt relief that he had finally decided. No more dithering.

Ronan had returned from the north feeling short-changed by his father in more ways than one. He figured things were about to change. He had reluctantly managed a swift there-and-back to *Eilean Donan* to collect the missing goods and was met with the sensational news at the gates of Castle Tioram.

Frederick and Sari had taken so long to set off on their journey, that their swift return had caused a lot of commentary and gossip.

"Perhaps it is not destined to be."

"Frederick is too old for this now."

"Sari should probably give up on the idea."

"Time to drop notions of grandeur!"

"Sari needs to find a husband before winter!"

They had that last one right, thought Sari when she got wind of all the theories.

Ronan felt compelled to go to Sari direct without even stepping inside the castle walls. But first he had to deal with his father. After an unceremonious debrief and disgruntled report of the journey, Ronan felt he had fully offloaded his duties. He was intensely annoyed at Reginald who had obviously conjured up this elaborate ruse just to get him away from Sari as she prepared for her departure. It felt like his father had sent the "treasure" north himself with a convoy passing through the previous month. A magnificent banquet had been laid on for the noblemen, and doubtless Reginald hatched his plan then and there.

Reginald obviously did not want Sari and Ronan engaging in any last-minute elopement or hand-fasting ceremony, so he roped his son into the farcical five-day hard ride to *Eilean Donan*. He also timed it perfectly, making sure Ronan's departure was several days before he knew Sari and Frederick planned to leave. This would protect his "investment," and prevent any last-minute regrets, engagements, or changes of plan. With Ronan out of the way heading north, the would-be lovers could adjust and move on.

Mindful that Ronan was a skilled horseman who could cover a lot of ground if the motivations were strong enough, Reginald added some finer details to his scheme. He figured that the main enticement Sari, was soon to be heading in the opposite direction anyway, so anticipated that his son would drag his heels and not want to return in a hurry. To ensure the snare was complete he also sent along an amusing coterie of young men with Ronan "for company."

Ronan had sneered when he saw his travel companions and instantly rumbled Reginald's agenda. These were notorious clansmen known for their hard drinking, who were likely to fall foul of the nearest tavern on a whim. He thought of aborting the mission on the spot. But knew within himself that he needed a diversion for a week or two. He figured that he may have to off-load this "motley crew" at some point. But, for the moment Ronan decided to humour his father and give the contrived task a semblance of legitimacy. It was undoubtedly a *fait accompli,* but Ronan figured he could ultimately use it to his advantage.

He was not his father's son for nothing, Ronan mused as he justified his compliance to himself. He resolved to "get this out of the way" and return with a fresh mind and heart.

If possible.

Reginald was quite sure that his eldest would be licking his wounds for some time to come and may even be gone a month or so on this fool's errand. Already strong in the knowledge that Sari was resolved to leave, Reginald reasoned that the round-trip of at least ten days would divert Ronan from her allure long enough to energetically cut the cords between them. Yes, it would possibly lead him into some questionable antics. But such indiscretions were easily dealt with when he returned home, especially if they all occurred in the north. The Clann did not have much business beyond the outer reaches of Moidart anyway.

Besides, the boy probably needed to let off steam!

The "treasure" that needed to be retrieved was predictably hardly worth the effort. It was nothing more than several silver goblets the kitchen had reported missing after a particularly riotous banquet. Reginald had known this. Ronan knew it was partly this. But he had been led to believe that it was also an important trip to retrieve a significant part of his legacy and some crucial documents. Despite his suspicions, he could hardly turn down the retrieval mission as he understood that one of the Tioram gold chests may have been compromised.

After the banquet on heading to his chambers full of red wine, Ronan had been aware of a lot of fuss outside his father's bedroom chamber where the chests were kept. He had peered through the door and saw one of the chests opened. So, based on physical evidence, he had no reason to doubt his father's word. Though he *did*. He had little choice but to ride it out. His fate was sealed.

Reginald had instructed him on arrival to ask for a James Matheson who knew the whereabouts of the held items. He was warned not to expect luxurious accommodations. He was briefed that *Eilean Donan* was a large "curtain wall" castle commissioned by Alexander II currently in development. The project was on a grand scale. But Reginald was not sure how much had been completed. He honestly did not know if Ronan would have to camp beside a wall, or if he would have his own chambers. Reginald at least expected Ronan to be entertained. James Matheson was a curious character who had travelled the world extensively and could allegedly "talk to the birds." Matheson had been given the job of overseeing this grand defense project, and rumour had it that he had sired an attractive daughter who lived with her mother nearby. Reginald thought Ronan would find James intriguing. This plus the "bonnie daughter" should soften the blow when he found out he was only on a mission on behalf of Castle Tioram kitchen staff.

As Ronan discretely rode out from Castle Tioram at dusk, he figured his father's manipulations were about to spectacularly backfire. The "bonnie daughter" had turned out to be a feisty curly-haired red-head with a generous waistline, smelly breath, crooked teeth, and a defiant gaze.

"More like a man in a dress if truth be told," Ronan had ended up describing her to his father.

The debrief did not last long. Reginald knew Ronan was displeased and simply listened to his complaints. He explained the compromised gold chest issue had been resolved. A castle cleaner had off-loaded some of its contents into another container to move the chest, and clean around the chamber. Forgetting to reassemble everything, "said servant" had promptly travelled off to see family in The Lothians without informing anyone of his actions.

"Really!" was all Ronan could manage to say to that fantastical excuse.

Goblets returned undamaged, and his account of events fully recounted, Ronan bowed out of his father's meeting room. The only useful thing that had come from the whole exercise was that he now knew for certain that Sari was his destiny. His father by diverting him from his heart's desire, had in fact consolidated it in his heart and mind. For the first time in a long time. Possibly for the first time ever. Ronan's thought processes and emotional inclinations were in harmony.

It would not take him long to reach Sheena's abode if he sped and galloped the whole way. After the long return journey to *Eilean Donan,*

Ronan was in horseback mode. Not in the least bit saddle sore, he was able to journey with ease and grace. In this groove he would not have been fazed if you had told him Sari was two hundred miles away. He would still have felt the journey was achievable in one day.

Slight exaggeration, he smiled to himself.

His horse loved the continual movement and the connection they made as they made swift work of the land beneath them. If Matheson could tweet to birds, Ronan could whisper to horses. He merged his energy with the magnificent beast as he rode. The equine engine and its capacity never ceased to amaze him. Ronan's favourite was his magical black stallion Merlin. Merlin was six yet had the movement and spirit of a younger three-year-old. Youthful enough to keep his stamina and energy well-paced. But experienced enough to deal with all weathers and terrains without noticing the difference. He could fly across the Scottish landscape as if he had wings. The rough ground and boggy moors did not faze him. He knew his direction and he knew that Ronan led him where he needed to go. The synergy and trust between horse and master was a wonder to behold.

The thunder of hooves enlivened Ronan, the hot snorting breath of the horse as they belted at full tilt through the damp dusk air was music to his ears. Merlin could sense Ronan's anxiety and perceived they were on a mission far more important than the one they had just returned from. Tedious in the extreme, Merlin had engaged his energy with workmanship for that long haul. This brisk gallop felt lighter more joyful yet earnest. Merlin could not wait to see what it was all adding up to. His master had seemed out of sorts the last several weeks, and he observed that the fresh smelling fragrant blonde with the wonderfully warm hands had not stroked his flanks or relieved his aching muscles in a long time.

Horse and master covered this ride with energy and enthusiasm, knowing something gorgeous and heart-warming awaited them on arrival. Both were primed in their expectation and this added extra speed, propelled them onwards, ever onwards, until suddenly in a clearing Ronan and Merlin came across a light-filled homestead. Warm laughter, chattering voices and the wonderful smells of bread and stew wafted out into the night towards them. Merlin was fully engaged in anticipation of warm hay and a deep sleep, hopefully alongside the handsome chestnut filly ridden by the woman with the soft hands. Ronan was eager to see Sari and give her the intense passionate kiss he had been replaying in his mind for days.

CHAPTER THIRTEEN

The Union

Yes! Yesss! Oh yesssss!!!" Sari moaned softly as she writhed in ecstasy. Her toes curled in tension. Anticipating that this just might go on for longer than she dared hope.

She was anxious to hold the energy. Prolong the intensity. This deliciousness. She did not want this to ever stop. Ever.

She could feel him moving within her. Expanding. Firmly. Earnestly. With conviction. Her loins rose to engage with his. She moved slowly to luxuriate the feeling. To hold him. Contained inside. She could feel the pulsating waves mounting. Her own climax approaching. Quickly. She did not want that final explosion. Not yet.

She wanted this moment frozen in time.

She curled her toes.

Moaned.

Bit her lip.

"Ronan, oh Ronan!" She whispered in his ear.

He did not speak. He let his body respond harder, more earnestly

86

in reply.

Her encouragement meant she was becoming rigid.

Ready. Taut. Waiting to gush and release. To yield to him fully.

Fully his.

Unconsciously she responded. She had not done this before. She just knew to follow his lead. She did not have to think about it.

They just *were*.

In the moment.

Out of time and space.

Their hearts untied.

Their worlds collided.

This was all she had wanted.

Everything she had expected.

Ronan and Merlin pulled up sharply as Sari ran out onto the sodden grass to greet them.

"Ronan!"

"Yes, my love! I'm here!"

Sari could hardly believe what she was hearing. His voice had taken on an effortless soothing tone, embracing her ears with warm affection. His energy jumped right inside her, penetrating her to the core. There were no more words. No need for any more words. The familiarity was instant, unrehearsed, and organically easy. Souls who had known each other many times before, finally conceding to a long-resisted embrace. What was between them was instinctive, telepathic, and complicit.

They had both been longing for and imagining this moment for so long. Ronan had played it out countless times in his head on his return journey. Sari had played it out countless times before she even left. She had hoped for this so many times. That Ronan would just reach for her without asking. Just draw her to him without thinking. Take her and claim her. Her breath used to rise and fall heavily in her chest at the thought of it.

She almost fell into his arms by accident or design so many times. She had just been waiting for the inevitable, knowing it would propel them to the next level. Into the other place, where words held no sway. Where souls met, where bodies flowed lighter, and minds connected, intertwining effortlessly with the other dimensions. Cosmically charged and mystically aligned.

It was such an enormous presentient feeling that she did not know what to do with it. In his presence she became energetically complete. The woman she was born to be. No longer the Oracle who served others. But complete. Fulfilled. Herself.

Sari knew Ronan overwhelmed her senses. He could do all this to her, and more. She had no doubt that the sweet surrender would be everything she anticipated. His ease of touch and grace in movement. The way he rode his horses. The way he smiled and caught her eye. Sari felt his touch all over her before he even held her hand. It had all played out in her mind and heart so many times.

It was real.

Yet.

Nothing.

Had.

Actually.

Happened.

Such was the curse of sensual intuition. Their meetings on the ethers. In dreams. In imagination. It had happened multiple times between them already.

And. Yet. Nothing. Had. Ever. REALLY. Happened.

She knew he felt the same. She could see it in the way his eyes held hers, lighting up when he followed the contours of her body. She felt undressed by him. He thought she did not know. She deliberately distracted herself with whoever they were attending. But she *knew*. She could feel his soul piercing her veil. There was no illusion in this secret

88

place.

Such was the intensity of their varied conjugations that she felt they had already consummated their passion. She had been both disappointed and relieved that their physical union did not happen. Her enlivened sensations would not have coped with any hurt or pain resulting from such a union. It did not naturally happen before she set off with Frederick. She knew if it had, she would have probably stayed. Neither of them seemed inclined to force it. It was a shared acknowledgment to recognize it yet not to act upon it. This was bigger than what either of them wished for. The "Lineage Contract" seemingly was bigger still.

What if the two elements could collide?

She dared not indulge this thought. Yet she felt it possible through to her bones. Perhaps all the interference and resistance simply reflected that they both already *knew* they had a special union and purpose.

How frustrating that for so long it seemed like the "sensible" options were the only viable ones: family obligations, paternal requirements, lineage expectations. What other people dictated could or could not happen.

Ronan dismounted his horse sweeping her up into his arms. Within seconds they were earnestly kissing. His tongue anxiously reaching to entwine with hers. All the passion that had been building between them found its expression at last. With the greatest of ease. A delicious, sensual lingering kiss, that sealed the deal within their hearts and souls.

Only the French could understand *Le Grande Amour*.

Tongues.

Sari could speak in tongues.

This embrace needed no translation.

The stable where they lay was warm and comforting. There was hay everywhere. In Sari's hair, her clothing, her curves had sprouted straw, even her womanly hidden places felt invaded by sharp pieces of straw. Such was their ardour she had not noticed these imposters in the throes of passion.

Ronan had been everywhere. All over her. Inside and out. So apparently had the straw. She smiled to herself at the analogy. Sometimes she had quite a warped sense of humour that she kept mostly to herself. Her brain worked quite like a man's at times. She probably would have been fine in the bawdy tavern with Ronan's cohorts. The beer, stench, swearing and lechery would probably be irritating. But cope with it she could.

She did not want to offend her Romeo by testing out her perversions in this situation. The scourge of that Scorpio Moon. She felt sure he could handle it. He had handled everything else. But this between them was what "they" call "romantic."

Sari decided to let her verbosity rest. She did not need to talk on this watch. She lay back savouring the warmth and connection. Lying in his arms felt secure, comforting and acutely erotic. She did not need him. She was quite able to take care of herself. But she adored him and desired him. She would quite happily ditch the "contract" obligations in favour of Ronan's fancy. She wanted to please him above all else.

She knew her destiny and obligation. Or did she? In this moment it felt as if *he* were it. She still had a hunch the two worlds could collide as their bodies had just done. Now was not the time for a serious conversation. Now was the time to indulge and fully recognize their love.

Ronan had taken her. Without ceremony. It felt perfect. She did not mind they were not handfasted or married. In her head and heart, they already were. She felt the familiarity of his soul from many lifetimes before. In this moment they were reunited not consummated. This was a reunion. A union in this lifetime. But a reunion considering the all the shared lifetimes of their souls.

Thankfully, the stables were a little removed from the croft. Admittedly shared with a few neighbours, fellow crofters in the community. But Sari concluded that most people were inside for the night as they led Merlin to his berth. The risk was exhilarating anyway. They were only aware of each other, and the loaded silence heavy with anticipation as they led Merlin towards the stable. They only had eyes for each other. Could only sense, smell and see each other.

The crisp night air and starry sky were discrete companions. It did not matter who observed them or happened up on them. This was about them only. Gossip would come from such a sighting but on balance they sensed it would not happen. Not quite yet anyway. This was their time.

Everyone in Sheena's croft was heading for bed. They all had supped on the stew and warm bread, leaving Merlin loosely tied to the bit loop hook on the wall of the croft. They were not contriving for alone time. But the household seemed to know and have an understanding that they would like to be left alone. Frederick was in bed from an early hour. He was resting as Ronan arrived. It would be a surprise for him in the morning.

One of several, Sari mused.

Still recuperating and resting, Frederick would probably have his supper later at some random point in the night when his sugar levels dictated.

Sheena gave a knowing smile as Sari and Ronan headed outside to bring Merlin to the stables. Sari did not indulge it and stuck to the laws of social politesse. She assured her they would not be long. Sheena knew different. She was not actually sure she needed to make up a bed for Ronan. She suspected not much sleeping would be going on that night.

Ronan contained her. Pinned her against the wall. Lifted her gently and lowered her to the ground. She was showing him the stable. The booth for Merlin alongside her filly Delphine. Merlin was pleased, snorting, and whinnying in recognition of his female compatriot. They led him into his quarters, which had a small way through to Delphine should he want to go visit and make his presence felt, gently or otherwise. She was not in season, so more serious engagement was unlikely. But who knew?

Sari turned quickly to smile at Ronan. He was right there his face moving quickly towards her. His arms reaching for her waist. Their lips met. More urgently this time.

Ronan pressured her forward against the wall. She various parts of his body growing taught, rigid, moving against her.

Before she knew it, she was on the floor, resting comfortably in the warm dry hay. She let the encounter take over. She did not want to spoil this with overthinking or questioning. She surrendered herself body mind and spirit to him. As he fumbled and loosened her corset exposing her left plump rounded breast fully, she lay there eagerly responding to him as he ran his hands all over her. His mouth descended onto her breast as she writhed in intense pleasure. Her groaning was soft and gentle as he explored every inch of her. She let him do whatever he pleased. The tension built quickly even though she wanted to savour every kiss, and caress. Thrusting gently, she could feel him pushing his member against her thigh. She wanted him. Now.

"It's okay Ronan!"

"Now!"

"Please. Now!"

Ronan did not need to be invited twice. He pulled up her skirts even further, ripped her under cover away gently but insistently. She helped him loosen her corset further exposing the second breast for his delight. He seemed to take great pleasure in her curves, moaning intensely as he indulged his delight in her.

"Sari!"

"Shhhh …. Take me Ronan! Take me now!"

92

She wanted him in deep. Quickly. He found her core and pushed. Gently pushed. He knew it was her first time. He could feel the membrane tear as he eased himself inside. She seemed to be okay. Responding moving. He knew he could just surrender. She was all in. Did not need coaxing. Did not need to be coached or coerced. She was in full surrender. His delight increased.

Feeling full and bursting with pleasure. Sari could feel his warmth inside. Growing building its intensity like a primal force beyond him somehow. Yet truly him. All of him.

Ronan could have released his energy so quickly into her. He could feel the waves of ecstasy building in him quicker than he had ever known. This was no chore. No mismatch or awkward fumbling moment. This was supreme and sublime. Everything he thought it probably could never feel like was here. Right here.

He had to hold back.

For her.

Thoughts of silver goblets.

Eilean Donan architectural plans.

The ginger haired daughter and her crooked teeth.

His annoying father, for whom he had nearly missed this moment.

All of this helped him stay his course as he waited for Sari to respond. To breathe more deeply. He needed to hear and feel that growing energy within her as her coming release built. He was not going to end this before she peaked. He would peak with her.

He waited as she built. He knew she could be as quick as he. But he also knew she wanted to fully live their union. To make it last for as long as possible.

Goblets
Treasure
Father
Teeth
Anything!

93

For some reason, the "goblets" enabled him to thrust with extra intensity. Fired in part by anger perhaps. He was not sure. But the cursed goblets enhanced his performance and held him steady.

He had finally found a valuable use for those damned things!

Ronan was aware of his horse Merlin not too far away. He could feel the warmth of his breath on his back and hear his gentle snorting. As the masculine conquering energy mounted in the stable, Merlin whinnied his approval. This was hardly an animalistic encounter. But the two animals were a very present audience. Merlin moved closer to Delphine snorting approval, nuzzling, and licking her. If she had been in season there would have been another consummation that night. The horses winked and snorted their approval intermittently as the heat between Ronan and Sari grew to a crescendo.

The horses connected telepathically to the mating were getting worked up and frisky. Ronan had given up thinking of goblets, increasing the thrusting as he sensed Sari's energy build simultaneously.

Boom! He exploded in the uncontrollable jerking movements of complete ecstasy. Sari beneath him was crashing and burning as the waves grew more and more intense.

"Yes! Yes!! Yesssssssss!" She screamed as she reached her peak. The passion within him surged and he melted. His warm fluid seed gushing into her. Far up into her. He merged with her life force. The etheric connection was complete. The seed was sewn. Their destiny complete.

They lay there in each other's arms. Their passion satiated for the moment. The night sky was cold outside. Ronan could see the stars flickering through the small stable window. Merlin was still heavy breathing and snorting to himself only a few away. Sari smelt so good. So sweet soft in his arms. He was complete. This was everything he never thought possible.

Here they were on a stable floor and yet they could have been lying in a four-poster bed in the grandest honeymoon chamber. This love

94

was all they needed. They were one. Truly they had found themselves in a sweet union.

What more was needed?

What needed to be said?

No-thing

PART TWO

2019

CHAPTER FOURTEEN
3rd June

Sarah's father died in the morning. 11.44 am. In a typically coordinated and respectable moment. Just in time for his usual lunch at noon. Except of course this was one day he would not be injecting insulin in preparation for the meagre hospital fayre. Sarah had done everything in her power to prevent this; even to the point of attempting to advise hospital consultants. She had researched obscure aspects of his complex conditions, hoping to apply relevant healing and delay what was looking increasingly inevitable. There was a sense of surrender and submission and compliance within the extended family. Sarah could tell that Pa did not want to be a burden, and although he really wanted to come home; he seemed to be resigned to longer and longer spells in the hospital. Within himself he was ready and waiting on God's timing. Indeed, he had announced himself to be at peace with 'whatever may happen' some years previously.

The last time she saw him, Sarah had managed to coordinate him being moved back into 22 with its spectacular view over towards the Welsh hills. A few days before she could tell he was immensely disappointed to be moved into room 25 with its supposed view of the back courtyard. If only he could have seen that. But nine floors up all he could see were the modern concrete walls opposite. True there was a sense of space, and he did not want to be repeatedly moved. But Sarah felt he would really appreciate being back in 22. Thankfully by the time her mother got there the next morning, he had indeed been moved, long enough to enjoy a day projecting his spirit onto the mountains in the distance. That night his system crashed. Quite gently and effortlessly. His breathing slowed and his heart gave up.

Roger called on his wife Joy. She was all he needed in his last moments. The journey they had shared together had spanned years. She needed to be there to kiss him on his way to his final resting place.

"Go safely on your journey love!"

"Wherever that may be."

She whispered in his ear hoping he could hear her.

He did.

This final release enabled him to let go and know that this was finally the time.

At last.

A long time coming.

Now he could go home.

Beinn Alligin beckoned.

His assigned Torridon mountain top for the great sleep.

Eternal rest.

His final breath rattled from his body propelling him into profound peace.

He shook off this mortal coil.

He suffered no more.

Roger Frederick was FREE.

Time Expired.

At 3pm right on cue on 3rd June the air raid Avonmouth emergency alarm sounded. At the same time every month, its plaintive siren startled the residents.

For 3 minutes at 3pm on the 3rd of the month.

Except this time, it was not a rehearsal.

It was real.

It came too late on this sad day.

Or right on time.

It was real.

333…

1982

CHAPTER FIFTEEN
Stirling

Sarah's dear old Nan Mary once advised her, "don't spend your life chasing rainbows!" Nan's handwritten note had been lovingly penned as Sarah was about to embark upon her university career north of the border. Did She listen? No, probably not. But She was assured that from her perspective in eternity, Nan would not now give her the same advice.

Standing beside the Bannockburn monument at Stirling Castle gazing across at the University Nan and Sarah contemplated the scene which was to encapsulate her rite of passage from introspective contemplative teenager, to independence, maturity, and adulthood. Well, in theory.

As they pondered the valley, which had seen many a skirmish and bloody debacle in the bid for Scottish freedom and pre-eminence, a magnificent rainbow illuminated the landscape. From the rugged peak of Dymyat, western extremity of the Ochil Hills, the vibrant rainbow emanated encapsulating the most vivid colours they had ever seen. The rainbow encompassed the campus below and highlighted Sarah's new student accommodations.

There was something magical about its timing. The vision gave her the courage to face the bleak reality confronting her, as well as confirming the promise of intriguing adventures to come. She did not want to be so far away from home. But the fates had decreed that her exam results, combined with the prospect of a largely coursework assessed degree, would see her settling into room 333 of Murray Hall for the foreseeable future.

Sarah's family had always loved Scotland. Weather-beaten holidays with elemental walks down gullies, over ravines and sometimes nearly off cliffs, had long been a feature of her childhood. Isolated terrain was a life-long compulsion of her father Roger's. He liked to push the boat out and set survival challenges like existing on porridge for two weeks on remote Hebridean islands, with geese, gulls, and canvas for company. Admittedly this recklessness was pre-wife and babies, but something of the maverick rock climber remained with him. Sarah could remember her mother Joy having a serious meltdown moment looking up at her father and younger brother scrambling on the rocks hundreds of feet above, without ropes.

Another time, they were all in situ in a typically elemental spot beside Loch Torridon, where her parents had honeymooned. Sarah had a middle-ear infection and mounting temperature, their tent was about to be blown off its pegs, and her father had decided to scale the heights of nearby *Beinn Alligin* in the fog. To be fair, it had been a fine summer's day when he set off. But by six o' clock in the evening, there was a freak storm raging; winds threatening to blow him off the mountain, and rain turning to sleet. Roger's blood sugar levels were doubtless low, regardless of Kendal mint cake, and her mother Joy was getting increasingly frantic. The mountain rescue was called out. These were difficult conditions for an experienced mountaineer, let alone a diabetic one.

Thankfully, they did not have far to go. The local farmers who had been sent out to find the intrepid Rog, met him sauntering back along the path, looking mighty relieved. By this time, his family had abandoned ship, and were sleeping and/or eating eggs in the nearby farmhouse. As Roger recounted his tale, his family started to pay a bit more attention. They learned that he had nearly walked off a precipice after taking a wrong compass reading. He had sheltered just below the summit and clambered down the cliff-face for a view of how to proceed. But the cloud was down to sea level, so he had to clamber back up the streaming cliff face. The compass was possibly waylaid by magnetic rock, yet he had to trust it to find the only safe way off the mountain, a narrow col between steep cliffs. An inner prompting, an earnest prayer and a pause for breath caused him to double check his bearings. Thank God he did. His previous course, arrived at by reading the small inadequate compass, would have sent him hurling to his death in the depths below. One wrong footing and he would have tumbled into oblivion.

Roger's route off the mountain was thankfully not *that* dramatic. He had to get creative though, as he had lost contact with the correct ridge path. Also, he was up against the magnetic rocks of the area, which can play havoc with a delicate mountaineer's compass, let alone a basic one. Natural intelligence kicked in, and a strong survival instinct. With the help of a map and the dubious compass, he found a steep gully. Scrambling quickly downwards as the gradient was steep, and the ground slippery and treacherous, he finally stumbled upon a more trodden route home.

By God's grace Roger was returned to his family in one piece. This brush with mortality was sobering and affected everyone deeply. Obviously, Sarah's father had used yet another of his nine lives. But the episode also showed them that we do not shake off this mortal coil, until it is our ordained time to do so. Roger clearly had a lot more to do in this lifetime. It was also clear that, more haste less speed and a charmed prayer in precipitous situations pays off.

Clearly a love for the wilderness was inherent in the genes. Roger's first recourse on holidays was to head for the hills dragging his family, in various states of willingness, behind him. Sarah certainly did not go reluctantly. Joy, her eternally patient mother struggled somewhat, home making in the series of damp, ancient and isolated cottages that came their way. She always did say that the best part of a holiday was getting home. But the kids loved the adventures, and the rugged nooks and crannies of obscure parts of Scotland and Wales.

Holidays were a thing of fun and excitement. They all rather enjoyed trying to work out what off-beaten track their parents would lead them down next. Rog-Route roads to remote accommodation at the end of eight-mile-long cul-de-sacs, were the norm. Walks in the freezing wind and rain, wearing florescent cagoules were the norm. Freeze-dried camping meals, to spare Joy the tedium of vegetable chopping, were the norm. The love of isolation, in the middle of a loving family unit, was the intrinsic paradox of their communal life. Sarah, Simon, and Rachel were the biblically named siblings who mucked in, with moss gliding, ice cold stream dipping, sheep chasing, building dams and sketching.

Sarah was so intrepid from an early age, that she had a temper tantrum, aged three and three quarters, insisting she be allowed to skinny dip in the arctic temperatures of Loch Sunart, on the South side of The Ardnamurchan Peninsula. She did not let up until she was able to do this. Her parents eventually conceded that turning blue and catching hypothermia would be a final comment on the matter, and a lesson learned.

On the same holiday, as they arrived in Scotland after an interminable drive north, their VW Camper Van came across the ruined Castle Tioram around six pm. So exhausted was Sarah by the journey, that she was insistent there must be a room for the night ready and waiting. She must have been overly tired, lost in a haze between times, or sensing a familiarity that felt like home amongst the ruins. But her senses were so primed and alert to the mystery of the place, that she was sure she had a room there, and would not take "no!" for an answer. Sarah, a young unusually sensitive child, was clearly picking up impressions from the etheric energies, atmosphere of the castle, and its environs. It was a potent, otherworldly, out of time experience she could vividly recall, and feel even years later.

Magical though her parents were, there was not much they could do to rustle up a bustling hotel reception in the dank, dark ruins of an ancient castle sitting on Loch Moidart's tidally compromised island. Indeed, it was imperative they got out of there as soon as possible, or a night on the island really *was* going to be a reality.

Clearly from a young age Sarah was full of the intention and belief that nothing was impossible, even despite any real evidence to the contrary. She was a feisty, determined, if not stubborn creature, who knew what she wanted in any given moment, and was going to do her damnedest to make it happen. Perhaps Sarah was 'entitled' and carried the energy of a princess who demanded that the world bend to her whims. She had the biblical name of Sarah, meaning 'Princess,' after all.

There was inevitably drama as a toddler. At the age of two in a Romford shopping center Sarah required a frog instead of a doll: "immediately!" Several stores later, antagonizing increasingly frazzled grandparents, clearly this Essex born aspiring witch, was not going to get her frog any time soon. Sarah had to settle a negotiation with her Nan, which involved her agreeing to make a cloth doll called a "Gonk," from the *Family Album Craft Book*, as soon as they got home. Being allowed to play with Nan's slippery, delightfully scented Camay soap in the bath before bedtime, was also a suitable compensatory gesture.

The frog incident probably rooted the seeds of the historic "chasing rainbows" comment, conjured up by her ever-patient Nan. Equally, Sarah was sure there were many such instances which gave her guardians clues, that she was someone out of the norm, who was going to at least try to defy the odds at any given moment. Doing things her way was an intrinsic part of Sarah's spirit from a young age. Her soul was defiant that rules were meant to be bent if not broken; especially if they did not serve a true, authentic purpose.

Sarah was obedient and helpful, but she did not like to be dictated to. Not much would put her off if her mind were made up! She was a pioneer for universal law, and spirited intentions before she could even read or write. At the age of six Sarah packed her little red suitcase, with only a pink dressing gown inside, and stomped out of the house. She was not sure why the pink dressing gown was so crucial, as opposed to warm clothes and camping equipment. But obviously it was a priority. She was leaving home. She had no idea where she was going; but leaving home, she was.

Joy panicked when she realized Sarah was completely serious.

"I have two problems in my life, Mrs. Rees the headmistress, and YOU! Anyway, The Bible tells me to obey God not you!"

Joy's response was a stroke of genius. She quickly called on the faith she knew Sarah had, even for one so young, and said,

"God also says 'honor your parents for a long and blessed life'!"

"Oh! Hmmm, yes. You are right. Okay then!"

And Sarah duly trundled back into the house.

If she had been equally smart, she would have said,

"But God does not say 'obey,' he says 'honor.'"

Then again, that might have seen her homeless at a very, young age, and there was time enough for all that. Annoyingly Sarah's mother had outplayed her this time. This was not by any means their last contretemps. But Sarah was generally more compliant after that. At least it meant she finally left home at a more reasonable age.

For some reason Joy felt she could never teach Sarah anything. Sarah assured her that this was not the case. Her mother was a wonderful homemaker, provider, and an exceptionally good cook. There really was no logical reason to doubt herself. Most her inadequacy as a parent, was a deeper self-esteem issue, which probably stemmed from the loss of her father in the war.

At the tender age of three Joy lost her father in The Battle of Crete. He was stationed on *HMS Warspite*, when the German raiders bombed the living daylights out of the fleet. Many lost their lives that day, and Sarah's maternal grandfather, who was Master Boatswain, died in a direct hit on his gun turret, while manning the guns in defense.

Nancy, Sarah's Granny, understandably shut down when news of her husband's passing reached home. Being personally acknowledged by His Majesty, King George VI would have normally gone down well. But in the current circumstances, the news was bitter rather than sweet.

The dreaded telegram was delivered from the war office by the Shamley Green post office lady:

"Is it? Bad news?"

"Yes! The very worst."

This formal message of condolence from The King was a mixed blessing. Nancy's reaction to the vicar who then visited to console her was, "and how will being proud help me to provide for my three children?"

Nancy, a practical Virgo, was left with the responsibility of engineering the best possible outcomes for her beloved young family on a shoestring. She had the help and support of near and dear friends. Aunty Frances, the lady whose piano was bequeathed to the household, was an ever-steady presence. Uncle Pete visited frequently with his serious moustache, and even more serious pipe smoking. For decades afterwards, Uncle Pete's chair in the dining room, had the aura he imprinted upon it, and the wonderful smell of the rich flavored tobacco he smoked. Pete lived to the ripe old age of ninety something, so no harm done. No filter.

The family home *Manelhe* was stuck in a time warp, a shrine to the early twentieth century. The old navy sword, proudly worn by Sarah's grandfather stood in pride of place. The antique brass, photographs, china, and fireplace were static, and unmoved, except for polishing, dusting, and sweeping purposes.

The old Grandfather clock Sarah used to listen to as a child, pervaded the house every fifteen minutes with its magically graded succession of chimes. Sarah would lie awake for long summer nights, listening to the cadences pace the house through the witching hours. If Nancy's specialty roast lamb was on the menu for the next day, the night was particularly slow. Her silverware was always laid out correctly, with the prerequisite white napkins; and there was a little button bell to announce the fayre, be it breakfast, dinner, or high tea.

Manelhe had a lot of magic to offer a young child. The coal tar soap in the bathroom and its compelling scent, was not quite so infatuating when being used to try to scrub off Sarah's birth mark in the bathtub. Nancy mistook this mark with the numbers 4, 11, and 26 at the top of her granddaughter's inside right thigh as mud. It took some persuading her, that it was not.

The Chinese pickup sticks kept at the top of the stairs in an antique china vase were fascinating, and it was a great treat when those were brought downstairs. The young siblings played snap, pickup sticks, and a card game "Happy Families," which involved getting all the animal suits of one family as quickly as possible. Sarah always aimed for the rabbits, and usually won.

The apple trees in the garden were charming, the sweet peas in the allotment and the peas in their pods, all captivated a child's imagination. But best of all was the croquet on the lawn.

One summer Sarah was unwell with a fever, and she remembered Nancy nursing her with a unique perfume 4,7,11. She hated the smell of it. Nancy dowsed her in it repeatedly, believing it would bring her fever down. Her pores were so clogged with this stuff, the virus was no doubt prolonged on a loop in her system. A twelve-year old is liable to shake off most things. But she was probably lucky to get through that in one piece.

Manelhe had a war time pantry, with a very distinctive smell. Nancy filled it with preserves, pickles, eggs, homegrown vegetables from the garden, and homemade purees from the windfall apples. It had a natural chill, keeping bread and milk fresh for days. The kitchen remained the same as it was during the times of air raids and rations. The big old roasting range, the off-white cupboards housing all the specialist crockery. The old yellowing boiler above the sink for hot water. The green back door with glass windows leading out to the clothes hanging area, and across to the apple trees, and allotment; then on down and down the long, long path to the tucked away air raid shelter right at the foot of the garden. All still the same.

Michael, Joy's older brother kept the memories alive for years. There was still a place set for Granny at the table, something sarah found endearing and charming, but which bothered her mother and their younger brother Chris. To quote Michael: "no death goes down well." Michael grieved in his unique way. There is no magic recipe for dealing with such loss. A staunch defender of his mother and mindful of all she had to cope with, Michael was loyal and true.

Michael the retired Deputy Head, who wore the same jumper for days, and kept the old square box television sitting behind the flat screen, just in case. Would not throw things away or tamper with the layout of rooms. He was required to step up as the man of the house and protect his mother at the tender age of seven, when his father passed. Little was changed since that time. Pretty much everything was just as Nancy left it. This was her space. Michael honoured that, so preserving her name.

Joy became a staunch Royalist, doubtless reflecting that her father died for King and Country. It must not all have been for nothing. There was a definite pride needed to be honored, despite the futility of Grandpa Harding's death. Sarah, Simon and Rache were unashamedly irreverent about their mother's penchant for all things Royal.

God Save The Queen!

But underneath it all, they *did* understand. The establishment was inextricably linked with Joy's father, and she had every right to be deeply proud.

When the bombshell of the passing landed, the drama of the shockwave tremor from a falling missile that had cracked the front porch doorstep, paled into insignificance. That air raid had brought the war close to home, but nothing could dissipate the sinister news that then entered and pervaded the house.

Joy was left coping with all sorts of issues, such as invasion of privacy, and having to be sure to "always do the right thing." She was provided for practically, and materially, but warmth of heart was somewhat missing. Nancy clearly died a little inside with the news of her husband's passing. After that nothing was ever quite good enough, and there was a permanent underlying stress at home. With her brothers Michael and Chris away at boarding school much of the time, Joy was left to fend for herself. This must have been very isolating and painful for her. But she weathered it, and as time marched on, she got some light relief hanging out with Hilton, cycling the leafy lanes of Surrey, and watching the cricket on the quintessentially English Shamley Green.

Once the war was over, Hilton's father Leonard increasingly became an important father figure for her, as she blossomed into a beautiful teenager. Joy felt a guidance and reassurance from this man, which brought her inner stability and calm. A timely comment when she was younger from an elderly missionary also enabled her to maintain her equilibrium. The missionary pointed out the magic of her name J.O.Y. Jesus, Others, Yourself. The words of this woman of God resonated with her. She took the message to heart.

"Yes, it is indeed such a great shame that your earthly father has passed. But there is a heavenly father up above, who loves you very much indeed." Joy, thus connected to a way of life, which she adhered to religiously. Exhibiting faith, hope, love, and impressive practicality in equal measure.

As her horizons expanded, she left Sweetwater Lane to train as a nurse at Saint Bartholomew's Hospital in London. There, she promptly met Sarah's father Roger, as he was carrying a bottle of urine across The Square.

Awkward?

Apparently not.

They chatted and fell in love almost immediately. Locking eyes, minds, and hearts at the famous fountain. Roger gave Joy a small wooden mouse, and their fates were sealed. Joy's brother Michael queried the modest gesture of the mouse; but Sarah's mother clearly found it charming and endearing. If only the course of true love were always that simple, and romantic.

Despite their backgrounds of considerable hardship, and on-going challenges, Roger and Joy forged a lasting bond, which saw them through some very testing times. Much of their married life became a quest to monitor and maintain and stabilize Roger's health. Diabetic since the age of seventeen, Roger confirmed his intention to train as a doctor, during his first hospitalization. He had to totally revamp his A level schedule, and ended up with seven A levels, in both arts and sciences, having aborted his original decision to be a land surveyor.

The bottle of urine he carried at his first meeting with Joy, proved to be symbolic indeed. The backdrop of the trickling waters of the fountain also added irony and pathos. Diabetics obviously check their urine frequently for glucose intolerance; so really it could not have been a more fitting "meet cute."

Joy, a patient, facilitating nurse, was just the right partner to practically maintain the status quo, through two episodes of blindness, quadruple by-pass surgery and endless in-growing eyelashes. "Joy Birds" and Roger are a testimony to lasting love; and nothing was quite as charming as Roger's proposal. This overlooking the fact that Joy was second on his handmade list of prospective wives.

Joy and Roger went through a lot together, but never failed to provide Sarah and her siblings with a wonderful, safe, loving, and nurturing environment in which to blossom. They were open-minded, never overly strict, or unreasonable; and endlessly patient with their three unusual children. Considering all their parents were contending with financially and health-wise, they were rich indeed.

As role models, Sarah's parents were pretty much perfect in her eyes. Simon, her brother had issues of Roger being a bit controlling in moments. But Sarah had no memory or recall of this. She thought it might be Simon's own internal pressure to live up to an expectation. A projection rather than a demand. Simon was talented creatively and artistically and could have taken a more left-field route through life like Sarah. But he went for the hard graft and bravely trained as a doctor. Even despite being taught the wrong course in Chemistry, Simon persisted, and eventually got all the results he needed to go and qualify as a medic via Sheffield University. That, plus an elective position for a few months, in the snake infested wards of a North Indian Hospital in the middle of monsoon season, and he made the grade.

Roger did not insist that Simon follow in his footsteps. But Simon certainly did a good job of achieving perhaps much of what Roger might have wished for, had his own health been better. With a general medical practice in The Highlands of Scotland, and membership of The Mountain Rescue team for Glenelg, Simon created an amazing life. The family traditions of splendid isolation and hard graft were wonderfully upheld in what he was clever enough to manifest.

Sarah knew she personally wanted to get results and achieve good things in life, but she did not feel it was ever demanded of her. The key was, they were all loved and understood. It made leaving home quite a traumatic event for Sarah in particular. Although she wanted to spread her wings and be independent, she really felt bereft of the background support her parents had provided. Of course, it was all still there in theory. But there was a sense of being pushed out of the nest to fly.

Stirling University was a mixed experience for Sarah. The idea made sense on paper. Here was a modern innovative learning center, set in beautiful and inspirational surroundings. Yet there was a melancholy about the place. One which did not go unnoticed, or unfelt, by a sensitive empath, such as Sarah.

Whether it was the ghosts of ancient struggles past; the imposing William Wallace Monument, the phallic majesty of which always commanded snickering whispers amongst the freshmen; or the lack of anything to do other than admire the scenery; she was not sure. But Stirling proved to be oddly disconcerting. Here was a place which really should have provided much stimulation and opportunity. Indeed, the courses, tutors, and curriculum were all exemplary. It was more the energy of the environs. When her head was not buried in a book, or distracted by an essay topic, Sarah was distractedly lonely there. It was impossible not to feel deeply the darkness and brooding backdrop, caused simultaneously by the geography and history. The fact that the campus accommodations were modeled on a Swedish prison, may also have had something to do with it.

There were rumors of the occasional suicide on campus. From her father's work as medical officer for the students of Bristol University, Sarah knew this was part and parcel of what happened when people left home and went to college. In the West Country there were several recorded attempts a year, where troubled students contemplated the jump to certain death off The Clifton Suspension Bridge onto the cliffs, road, or murky river below, depending on vantage point. This had not been the intention of genius Isambard Kingdom Brunel, when he designed this magnificent feat of engineering. But it was the obvious spot in Avon, for those looking for a way out.

Sarah was miles away up in Scotland and not that way inclined. She was not about to travel home, and avail of this beauty spot. But clearly depression was potentially an issue for a sensitive creature cast adrift, a long way from home. This was all within a norm, she logically told herself. A natural part of the adjustment young people had to make leaving the nest to embark upon their adult lives. It was not so much about chasing rainbows, as getting bogged down in the quick sands of the swamp. It was safe to say, Sarah's feet were going to remain firmly planted on the ground with all that she had to contend with.

CHAPTER SIXTEEN
Posset

There were a few enticements which made Stirling an appealing prospect. Sarah's summer camp, Scripture Union friend, aspiring actor Jack was there. His infectious humour, and crackling laugh, would always make her smile. But it was odd to arrive at Stirling and find him somewhat standoffish, sporting a fake Scottish accent, and harboring no interest in helping her to settle in.

On reflection she could understand this. The Scottish were not madly accepting of the English, and Sarah observed that the young males from south of the border found their reception particularly frosty. Sarah could not say that she had any problem with being English in a Scottish university. Quite the contrary. It all felt spookily familiar to her. But she understood why someone like Jack would want to go under the radar and take on the mantle of pseudo Scottishness. Why, he even played Macbeth in a university production, so not much love lost there then.

Jack was already established, and had done his settling in. There really was no reason he would pay Sarah much attention. Clearly, his baby blues had moved onto greener pastures. and perceived Sarah as out of context in this environment.

The compartmentalizing brain of the male species could only cope with so much, she concluded.

I was Jack's summer-camp girl, not his term-time partner.

Jack had been a dreamy summer romance, a wonderful kisser, charming, beguiling and lots of fun. All the girls at camp, in The Quantock Hills, had liked him. But Sarah's friend Sally won him over, first and foremost. Sally, a lithe, leggy brunette tended to take the lead, and got the first pick of the boys for some reason. For obvious reasons really. Jack and Sally used to sit up talking until the campfire burned to ashes; then did a sprightly sunrise walk up Will's Neck before everyone else got up. Somehow, after all that, there was Sally lively and full of energy at breakfast, as if she had just had a full night's sleep. High on Jack's company no doubt. Sarah also later found out the kissing was enlivening; so that explained it.

Sally had first dibs on Jack, and Frank, the rugby playing team leader. She also had the run of the kitchen and the chores. Many years later Sally could still be found running camp as part of her nurturing empire, and Christian ministry. Married to a minister, Sally took the correct route through life, remaining within the safe boundaries of church and family. Sarah probably should have done much the same with longer term boyfriend James. But there was more adventure and karmic adjustment to play out. Clearly, Sarah had to walk the line, and chase those rainbows.

Jack was not hugely cool or buff, or jaw-cracking handsome. But he was vibrant and mischievous and had something about him. He had told Sarah that hazy summer that he had prayed to be sent a Christian girlfriend. His prayer was answered in the form of "Sarah." But by the time she arrived, he appeared to have retracted his desire for something seemingly wholesome. Jack did not seem to find the option Sarah presented pleasing enough to risk losing face in front of his compatriots. She embodied a "be careful what you wish for" moment. Jack was friendly enough, but basically, Sarah was relegated to some "hi and bye" moments on the lake bridge between lectures. She harbored no hard feelings. Jack was eminently likeable.

Sarah's father had liked Jack a lot, and once tried to steer things slightly saying,

"I think he really likes you."

But that was about as proactive as he ever got in encouraging Sarah to keep company with anyone of the male species. Roger was usually more protective, flickering lights when she sat outside too long in the car of her hunky welding boyfriend David. She was fifteen, and David MacGillivray, suitably Scottish, was twenty-one. She found it on balance, reasonable paternal behavior.

Her father at a later point was concerned again at the level of her physical relationship with boyfriend James. But really, he need not have been. Sarah was eighteen, and James was twenty-one. They were serious about each other, and not much was going on. She was brought up to be respectful and never to treat sexual intimacy lightly. She never did, and she never would. She found sex for the sake of it as equally abhorrent as her father did. She was a very trustworthy young girl.

Having said that there was a near miss when James first arrived at "Conifers" the family home, for a visit. Sarah's high school boyfriend was a boy named Luke. Easter time of her eighteenth year, Luke had just left Conifers after one of his regular visits. Zooming down Fircliff Park on his scooter, he would have been intrigued if he had noticed the broader, more chiseled frame of James walking up towards him.

Woodhill Road, the main route from Portishead High Street which aligned at right angles to the cul-de-sac Fircliff Park, which was home. Jack and Luke missed each other by a couple of minutes. Dominated by a picturesque Georgian Terrace, Woodhill Road was a fine example of old Portishead. As school kids, Sarah and her friends could be found sketching the various town landmarks for their local history lessons. Woodhill Road was a favourite, as was the old farm in the heart of the village run by Gertie Gayle. The Church of Saint Peter's beside this Elizabethan farm, with several old coach houses and historical cottages in its vicinity, dated to the thirteenth century. Courtyard Farm adjacent to the church was eternally evocative and magical. A charming enclave, where time stood still.

The twenty-one doors in a row of the fine sandstone sculpted terrace of the wooded hill road, whispered stories, to the school kids as they sketched them from the outside. Sarah would pick up spooky impressions, imagining domestic scenes from days gone by, and could almost hear the chink of the china, interspersed with the banal but compelling gossip, of numerous sedate civilized tea parties. Frequently she walked up the hill tired after long days at school. passing the houses one by one in anticipation of the long cool drink of orange juice awaiting me once she crossed the threshold of home.

The interiors of these dwellings would hold endless fascination for Sarah as she ascended the deceptively steep hill. She would strain to hear the abstract voices on the ether floating in and out of her consciousness, as if she might glean messages, clues and assistance from the ghosts, and entities that frequented these buildings. This environment was fascinating for a young psychic who was intrigued by other times and dimensions. Aesthetically pleasing too, the houses had spectacular views out across the Bristol Channel, which on a bright sunny day looked less like a muddy brown river, and more like the smooth luminous waters of the Rhine. (They were taught creative thinking too).

In Victorian times, Portishead had a healthy rivalry with the nearby town of Clevedon, for the affections of those who indulged the tradition of a promenade walk along the sea front. Clevedon boasted the iron clad molded, wooden-slatted pier. While Portishead had

Battery Point, and the ancient East Woods, which were prime spots for logging the movement of ships in and out of Bristol Port. In later times, the shipping lanes worked somewhat differently, and the huge freight liners embarked at Avonmouth, instead of navigating the treacherously variable tidal waters of the river Avon beneath The Clifton Suspension Bridge. With one of the highest tidal ranges in the world, The Bristol channel accommodates a vast volume of commercial carriers into Avonmouth harbor. The cruise-sized ships sail close to the jutting promontory of Battery Point, and the view afforded is quite surreal.

Portishead, situated at the foot of the Gordano Valley on the west side, had a lot of appeal long before the Trip Hop band of the same name hit popular consciousness.

Undeniably an impressive experimental keyboard fest, the dirge like predominantly depressing tones of *Portishead* the band, would give the impression that all the town's inhabitants were on the verge of suicide. Nothing could have been further from the truth.

For growing teenagers Portishead was perhaps a bit dull and suburban, but it was also a place to grow, explore and flourish. It was somewhere all the kids knew they would probably leave. But it was undeniably a good place to bring up a family. Offering a safe and secure environment for children especially, the schools were good, and the community spirit was conducive. A modest sized dormitory town, Portishead served as a place of sleep, rest, and recuperation for commuters at the end of a busy day, and at the weekends, it was conveniently placed for excursions further afield. The Mendip Hills, The Quantocks, Cheddar Gorge, or even The Brecon Beacons in Wales were all within easy reach, if feeling adventurous. London was not much more than a couple of hours away on the train. Sarah's father chose this prime spot for his commute into work at Bristol University, and it served well to create a safe bubble for his family life, at one remove from the bustle of a big city, and the working day.

In more recent times, the development of a huge Marina where the old phosphorous factory used to be situated, brought a huge influx of new blood, and vastly swelled the real estate values and population of the town. Portishead became less personal, but was still, a friendly and vibrant community.

James from Bath was probably pondering all of this as he climbed the hill to Conifers. He had taken it upon himself to come and meet his pen pal from summer camp: Sarah. There had been a growing connection by post, but Sarah had not given it much thought. She was "Luke's Girl," or so she had overheard a group of his friends say as she sauntered by on a freezing night at The Victorian Christmas Evening in Portishead.

"There's Luke's girl!" was the comment that had wafted across the crowded walkway to her little freezing newly pierced ears, courtesy of someone not particularly competent in The Precinct.

Psychics generally have spectacular hearing. They do not need to lip sync. They just read the energy, and thereby know what is being said. They also generally have amazing physical hearing too. Sarah used to be able to make out most of what her parents were talking about up in the kitchen with the door closed, from her bedroom tucked away in the lower part of the house; and if she could not, sitting at the bottom of the stairs would more than suffice.

Sarah was dressed in her big brown bear coat, armed against the cold with woolen gloves and scarf. She would have had on the required eye liner and lip gloss. Her blonde hair, highlighted with "hint of a tint," was mildly wavy. She probably flattered herself, but there was a bit of the look of a young Princess Diana about her. She had the "Princess" name, Sarah, but no aspirations to be royal. Her mother would have been delighted of course. But overall, it is just as well she did not go too near Buckingham Palace in those days. She would have been even more of a rebellious disaster than Diana, cornered by all those rules and regulations.

119

It is a shame that Luke had not cleared this being-his-girl thing officially, as they might have made something of it. They got on and were definitely "seeing" each other. But Sarah did not think either of them assumed it was a long-term thing. They were still a fairly young age. Even though it was an innocent, kiss-and-cuddles-babysitting arrangement, Sarah really liked Luke. They used to be left to baby sit his younger sister. They would play Genesis, Marillion, and other magical other-worldly sounds to pass the time. Nothing much happened, though it had a very charming feel to it. Sarah was not feeling a grand passion, but there were the stirrings of mild romance. Suddenly there was a choice to make. James or Luke? Should she choose her school mate or the nice Christian guy?

James was the dark, thick haired handsome rugby player, with the finely shaped nose, and dancing eyes. Luke was tall, dark, sensitive, who wore a burgundy jumper. He once made her lamb chops, peas, and mash at his house. It was a bit of a no brainer, especially as Sarah's family was largely vegetarian in inclination. James was more congruent with her background and romantic expectations for the long term.

She hurt Luke with her decision. He told her he was, "all churned up." She felt bad. But needs must. Her first serious relationship had arrived on her doorstep.

All is fair in love and lamb chops.

Sarah had liked James a lot after he threw her in the swimming pool at summer camp. But that tumble into chilling water also jolted her sensitive system and seemed to kick-start on-going ventricular contractions. The Dr put them down to too much caffeine and lightly dismissed what was potentially a "murmur." The accompanying symptoms were random and alarming for a sensitive teen, and when she gathered that her Nan had a heart condition inspired by Scarlet Fever in her youth, she grew further wary of all things medical. Sarah became alarmingly self-monitoring and anxious. It was a long time

120

before she dared even verbalize her concerns. A shock to be plunged into that cold water after a struggle, it was a baptism of sorts. A sign of the heart skipping in other ways too, in time to come, and the birth of her background worry about her "heart."

Aside from the ectopic beat inducing scuffle, James did not hang out with Sarah at camp. She was quite introverted socially, and insecure perhaps too; and he seemed diverted by a couple of the older girls. She did not hold out much hope. She wore her red dress, black spurred riding boots and cream mohair jumper knitted by Joy on the last night of camp. But to no avail. The last night of camp, was a bit like the prom, you generally tried to hook up with someone for a bit of a kiss and cuddle.

"In your dreams" was more the reality.

Expectations were high. Sarah did not think anyone, but Sally got anywhere. Sarah was never madly successful at the last night of camp thing. There was a tradition of walking up through a claustrophobic, dank tree-bush tunnel, in the dark as a group. The idea was this was a scary, fun thing to do. They all saw it as a challenging obstacle course, with the promise of a delicious prize at the end. In other words, a means to get their "wicked way" with the guy or girl they had been eyeing up all week.

This was a Christian camp, so nothing untoward went down. But as teenagers, they all still had hormones surging through their systems, so romantic possibilities were highly charged. The previous Easter, before meeting James in the summer, Sarah had received her first proper romantic kiss from Steven at a muddy Youth Focus camp. Steven lived in Rugby. Steven and Sarah had walked around the mile-long track which circuited the camp in the dark, in their Wellington boots. No doubt they chatted animatedly. Sarah could not remember about what. In retrospect, there was an unconscious agreement that they were each-others' rite-of-passage moment. As they neared the gate to head back to the cabins, Steven zoomed in for "the kiss." Her first "proper" kiss.

So that was it!

It was the beginning of that strange fluttering feeling that Sarah came to love when connecting with a guy. The romance of the first kiss was *everything*. She was still a teenager, so it was an understandable misconception. It was not until she grew up a bit, that she found out that not all guys even like to kiss.

The following summer, James had no eyes for Sarah that she was aware of, but she reached out with a letter, and he was apparently delighted she had done so. He told me he could not have been more pleased to hear from her, and that he had hoped the strange letter which popped through his door was from her.

James and Sarah shared niceties, thoughts, and general chat by carrier pigeon. But there was not really any chemistry or frisson in the words exchanged. This was a nice guy who shared her faith, and who was at least a brother-in-Christ. She thought this way in those days. It was tricky to think outside the box of the secure, smiley, happy, joyful Christian bubble she was raised in. Her eyes were not yet open to the ways of the world. Sarah was a good girl if a bit stubborn. She was obedient, generally thoughtful, and hard working. But she struggled with anxieties and worries. What she did not consciously realize, was that in her hyper-sensitivity, she was picking up a lot of background stress from others. She was psychic, sensitive but still unconscious ones and not fully developed. Sari absorbed energies like a sponge. She was gifted and creative. But also, somewhat withdrawn, introspective, and creative.

For Sarah, listening to the news with its commentary about nuclear weapons and their development, inspired great fear. She was not logically sure how much of a potential threat nuclear annihilation was in those days. But the reports of the cold war with Russia, and the analysis of the damage impact of these weapons, did not make for restful sleep. She used to lie in her bed at night, terrified of a huge atomic bomb going off over Bristol. It was in those moments deep in the night that she wished she had not been born. she had not asked to be, and she was really terrified of death. It may have been that as children being aware in the detail of the implications of a long-term disease like diabetes, was an ever-present reminder of our mortality. But Sarah's naive rationale was that having *been* born, and now *being* alive, she should be allowed to *stay* so.

Sarah used to tell her parents that she was going to ascend not die, and she reassured them that this was in fact a very biblically correct possibility. Of course, she had to make sure she was eligible for the "rapture" option, so she needed to toe-the-line.

At school there were the energies of twelve-hundred fellow pupils to integrate, and at home there was endless worry and concern about her father Roger's blood sugar levels and general health.

The morning and evening ritual before meals was quite the ceremony. Sarah often asked to do the honors. Like all type one diabetics, Roger had to frequently monitor his inner sweetness. It was always a great relief to Sarah, when the tablet fizzing in a small sample of his urine turned blue. She got inwardly alarmed when she saw it go a hideous green or gunk orange. It used to mean he needed to eat immediately, or else go and lie down, depending on the interpretation. At church Sarah would sometimes hear the rustling of the glucose tablets in Roger's pocket, his emergency supplies for when the blood sugars were plummeting. Sarah knew when she heard that that they would likely not be held up with too much chat after the service on *that* occasion. Good. Lunch would be quicker today.

Her father's diabetes was like a thermostat for Sarah's well-being. When Roger was okay, all was well in the world. If something was up with him, the security bubble was under threat. Roger's words were pretty much gospel to Sarah. His voice was soothing, reassuring, and edifying. If a father were a demonstration of God's love, Sarah's father got the A' grade. But his health concerns became hers, and much of the time she was concerned that she too would develop diabetes. She used to get very worried if she had extra thirst or ran to the toilet once too often. She used to secretly check her own urine, and it was equally a great relief to see that fizzy tablet turn, deep dark blue, the colour of her eyes.

On first arrival at Stirling University, what sealed the deal for Sarah was a random chance comment by the English professor doing a meet-and-greet for her and her father. This professor was eloquently selling the benefits and wonders of the English courses, and Roger was asking many pointed questions. The professor probably was sensing some of Sarah's reticence and discomfort, and asked her father was he attending, or was she? This was a bit harsh and rude Sarah thought, and she nearly called him out on it. But what he said next was one of those synchronous comments that make your hairs stand on end. On describing the stronger points of the semester system, the professor said it was all designed to facilitate visits for "Mr Wonderful from Canada," as the structure exactly correlated with the education system across the Atlantic.

OMG? How could this man have known?

Sarah had literally earlier that year fallen for a Canadian artist at the *L'Abri* study center in Hampshire. At *L'Abri* she had spent much of her "gap year" studying, cleaning, baking, and communing with like-minded people. She had had quite an active row of suitors lining up. Her Christian boyfriend, rugby-playing James, was finally getting fed up with her after a year and a half. He had not wanted her to accept the place at Stirling University for the following fall. It was so far away from Welwyn Garden City where he was a budding business IT type. He had marriage and family life in mind for the long term. There were even informally engaged for a time. But really, Sarah knew her destiny involved a more elaborate path than anything quite so straightforward and sensible. James threw in the towel when Sarah went to *L'Abri* and

124

started to get diverted by all sorts of interesting people.

L'Abri is an all-embracing Christian community set up originally in Switzerland by Dr. Francis Schaeffer, a fundamentalist Christian theologian. The intention of his communities in Switzerland, Hampshire and USA is to "shelter" those who need time out and inspire those who are searching for life's deeper meaning. Sarah was in her element, aside from resenting the dubious daily tasks and chores. One time she had to de-gunk all the drains right around the periphery of the property, the contents of which were very smelly and wormy. But she relished the vanilla cake, corn breads, and other Transatlantic cuisine. She throve on the study of cults, multiple diverse religions, and Christian theology.

Sari was quite intense and nerdish as a late teen. Her time at the red-bricked Manor in Greatham, set her up for her university career. It gave her independent study skills, broader perspectives, as well as original angles on ancient questions. She met some wonderful souls from all over the world, and the breather from formal education, opened her eyes, and expanded her horizons.

She also realized she was not emotionally fulfilled, nor was she in the right relationship. The time had come to spread her wings. James returned all her photos with a flourish, along with a statement, that he "did not want to now know the real Sarah." He promptly took Sarah's cousin to the cinema instead.

Oh well.

Just before 'Mr Wonderful from Canada' arrived at *L'Abri,* Sarah had been romantically linked with a much older artist called John from Aberystwyth in Wales. There were discrete smooching sessions in the small lean-to kitchenette upstairs and copious hand-holding moments, despite disapproving glances, frowns, and whispers in corridors. Sarah was eighteen, John was thirty-one.

John had a long back, big warm hands, ice blue eyes, and a big nose. He wore baggy dark blue jumpers, and a rather glum expression on his face. Sarah was not quite sure what need he fulfilled in her. It was one of those things where a guy seeks out solace and healing, because basically he is still in love with someone else. In this case, that someone else was called Pearl. All Sarah got out of this fine romance, were some dreamy moments; a coach ride to Aberystwyth; a steamy movie viewing, during which John watched her reactions somewhat creepily; and an assurance that she had healing hands. Not, as bad as it sounds. She was simply able to lift his Pearl-induced headaches with a mop of his brow.

"Mr Wonderful" represented something far more enlivening, and Sarah thought the connection was potentially progressive. She quickly distanced herself from maudlin John, who feigned further deep hurt, sorrow, and compounded problems.

He had really liked her after all.

Too late.

No girl likes to hear about her beau's ex with every waking breath, whilst enjoying the tentative throes of a new romance. That bittersweet game Sarah was to meet once or twice more. It never got old apparently, or perhaps she did not really feel she deserved the best. She certainly did not seem to be attracting it. This was a pattern she was going to have to resolve at some point.

Mark from Canada was particularly captivating, and interesting to Sarah. He had a similar energy to her father. The same intelligent conversational ability, and artistic integrity. He was a professional artist visiting the United Kingdom from Toronto, taking time out from his relationship. He needed to decide what to do with his life, including whether to make the huge decision to marry his girlfriend. Clearly, Sarah helped him to do just that. Because, despite numerous twilight-walks down flowery Hampshire laneways, and deep conversations into the night, Mark went ahead and fixed a date to marry on return to his home country.

One evening Sarah had found him sketching two girls, a blonde and

126

a brunette, as if he were trying to make up his mind, and the answer lay in his pencil. Seemingly it *did*. She lost out to a brunette, a phenomenon which established a cosmic ripple effect, which would reverberate, repeat, and amplify, for some time into the future. In a bid to explain himself, Mark told Sarah he looked on her as a sister.

One who helped him solidify his feelings for his girlfriend apparently!

He also was deeply grateful for her company, and the way she had helped him sort out many of his spiritual life dilemmas.

Glad to be of service Sir!

Sarah was quite emotionally at sea on her arrival in Scotland for two reasons. One, she was about to be four hundred miles away from the safety and security of home; and two, she was really feeling the separation from her good friend Mark, "Mr Not-So Wonderful," with whom she had really bonded. The random, synchronous comment of the professor was enough to give her a slither of hope that Mark would return for her, realizing the error of his ways.

In the end, he just sent some thought-provoking poems and his annoying younger brother instead. The poems Mark wrote showed recognition of an emotional connection. One called, *What A Tragic Night It Turned Out to Be*, revealed that he had felt a surge of feeling, but too late. Typical. The "too little, too late" thing began to set a precedent for much that was to come. At that point Sarah was still upset rather than jaded.

Well at least he acknowledged the moment, was the thought she consoled herself with.

Some months later Phillip, Mark's brother, was over on a European jaunt for his rite-of-passage year. He manifested as a major irritant towards the end of the second semester of Sarah's first year at Stirling. *L'Abri* obviously was not on his radar, and he wanted to do something more traditional and "normal." Mark had assured him Sarah was a marvelous tour guide.

Post-*L'Abri,* Sarah had shown Mark and another brother Dave around Wales on a whirlwind road trip, which had worked out brilliantly well. The notion had raised eyebrows amongst the *L'Abri* infrastructure. But the powers-that-be were good enough to lend the intrepid trio transportation, nonetheless. They had signed-off officially from their studies, and the open road beckoned. The possibly irresponsible whim quickly transmogrified into an invigorating, seasoned adventure, which was inspiring for all, including the green VW Beetle, their trusty steed, which clearly needed a good drive.

The only embarrassing low point had been Mark stumbling upon Sarah white trousers down around her ankles, trying to have a discrete pee around the back of a church they were investigating. The night they all shared a tent was not much more conducive. Mark slept affectionately, with his finger placed on Sarah's head to stake a claim. But it really was quite pathetic in terms of permitted physical contact. With his larger, thicker set, snoring brother Dave alongside, things were not about to get frisky any time soon.

Sarah was overall annoyed and hurt by Mark, so was not about to repeat such hospitality for yet another brother, while still pained by his lack of action. Mark had sent lame attempts to respond to her feelings in the poem. But that really did not cut-the-mustard. He was still engaged to his girlfriend, and about to be married. His younger brother Phillip could feel the full wrath of her anger instead. Sarah was not going to play ball with Mark's inadequate, and somewhat insensitive fob-offs.

Mr Wonderful was MARK, not Phillip!

The joke really was on Sarah. There was no getting away from it. The universe had timed the tutor's pointed comment to perfection. In fact, if not for this comment, Sarah had been on the brink of asking her father to take her back to Somerset. If not for this uncanny professor, Sarah would not have stayed in Stirling a moment longer. The Spirit world was clearly up to something and exercising its right to spin a bit of dark humour at her expense.

The whole Mark thing gave Sarah a big demonstration of how things were going to roll. It showed her clearly, that however disappointed she turned out to be, she still had faith in life, the universe and God, to steer her in the right direction using signs, signals, and synchronicity.

That a random comment from a professor was enough to commit her to a preordained course of action, should have made her wonder. Instead, it filled her with awe at how life works in uncertain moments, revealing how the smallest thread, can in fact be the most significant lead. At least it showed she was listening and responding to guidance as her spiritual legacy required. This intervention happened to ensure she stayed in the right place to fulfil the correct destiny path. Sarah was meant to stay in Scotland and God had used her misguided emotions to bait her into doing so.

Clever, if annoying...

CHAPTER SEVENTEEN

Karma

Ingrid was petite, blonde, German, germane, and a decade older than Sarah. But the two of them instantly connected at Stirling, becoming great friends. Ingrid taught Sarah how to stay trim by stir-frying carrots in lemon juice, with a touch of sugar. She ate that rather a lot in the first term; along with the prerequisite student diet of pot noodle, and intermittent attempts at canteen food, which roughly translated equated to various manifestations of "stodge."

Sarah once saw Jack coming out of Ingrid's room at a strangely unexpected hour. So that got her thinking. But there was an innocence about her at that stage, so she did not make any obvious enquiries, and parked any suspicion or retort. Usually she found a wry, curious, quizzical smile was enough in such circumstances. Perhaps she would have got further with "the birds and the bees," if she had been more dramatic, feisty, and determined in her dealings. But at that point, she was the well-behaved Christian girl, who saw the best in everybody, and believed that every situation was redeemable, even when it was possibly dubious.

Sarah probably fell between two stools with many things to be honest. For some reason, Old Testament lecturer John Drane had found her very atypical of someone who should be attending a University Christian Union meeting. When he targeted her as a very unlikely member she retorted: "there are two sorts of Christian: open and closed. And I'm the first sort!"

I guess he might have sensed a pagan, wiccan type nature connection, inherent in her energy field. But it just goes to show, you should not judge someone on appearances. He was right though. Sarah did not particularly relish those meetings. Even so, she showed willing, and was useful ferrying people to and from the local Baptist church on Sundays in her beat-up white Morris 1100.

She had driven all the way up from Bristol in that car with Ingrid and Jack following the first mid-term break. It was bought from an old school mate Colin Leaker, who had attempted to romance her in the sixth form common room by playing *Stairway to Heaven* by Led Zeppelin on a loop. That did not work. But the car sort of did. The irony did not escape her when, as they approached Stirling, after four hundred miles of motorway, and eight hours of driving, the brakes failed. On another such journey, this time with her brother Simon, the clutch gave out at Carlisle. The car, the universe and Colin were probably trying to tell her something. In the first instance, Sarah had to gingerly handbrake her way back to campus. In the second, her and Simon arrived in style on a pick-up truck, car incapacitated in full rescue mode.

The back-street garage Steering and Suspension rectified the issues on both occasions. But when she finally had to scrap the car for ten pounds, she got the point. That vehicle was not fit for long journeys. It was a run-around to enable her locally, and she had killed it prematurely by demanding too much of it. Again, the symbolism - not lost.

Morrissey, the white Morris, not only failed her on a couple of occasions, it also rescued her in some serious moments too. She had been feeling left out and isolated in Stirling, most especially since the boyfriend John she had hooked up with in second semester, was proving challenging to say the least.

When she had first phoned her father about John, probably somewhat fretfully, Roger had said, "do choose not to fall in love with the guy. You do not have to go there."

Easier said than done, she thought.

Does one choose who to fall in love with? Is it really all that contrived and deliberate? She did not think so. But this pragmatic Aquarian approach of her fathers,' raised all sorts of doubts in her mind.

Was love just an informed choice?

Roger's paternal instincts were clearly good as she was soon reminded.

Well, he was his mother's son after all.

Regardless, Sarah felt compelled to see where she got to with this darkly dangerous person who had crossed her path.

Sarah's father was a highly intelligent ex medical officer, writer and counselor, son of her intuitive Scorpio Nan, whom her grandpa affectionately called a "white witch!" Her father had instincts, wisdom, and advice, which they all ignored at their peril.

With the John situation, Sarah thought it was time to take matters into her own hands and be a bit more independent. Even though she knew her father always tended to be right, she went ahead with John anyway. Just to see what would happen. She was committed to chasing those rainbows, wherever they would lead. So, in her loneliness, she was intrigued enough to give it a whirl.

John had caught her eye with the sexy scar over his lip, wry grin, beautiful but troubled green-brown eyes, a certain shyness, and his uncanny resemblance to the lead singer of a famous Irish rock band.

(On a good day.) He was also Irish, crazy, and highly intelligent. A lethal combination. A black-belt karate expert, born and bred in Derry, John seemed to take the Northern Irish troubles out on Sarah in ways she had not seen before, nor since.

They had met in the smoky, den of iniquity on campus which went by the name of The Grange. It had one slot machine, on which Sarah once won the jackpot of twenty-five pounds, a darts room, and some lucky students had their accommodations above the dance room. Not sure much work would have been done in *that* environment. She observed John being amused at some slim, red haired, pole-dancing type, who was touching herself dancing in front of him. God knows why, he gave the sweet short-haired blonde Christian girl the option on his company instead.

Their first date had been to a gig of the famous Irish band in Glasgow. Sarah was captivated by the bright blue eyes, and energy of the singer Paul. His cocky confidence, Christian faith, and musicality were a winning combination for her. But she had alongside her what she thought was a handsome enough consolation prize, if not booby prize. Besides, she was not a groupie, she simply liked her music, and anyone who appeared to have the same world beliefs, and approach to life as her, was compelling for reasons other than the obvious.

Sarah had been given a single by the band for her eighteenth birthday. She did not quite get what all the fuss was about. She knew they were a Christian Rock Band from Dublin, and that there was quite a buzz about them. Her brother, a punk rock connoisseur played this band's music. So, the fact that this Irish rock wafted out of his bedroom, along with Magazine, Joy Division, The Stranglers and Killing Joke, said something. They must be good. Simon, Sarah's brother, was a cool, rebellious, handsome Christian lad. A May-born Taurus like Paul, he looked vaguely like him too, with his pale blue eyes, and enigmatic middle-distance stare.

Back in the day, Simon spiked his red titian hair with sugar for

133

maximum effect, and then headed off to church in holey green jumpers, and bondage trousers. He drove a blue pickup truck with souped-up engine, which on purchase he immediately took apart, so that he could understand how the engine worked.

Simon was cool.

Christian Rock back in the eighties, was usually bland, sickly sweet, and insipid without a beat. The live wires from Dublin, seemed to know how to channel something from the great beyond. They were magical and captivating. Their live show convinced Sarah of that. Never mind the disc she had been given for her coming of age birthday, here was something she could really relate to.

John turned out to be nothing like Paul. He was a wolf in sheep's clothing. Paranoid, edgy, demanding, leaving Sarah incredulous on more than one occasion with his actions and behavior. She was in shock if truth be told. She had left a loving home and family, and suddenly life in the cruel outside world had got challenging. She needed stability and good friends. The universe had connected with her the tumultuous whirlwind that was John.

Great.

Probably those who met him, would not understand, or compute her experience of him. He was on the surface funny, brilliant, and good looking, and wrote a column for the local newspaper. What was not to like? The John drama became was one of those scenarios, where what went on behind closed doors belied the appearance of the thing. Sarah and John were two handsome people in the prime of life, yet emotionally she felt bewilderment and chaos churning up inside her. She was being emotionally abused and kept on her toes in a bid to keep his favour. God knows how a well-balanced Christian girl, with oodles of love and support even got into such a situation. But God knows she did; and she needed help. Fast.

Sarah's family were visiting the area for the Easter vacation of her first year at Stirling. They were of course tucked away in some obscure hidden spot down towards the borders, which they could not find. John and Sarah had driven out from Stirling in the white Morris 1100, and it was getting dark. Any psychic sense of direction she had was completely failing her. Clearly John had disempowered that too, amongst other things.

Sarah was beside herself. It was snowing, the roads were treacherous, and the windscreen wipers had just broken. John was having one of his psychotic meltdowns, and she began to be afraid of what might happen.

The battery of the car also failed. Completely inert. Dead. It looked like they were going to have to spend the night in some verge, on an unfriendly, potentially dangerous, stretch of road.

How was she going to start the car?

John would not have had the patience to wait for motor rescue. She did not have the patience to deal with his fear-inducing temper tantrum. She prayed. She prayed for what felt like the life of her. It was something she did many times in that relationship.

Divine and angelic assistance was hers that day. Not finding her family had rubbed in her depression and isolation. John's madness compounded it further. But it was confirmed that she had God on her side, when push came to shove, as it quite frequently did.

Sarah's prayer was literally a matter of life or death, or so it felt to her.

Please God. Please. You can see what is going on here.

Please get me out of this in one piece.

She did not just mean the present scenario of being stranded on a verge on a dark, snowy night. She needed a divine intervention.

The prayer was answered on the third turn of the key in the ignition. The car started. Sarah told John that she had prayed. He was having none of it. But completely against the odds, like a bolt out of the blue, a spark of life revved things up, and the engine turned over. It was the required boost to get them moving and back to campus in one piece.

Gott Sei Dank!

The prayer, and Sarah's reaction to the situation might have sounded over-the-top dramatic. But earlier the same day, she had nearly been flattened by a huge double-decker bus doing an incredible speed, at a busy junction in Glasgow. She sat motionless in the middle of the crossroads, knowing that any movement could well have been fatal. The hurtling, oblivious bus missed her on the driver's side with two inches to spare. She was understandably primed to be a bit sensitive. This, plus John's increasingly antagonistic disposition, and she felt justified to call on divine intervention in that moment.

Things were looking increasingly dark and challenging for Sarah, and although she was looked after in moments such as these, it was difficult not to also resent her situation a little. In all things she was doing her best. Despite a descending depression, largely thanks to John's incredible behavior, she still got good grades and performed well in all university activities; and as her mother said at the time.

"If you can do all this without trying or thinking much, look at what you might achieve when fully engaged."

Sarah's did not really know what she was struggling with, or why things had all gone so peculiar. She kept it all very much to herself most of the time. She was biding her time, waiting to find a suitable way out. She needed a way to strengthen inside and gather her resources to leave John. He had unfortunately become a make-shift family, along with his circle of friends. But things had to change, or she probably would not come out of this alive.

On the upside, John was the person who introduced her to Edinburgh, a place she really came to love and enjoy on her own terms. John had moved there on graduation, and although she enjoyed the ambience and charm of the city, she also got a semblance of separation, still having room 333 to retreat to, and her university degree to complete.

Being locked in John's pokey bathroom on Albion Terrace, in full view of Arthur's Seat, on her twenty-first birthday, was really the last straw. She built her escape plan. She needed to retrieve Archie the cockatiel and get the hell out of there.

Archie liked to swoop into a pan of boiling potatoes as a kind of sport. God only knows how he did not boil his feet in the process, but he managed to get his pieces of potato using his talons, and extended reach. John used to like teasing him with a broom handle, a game which probably amounted to stress for the bird, and amusement for John.

Sarah packed all her belongings up and hid under the stairs in the main stairway, until she ascertained it was safe to leave there for good. She somehow managed to navigate the train platforms at Waverley Station, with a bird in a cage, several items of luggage, trying not to exhibit a highly charged emotional state.

She did not know it then, but John was clearly a sociopath. She thought he had no clue that what he was doing was wrong. His behavior was totally justified in his own head. Sarah was after all a live wire, totally uncontrollable and a liability, if not a complete danger to herself.

One time, Sarah had arranged to meet her brother, and his girlfriend Caroline, in Princes Street Gardens, with John in tow. John had throughout that morning been typically abusive, and active in whatever the current torture was designed to make me cry. Sarah was sure Simon must have noticed her distress, but apparently not. She could not give a clue to him about the danger she was in, whether real or imagined. She felt so relieved to see her lovely brother and his wonderful girlfriend. But must have seemed stilted and guarded. Again, apparently not. Sarah was also a better actress than she had realized, clearly. It just goes to show how the scourge of domestic abuse can be so silent and deadly. There were times she felt in fear of her life. She was at this guy's mercy. Even amongst friends or family, she had no way out, or means to tell. She was totally under a cloud and controlled by this person.

Sarah brought Archie back to room 333, and shortly after, as if by magic, a Java Sparrow, flew in through her window to complete the avian unit. Arnold, her blue Budgie, had been decapitated in the triangular metallic spring door, of John's community flat on campus. But Archie was a survivor, and with Finch, he now comprised her family, who were feathered.

Finch, obtusely named in that he was a sparrow, was a character. He used to play dead if you held him extended in your hand. He would just lie there motionless for minutes at a time; only coming alive if you wrapped your hand around him. Simple pleasures. Sarah was not sure who taught him this circus trick. But he performed it like a charm, right on cue.

This was probably the beginning of Sarah's use of animals to build a sense of belonging. She had been known when younger to breed frogs in a bucket in her bedroom, and bring home litters of kittens, because she could not decide on just one. She had had a rabbit named Flopsy, and a guinea pig named Patch. She was in the Animal Defenders, linked to the *Royal Society for the Prevention of Cruelty to Animals*, and loved all things feathered, furry, and fluffy. As humans were proving increasingly problematic, and uncooperative, animals proved a valuable, rewarding connection for her. She had always loved them as a child, but as an adult, they began to have a role of support, and allowed her to express her nurturing side.

CHAPTER EIGHTEEN
String of Disaster

From the inside out, Sarah understood what it was like to be a woman who loves too much. The experience with John, gave her an armory of resources. A depth of understanding to help her reach women in the same situation. Through pacing herself she strengthened and detached from what had become an incredibly dysfunctional, co-dependent relationship. In her own time, she extricated herself from the emotional web she was caught up in. She would say, no harm done. But clearly this was not the case.

Her former best friend Em, whose job she took as a chef at Lilligs the German restaurant on Victoria Street, had quickly noticed the tell-tale "frightened rabbit" look of an abused woman, as they bonded over sauerkraut, bratwurst, and schnitzels. Em knew she had to step in, and help a girl who was presenting as vulnerable, scared, and at the mercy of a boyfriend, who probably did not even know consciously, that he was mistreating and terrorizing her. This she did, and a valuable sisterly bond was created between her and Sarah, which ran through many years. Sarah was family to her, and she, along with her daughter "Nip" were support and family to Sarah.

On graduation from Stirling University, Sarah relocated permanently to Edinburgh. Stupidly, this involved sharing a dingy basement apartment with John, and two other Stirling graduates, Northern Irish Colin, and Ron. This was a much better domestic situation than the isolation she had felt in Albion Terrace. John was also initially better behaved. It was an odd arrangement though. Sarah did not have a bedroom and slept on the floor in John's room. Her stuff was kept under the stairs in a damp, dusty, dingy cupboard. This set-up was completely ill-advised. But Sarah did not have the means to get her own place. At least the presence of Ron and Colin made her feel a little safer.

She recalled Colin even banging on the door one night, when he heard the commotion of John threatening to pour water all over her as she slept. In fact, he must have already drenched her, and woken her, since Colin responded to the noise of her protestations. The point is, she was minding her own business. She could not even remember why John did these things half the time. Clearly something had fired his vivid imagination and paranoia again. Sarah and John did not answer the door to Colin; but Sarah noted that someone had finally *heard* her. Finally, a male of the species, responding to an injustice, had stepped up, and attempted an intervention. Something was not right here, and Colin was brave enough to call it. But still, Sarah did not tell anyone, or talk about it, or report it.

There was no sex between John and Sarah. In fact, the whole relationship had been devoid of it; the exception being, a real push, to steal her virginity on her return from a summer break. That did not work out so well. He did not know what he was doing. He was probably a virgin himself if truth be told. He was a bit rough. There was an incident in her room, which drew blood. Sarah phoned her father in distress and he reassured her. But hmm. Not much gentle

140

romance was going on, that is for sure.

John laughed cynically after another similar attempt in his quarters. *Hardly the stuff dreams were made of,* she thought.

There were no hugs, no kissing, no affection, no nothing. Really thereafter, the whole thing descended into a power play. Even the minimal physical encounters were about control.

One time, Sarah had been doing John's laundry, and one of his disgusting brown towels with cream trim got mislaid. She was frantic, knowing that he would throw all kinds of accusatory nonsense at her. She kept going back down to the launderette to see if it had reappeared. This suspicious behavior was noted by John, and he immediately started to bully her for flirting with someone, whose existence she was not even aware of. Clearly, he had noticed a guy called Paul looking at her. Clearly, she had not. When John finally pointed him out to her, she was incredulous:

Not even my type.

Duh!

It just goes to show the measure to which she was intimidated. In anger and frustration at his behavior, she ran out of his apartment, and aggressively bashed in the fire alarm, breaking its glass all over the stairway.

Boy, that was loud and effective!'

In super quick time, the Stirling Fire Brigade appeared, and she felt incredibly awkward at having caused such a commotion. She thought she had better reassure them there was *no* fire, for safety's sake. The whole building had been evacuated, and everyone was out there shivering in nightclothes.

Oops!

She dithered because of the possible consequences. But she had been irresponsible and needed to sort this. She found the chief and confessed her misdemeanor. Thankfully, he had mercy. She apologized, explaining that she was being bullied, and to please not tell anyone why she had done this. He honored her in her desperation and did not press charges or report her. He was incredulous, not that she had done the deed, but that she had *told* him about it. He observed that it was, "most unusual that she would confess such a thing."

Ironically, she seemed to impress him, and he clearly had sympathy for her plight.

John's intimidations took an even darker turn by the time Sarah was living full time in Edinburgh. He would threaten to rip up her nicest things. Her books, clothes, photographs, valuables, indeed anything that she *liked*, were all under threat and at the mercy of John's volatile temper. Sarah sensed John had rumbled her attraction to Harry Horse, the front man of *Swamptrash,* which she did confess was *real.* All the same, it was none of his business really. They were not together by this point, and still he was trying to dictate to her with his bullying. She was not even sure what inspired his actions. She was hardly a difficult person to get along with. In fact, she was most obliging, amenable, and a good support to her friends and those that loved her.

Clearly there was abuse in John's past, which was triggered by the slightest flicker of independence in Sarah. The psychological reasons were no doubt complex. But it was horribly real and intimidating in the extreme. John made mention once of an uncle who used to beat him on his lower back. Beyond this, she could not hazard a guess about what prompted his behavior. She certainly did nothing at all to warrant it or provoke it.

Harry was dark, gothic, and intriguing. Real name Richard Horne, he had a posh English accent in reality; but at any given opportunity he would fake a Southern American drawl, as if he had stepped straight out of the swamp. Harry was something of a genius. A talented artist who did pen and ink political satire cartoons for the main Scottish newspapers. Sarah commissioned him to do a *City of Ghosts* pictorial map for her brother's wedding. The result was stunning. It was supposed to be a first edition exclusive. Harry being Harry printed copies and sold them liberally on the streets of Edinburgh. The passing tourists were pleased, Sarah was *not*. But she understood his entrepreneurial streak had to take advantage where it could.

In the end she was pleased to have given him the idea of a pictorial historical map of Edinburgh. It was a good money spinner for him. One of Harry's gripes was that, despite his many talents, he was not making the money he potentially could. Harry was the son of quite a wealthy English family who lived in the Midlands, somewhere near Rugby. The demeanor of struggling artist wore well on him. He could tread the boards of the next offered stage, earn a crust performing for gratuities at The Mound, or sell his pen-and-inks, rolled in scrolls, down in The Grassmarket. Edinburgh needed characters like Harry. He suited the bohemian, haunted, brooding energy of the city. Sarah did too, but in a different way.

Harry was exotic with long wavy hair, tall and melting brown eyes. Sarah was sold. He totally captivated her. She was not quite sure *why* in retrospect. But at the time he was very alluring. Dangerous, mysterious, psychically connected, intuitive, and very musical too. He took Edinburgh by storm with his Cajun band *Swamptrash*. Their gigs were a complete hoe-down. A maelstrom of whirling dervish energy. The magic was palpable. The music scene in Edinburgh at this time was just what Sarah needed. She felt as if she had come alive once again. The music had started to save me. It was a trend that was surely set to develop further, as the musicians and their notes, lit the way ahead.

The "thing" with Harry was somewhat unrequited. It was sort of awkward whenever they were in each-others' company. Nothing was going to happen. Sarah thought they were both a bit too reserved and English, ironically. She liked him a lot and he knew it. There was only one time she felt he let his guard down, and that was when he walked by the public launderette on the main cobbled street of Stockbridge.

Stockbridge was the trendy, bohemian down-town part of

Edinburgh, between Princes Street and Leith. All the artists and musicians congregated in various apartments. It was a magical and vibrant community. Not as historic as the haunted old town up by The Castle. But certainly, atmospheric, and compelling in its own way.

Harry's eyes met Sarah's.

Woah! Okaaaay.

But *no*, they were not in business. Nor were they ever going to be. Harry's very Scottish girl friends were always in the way. Kimberley, a gothic brunette, was a bit of a nightmare. She was openly jealous, and sometimes deliberately vindictive towards Sarah. She turned down a conciliatory kitten Sarah bought her to compensate for her dead cat, who just got run over. Sarah was being kind, and obviously naive, considering her behavior towards her. Not surprisingly she was left "holding the baby," as Harry so aptly put it. "Travesty" the cat, astutely named by Sarah's mother, then had to travel to Bristol with her on the train, to be homed unceremoniously with friends of her parents in Portishead. Sarah could not really manage two cats. Mellish, her black and white cat, who thought he was a dog, was profoundly jealous. Travesty was not destined to live with her, nor anyone, in Scotland. She had clearly been somewhat stupid to think she could replace one dead cat with another random live one.

On reflection, Sarah was well protected regarding Harry. He was under the skin quite prickly and odd. She often used to wonder if he was concealing that he was gay, but there was never any rumor, let alone proof or admission that he was. He was just "British," which lends itself to some ambiguity; especially in the artistic communities, where eyeliner, tight pants, and feminine gestures were pretty much the norm amongst glam rock devotees.

Harry's genius left him open to much torment. He was complex and brooding, and never really seemed that happy. Years later in a looking back over her shoulder moment, Sarah looked him up on-line, and found that he had relocated to Shetland with the beautiful Mandy.

144

Mandy was the softly spoken Shetlander who had artfully captured Harry's heart after Kimberley slopped off into the shadows. Mandy was luminous and ethereal, and quite frankly Sarah considered herself no competition. Harry clearly preferred the dark, sultry brunette look. Sarah needed to find someone who liked *blondes* as this was becoming a bit of a habit.

In her next life, Sarah decided to come back as a brunette. She thought she may have a more straightforward time of it Being "blonde" was obviously proving to be challenging. She perceived that people expected her to not to have an opinion or a brain. She was *blonde*. So, what else did she do?

Time and again, it really seemed like she was victim to her blondeness. The men she was attracted to, all settled for, or were already with, women of a dusky hue. Sarah was the danger zone. Blonde and carefree, and a whole lot of trouble.

She obviously needed to make better use of that brunette wig.

On trying out said wig one time, much later-on in Dublin, "Rockstar" Paul had looked visibly shaken and panicked, that she might have dyed her blonde hair a rich brown/red. While his wife graciously said it suited Sarah, Paul looked relieved when she reassured him it was a wig that she donned from time to time. "You little minx," he said, doubtless ironically. But that experiment was interesting and showed Sarah that at least *one* person in her circle liked blonde hair.

Back in Edinburgh, in what seemed like another lifetime, Graham the dishwashing kitchen-assistant who took ballet classes, also seemed to like blondes. Graham enticed susceptible girlies with his specialist cheese sandwiches made with precision and care in the back kitchen of The Antiquary, a bustling, beer-filled watering hole situated in a Stockbridge basement on Saint Stephen's Street. Of course, the red leg warmers, and dance lessons should have sent alarm bells, and Sarah's "gaydar" ringing off the scale. But for some reason she missed this red flag which was surely as bright as his dancing gear.

Graham probably hated women. He was troubled, smoked pot, slept with his sister's friends, and put his fist through windows. Sarah's hunch was that he had a background of abuse, for he was certainly abusive and messed up. Bob, the chef had warned Sarah in his Christmas card to

"watch out for the cheese sandwiches."

Sarah did not listen and chased this tarnished rainbow for a wasted month or two. No, she did not join in the smoking. Everyone around her smoked weed. Sarah did not. However, she did stupidly spend way too much time trying to help and settle this guy. Graham was potentially good company. An off-beat handsome chap. But there was an intrinsic sense of humour failure, a screw loose, and a tangible darkness within his energy field. He was a foppish private school type, with a permanent frown, restless pale blue eyes, and his mouth in repose resembled, for want of a better way to put it, a cat's bottom.

Eventually, Graham announced himself to be gay, which explained everything. A couple of years down the road, Sarah randomly met him when she was making her way to her boyfriend William's apartment. Graham intercepted her attention insisting she come see his "love nest." Graham had set up home in a dilapidated, mold-infested hovel in the bowels of Leith; had hooked up with some guy who "tickled his fancy," and just as irritatingly as ever, wore a defiant defensive grin having further perfected that sneering glare from those menacing baby blues. Problem solved. Sarah was well rid of this one.

Thankfully, she had not got too involved with Graham. He was just another kind of emotional abuse Sarah had stumbled upon. Not as intimidating as John's manipulations, but still somewhat disturbing. The signs were all there in retrospect, but subtle this time; easily missed in other words. As with all the challenging things met along the way, it was easy for Sarah to be wise after the event. She did what she did, and although her life experiences shaped her. They were not who she was. Most definitely not.

146

As the few months of the Graham interlude had progressed, it was easy to see that he was indeed as f*cked up, as he said he was. He also enjoyed getting f*cked up, even more than talking about it. Graham's most annoying trait was to say that something was "important" when he thought he was making a valid point. The "girlies" were supposed to hang on his every word, pondering what was "important," and making sure they understood it.

Whatever "it" was Sarah was never quite sure. But that was her inherent failing apparently. She would literally wrack her brains lying awake at night trying to understand this guy. It really was a pointless exercise.

On the few occasions they had sex, she was paranoid about getting pregnant. She enjoyed the intimacy. But really that would have been the worst mistake of her life, and she knew it. After a session, in which he experimented on her rather than connected with her, Sarah would jump into the tub, and purge all trace of him from her being. She was not about to be caught off guard by this crazy fellow.

On the upside, Graham had a wickedly appealing laugh, and was compelling enough in his perversity. He stirred up controversy and provided much food for thought. But the experience was uncomfortable, and nothing whatsoever to do with love. Graham's circle was falling foul of a basic gas-lighting attempt.

Graham was a novice at manipulation, except with those who fell for his surface charm. It was difficult to pinpoint exactly what his appeal was. He was not classically good looking. He was a spotty youth really if you objectified him. An angry young man, who was trying to process his karma, whilst dragging others along with him. He did have something alluring in his energy, and intensity, but his contrived grip then fed on those who had complied. A kind of vampire, he fed on people's distress and confusion, because of his own need for attention. He was probably reeling from mother issues, and not being understood. Sarah had no doubt he was a bit of a magician too, a necromancer from another lifetime, who all the girls would have done well not to meet in this one. He was a challenge; but then all narcissists are.

Graham probably needed a course of medication, counselling, and a spell in the army. Instead he prayed on the vulnerable and projected his issues onto whoever would listen. His sister Kathy was fun and cool. But she had her work cut out dealing with him. Sarah did not think he did her any favours either. He tried to be everyone's psychologist, priding himself on being a Charles Manson type figure. He claimed to be able to plummet your psychological depths and inadequacies. But really, he was trying to work out his own.

Sarah was ironically named "Dolly." Em and Colin from Lilligs, had originally christened her "Dolly" when they rescued her. She did not mind, as her beloved Nan had also had the moniker "Doll" bestowed upon her in her East End days. But Graham and his harem then proceeded to twist what had been meant as a term of endearment, into a term of torture. Graham's ex-girlfriend, an intermittent double-breasted comfort cushion for him, had the nerve to write a poem about "Dolly Daydream and her cat."

"Dolly" was apparently lost, lonely, pathetic, weak, broken etc. Sarah was *not*. But this group of young upstarts projected their drama and pretention onto her, to the point when it began to be undermining. She allowed it. It was a toxic situation. Sarah was privy to what was going on and could still objectify it and distance herself. But it is amazing what boredom and loneliness will do to a person. The Graham saga also shows that groups of people tapping into the same warped energy field, are just as detrimental as the individuals who endeavor to control things. There is not always safety in numbers.

The whole thing was a regressive nightmare, which never should have happened. Sarah was better than all of this. It was also impossible not to wonder what she had done to deserve it. She began to think everyone in Scotland was less than *compos mentis*. It was hugely detrimental, and a complete waste of time, to hope for anything sensible from a group of immature kids, who were many years younger than herself. Sarah was in her late twenties at this point, going on thirty-six, and Graham was twenty-three. The girls were younger still. Instead of going for older guys, Sarah was starting to choose the 'toy boy' route. But really, she was still too young for that. She made a quick exit left, when she realized the depths of Graham's depravity, and the extent of his experimentation with people's emotions.

Sarah's brother and sister stumbled across their own lessons in abuse down in Sheffield at around the same time. Simon, Rache, and their circle of friends all became heavily involved in *NOS*, aka, the *Nine O' Clock Service*. They acted in predictable 'left-field' fashion and chose to attend this church service, which was to all intents and purposes a nightclub, hosted by a wannabe rock star.

The worship in the alternative communion services was generally quite awe-inspiring. Here was a vibrant young Christian community led by an inspiring charismatic leader. The energy and spirit of the project was fresh and innovative, and the air was thick with excitement and expectation. When Sarah visited a service in Sheffield, she certainly experienced the tangible and magical feeling first-hand. It was not a typical church service, that is for sure. This was something different for young people who wanted to make a difference. The emerging social consciousness of this group was applied in practical ways to benefit the broader community; and the church's ethos was to actively reach out evangelically, as well as to help those in need. The intentions were all good.

What then unfolded over time was nothing short of tragic. It all became a bit of a mess. Some years later, a horrible truth emerged that certain people, mainly young women, had been abused and taken advantage of by the vicar, who Sarah's brother came to call Voldemort. This experience was painful to many, and some still hurt to this day because of this man's actions. Yes, it was all a long time ago. But abuse of any kind does not always get processed easily; particularly not when exercised by someone you are supposed to be able to trust. Are some things unforgiveable? If so these acts of treachery may have come close to being so. They certainly did nothing to instill confidence in people spouting the word of God in hypocritical fashion. In a similar way to the scandals inherent, and subsequently exposed, in the heart of The Catholic Church, this sad reality damaged many people.

Rachel, Sarah's sister who had studied History of Art at Manchester University, had moved to Sheffield to be near Simon and his young family. Rache in her teens was "Rache H, famous fashion designer of the future," to quote her art teacher. Rache H was prone to bringing out the natural colours in her hair using various dramatic hair dyes. A natural brunette, her colouring ranged from bright red, through purple, sometimes black, and other times blonde-streaked.

Rache was artistic like her siblings, and liked alternative music, also like her siblings. She chose to do her high school years some distance away in Bristol, because she did not want to hang out with the "false nail brigade" in Portishead. Sarah and Simon cannot have minded the "townie" Kardashians of Portishead quite so much, as they both finished up their designated terms at Gordano, the local comprehensive school. Thanks to the more elite Cotham Grammar School, Rache was able to get the correct grades she needed to further her studies at University.

Gordano School, named after the "arrow-shaped" valley in which it could be found, was a good school, with an impressive array of open-minded teachers. It was big for local standards, and it was easy to get lost amongst twelve hundred people, and the warren of corridors. Built in the sixties, Gordano was designed to serve the local community, and the surrounding villages in the valley. The layout of the school was complex. At the top of the ramp were the science blocks on the right, and on the left, the arts buildings housing music, art and drama. Maths tended to be in the oldest part of the school, along with home economics, and languages. The sixth form was more informal than the rest of the school, which was appropriate for those preparing to graduate and go to college, or university. Found by the library, the common room was also near the exam rooms, computer rooms, and the staff room at the top of the vertiginous wooden slatted stairs.

Sarah enjoyed her arts teachers Mr Hallam, Mr Porter and Mr MacDonald in particular. Miss Plimmer, the English teacher was a sight for sore eyes, with her long red nails, peroxide blonde hair, skinny jeans, and little lap dog. But Sarah was somewhat of a loner at school, and often chose to take her lunch break reading up in a classroom on the first floor. Obviously, a natural introvert, she hated team sports, and group activities. She only came into her own when on familiar ground up in the mountains or playing pool with all the handsome guys in the sixth form common room.

Sarah was much more of a "boys, girl", though had some good close girlfriends in the form of Ginny, Jan, Bev, and Australian Vanessa. These were the "cool" girls who were in it for laughs, as opposed to the "bitchy" girls, who would persecute and find fault. Vanessa and Ginny were the girls with the long blonde hair Sarah envied as she was never allowed to grow mine long; because she had a nice neck, "like Granny."

I have heard better excuses.

Jan was spectacular with her blue eye-shadow, and long nails, invariably black or blue. Sarah was good with the lipstick. But the darkest shade she was permitted to go with her nails was a rich chocolate brown, which made them look positively edible or disgusting depending on your mind-set. Sarah was not very forthcoming or extravert at school. She felt uncomfortable in morning assembly, and generally did not like crowds of school kids, or activities involving big groups. She was too sensitive, and the bombardment of the senses in these situations she did not always know how to process. This young "sensitive" preferred to skip gym, school trips, and any hectic

151

participation activity. She would much rather have her head in a book, or be doing her art homework, or perfecting an essay assignment. Sarah was fine if she had something creative to engage in. But she did not like socializing except with close friends.

She had always been better one-to-one. Even in later years Sarah still preferred a quality interaction with one person, to an overwhelming over stimulating group event. As a mutable Virgo she was variable though, and sometimes would shine and perform well on the days her confidence peaked.

Mr Ackland her House Head Teacher had been glowingly impressed and proud, when she led a small school camp along the ridge heights of *Crib Goch*, on Mount Snowdon in Wales. There are a couple of ways up Mount Snowdon. Most of the party had chosen the slow, methodical route, *The Miner's Track*. Being her father's daughter, Sarah chose the precarious, precipitous ridge route that is *Crib Goch*. With sheer drops on either side, this is a tricky climb, and not for the faint hearted. She was not actually sure why a school party were even attempting it. But there they were in the fog and rain, with dusk descending rapidly, without ropes or a compass. Understandably, the party were a little edgy, nervous, and panicked, and feeling varying degrees of discomfort. Sarah had already done this route before, so she confidently kept her cool and took over. In respectably quick time, she guided everyone across the ridge safely.

Sarah was perceived in a new light after that. It just goes to show, a kid needs just one chance to come good, and everything can change. Her confidence increased, and somehow, she had made the connection between home and school life. Yep, she truly *was* her father's daughter, and thereafter recognized that her private and public self, were one and the same. Life needs an integration point like this. In that moment Sarah grew up and became independent.

All three siblings, Sarah, Simon, and Rache, had a penchant for risk taking and choosing more alternative approaches to life. Brought up in the punk era, they all had spiky hair, and at one point all pretty much had the same prerequisite mullet. Sarah's was always blonde, her brother's ginger, sorry titian; and her sister varied hers to match her mood or her clothing. They were victims to the trends just like anyone else. They all loved their music, shared similar tastes in fashion, and painted on their bedroom walls at home. Rache splashed hers with abstract flicks of red, green, yellow and blue; Simon painted a spectacularly OCD Hot Rod with not a blurred line insight; and Sarah painted hers bright orange, which did not quite work, so she promptly pasted it over with a magazine montage. Obviously her glamorous, media-friendly sensibilities began in her teens. This collage was full of painted lips, high-fashion, musicians, and beautiful scenes.

The music which floated out of these downstairs split-level bedrooms was assorted. Joy their mother upstairs in her kitchen could hear a curious blend of Fleetwood Mac, Elvis Costello, and The Stranglers. When teatime came, a loud bell placed strategically at the top of the stairs, was required to drown out the music, and imprint upon our eardrums that food was served.

Sarah, Simon and Rache were all artistic, creative, smart, and generally cool. At school Sarah was in the top stream for all subjects, but there was a definite mismatch with the maths. She managed the course work but needed three attempts at the GSE to pass for university. Finally, she managed to make the grade, as she simultaneously studied for S' level English to help boost her application for Cambridge University. Her father had done his medical training at Cambridge, and Sarah fell in love with it when he showed James and Sarah around. Gordano school was not primed to prepare students for Oxbridge, but Sarah was guided to see how well she could do in the entrance exams. Jan was horrified that she had chosen a question *not* taught in our English class for the A level English exam. Sarah assured her it was fine, as she had been independently studying for the Cambridge entrance exams. She had not liked the questions on the books and subjects we had covered in class, so she intuitively chose a general Shakespeare question. It worked out, and Sarah got a B1 for English, which was a "score," as Gordano did not teach the S level either.

What it showed Sarah, was that she was a natural student, who could self-teach on subjects that were of interest to her. This independence set her up nicely for the three academic degrees that were to come. She did not manage to get into Cambridge for undergraduate work but was offered a place for postgraduate teacher training on graduation from Stirling University. She turned it down. By then, she was too deeply embroiled with all the prerequisite karma of the Celtic Countries. The Rainbow Road was leading her in a completely different direction.

Sarah's entry in the Publishing Studies yearbook published on graduation, stated that her ambitious life intention was to:

"Live in Dublin, to work at The Kitchen night club; and to possibly take up PhD study at Trinity College Dublin or University College Dublin."

This statement shows where her energies and ambitions were leaning. Sarah was on a mission to call in her Irish karma and make some soulful connections.

CHAPTER NINETEEN

Cathar-tic Purge

The *Nine O' Clock Service* had all the hall marks of being an exciting experiment when it first began. Brian, a young apparently brilliant, funky, open-minded aspiring vicar had been given charge of the young people in the congregation of St. Thomas' Church, Crookes. This innovative measure inspired many people, and the *Nine O' Clock Service* (*NOS*) gained recognition for its innovative worship nationally, if not internationally, in Christian circles. Brian was fast-tracked to clerical status without stepping foot in theological college.

Paul told Sarah personally that his band's tour and light show had been inspired by *NOS*'s use of projectors, words, and flashing images in worship. This confession of Paul's surprised her. But she could see what he meant. *NOS* was essentially a nightclub come to church. The ethos was designed to accommodate youngsters who loved music, who would not usually hang out in a church.

The creationist theology of *NOS* was also a bit more all-embracing and forgiving than narrow fundamentalism. It had a broad appeal, for those who found traditional services staid and lacking in joy. In short, *NOS* caught imaginations everywhere.

Paul had been a member of a similarly innovative Bible class in Dublin and was always on the lookout for refreshing worship ideas, and non-stifling ways to express a love of God. He talked freely about his love for the Glide Memorial Church in San Francisco, where the rubber meets the road merging musicality, message, and soul. "Radically inclusive, just, and loving," is the consciousness of this innovative church. Paul equates it to a voice of freedom, for the people. When a church is authentic and works from a place of honesty, integrity, and commitment, it is a political, social, and personal weapon of strength.

To observers and participants alike, it seemed that the *Nine O' Clock Service* was onto something. An energy was generated at these services, not unlike that of a spectacular rock gig if truth be told. Brian was one of the first Christian leaders of modern times, who could whip up a frenzied energy in a communion service. While Paul was a master on stage, who channeled God, even singing in tongues for his devoted fans, it was easy to see how his band may have tapped into some of the presentation tricks of innovative worship. Indeed, Paul basically told Sarah they had done so. She is not sure she would have noticed the connection otherwise. One would have assumed it was more likely the other way around; that Brian was inspired by Paul's rock band, instead of visa versa.

If truth be told, Brian's energy was probably more that of a druid, than a rock god. The Church of England would have been truly alarmed if they had worked that one out more quickly. Brian was open and tapping into some universal energy that is for sure. But was it purely pagan and overtly all-embracing with no boundaries? This might sound ideal to those who choose to believe all is equal under the heavens, but to those who are aware that being open to a fault is dangerous, this was indeed a potentially alarming approach. Being a channel for spiritual energy is an admirable pursuit when discernment is employed. Ditch wisdom, healthy boundaries and a holy reference point, and all hell can break loose. Literally.

The *Nine O' Clock Service* was a family concern for many. Those who were twenty-something, met and married at this Godly nightclub; Sarah's brother and sister included. Sarah's parents had understandably been concerned about her Edinburgh shenanigans, and urged her to consider a move to Sheffield. It could not have been worse than some of the things she was encountering. But Sarah did not completely warm to Brian when she met him. He had all the right accoutrements. A thick head of dark wavy hair, piercing eyes, and a lanky tallish demeanor. In theory she would have normally found him appealing. But he could not look her in the eye. She saw a hidden, secret element within him that she did not warm to. It was as if she saw through him. A memory from another time perhaps. She gazed into his soul for a moment and did not like what she saw. She did not judge people, but if she got such a warning sign, she kept her distance. She did not feel the pull to move to Sheffield, that is for sure.

Sarah's perception of Chris was a bit ironic with all she apparently missed up in Edinburgh. But if truth be told, Sarah did not miss things. She simply walked into tricky situations eyes wide open. It was a choice really. She owned it. The Edinburgh scenarios felt karmic, and she was emotionally engaged to learn and grow. She did not think any of it was a waste of time. It gave her an armory of experience, which she was able to then use to help people. It was not such a raw deal. Sheffield was not Sarah's learning curve. Edinburgh was.

Things ran smoothly in *NOS* for quite some time. Long enough for the newlyweds to start families and commit to a community vision for the church. An ethos, plan, practices, and approach were agreed. But

157

the overall point of concern was that Brian was given free reign. He answered to no one in the church hierarchy and was left to do his own thing. The congregation *NOS* was initially an observed experiment, performed advisedly by The Church of England. But, somewhere along the line, the truth got distorted, power went to someone's head, and megalomania set in. If the gossip is to be believed, a small select group of women started to tend to Brian's needs beyond the call of Christian duty. Brian had a set of darkly clad handmaidens who gave him massages; or so the rumors went. If the tabloids were right in their conclusions these massages invariably had a "happy ending" too. Girls started to feel used and emotionally toyed with, and one day someone blew the whistle.

Of course, the fragmentation of *NOS* was excellent tabloid fodder. Probably much that was printed in newspapers was an excuse to sensationalize the situation. Yes, things had gone horribly wrong. Many felt hugely betrayed once Brian's antics were uncovered; and many then fell away from faith in God, because Brian had let them down. This was a classic guru scenario, where the people had become over reliant on one human being rather than God himself.

It was not strictly right or fair to blame everything on Brian. But he did take advantage of his God-given position. No one really knows the extent of any abuse or manipulation that went on, except Brian himself. Winnie, his wife at the time, claims to have known nothing about it. What apparently went on under her nose, was well hidden, and subsequently covered up. No one knew quite what to believe, and the testimonies of the abused, obviously had to be proven and substantiated. The rumors and stories were damaging enough.

Just as people were originally united through *NOS*, they then became torn apart through the same channel. This was all so devastating and ironic. What had started as a wonderfully refreshing movement inside the church, became abusive and misleading. *NOS* had started to serve Brian. He had lapped up the attention apparently, and had started to take advantage, feeding a lavish lifestyle of travel, designer clothes, and those handmaidens to alleviate exhaustion. God was nowhere in sight by the time he was uncovered.

When it all fell apart, Brian had nowhere to go. Technically he could have been arrested on charges of embezzlement, abuse, and fraud. But the Church wanted him to lie down quietly and disappear. This whole thing had become a huge liability and embarrassment. True to his innate loyalty as a Taurus, Simon, Sarah's brother, protected Brian, and gave him shelter in The Highlands. Simon was the one member of the congregation who stood by Brian, Winnie, and their daughter. Even though Anne, Simon's first wife, had been close to Brian, Simon decided to remain true and supportive to a guy who now had no friends, and no future.

Until the dust settled on the sorry mess, Simon gave Brian the benefit of the doubt. He was godfather to two of Simon's children, and things were by no means clear in the immediate aftermath. Simon's sainthood is probably lined up in the heavens, to be bestowed at some point, as God sees fit.

Sarah's sister Rache, and her husband Graham did not have any such tolerance for Brian. They knew more than Simon did in the initial stages of the scandal, as some of their closer friends had been directly involved. They wanted nothing to do with Brian, and saw the devastation first-hand, of how Brian had manipulated and taken advantage of his position.

"Simon de Montfort," as Roger, their father called him, clearly had some sort of Knights Templar brotherly karmic contract to uphold with Brian. He did his best in a messy situation. Anne his first wife departed, to spread her wings and explore her independence, leaving Simon with mutually agreed custody of their three kids. Two divorces and a wedding later, and Simon was soon enough, happily married to the wayward vicar's wife.

Result!

CHAPTER TWENTY

Not Meant to Be

arry Horse had been Sarah's background daydream and
fantasy, throughout the Graham saga, and indeed during the
last throes of the John nonsense. He was an emotional
thread and reference point during her time in Edinburgh. Darkly
alluring, brooding and mysterious as he was, Sarah also loved that he
was doing his own thing. He was a highly creative artist and musician.
Essentially, Harry was a storyteller, who led a magical existence fired
by his imagination and natural intelligence. His life was certainly not
an open book, and he was far from clearly readable. But he was
compelling. Unattainable.

A misfit, who was somewhat out of place in the twentieth century,
Harry looked like he was from another century, and Sarah was sure his
karma was playing out from another time and place. He dressed like a
dandy from the Renaissance, with ruffled billowing white shirts tucked
into black cloth breeches, which were in turn tucked into black riding
boots. He really looked like he had stepped off the set of *Dangerous*

Liaisons. That scene where John Malkovich uses pen and ink to write on the back of a prostitute? *That* was Harry.

Sarah would see Harry and Mandy walking arm in arm around Stockbridge. He was much more receptive to Sarah than he had been when he was watched like a hawk by Kimberly. But he was all about Mandy. She did not live with him permanently. They had a to-and-fro arrangement which involved him going up to The Shetlands for part of the time. Sarah lived on the corner of the main street in Stockbridge, and Harry lived in his garret a few doors up on the right. Her building was somewhat bulbous, jutting out into the thoroughfare, which accommodated traffic running from Cramond up into the New Town, the steep cobbled streets which connected with Princes Street.

The cracked window of her wooden-floored, wood-lined, and wood-paneled room had a view right up the streets to the left and right. Mellish the cat used to sit on her pine desk surveying the landscape, before opting to brave the communal stairs to go outside for a reconnaissance expedition. He was lucky not to have been run over in this bustling corner, at the intersection of five roads. But he had a way of disappearing out the back, over the walls, and down the path which led to the Water of Leith. In the evenings, Mellish would trot along the street beside Sarah to get their groceries from the store. He was permitted to accompany her around the aisles also. Basically, he was a dog that purred.

Sarah visited Harry in his garret once to drop off a pen and ink picture she had found for him in an antique shop on Dundas Street. He liked the picture. But did not like her apparently. Not in *that* way anyway. He had ample chance to take advantage of her as she sat uncomfortably on a wicker chair in his tiny attic flat; and did nothing. It clearly was not in any way "happening."

Sarah lost contact with Harry for years after that. But on searching for updates at one point, she found that he had published several illustrated cartoon books, and had a documentary made about himself,

Mandy his wife, and their dog Roo. She was delighted to see that Harry had achieved this level of success with his work. He had cut his hair, put on weight and in his domestic bliss, was much less attractive. He now looked like he belonged in the twentieth century, so had obviously worked through his Renaissance karma efficiently.

At least he was happy, she mused.

The next articles she found about Harry and Mandy were much more worrisome. A few years on, in some dark, full moon moment, Harry had murdered Mandy, who suffered from multiple sclerosis, and all their pets, before then mutilating himself fatally. What was initially presented by local papers as a suicide pact, born out of frustration with Mandy's condition and their isolated circumstances, was in fact a brutal murder.

Omg!

In that moment Sarah realized, she had been protected from another John type scenario, which could have turned out even more violently. What a tragedy and a shock. What a horrendous story, and such a grizzly end, for two talented, handsome people with so much potential. Reading these pieces gave Sarah her "there but for the grace of God go I" moment. Hardly an appropriate time to voice "it should have been me." But thank God it was not. She felt suddenly protected by all the things she had wanted to happen which did not.

Harry must have been high on a hallucinogen that fatal night. His impotence in the situation with Mandy dying of multiple sclerosis before his eyes, got a ruthless grip of him. He became possessed by a dark force. This would make sense of all the energy he stirred and conjured during his lifetime. Harry was wont to walk on the dark side, and Sarah intuited that a fleet of entities piggy-backed his existence if truth be told. Sometimes such energies can take over, or build to a crescendo point, and *BAM!* The outlet is not pretty.

Thankfully, latterly, Sarah chose to hang around with *Pierre Le Rue* instead of Harry. Harry had turned her down and was never going to make a move. She certainly was not going to inflict herself on someone not interested, so she moved on. *Pierre Le Rue*, or Pete The Street, was much more wholesome energetically, and a more talented, authentic musician also. Harry was a showman and travelling salesman. Pierre was the real deal, straight from the Bayou. Well. Albuquerque, and the deserts of New Mexico.

Pierre really *was* American, and a skilled Cajun fiddle player. He had a similar tall and lanky vibe to Harry, but even deeper meltingly chocolate eyes, revealing a depth of soul. Harry had clearly modeled himself and his *Swamptrash* story on Pierre, or at least taken huge inspiration from his ilk. Sarah came to much prefer the kosher version, as opposed to the fake. Harry had to act and compensate for quite a bit. He was immensely talented and driven, but also thwarted and ultimately doomed. Pierre was apple pie in comparison.

Pierre was a true gentleman, and an intelligent, humorous companion. Harry was apparently the type who would have locked Sarah away in a tower; and then murdered me. Pierre took her on the road. playing his fiddle joyously. Magically night after night her soul and vibration were lifted. After all the drama it was a gift from the heavens.

Sarah's eyes were opening. There were other interesting men out there. She was never an easy option, for a guy and was always somewhat "proper" and well behaved. Boring you might even say. Except she was *not!* She was the girl who would stand in the bar and not drink. But who would dance, and socialize, and have lots of fun! She did not need recreational drugs, nor drink, nor meaningless sex. She was into music, and people, and soulful connections. z\

Before the Pierre chapter, Sarah had warmed to Charles one of the managers of a German restaurant on Victoria Street. The Edinburgh restaurant family opened her up to some company, love and support, and psycho John did not like it. Sarah was a prolific chef. Her dishes filled the fridges to overflowing, and she was well liked. She enjoyed

163

the camaraderie the restaurant afforded. It was hard work; but it was also social and intriguing.

Charles was fun, but he had a connection with and fixation on someone else. That somewhat unrequited affection was not dissipating any time soon. Charles was on his own journey with his personal situation, and clearly not about to be diverted. He had a formidable live-in partner, the very German Inge, who was fielded by her even more formidable Germanic mother. This Teutonic duo were the force field and hub of the restaurant. They did not crack the whip, or rule with the iron rod, but it was all run very efficiently. There was strudel for breakfast, soup for lunch, schnitzels for dinner, and stuffed savory croissants at any time of your choosing.

Charles was tall, lanky with piercing blue eyes, and deep auburn wavy hair. Not really Sarah's type if truth be told. But his voice was wonderfully deep, soothing, and resonant. He was playful and entertaining, and liked his food. Sarah's exotic, spicy *Kusherie* dish was one of his favourites. She greatly enjoyed his company, but of course wished for something more. In her head the Charles thing was important for several months. An energy link to muse and dream about, even while knowing it was not ever going to be a reality. Sometimes she indulged her Pisces ascendant in these ways. Such reveries were a means to get through boring or demanding times. After all there is nothing wrong with a bit of fantasy. It can play a valid role. Sarah knew the difference between someone she was dreaming about, and someone who was *there* for her. Her feelings for Charles were nothing overwhelming or overtly powerful. But they were important. She did not want to diminish the connection; but it was an attempt to move on cleanly from John, and innocently enjoy someone else's company.

Between them Charles, Simon and Em hatched a rescue plan to deliver Sarah from John's clutches for good. Simon was a talented ginger artist in his own right, and yet another restaurant partner. There really were too many chiefs, and not enough Indians running this place. It was a vibrant place to work, and visit. But eventually it inevitably went out of business, simply because too many couples were draining its resources. It was hard work for them all, without much return. Sarah learned first-hand that running even a successful restaurant is no guarantee that the books will balance, let alone generate a profit margin.

Scottish Simon pronounced Sarah a "delicate flower" that needed careful feeding, nurturing, and rescue. She was permitted to sleep on the floor of Emi's flat, which she shared with Simon. Strangely this was just around the corner from John. Small steps. She was only yards away from the boys, but it felt cataclysmically important. She had some personal space, but of course only through invading the space of the generous Simon and Em. Clearly, she would not be able to sleep on the floor of their small sitting room permanently. But with John? It. Was. Finally. Over. Sarah never went back into that dingy basement apartment inhabited by John, Colin, and Ron. But ended up instead in the attic flat of the same building.

Amanda, a social worker, single mum, who had recently given birth to a gorgeous half Chilean baby, needed a roommate. Sarah jumped at the offer. Of course, she ended up being a surrogate mother, and helping a lot with the lovely five-month-old Luce. But she did not mind. She had a healthy degree of separation from John, and life was picking up.

Sarah really enjoyed the nurturing experience of bonding with a young baby too. It was therapeutic, and obviously helpful to her roommate. Luce was the most beautiful baby she had ever seen. Her half Chilean genes gave her a wonderful depth of caramel complexion. Her hair was dark, silky, and smelled delicious, and her eyes were big orbs of soulful deliciousness. Sarah had always been good with both animals and children. They tended to fall asleep on her. Her healing energies make them feel safe and secure, and she could quickly calm them with the use of her hot hands.

John was still attempting to monitor Sarah's movements in and out of the attic flat. Sarah needed to wean herself away from the claustrophobic situation in Gayfield Square. Several times she had managed to sneak out unnoticed and go spread her wings at some gig or other. She was living dangerously and doing her own thing. Those that would control her did not like it. Everything John had tried to squash or stop within her was coming back to the fore. She had the music in her.

John had panicked and cried like a baby when he saw that Sarah finally had the means and confidence to leave. She even felt sorry for him, and there was a flicker of remorse. He finally looked vulnerable after years of bullying, and she felt some defense within him was down. Perhaps he would even get help. John was finally forced to at least contemplate his behavior. Or not. John hated Em and all the Lilligs crowd. He had baited Sarah mercilessly about them. Essentially, he tried to put the doubt in her mind about every good thing that would threaten to take her away from him and diminish his control over her life. Finally, the shoe was on the other foot.

Agoraphobia had become something of an issue as Sarah sought to expand her horizons and spread her wings after the John trauma. She had been in an obtuse energetic funk, and trapped confinement in the unnaturally stifling situation. She was contained in chrysalis form, and her hatching was a real stop and start affair. She had to take a few months out from postgraduate studies at Edinburgh University as she was not able to successfully get up into the heart of the city without having a panic attack.

Taxis became her safe mode of transport. Whenever she had to get somewhere which felt in any way awkward, she would manage it only if she could, "wrap a taxi around her," to quote her father. That tendency has not changed much over the years. She still much preferred to get somewhere independently than brave the hordes of

166

commercial travelers on planes, trains, and automobiles. She sought the smooth, easy, hassle-free way. A legacy of the John days. A legacy which affected quite a lot. But thankfully the psychological damage was not as lasting as it might have been. The gift in the situation was that she could now understand and help people with post-traumatic stress disorders, anxiety, depression, and agoraphobia. She was perfectly fine, and the trauma feels like another lifetime at this stage. But having been there herself, and emerged through the tunnel, she was able to help others shift those tricky energies and get their healings much more quickly than she had been able to.

Sarah had to manage much of this aspect of her journey independently. She refused to approach a doctor for medications she did not need. She wanted to confront, process, and experience all she was going through without dampening it down in any way. She cannot imagine what it would be like to go through something like this in a medicated fog. She felt she needed her wits about her, and it was imperative that she was fully engaged in her life, even though it was difficult.

Sarah attempted spasmodic counselling at one point. But it was basically useless. She was open, honest, and not in the least bit defensive or evasive. But she was able to run rings around the counsellors with her answers for everything. Something her mother had always said about her, proved very pertinent in this situation. She really did have an answer, an excuse, or at least an intelligent explanation, for everything. She could easily justify her decisions, reactions, and behaviors, as she was fully conscious throughout of why she was doing what she was doing. Her inner stability required that she back off slowly and deliberately from John and his obsessive monitoring. Going cold turkey and disappearing would not have completed the karmic loop on this relationship. For some reason, she needed to see it through, and come out the other side through a choice which ultimately led to her empowerment not her diminishment.

Knowing what she knew did not always help. Sarah did not actually need insights. She could verbalize insights and analysis until "the cows come home." What she needed to find, was *how* to change things. Sarah really needed energy work, and energy shifts, to finally sort the trauma. The emergent path she took to master healing, and her psychic abilities, became a means to cope. It proved to be an education, and a way of transmuting all the negativity.

Sarah began researching readers attending regularly for readings at The College of Parapsychology in Edinburgh and started to visit commercial psychics. Her phone bills were rather scary from all the phone calls to psychic lines, and she certainly got a schooling in how *not* to read. In different ways, she began to look outside of herself for perspective and answers. She hoped she was not looking away from God for those insights, but her journey spiritually certainly had become much more complex.

Celia was an amazing grassroots Scottish psychic that Em and Sarah visited quite regularly. Sarah asked her about marriage at one point. Her response? "You don't need a man!" Sarah guessed that was one of the most pertinent things she ever said, because she sure as hell had to manage without a partner for much of the time. In the name of research, Sarah was taught first-hand to understand the "when, when, when," of desired future events. The "when" of something was a persistent question which pervaded most of her clients' issues subsequently.

Sarah had asked that question herself frequently. But it was some time before she learned to stop asking for the "when," so that the "why" might become apparent. As she searched for the healing she needed, she essentially became an apprentice in the healing and psychic arts. Her understanding of psychology amplified, and her life skills grew. It was initially very much a case of, "do as I say, not as I do." But as she developed, her road became increasingly congruent and authentic, and she began to "walk her talk," understanding just what that meant.

Sarah's suffering had become the means to help people. Through not giving up, she began to turn her story into a tool for guidance and healing. She obviously needed to learn to apply her skills, gifts, and insights for other's benefit. She needed to know she could speak accurately and with authority, and not be wrong. She had listened to a lot of nonsense during her research quest. She wanted to provide people with a service that was relevant and helpful. A path of spiritual responsibility was unfolding. She had not planned it. But it was the upshot of not taking the suicide options, which had presented rather frequently if truth be told. She was never *ever* going to take that route. Times were surely dark, but the flicker of the flame of hope was never extinguished.

Whatever happened to her, the love of God never left her; nor did an implicit faith in his/her ability to deliver. The dark night of the soul was an ever-present reality. She did not baulk. She knew the night was darkest before the dawn, and she was not going to waiver in her faith. Nor was she going to run away from her calling. The road less travelled had certainly taken a hold of her, and there was no turning back.

CHAPTER TWENTY-ONE
Dublin's Fair City

S arah arrived in Dublin, dishevelled, despondent and more than
a little knackered. The drive down from Belfast had been
interminable. So tedious in fact that Sarah and William had to
halt the journey before reaching their destination. At a castellated hotel
perched on the approach road they stopped off for a night's rest to
gather thoughts, energies, and intentions before driving into Dublin's
Fair City the following day.

Over a sleep-inducing pint of Guinness in the downstairs bar they
contemplated their big decision to up sticks and head for the Republic
of Ireland. After a curious and intermittently disturbing chapter in
Scotland, Sarah was more than ready for a change of scene. This lure
of Ireland had long been enticing. She felt her destiny would play out
in The Emerald Isle much more productively than it had in Scotland.
But Sarah was feeling the enormity of what was about to happen, and
she did not fully like what she saw.

It was a big step to pack up and leave Edinburgh, a city she loved, relished, and adored. Moving to what was essentially another country took courage, and it was much more disarming than she thought it was going to be. Although so close to the United Kingdom, Southern Ireland has a totally different energy. Travelling through the North stirred up many anxieties, as it was in the days before peace talks and uneasy resolutions. There was an ever-present feeling in the air, that something "bad" was about to happen.

Many impressions bombarded Sarah's psychic sensibilities on arrival in Northern Ireland. The all-pervasive heaviness was tangible. This sensation, combined with the observation that anyone she had ever met from the north was always slightly unhinged, did not help. Her psychotically disturbed, paranoid ex-boyfriend John was a case in point. Enough said.

Was it safe at the cross-border check? Would the authorities, question who they were in a laden white van heading south? Was there a crackpot border raid, or ambush about to take place? The feel of the atmosphere at the borders had all this potential swirling. Northern Ireland did not strike her as safe. There was something in the ethers inducing a fiery, twitchy, heightened jumpiness, which would surely drive someone over-the-edge given enough time.

Sarah had panicked at the ferry terminal, and this discombobulating energy that greeted them probably did not help. She had a compelling wish to turnabout. Never a good sign. Although the overall decision to move felt compelling, it also felt uncomfortable. She felt a destiny calling linked to the south, an inexplicable pull. She could not turn back. This move was a leap into the unknown, especially as it was done "holding hands" with someone, she did not even know she had a future with. In retrospect William was delivering her to where she needed to be. She would not have undertaken such a big task and upheaval alone. Even in the company of a good friend, which William surely was, it still felt challenging.

Sarah had had the notion about Dublin for some time. But it was just an intriguing thought, which floated through her consciousness intermittently. She just as quickly squashed it and parked it for later perusal. In truth this move had in fact been precipitated by a restless boyfriend. One who could not face life in Edinburgh with her in a small, potentially floodable, cottage apartment by the waters of Leith. Fair enough. Sarah was clearly his ticket to a bit more excitement than that. Said boyfriend needed a change of scenery.

Sarah had been cautious and in two minds about the whole thing. It did not seem practical or doable. It was back to that not chasing rainbows thing; the very definition of which is not to embark on anything impossible or impractical. She had her masters in Publishing Studies at Stirling to complete and was not looking forward to commuting all the way from Dublin for exams. Plus, she had the small matter of a thesis to wrap up.

Making an Impression!

The restless boyfriend syndrome in the amenable form of William was inconvenient to say the least. What was most odd about the whole thing, was that Sarah's tutor at Stirling supported the requested upheaval to her schedule. In what was an unprecedented agreement, the media expert instinctively realized that Sarah was about to step into an environment that would afford her opportunities to apply the principles of the Publishing Studies course. Scroll forward a few months to Sarah working in the cloak room of The Kitchen night club, and she was less sure he was right. But there was no turning back by that point.

The tutor at Stirling, had felt that she should just roll with the opportunity resenting itself. That the time was now. William had spoken, the tutor had spoken, and destiny it seemed had everything in hand. William had issued one of his ultimatums. Nothing too heavy. Just a threat to scarper if this life change did not happen. Spain or Dublin it was. Him to Spain. Or the two of them to Dublin.

William had recently come back to Scotland from an extended trip

172

to Spain. He had not wanted to return, and probably would not have done, only the summer season was done, and he was at a loose end financially.

At the time of William's departure to Spain, they had only just moved into Warriston Terrace, out of a much-loved communal flat shared with several of Edinburgh's finest Goths. Sarah had loved the shared life with this gathering of dark musicians, who ate scrambled egg rolls for breakfast, and who raided the bakery across the road at two in the morning for as many freshly baked goods as possible. Two pounds passed into the hand of the on-duty baker would see them all carrying bags of warm yummy goodies back to the apartment.

Not much sleep happened in that huge high ceilinged, corniced second floor apartment. The toilet was cracked, the bath was slippery and dirty, and the kitchen was a health hazard. But we all muddled along with a mutual understanding of the conditions, and some slap stick camaraderie. Sarah had painted her room cream, lime green and pink in a bid to be creative and add to the flavor of what was essentially a dump.

Sometime before, Sarah had visited her drummer lover Greg for a few hot and sweaty months in this apartment. Not much sleep was had then either. She had had to agree terms that Greg would be allowed to see his ex on Sundays for a cozy roast and time with her mother. But like most cool, aka "stupid," girls Sarah had a bit of the "whatever" about her, and she accepted the conditions.

The days of William the bass player rolled differently. There was a good friendship connection, as well as physical satisfaction initially. Sarah had not had an orgasm with Greg, even though he was a good lover and kisser, but she immediately did with William. Probably she held that part of herself back from Greg because he was still seeing his ex, once a week. But aside from that, she had no complaints. They had appreciated each other for a time, and the connection was intense; probably too intense to go the distance. William was also interesting.

Whereas Greg had been the groovy drummer of a gothic rock band, William was the bass player of a semi-successful mainstream rock band. He was hot, slim, and leather clad; with long layered black hair, off-set with green eyes, and a cheeky grin.

Never mind the good sex, the developing emotional link with William was fraught. He was in resistance much of the time. and totally preoccupied with an ex-girlfriend called Julie. William was initially a torturous nightmare to relate to. There was all the emotional turmoil of his lingering infatuation with Julie, which hardly enhanced the potential relationship. Then out of the blue one night, he announced that suddenly he just "tends to go off sex." Sarah laughed and thought it odd seeing as they had been having *no* complaints in that department. She did not believe him, so incredulous and unexpected an announcement was it. But sure enough. Off. It. He. Did. Go.

On reflection, William was probably the type who liked to have sex with strangers. Girlfriends tended to become sisters to William. He got emotionally bonded, and then some block occurred within him, and he found that his situation was not "sexy" anymore. Over his time with Sarah he always had an internal conflict about being attracted to women he did not know very well but worked with. Every time he got a new job, Sarah would wonder who the new flirtation was this time; and more-often-than-not she guessed correctly. Sorting out that week's laundry, she would find the relevant phone numbers in pockets, and William would have made some connection that ended up making him confused and upset. Not to mention that it always annoyed her greatly.

A particularly annoying phase came a couple of years after they had settled in Dalkey a few miles south of Dublin. William was helping a local creature with her singing demos. Suddenly, William was a dance keyboard pro, and she was the next best dance act. William spent long hours with this "wannabe" up at Strawberry Hill, a magnificent white Italianesque mansion on Vico Road, situated between Dalkey and Killiney. The views from this vantage point are spectacular across the bay. The sweeping flow of the green-blue water, and the soft lilt of the land culminating in the distinctive peaks of Great Sugar Loaf in the distance, create a breathtaking vista. This landscape was Sarah's heaven on earth, her "home from home." It really was the ultimate place to live, and Strawberry Hill was the ultimate roof over one's head.

The wannabe had the right to stay in her marital home for the duration of her divorce proceedings from a bass player with a well-known rock band. She obviously had a thing about bass players. Sarah was not allowed up to the house with William, and he made a point to gloat about it. The great irony was, within a few months, Sarah's best friend was living in Strawberry Hill, as the rock star's partner. His divorce had finally gone through, and he had got his house back.

Sarah was warmly invited for tea, whenever her friend wished it. She also got to spend Christmas Day there with the young family. After yummy crisp well-cooked turkey, they had sat through *Titanic* on the big screen, sipping wine, and wondering why her friend was spending so long in the bathroom, possibly throwing up her food. Her friend came back just in time to catch the close-up of the ancient actress' eye, emerging from the youthful form of Kate Winslet, extended on the chaise longue being sketched by Di Caprio.

There was also a memorable party night at Strawberry Hill where the cream of Dublin glitterati gathered to celebrate a birthday, and some well-known musicians led a singsong around the piano. With its own fully stocked downstairs bar, Strawberry Hill was a rockers' paradise. Alongside the gym, master bedrooms and games room, the social quarters were more than substantial enough to entertain and satiate the magnificent among us.

The lead singer of the bass player's band was between wives and girlfriends, and Sarah's friend had the notion that he and Sarah would make a fine couple. Her friend was looking for longevity in this well-established rock band's "camp," and such a union would potentially give her the security and solidarity she thought she needed. Sarah was fully in the throes of angst over Paul, the lead singer of another band. Her friend had obviously told her partner's front guy. This tall not unattractive singer, with a very lived-in energy, followed Sarah up the stairs from the bar crooning irreverently in a style evocative of her unrequited love, in a bid to make her laugh, or at least catch her attention.

Sarah was too seriously involved, in her heart at least, to make light of his gestures, let alone respond. Even though the two of them were the last to leave the party, Sarah politely said "goodnight," as he lingered watching her at the gate. Sarah had a sense that her friend might be watching through the intercom camera, so she effectively dismissed him, sending him off into the night to find his vintage gold Porsche. Even though Sarah's Irish ancestors shared the guy's surname on her mother's side, the familial feeling did not seem to be present between them both. Yes, he was tall, handsome, and strong. But he was also blond, from the United Kingdom, very northern, and not in the least bit mystical. It was not happening. Sarah's friend decided to secure her future with her bass player by getting pregnant instead.

Every time William got diverted by one of his work colleagues, a little piece of Sarah died inside. Every time it happened, she distanced herself further from him. He was not a bad person and would end up getting quite distressed and upset about his latest encounter. He felt stuck, emotionally involved with the person, and unable to do anything about it. She ended up being his therapist, healer, and counselor, as he processed whatever current emotion he was dealing with.

One time, Sarah found a phone number of a girl he had spent the night with down the road from Dartmouth Square in Dublin, in a hotel on Leeson Street. Dartmouth Square was the red-bricked Victorian apartment they shared with their sausage dog Freddie, prior to moving out to Dalkey on the coast. It was a spooky eerie location, and Freddie used to anxiously await her return from The Kitchen night club, gazing out the window, steaming up the glass from the inside with the warm

176

breath emanating from his huge snout.

William worked at The Pod nightclub and generally got home much later than Sarah did. On this night he did not get home until late morning. The Spanish girl he had been in *flagrante delicto* with, had apparently bashed her head off the headboard until it bled. He then got embroiled in an accident and emergency incident, and not for the last time either. His drinking was fast becoming a problem. Like all Scotsmen he drank until he was "finished!!

Sarah was mortified. She had found a phone number in his pocket, as per usual. This had become a habit she usually witnessed with resignation and a "sigh." But this time she was angry enough to do something about it. Acting somewhat out of character. She phoned her, reprimanded them both, and then dumped him. Sarah did not get intimate with him much at all after that; once or twice maybe. The years passed. Sarah seemed to be good at picking guys that she ended up not having sex with.

She had become more and more fraught and upset, by the apparent nonchalance that William had for their relationship. He did not seem to be able to put the brakes on when a new flirtation came his way. William was a typical astrological Cancer type. He did not know what he wanted until it was too late. He used to constantly cast his mind back to the past and in bleak moods, dragged around a bucket load of pity and regret. It really was at times quite exhausting and exasperating. William could never quite engage fully with what was under his nose. With every passing minute he was stacking up the future regrets of tomorrow. Sarah used to say to him repeatedly "one day you will be lamenting the loss of me also." Sure enough, this happened. He randomly texted her once during a drinking session while he was listening to the song *Let Her Go* by Passenger. Those vodka induced wedding proposals came way too late, and spectacularly out of time.

Scotland had bene a learning experience. Sarah certainly was beginning to understand men. Musicians, anyway, Messed up Scottish musicians with commitment issues. Dick was another one. Sarah worked for Dick in an Edinburgh nightclub every so often as a hostess. He eventually got engaged to the luminous, lovely, leggy, blonde Karen. Sarah had babysat their daughter as an infant. There was an easy jovial connection between Dick and Sarah. He was William's old school mate, and someone William aspired to emulate in terms of worldly success. Dick was fast becoming a millionaire with his band nights, nightclubs, and promotions. Sarah was not overly impressed, but his attentions were warm, friendly, and amusing, and often cheered her up if truth be told.

Dick was always pressing Sarah for smooches, intimacy, and any kind of bodily contact he could get. If she had not liked him, it would have bordered on sexual harassment at times. But she did like him. She valued him as a friend, and was attracted to him, most of the time. Sarah loved William, and it conflicted her that she got more in the way of physical attention and appreciation from Dick. It was irksome, upsetting, and sometimes tempting.

One day though, it suddenly became distinctly unfunny. Sarah had been helping Dick and Karen decorate their bedroom and hallway in their ground floor apartment. For some reason she had agreed to assist. She liked to decorate, and she thought she might as well offer, seeing as they were both busy. One evening Dick called by to assess her progress, and "something" happened. There was a physical connection, on the floor in the front room, windows open, curtains not drawn.

She had said "no!"

He did it anyway.

She did not know what had happened. Her mind was in a fog, and it was over so quickly. Almost like nothing had happened. Except that it *had*!

This was one of those shades-of-grey type scenarios, where the guy could so easily have said, "she was gagging for it," and that, "no meant yes." But this was *not* the case. Sarah had an emotional pang for William, in that moment, and she wanted him to STOP.

She had permitted some snatched snogging before, but even that conflicted her and of course it was also all kinds of wrong. Sarah was not the type to engage in an affair, so this was strange territory for her. Technically it was not an affair, Dick was not married. William had not made a move on her for months. But it was crossing a line she was not comfortable with.

The next time she saw Dick he said it had been "like a dream," and that he hoped she was not pregnant.

Charming.

Dick obviously thought something significant had happened and wanted to make it clear that he could not take the whole thing further. Sarah in turn shrugged the whole thing off. Being kind of shell-shocked she was not sure if it classed as rape or was something she had wanted regardless. She had said "no" because of William. But it still happened. She had not wanted it to. End. Of.

Sarah could not fairly isolate this incident as a unique one. Sometime after that, they were together again; and then again. The next time was with her *full* permission. They had sex in the front seat of his car on the way home from a night's work at the nightclub. Their encounters then became a bit of a habit. Dick smooched her all the way home from some gig, and then made more definite moves in her apartment before work. She did not put up any resistance, verbal or otherwise on those occasions.

The connection was strong enough with Dick. But it did have a take it or leave it element. Not least because of William and Karen. It could have been a choice, or a wife swap scenario. But once Dick made his full commitment to Karen, Sarah took herself out-of-the-running.

Dick and Karen finally got married, after the longest engagement in history, and William and Sarah attended. It was odd for her to go, but not too much to cope with. Nothing ever happened between them after that.

Sarah tended to walk on the dark side with her love life. It was not intentional. But she certainly processed some karmic lessons and experienced an intense learning curve. Much of the knowledge she acquired came to enable her to help people come to grips with their emotional struggles. She became an effective guide for clients on what they need to do to stay with their partners and make it work. Equally, she could help them leave with their head held high, that were required. The upside and reward of her colourful experience, was that she got to apply it in productive ways to facilitate others.

With the disintegration of the gothic nightmare, Edinburgh started to wear thin, and the time had come to take serious action. The left field community of black-clothed, eye-lined, hair-plaited Goths had been ordered to leave their sanctuary and thus ended an era. In real language, the "kip" rented to sarah and her friends by one of Edinburgh's finest doctors, was long overdue a refurbishment. The days of that cracked toilet, and bug-infested kitchen, were most definitely numbered.

For all of them, the notice to quit was the bottom falling out of their world. Despite its dishevelled presentation, number eight Brandon Terrace, top buzzer, was home. It had most definitely been a comfort through unsettled times. True, Sarah had nearly died there when Greg's unhinged jealous girlfriend had soaked her liberally with a bucket of water, as she sat beside an electric heater. Greg got her to apologize several months later in a night club. She offered to let Sarah throw a pint over her for a measure of revenge. Sarah declined. The volume of liquid proffered was not a match that would compensate for the humiliation. It would have taken at least six pints to be fair. Retaliation and pettiness were not Sarah's style, so she passed on her not-so generous offer.

Overall, times were pleasant enough on the terrace. In the previous couple of years, Sarah had liked being able to just turn up and sleep on the sofa. Sometimes things got a bit lonely and intense in her ancient haunted apartment on Victoria Street, so when she was able to move in with William and all her friends, she thought she had finally found a safe-haven and family setting in the north. It was hardly the projected vision her teen self would have found comforting. But in an odd way it worked.

They say change is good. This false, somewhat otherworldly, chill zone had to come to an end just like they all do. With ultimatums flying around, Sarah found herself and William a lovely ground floor apartment with cottagey feel, by the flowing waters of the River Leith. It was just across the road from the gothic haunt, so there was not too much to deal with in the way of lumbering luggage. Though according to William, Sarah possessed more books than it was humanly reasonable to own. An issue that surfaced with every move thereafter.

William lasted about five minutes in this somewhat claustrophobic damp lower level apartment. The Warriston Terrrace accommodation was small with a wicked mold problem in the bedroom. Very quickly William announced he had to do something different. He did not like anything which smacked of commitment and would not be persuaded to stay. No wonder Sarah was vulnerable to the attentions of Dick, who seemed to *like* her and enjoy her company!

Before you could say "Jack Rabbit," William was off to his brother's time-share in Benalmadena to work in Spanish nightclubs for the summer. Banal was indeed the word, for this built-up tourist resort on the southern Spanish coastline. They had enjoyed a two-week holiday there as a couple the year before. But it was certainly not Sarah's desired scene for any long-term working vacation. Besides, she was not invited.

William loved to drink, loved the sun, and loved the night life. For him this was a no brainer. As for Sarah, she finally admitted to herself that she had hooked up with a guy who was happy to drift along, to not settle down or have family, nor commit in any way, shape, or form.

Clearly it was time to start letting go of the notion of finding a soul mate for life. Celtic guys just did not seem to be wired for domesticity. Sarah had lived and breathed in Scotland for some time. Here the men were footless fancy free and had a thing about their mothers. Even once they were married with five kids, the dynamic tended to stay the same. There was no competing with that really.

A move to another Celtic country was worth a shot.

CHAPTER TWENTY-TWO
Thunderbolts

What Sarah knew about Dublin, she could recall in a sentence or two. She knew she was drawn there energetically, and James Joyce's *Dubliners* had given her a taste of what to expect. Apart from that, she knew that the River Liffey flowed through the town center and that a famous rock band lived there, along with Van Morrison, and Enya. Sarah did not know what any of it would mean for her. But one thing was for sure; she was going to find out, thanks to William's restless nature and consequent ultimatum.

Sarah had always found that certain places of significance stuck in her consciousness, and when they really stuck, she usually ended up living there. Dublin was just such a place. She had had no active plan to move there, since she was quite content with her lifestyle amongst the artists, musicians, and rockers of Edinburgh. But she always knew on one level that Dublin's fair city would offer some important and fateful experience. Boy, did she turn out to be right! In ways that not even her strong intuition could have anticipated, Dublin was about to hit her squarely between the eyes.

By invitation, William and Sarah attended the wedding of a well-loved Dublin couple. The handsome groom was part of *Lypton Village*. A group of Dublin artists and musicians who gathered, much as we all had in Scotland, to rail against the dying of the night. *Lypton Village* were a motley crew. The lineup included Paul, Guggi, David, Strong Man and Gavin, to name but a few. These were brothers-in-arms, who had each other's backs. Their art was experimental, and in 70s Dublin somewhat risqué, if not offensive to those who did not understand it. They dressed as women, pushing the boat out, and testing people's boundaries with their performance art, politics, and antics.

Sarah found it very charming that half of Dublin, and the whole of Cork, seemed to hook up with their first love, and stay with them for the duration of a lifetime. This was the way it should be. The way it was in the good old days, and the way Sarah had been brought up to expect it to be. Although very unadventurous, such simplicity and normality, was also refreshing and inspiring. She was used to seeing her contemporaries drift in and out of meaningful monogamous, and not so monogamous, connections.

No dour messed up Scots on the prowl here then, was her thought, as she looked around the wedding guests in attendance.

Oh, except the one I brought with me.

Hmmm...

The groom looked handsome and glamorous in a crisp white suit with a huge sunflower tucked into his lapel. He seemed a bit tense and hassled though, anxious to get the drinks in for his select corner. With a supermodel draped on one arm looking eminently feline, and his new wife obligingly demure on the other, he looked dapper, and quite the dandy.

The sharpest dresser, and probably the coolest guy in town, Sarah concluded. This was the guy you wanted in your corner. He seemed to have a radar for "bullshit," and minimal tolerance for wannabes.

Things started to heat up as the drinks flowed in The Kitchen. Little did Sarah know it, but she was experiencing what was to become her primary habitat for the coming years. The Kitchen Nightclub was so called because it was renovated from the old, cavernous kitchens of the boutique hotel above. The main reception for the wedding had been upstairs in The Tea Rooms of The Clarence Hotel. The Charles Rennie Mackintosh inspired wooden and white decor of the tearoom, gave an elegant backdrop to the wedding reception, where the elite of Dublin and the big wide world, had gathered to celebrate the nuptials.

Just before the party settled into its groove, there had been a kind of crisis. A beautiful doe-eyed super model, with a smiley mouth full of immaculate teeth, had been inconsolably distressed. Sarah thought it rather weird that a woman of her class and poise should have freaked out whilst tumbling out of her limo onto the pavement. The drama which threatened to over-shadow a joyous event, was averted by the limo driving a couple of times around the block, so that its glamorous contents could reset and re-present.

Spirits were soon lifted by the mounting energy in the room, rather than by any white powder that may or may not have been consumed. Sarah found herself playing the role of hostess and was charged with the responsibility of ensuring a healthy flow of white wine to Paul's table, and to Paul in particular. Paul was disconcerted that someone kept walking off with his wine and commissioned Sarah to keep him fully replete throughout the night.

William was in seventh heaven at the wedding. Long time buddy Anthony was in tow, along with a wiry, silver-haired character called Diarmuid. Between them, this old-boys club eyed up every super model that passed by their drinking corner. These old die-hard Dubliners, used to letting it all hang out at The Pink Elephant, had never had it so good. Their years of trawling for talent had finally reached its fulcrum point; and William seemed more than slightly bemused that he had landed in Dublin and was sharing his first Irish shindig with the likes of Christie, Naomi, and Kate.

Surely, he had died and gone to heaven?

The wedding was a joyous occasion. Sarah engaged in the energy of the event and offered to help with sustenance and fluids. She was generally happy enough to flit around making sure people were fed and watered. She never did really drink herself, despite long hours and nights at gigs and nightclubs. She was content enough to just get a feel of the place and enjoy the ambience. By this time, the center stage karaoke machine had been switched on and the weirdest duets and ensembles began to pervade the night air and massacre our best-loved songs.

How bizarre. Here I am in Dublin listening to Paul singing karaoke with a drag queen called Mr Pussy, and he is not sounding much better than your favourite uncle, if truth be told.

She remembered all the white wine she had plied him with, and immediately gave him an excuse.

"The Band" had been Sarah's musical landscape during her tricky times in Scotland. She had a strong sense of Paul's energy as being familiar somehow. When they met at the wedding, and then again at the opening of the nightclub the following Valentine's Day there was an immediate comfort and recognition. She was sure his fans worldwide would understand and identify with this "assumption." She was not trying to factor herself in or conjure anything up. But she did *feel* it if truth be told. The way he looked at her with warmth and curiosity, showed he acknowledged something of the same energy. He seemed to be double-checking himself. Slightly confused as if he was trying to place her also.

At this stage Sarah's musings were innocent and not in the least bit contrived. Of course, they were never about to be "contrived," since she did not do superficiality in any guise. But, one thing was for sure,

186

Sarah did not fully appreciate that this wedding was going to be just as much of a watershed moment in her life, as it was for the bride and groom.

Obliviously floating around in her "bubble," Sarah was always one for observing, watching. and connecting with people. But all this felt a bit different. Something more was engaging her underlying attention. This was deep and interesting, an experience she had not bargained for. She knew there could be a mutual warmth. She could tell this through the kind of soul he was displayed through his music. But quite honestly feelings were stirring that she did not want to deal with. Something was evoked like a distant memory and her heart was unwittingly involved. There was a quality of energy in the air that she had not experienced before. Well not in *this* lifetime. This was the real deal.

Never mind all those Scotsmen.

As usual William managed to annoy Sarah by chatting up the nearest model. Not Naomi, Christy, or Kate thankfully. No, he had grabbed the interest of an attractive red head, over from London with her mother especially for the wedding.

Safe enough, she thought.

But duly observed and noted too.

Besides, she had other fish to fry. For the first time she was consciously aware that William had serious competition for her heart. Even though she was only just waking up to the fact, she amused herself with the notion that Paul had apparently taken quite a shine to her.

It was all William's fault. They should not have even been there. Sarah had a degree unfinished in Scotland, and somehow here she was in a Dublin nightclub dishing out wine and sorting out coats in a cloakroom. She had been quite happy with the prospect of settling down and enjoying William's congenial company back in Edinburgh. She loved and missed the old historical town which had inspired her senses and stirred her soul. But here she was serving drinks at a party in "dirty old town" Dublin, with a special request from Paul to keep him plied with wine, as someone kept marching off with his bottle. You could not work that out or plan it if you tried. A most bizarre subterranean triangle with echoes of another time, another place was beginning to play out.

Sarah was not ready for this karmic destiny moment. No wonder she freaked out on the ferry from Stranraer six months later, when the time had come to face the music. She had fallen under a spell or into another worldly dalliance at the wedding and was loath to come over to Dublin to see what it was all about. It was compelling, but also dark and inexplicably dangerous. The whole scenario felt uncomfortable, panic inducing, and beguiling in equal measure.

Little did she know it, but she was experiencing one of those multiple-choice scenarios you sometime get in life. Depending on how she reacted, one of several things could happen. She could get seduced by the glamour of the fashion jet set lifestyle in Dublin; which was not really her thing; she could return to Scotland with, or without William, and then split up with him as he scarpered off abroad again; or she could sit with the new connections she was making and see what happened.

Sometimes you walk into something that is the exact opposite of what you really want or intend. You get embroiled in an emotion from which it is difficult to retreat. A masterful web is spun, and you wait for an answer, but none is forthcoming. It is the magic of a compelling and powerful alluring moment that causes you to hang on for dear life; and such is the charisma of a good man on a good day that you are happy to oblige, or at least wait and see what it is all about.

Sarah found the groom's magnificent Sunflower later, on his wedding night. It was discarded and crushed on the night-club floor, muddied and lifeless. She retrieved it for the newlyweds, hoping it was not a bad omen for their union, and resolved to put it in water, and then dry it out when she got home.

The nightclub in this form only saw one night of entertainment. Having taken months to renovate and create a wonderful eclectic space, the owners decided to unceremoniously rip it apart after only one event. The nightclub reopened on Valentine's Day five months later as a mysterious winding cavern complete with nooks, crannies, water features and moat. The moat was a new design flaw which was impossible to keep clean for any length of time. But enough energy had been wasted getting the club in order. It was now down to business.

The club was re-launched officially amidst a flurry of fuss, and the prerequisite supermodels were in attendance. This time drama was kept to a minimum. Paul was sober and on his best behavior. With the press present, this was a "Zoo," to use his words. The "band" were on display, and their night club had come of age. Paul looked cool, drink in one hand, cigar in the other. His wife, glamorous as ever wore a big furry off-white jacket which off-set her raven black bobbed hair.

Sarah was slightly confused and bedazzled. She had not exactly chased this rainbow. But it had certainly been sprung upon me. The creeping sense of wonder and connection was only just beginning, in her head and heart. She was not star struck, but her heart sure was enlivened.

CHAPTER TWENTY-THREE

Echoes

When she was younger, Sarah thought it was normal to know who was on the end of a ringing phone, or who her sister's next boyfriend would be. Her sister used to get cross that Sarah knew her mind better that she did when it came to her love life. She did find herself saying, "see I told you so," rather a lot.

It was during her twenties that a fuller awareness of her Gift developed. Sarah would find strange things happening, like when she looked at a picture of The Crows in the local paper. Thinking they were all rather cute, she got a flash of a wedding ring in her mind's eye, and promptly went up to the gig. Sure enough, Dick the guitarist's engagement was announced, and shortly after that Sarah started dating the bass player William.

What was a possible one-night stand for William - she gathered that was his intention - turned into a lengthy relationship! Even though she did "pick him up" at two-thirty in the morning in the nightclub next to her apartment, she knew it was a safe thing to do. What were the chances of that working out? It really went against all logic. Sometimes she found her deep knowing could cut corners and be useful indeed.

Sarah found increasingly it was a case of when she knew, she really *knew*. This was clearly annoying for some people. Family, friends, and clients alike loved to test out her insights and challenge her suggestions. More fool them. It did not get them far, even though it amused them to try. Sarah was formidable with her intuition. It fast grew into a weighty responsible, she did not quite know how to manage. She did have an implicit sense of trust in it though. She observed she really was always right when the knowing came upon her.

It was not her anyway, she reasoned. She knew the information came from The Divine. It all felt profoundly familiar to her. Like she was remembering rather than learning. The experiences of knowing became ever more prolific and Sarah found she was able to effectively guide people, even daring to give judgement on quite intricate and complex issues. Against odds, and against expectations. She became accustomed to it all again. It was what being a living breathing oracle was all about.

Most of the time it might have been better for her to keep her mouth shut. But she also had to live, breathe, react with people, and be normal. So yes, predictions flew out of her mouth from time to time before she thought twice about their implication. Strange things occurred, as a norm. Reluctantly she had to relearn to develop and master it. There was no point having such a Gift and then not using it to the maximum to help people.

Why reluctantly? Well, being a commercially viable psychic out in the world was not the game plan for her life. In her upbringing Sarah was academic, bright, had Christian faith and boundless optimism despite challenges. She also had great sensitivity, perception and randomly knew things that others did not. Even in childhood it was always controversial when she picked up something against the odds or unasked for. From an early age, she noted the mixed receptions the phenomenon got.

It was all very well helping people when asked to do so. But sometimes she was required to intervene so that others did not make mistakes, or harm themselves. Try implementing that that when your message is not well received. She found it sometimes demoralising. Thankfully, she learned ways to intervene on the ethers, and through the hidden dimensions, by tuning into a person's higher understanding. It was not always necessary to actively explain things to the nth degree.

Sarah found the whole oracular "contract" thing challenging in the extreme. It had to be responsibly mastered, ethically understood, and applied effectively. She had to always deliver. Plus, she was expected to be accurate to a fault, and have that inner confidence where she just *knew* she was correct. Done in the wrong way, this could come across as egocentric. She could not impose this on people. Indeed, that was the last thing she wanted to do. But she did feel *obligated* to use it, even in risky moments.

Thankfully, Sarah could tell that people generally understood her approach most of the time. She noticed too that spirit guides, most significantly the Holy Spirit, brought the correct people to her. She did not ever go looking for work. It came to her. Contracts she had to balance and complete. Whether by word of mouth, because of her reputation, or because of a prompt within themselves, people found Sarah. Those that found her were rarely testing. They knew that she knew, and that she could help them. For reasons she had not quite worked out, she instilled trust in people. They had an underlying confidence that she could help, whether it be for information, healing, or energy work. This turned out to be a correct instinct, time and time again.

"Human I am, God I am not."

"I deliver to the best of my abilities, with God's grace and help." Sarah would explain to those asking.

For much of her time in Ireland there was a huge roadblock which prevented her from leaving Ireland, even for visits home. It was as if she had a contract to the whole country. A penance that needed to be paid, so that she could fulfil her destiny. It was as if she was meant to hold the faith, in the belief that despite appearances all was safe and well. This especially applied to her father's health. There were a few times when the family thought his passing might be immanent. Sarah could not get home. She felt and trusted that all would be fine for the moment. "It was not yet his time," she would reassure her mother, even though she was aware that such a personal prediction could misfire. She tried to feel it as confidently as possibly. Thankfully, she turned out to be correct. It was not an ideal situation. But it was unavoidable, and it was tricky weighing up if to stay or go. Destiny had brought her to Ireland. Was it appropriate to even leave? At times it seemed most definitely not.

Sarah found healing to be a mysterious art that she could not fully explain. She did not understand all aspects of the challenges she went through. At times it felt like a fight for survival. Her contract with The Emerald Isle was deeply challenging. At times it felt like a battle for her very Soul. She was cornered by circumstances, or so she thought. But as always, an elegant exit presented itself exactly at the right moment.

For a long time, and for complex reasons, largely linked with her work in Ireland, Sarah seemed to be thwarted every time she tried to get home. A deep part of her knew that if she *got* home, she would not be able to return. It was easier not to leave for a while. She carried on in faith, knowing and perhaps assuming, that the way ahead would clear itself at the opportune moment. Which of course it *did*.

Being from a Christian home, Sarah was not the sort of mystic to be madly interested in haunting or *séances*. You could call her a "reluctant psychic" in this respect also. She disliked and recoiled at a great deal of the things normally linked with her profession. She was an old school mystic. From another time, where the healing arts were called up without question, where the local wise woman and oracle was largely needed and respected, though looked on with suspicion by The Church. There had always been tests and persecution she remembered. But these modern times brought a different set of challenges.

Even though Sarah did have mediumistic ability, she tried not to use it except when she was really called upon to do so. When she had lived in Edinburgh there was a lot of energy activity still live from other lifetimes. Sarah would simply observe these happenings. She lived in the heart of The Old Town on Victoria Street. This steep cobbled road which links The Royal Mile to The Grassmarket. Victoria Street was an ambient laneway lined with restaurants and colourful shop fronts. It was a world set apart, and its environment was steeped in the energy of historical muggings, hangings, haunting, and murders. The gradient of this quaint ancient slip road was steep, mounted on either side with high buildings which towered over unsuspecting pedestrians, threatening to intimidate them with daunting intensity, if only they would look "up!"

On one side of the street stood Victoria Terrace, which disconcertingly allowed passersby to gaze into the top floor window of Sarah's flat opposite. Walking along this precipitous path, even the most unobservant tourist was confronted with the majestic height and impressive curve of the West Bow. It was impossible to climb Victoria Street musing at the shop windows laden with antiques, secondhand books, or the latest ethnic outfit, without the accompanying sense that a loose slate might career from the precipitous buildings above. This sensation was rendered more than a paranoid imagining by the wind tunnel effect, notorious amidst the Wynds and closes of Old Town Edinburgh.

Victoria Street was to be found just below George IV Bridge, a busy road which crossed the Royal Mile, and connecting The Mound leading up from Princes Street with the University Buildings, and various training hospitals. This unique street offered an instant impression of depth and serenity. Despite its noisy cobblestones, busy Aztec Indian craft shops, cafes, and night club venues, it possessed the peace which commonly emanates from an ancient monument.

If walls could talk?

Sarah knew that many spooky experiences had been reported throughout Edinburgh's history, but she did not expect her own flat in Victoria Street to be troubled. In the middle of a "Highlands and Islands" tour she had booked for the American Cajun fiddle band *Le Rue,* the band were all lazing the morning away in her flat before an Edinburgh Festival performance the following day. Sarah was talking to the banjo player, Martin at about noon, when suddenly this hideous demonic voice spoke over them. It was clearly audible, as loud as you like. They both heard it, looked kind of incredulously at each other, and simultaneously said, "no way!"

Early the next morning the older members of the band, who had not believed the account of their experience, were themselves freaked out when the heavy solid door of the front room opened all by itself. Sarah's bedroom in Victoria Street overlooked the famous Greyfriars Bobby graveyard, and there was of course a history of devastation by the plague in this area of Edinburgh. Sarah did not think much of it at the time, but there was always the intermittent smell of rotten vegetation in her bedroom, which she would effectively get rid of by saying:

"F*ck Off Ghost!"

Weird, but it worked.

What seemed to confirm the relevance of this strange technique, was that from time to time Sarah would remember that she had not smelled-the-smell for a while. As if by magic it would almost immediately recur, almost simultaneously, as if telepathically coinciding with the thought. She would then have to use her simple banishment, and there you go.

Gone.

Once again.

Sarah found being psychic useful when she needed clues about the way ahead in her own life. This gift was not just for the edification of others. It did have its helpful moments supporting her too. She was always able to find gigs in strange towns without knowing the precise address; a very handy skill when there was a bunch of tired moaning rockers in the back of a van. Similarly, she always had a strong sense of where she would live next. On the way home from the family holidays of her youth she would pass through Stirling. She knew it was going to be a significant place for her. Sure enough, it is where she saw the rainbow with her Nan, and where she eventually studied for a high-level BA (hons) in English, Philosophy, and Religious Studies, as well as an M. Phil in Publishing Studies.

Sarah was also precognitively aware that she would live in both Edinburgh and Dublin well in advance of the times she spent there. This pre-cognition of important places also applied to specific addresses. The German restaurant where she had worked was directly opposite her haunted Victoria Street flat. For several months when she still lived down in Stockbridge, she would look up at the flat, while chopping vegetables and bashing schnitzels, thinking,

I sure would like to live up there one day.

The flat was high off the ground, and one of only three properties available to rent in the street. Eventually Sarah's future flat mate Paul came into the restaurant looking for a place to pin his Ad. for a roommate, and she staked her claim. She did not even let him put up his advertisement. She gathered later that he had subsequently fallen in love with me, which was something she did choose to miss at the time. Paul never told her, but he *did* tell Em, who only told Sarah years later in Dublin.

Hmm. Sorry Paul. Not meant to be.

Similarly, the first time Sarah got off the train in Dalkey, a year after she had moved to Dublin, she mused that she would like to live on Railway Road, the road which gently curves and inclines down into village. At the time this was not an area of domestic rented property. But there she was, a couple of years later, living just where she had envisaged. They had built and converted apartments as if by magic in the interim.

As soon as Sarah saw the Dalkey apartment she knew it was the right place for her to work as a healer. The energies in the Dalkey and Killiney area were unique and powerful. They really lent themselves to psychic and healing work. Both the apartment and the layout of the village itself, proved crucial to the success of her subsequent work and practice. Aside from the friendly sense of community, Dalkey provided some twinkly, "minkly" intrigue on the ethers. Life was to take on new layers of meaning in this magical place, which resembled a Cornish fishing village rather than a Dublin suburb.

Sarah's healing work required a conducive energetic environment. It was not ideal to work just anywhere. The beauty of living out of town was that she could clear her head on the beach after appointments. This simultaneously kept her sane and enabled her to effectively do the work. She would not have been able to function so easily as a healer in the heart of Dublin City. Dalkey proved to be perfect.

Sarah found that if she followed her inner guidance, things happened. She was never one to do the obvious or conventional thing. She completed her publishing master's degree and went to work in a Dublin nightclub. Against the odds she got permission from the department to study under her own steam, and to finish the studies from a distance. She managed to convince the powers-that-be, that the move to Dublin was too good an opportunity to miss. You can imagine that she did then question her judgement when she was initially put on cloakroom duty in The Kitchen, when she had originally been in line to manage the club. But ultimately the decision to move to Dublin was validated. She was sure her parents thought she was mad moving on spec like that with a restless partner. But over time the opportunities to write and publish herself began to surface. It all started to make sense. Except when it did not.

CHAPTER TWENTY-FOUR
Muse-Worthy

It became more and more clear to Sarah that the spiritual, intuitive route through life was not the most logical. But at least her life path had been interesting. It clearly paid to have some idea of what lay ahead, but it was ultimately best if the details were left to look after themselves. Otherwise life would have had no mystery at all. She did like surprises! She realised that God laughs at our best laid plans. But she still had a post-it-note written by her father before she set off to Stirling University.

"For I know the plans I have for you," declares the Lord, *"plans to prosper you and not to harm you, plans to give you hope and a future."*

Jeremiah chapter 29, verse 11.

Sometimes Sarah found her knowing moments could be a bit sad. For instance, she did not feel she would inevitably marry in this lifetime. She sometimes reviewed her chequered history, and catalogue of karma which had played out.

I must be romping through the list of checks and balances. She mused.

Rationally she figured this awareness may not be sad but a kind of protection. She could appreciate that she had survived some interesting near-misses. She also hoped secretly that someone warm, vibrant, and magnetic would want to prove her wrong. What she did not want to conclude was that her Soul Mate was "In Spirit" and had not incarnated to find her in this lifetime. She shuddered when she thought this might be the case. But as the chapters multiplied, and the searching got ever more obscure, all her wisdom came back to her. She concluded that it could indeed be true.

Ronan, where are you?

Sarah jolted herself a sleep one night when a particularly passionate encounter sprung upon her on the ethers. This energy invaded her dreams. She had discovered some time before that astral sex could be amazing. Sometimes even better than the real thing. This time she sensed a familiar sensual feeling. She did not fully see the man's face. But she knew his energy. Oh. So. Well.

The pattern of Sarah's relationships had re-enacted many spooky twists and turns, some familiar, some bizarre and incongruous. The upshot was that she had learned to be amused rather than disappointed a lot of the time. She had fallen heavily for "Mr Wonderful" the wonderful Canadian when she was eighteen. He had been "on a break" from his girlfriend, so she gave him something to think about and the whirlwind tour of Wales instead. Then there was the sexy American Pierre, who was married a week before she met him. So, she went on tour as an accompanying oracular presence, and became his "Scottish agent," rather than bust up a marriage.

Sarah was sitting in Pierre's company in a bar in The Grassmarket, when a band member rather pointedly asked him what he would do "if a Mermaid fell in love with him out of the blue."

Rather aptly and wittily he replied: "why, I would take her on tour." And. so. It. Was.

Pierre fiddled his way around much of the United Kingdom, and parts of Ireland and Europe with Sarah in tow. Nothing untoward happened. Something *nearly* did a couple of times. But vague opportunities were only half-heartedly noted and were duly intercepted by people on the lookout for his wife.

Fair enough.

One time in the middle of nowhere at The Aultnamain Inn in the Highlands, there was a crackling chemistry building between us. There was literally a luminous ring around the moon that night. The Highland's other worldly, and mystically evocative atmosphere hung heavy in the air. Pierre in gallant fashion was attentive, and pointedly knelt before Sarah lifting the glove she had accidentally dropped to the ground. He literally handed her his "favour" on bended knee, just as a knight would propose to his lady.

It was very moving and romantic She thought. A special moment. she gathered later that it was symbolically bad luck. But it felt magical at the time. She mused it could not have been much worse luck than meeting him and falling in love with him only a *week* after he had married. Sarah felt ill-fated for sure in her love life.

That night Pierre, who was prone to sleepwalking, walked right into her room naked. Sarah pretended to be asleep and nothing happened. She would never know if he was literally sleep walking or pretending to. Her suspicion was that it was a genuine sleep walking incident that she could have taken advantage of had she been that way inclined. Instead she kept her eyes firmly shut and remained studiously asleep.

Another time Sarah was in the top bunk above Pierre on the Dutch Island of Terschelling. They all had to wake early to catch the ferry back to the mainland. She awoke in the early hours to find him standing gazing at her face, and she asked for the time. His reply? "Time enough." That comment sort of held a resonance for her, and she relaxed deep inside.

Of course, yes: if something is meant to be, there is always time enough, and no rush whatsoever.

Sarah was something of an innocent, and certainly a well-behaved girl. She kept her mystique, and her urges went unfulfilled as the tension grew. She gathered that her presence in the van on tours had become a bit of a puzzle to the other band members. She picked up that she was sometimes resented, and certainly not always understood. One particularly annoying time was when Alfred, Pierre's brother in arms from America, was travelling with them. Alfred was a lovely man, but he was looking for a wife, and in the back of the van Pierre pledged to play at the wedding should Sarah consent to marry him.

How did it go from people in Bruges, Belgium asking me if Pierre was good in bed, to Pierre offering to play at my wedding to someone who was trying to facilitate a visa!

Pierre had obviously become annoyed with Sarah after a while and was apparently looking to offload her onto one of his band mates. Either that, or Alfred's studied verbal devotion to me gave Pierre the perfect excuse to hide any residue of feeling he might have. When they reached Belfast, thankfully the pressure eased, and Alfred met his match at a gig in a bar in some dark dingy corner of a grey area in the city. Sarah was not sure how safe they all were hidden in the staunch protestant enclave, with flamboyant, republican mandolin player Fergus in full flow. But they weathered it and got out of there alive. Alfred realized the love of his life, had morphed from a bewildered mystic into a buxom blonde barmaid who warmed to his friendly advances.

Okay, good, Pierre could play at that wedding instead!

After Belfast they headed across to The Netherlands. Arriving back to Dover on the ferry after the Bruges gig, they were hauled in for a thorough search by customs. Alfred had been drumming with *Le Rue* for some months and had clearly overstayed his visa option in the United Kingdom. He should have had a work visa. He did not. So, in an incident which was very distressing for all of them watching, Sarah's ex future "husband" was exported off to Paris, and then unceremoniously across to the States. Obviously, the universe had other ideas about who Sarah was going to marry, or not marry. It was not going to be to a random drummer looking for a visa extension anyway.

All on board the tour bus, were friendly to Sarah and she had a good friendship with most of them. But, Mark, a former bass player with The Psychedelic Furs, was a bit of a problem. Mark directly confronted her about her presence on the tour in Southern Ireland and upset her immensely. Nothing was going on. Sarah just enjoyed the company of the lads and the music. He annoyed Pierre even more apparently, and Pierre told Sarah privately that he was about to get his marching orders. This bullying event gave Pierre the perfect excuse to ditch Mark, rather than "The Mermaid." Sarah was okay with that.

Yes, Sarah was in love with Pierre, but she also meant well, and certainly was not going to break up his marriage or disrespect his wife. As usual, Sarah turned a situation which was disappointing romantically for her, into something constructive for everyone. She booked gigs for the band in Scotland, and she designed a T-shirt for them, and sold it at gigs. All very wholesome. There were moments of frustration and temptation, but nothing got out of hand. Neither Pierre nor Sarah were into causing any problems for anyone. Pierre had a job to do, and Sarah was enjoying the camaraderie, and dancing the night away as they played their intoxicating music.

Pierre was immensely talented. He had worked originally with Queen Ida in America, and is a real deal, grassroots Cajun player. Sarah loved the music and energy conjured up by *Le Rue*. It made her happy and gave her a purpose she had been lacking for quite some time. She had a lot to get out of her system and being able to keep company with these musicians enabled her immensely. She was aware that her presence was resented and challenged by some of the team. But #whatever. Pierre himself, did not seem to mind, and that is all that mattered to Sarah. She even overheard him turning down his wife's request to "get rid of Sarah," one night when they were sleeping in adjacent rooms after a New Year's gig at Hebden Bridge in Yorkshire. Pierre was an all-inclusive gentleman, and really there was no need to be mean or a "bitch" to The Mermaid.

At the beginning of this Christmas and New Year Tour, Sarah had booked a gig for *Le Rue* at The Preservation Hall in Edinburgh on Boxing Day. She prepared a huge Christmas feast for everyone on the off chance they would accept it. Tina, Pierre's wife looked like an alarmed rabbit in the head lights, when she met Sarah at this seasonal time. Sarah felt jolted emotionally too and surprised at Pierre's taste and choice of wife on first impression. Of course, Tina declined the Christmas feast, and Sarah was left with a lot of turkey to consume alone. Mellish, the cat was pleased indeed, and Sarah was left upset, feeling something like a loser. She had chosen Christmas alone to be on hand for the gig, and the band were then blocked from accepting her hospitality by a jealous wife. She was not best pleased. But she had no intention of giving Tina a real retaliatory problem to deal with.

The gig, the day after Boxing Day in Shotts, saw Pierre changing some song lyrics as he was singing about *Billy the Kid.* He sang of a wrong road taken, and Sarah knew when she heard the lyric switch that he felt the same way as she did. She was sure that being wrongly accused would have been a big part of his frustration.

Keeping company with all these men, as a friend most of the time, taught Sarah much about their ways. Sarah ascertained that men were essentially simple creatures, who wanted a simple, stable life. She figured that Pierre liked her calm energy, presence, and support. They were friends and kept a respectable distance from each other. But the connection at times felt quite compelling. To Sarah anyway. Pierre never told her to leave. She was sure if she were ever not welcome, he would say something immediately. That was approval enough for her.

Sarah got signals of the deeper levels of feeling whenever he played

Jolie Blon. Pierre played his own version of this Cajun anthem adlibbing with phrases like, *Jolie blon, my little darlin' you are the flower of the bayou and my sweetheart.* At the time Sarah mused that it might have been sung partly for her benefit. It probably was not. But a girl can dream.

Sarah enjoyed being a kind of musician's muse, in her own head at least. She loved music, and its players. Music, the company of musicians, and the energy they conjured made her heart soar, and her soul sing. She needed this diversion after all the traumas and dramas, which were in sequence, John, Harry, and Graham. It was her way of processing a whole load of nonsense without having to think too deeply about it. She was into having fun! Not sexually, but musically.

She. Just. Liked. The. Music.

CHAPTER TWENTY-FIVE

Two Stools

Once Sarah had arrived in Dublin, her "stuff" sat for two weeks in what is now the resident's lounge of The Clarence Hotel. Nodd Mc Donagh, the Scottish manager of The Kitchen nightclub, kindly allowed her to camp in the hotel until she and William had found a suitable flat in Dublin. Sarah quickly settled in and became more established in Dublin. But it was a huge adjustment. It was mainly Paul the Rockstar's friendship that settled her down and cheered her up. It was he who placated her and made her feel emotionally safe and secure. He was actively concerned that she was okay and not feeling too isolated. What a Gent.

Sarah used to work in Edinburgh at The Cathouse for her friend Dick, so she felt quite at home in nightclub land. Weirdly though, she did not smoke, or drink. She would manage an inch of something and had never been drunk in her life really, always stopping short as soon as she felt it going to her head. Sarah just loved music, being sociable and dancing. But she realised that her lack of curiosity regarding drink, drugs, and general debauchery made complete sense when her path as an energy healer emerged. To be effective she knew she had to be a clear, accurate channel. Substance abuse, though she was not in the least bit judgmental about it, never interested her. She knew she was strange enough already.

From the start in Dublin, Paul was kind, friendly and interesting. He included Sarah and she was so grateful for this. If he had not done so, she probably would have returned to Scotland very quickly. One time, he had been dining, and had been really perturbed at the quality of the music playing in The Tea Rooms. Sarah was commissioned by him to go out and source a broad range of traditional jazz music to spice up the dining experience upstairs. Her brief was, to make The Tea Rooms more ambient, and a whole lot classier. Sarah loved that Paul instinctively knew she could do this, without seeing any resume or credentials. He was right. She could. Paul had such heightened senses that he could truly "see" people. Years on the road had honed his skills of perception, and he could read a room, and a person, in an instant.

Some people seemed to be wary of Sarah's link with Paul, and interference began in subtle ways. Sarah was made to feel so unwelcome at one point that she penned a farewell note to him. She had been deliberately barred from socialising with *The Lypton Village* brigade because under a new staff rule, staff were not allowed in the VIP bar. Sarah was the only one who used to avail of this anyway, so it seemed to be deliberately targeted to cut her out. She finished on the door in her selling tickets and hostess role, sooner than anyone else, so this was a deliberate ploy to keep her separate from her friends and was clearly the manipulation of someone jealous. She knew who.

Perhaps Sarah should have left the nightclub whilst the bad vibes were going on. But she was already totally in love with Paul by then and felt she should stay around. After a while, he was really the only reason she stayed put. Ultimately, Sarah got on well with the door men, and the unfriendly phase only lasted for six months or so; the duration of one assistant manager's reign in fact.

Sarah had long ago decided she had no desire to manage the nightclub herself. It was a great relief ultimately that she had not been given that position in the end. She would not have liked the long hours, and she needed to look after her health and well-being. The schedule was too gruelling to sustain for long. She was happy with being a meet-and-greet person. Chats on the door, selective socialising, and an earlier bedtime than her fellow workers enjoyed, suited her fine.

Nothing untoward ever happened between Paul and Sarah. Nothing of a sexual nature occurred. She never tried to break up his marriage; nor would she ever do such a thing. She had the utmost respect for him, his work, and his family. At times, the expressions of affection were intense; for her anyway. But Paul was a perfect gentleman and such a kind guy. This was an emotional and spiritual link, which left her reeling. It was tangible and real, and not in her imagination, as might have been tempted to conclude. But there were serious problems in giving this soul link so much priority. If not for Paul, Sarah might have married and had her own family. She could not though, as this was what in her heart she wanted with Paul. No one else measured up. It was her decision and nothing to do with any requests or implications made by him.

Sarah remembered William interrupting an evening session in The Kitchen. Sarah had been sitting beside her, and William showed up. Paul made a quick exit, grabbed her hand meaningfully in farewell, and scarpered. Sarah was annoyed as she was feeling particularly bonded with him in that moment. William turning up was most inconvenient. Paul's action showed her he was awkward in the company of her assumed boyfriend; so again, indications were, there was some level of involvement. Sarah assumed their chaste but intense connection was meant to be for a time, or it would not have happened. To the onlooker she was in a long-term relationship with William, the Scottish guy she moved over with.

Throughout this time, Sarah and William remained companionable and good friends. More like brother and sister if truth be told. Sarah did not understand what was happening with Paul; but loved William as family and was still annoyed whenever he was unfaithful. It became less and less of an issue though, as time proceeded. She really should have ended it with William much sooner than she did. Probably she held herself in stasis by not being brave enough. Essentially, she was vulnerable, living abroad, and needed that sense of belonging. She would have been more independent in retrospect. But easy to say after the event.

William was Sarah's family in Ireland: Paul was her spiritual dalliance. But this was way more than an inconsequential dalliance. Paul was her grounding rod, security, and reference point. The quality of emotional connection between them was everything to her. There is no doubt she would have been long gone from Ireland if Paul had not embraced her. Literally and practically.

CHAPTER TWENTY-SIX

"Sarah Love"

At five o'clock in the morning, the night before Clinton's first trip to Dublin, Paul asked Sarah to slow dance to a strange Howie B mix of Elvis's *Silver Bells*, and Madonna's *Like a Virgin*. You could not make it up if you tried. A strange combination, but somehow the genius that is Howie B made it work. This was Sarah's first and only slow dance with a guy ever. She had not experienced anything so powerful either before or since. It was truly magical.

Earlier, Sarah had seen Paul watching her sway to the music somewhat transfixed, and she thought to herself

Surely not!

She was feeling particularly "Mermaidy."

There was warmth and "minklement" in the air. She had previously caught him eyeing her across the room on an interlude visit home during a long gruelling tour also. That time she was wearing a black velvet dress with gold shimmery cosmic motifs. She had declared her

210

feelings to him before he had left, and he still seemed to be engaging, if a little distantly.

Paul had always been affectionate and connected whenever they crossed paths. But his attentions were apparently stepping up and had a different deeper quality. Obviously, these were her perceived responses, she had no idea what he was really thinking and feeling. Suffice to say, the night of the slow dance, she fell hook, line, and sinker for him.

Sarah was wearing a red Chinese top brought in George's Arcade - the bustling bohemian enclave between South Great George's Street and Drury Street - and her mermaid tail, black velvet skirt. She hoped the magic of this red brick gothic area of Dublin, situated in the back streets behind the famous Grafton Street, would work like a charm.

The bottle green warren of an Arcade housed sweet smelling incense shops; a wicked cafe, full of bakery goodies and the most ridiculously good fry up materials, a stall of obscure luscious olives, numerous colourful stalls over-loaded with odd clothing, and a gypsy tent, which housed in coordinated sequence, a family of seven psychic sisters. Of course, she checked them out, and found them curious and beguiling. They supplied relevant insights and entertainment more than gut wrenching details, or accurate predictions. Sarah was not sure anything they said regarding the future happened; but they did give pertinent advice.

The White Witch of Wicklow, a visionary Aquarian, was the winner hands down when it came to picking-up glimpses of the future. She was uncanny. Noel the tree surgeon in Phoenix Park, with no lines on his palm, was a close second, if not an equal. He got upset at Sarah's reading, because he picked up on Paul in her energy field and identified their connection. It triggered the memory of a personal situation for him, and he found it too traumatic to go into.

Paul smelled gorgeous and was so sensual and inviting. People were pairing off for the slow dance, amongst the small select crowd in the nightclub. Paul crossed Sarah's path, beside the moat and gestured to the dance floor with his hand. He chose Sarah, and in a very gentlemanly way led her to the dance floor. Was this his way of "taking her" in the only way he could think of?

Possibly.

This night turned out to be the highlight of her life up until that point. It might sound a bit pathetic, but Sarah had not had much experience of romance in her dealings with Scotsmen. There was always something coarse and rudimentary about their approach. She guessed they were refreshingly real, and without affectation. But they really would not win prizes for romancing a woman. Paul, on the other hand, would get the trophy. He has a way of making a woman feel like the center of his universe. A special talent.

It was a very rude awakening when, the nanny of Paul's children, butted in and broke up our energetic union. She had obviously been commissioned to be on guard duty and intercepted Sarah and Paul at her first opportunity. Either that or she rather liked him herself. Sarah just knew she felt bereft to be thus separated. There was a tangible quality to the sensuality of our closeness that she did not want to end. Sarah did not know whether to be moved, delighted, or embarrassed. In truth she was all three, in probably equal measure.

She knew there was a chemistry between them already as every time she saw Paul her heart leaped. Whenever he planted a smooch fair and square on her lips in greeting, the warmth and feeling, was electric. For her anyway. She loved that he had no shame in expressing his affections. She watched to see if he kissed other women on the lips, and he did not seem to. Though Paul is undoubtedly a very warm and sensuous Taurus, he did *seem* to save Sarah some special attention. One time quite soon after her arrival in Dublin, he gave her a lingering hug as he was leaving the nightclub. Paul's wife was waiting for him and moved discretely out of the way to get into the car.

He. Would. Not. Let. Her. Go.

Sarah was embarrassed and moved in equal measure. But also confused. Perhaps his wife saw things like this a lot and had endless patience. She may have put it down to a rock star embracing a fan. She did not know at that point. She still did not know.

The energy charge whenever they connected, was electric. Sarah had noticed a strange frisson when Paul had caressed the inside of her lower arm, on arrival at a private gig in The Pod nightclub. He had walked up to her at the door, where she was attending to the guest list, and intimately stroked the inside of her wrist with his forefinger. She did not know that a fleeting touch with a mere finger could be so sensuous and sexy.

Taurus, though. What do you expect?

Sarah did not understand what was happening. She just knew it was a chemical romance of sorts. Paul's wife was with him. She walked in ahead, and he managed to artfully do this without anyone noticing. It was intimate and highly charged. Paul sure did have a way of making a girl feel like she was the only one getting his special attention.

Sarah could not remember at what point she declared her feelings to Paul in a note. It was certainly after all of this. Indeed, all of this probably *prompted* the declaration. There was certainly some serious reciprocity going on by this time. These encounters spanned a few years. Each one more delicious than the next. He was nothing if not consistent, and for Sarah the feeling grew steadily. There were interactions too numerous to recount; and Sarah was floating and slightly bedazzled by the quality of the feeling. This was a Scorpionic meeting of hearts and minds, stirred by the interaction of our two Scorpio moons. "The Mermaid in The Kitchen" was coming alive and feeling deeply charged from the inside.

Others noticed the obvious affection between them, and there were whispers in corners. The slow dance had been unceremoniously intercepted. But Paul still found Sarah later and held her hand affectionately and unashamedly for quite some time in a corner of the nightclub. She did not know what to think. She only knew she liked it. Her heart was his for sure.

Emotionally, Sarah had not been having an easy ride. William her long-term partner had been unfaithful the odd time since we moved to Dublin. Even in Edinburgh, her love life had worked its way through a catalogue of betrayal and confusion. Not through any lack of clarity on her part. She just did not seem to make the most intelligent choices. But she always did follow her feelings, wherever they would lead. Sarah made a direct link with Paul as soon as she met him. Their eyes locked, and there was a sense of having known this person before. There was a feeling of familiarity and comfort, as well as a charged-up energy. He felt like "home."

As Paul got increasingly touchy feely, she found it difficult to keep her emotions on an even keel. He would always greet her with a lingering kiss full on the lips. She remembered being quite embarrassed when he once smooched her well beyond the time limit of a socially acceptable peck, whilst his wife was in the same room. He was about to go off on tour, and obviously found the thought a bit emotional. As did I. Paul wore his heart on his sleeve as those who loved him knew. He is a gutsy guy unafraid to show his feelings. Even fans get a flavour of this when he pulls the requisite girl on stage during gigs. One could say he collects hearts, perhaps energy too. But all in all, he is a genuine well-meaning person. His major smooch was a direct response to the declaration Sarah had made to him a few weeks previously. She had been finding it impossible to cope with her feelings and had to tell him. Not in the hope of busting up his marriage. But simply to try and make things easier and more fluid. Somehow. It was probably a naive thing to have done. But he was gracious and warm in his reaction. For a while he had kept a polite distance. But the smooch Sarah took as a direct more unguarded response. A signal that his emotions were also engaged.

214

One hilarious moment occurred at a small party held in Simon's rather pokey bleak red brick flat. The ex The Golden Horde singer, Simon, lived amongst the back streets of dilapidated urban Dublin, hidden away in a large warren of apartment blocks. It was a curious place for a seasonal gathering. Fairy lights softened the atmosphere, and a cheery warm coal fire burning in the grate soon raised temperatures. "Bad Dog Reggie" kept urging Sarah to warm her freezing hands and seemed quite concerned at her body temperature. He was right, Sarah probably was running a metaphoric fever inside, for reasons unbeknownst to him.

Michael Hutchence, rock singer with INXS, was off to the side doing his thing, flailing all over a model type called Antoinette. He had been playing with her, now substantially holey, tights all the way from The Kitchen nightclub to Simon's house in Paul's car; and by the time they got there, she looked dishevelled. All sorts went on at the party; mostly in the rest room Sarah suspected. But then again, she was not privy to all that.

Paul had stomped in late, in a strange mood, and climbed straight up to the elevated platform bed, to be quickly joined by Antoinette, Simon, and Michael. Sarah could overhear a somewhat sycophantic, attempt by Antoinette to fish for compliments and reassurance from the men surrounding her. Sarah dared not climb the rickety wooden ladder to join in. She was not inclined to do so, and certainly was not invited. She could not quite work out the dynamic of Paul on a bed with Simon, Michael, and this opportunistic girl, who had tagged along for the ride. She was sure it was totally innocent having said that. She thought Paul was tired if truth be told, and simply wanted a lie-down rather than all this unwanted attention.

On reflection it must have been tedious being Paul sometimes. Privacy comes at a premium and is often impossible to find. Probably in every waking moment someone wants something from him. Sarah suspected he selected his "irritants" carefully. She knew he was grateful for the life his fans bought him. But sometimes you just cannot put a price on a quiet moment alone. A moment it seems he never got. Ever.

After a while Michael came down to join Guggi, Reggie and Siobhan, Sarah, and a couple of others. He chatted to Sarah about his attempts to record in Dublin. A heavily pregnant Paula Yates was apparently being supportive of his times away from home.

Quite! Thought Sarah.

Michael was a nice guy. But he struck Sarah as a little insecure, and he did not seem to be able to cope with a woman who was not fawning all over him. He was cute alright; but clearly felt more comfortable just flirting and fooling around, than talking philosophically. Sarah did not fancy him enough for the rolling on the floor part, and besides Antoinette was doing all the running on that score. Sarah was also totally straight, not being a drinker or a substance user, so again, not much energy connection there.

Instead of clucking around Michael and Paul, Sarah used her time constructively at the party, and re-established her ability to call in the lucky numbers. An incredulous Guggi kept testing her on a mini roulette wheel, and she kept the hits coming, getting three red sixes in a row. Guggi was gobsmacked. Sarah did not really understand what had just happened, as such things were normal for her. He proceeded to explain that she would now be a rich woman if only she had backed those three red sixes in a casino.

Sarah was not a gambler. But here was some food for thought. Her only experience of anything with numbers previously had been when she was eleven years old at the school fete. She just *knew* the number five was going to hit on the spinning wheel. She must have a penchant for tuning into the energy of a wheel, as sure enough five came up, and she proudly took the bottle of Champagne she had just won home to her parents. She recalled her parents rather downplaying her enthusiasm when she told them that she *knew* the number five was going to hit. Perhaps they already were aware that they had a psychic daughter on their hands and were not sure quite how to handle it. Her mother certainly must have been *au fait* with the skills of The Grail Line. But they seemed to be conscientiously taking a different direction in their lives. In some ways, though profoundly spiritual, they were choosing to be unconscious of what these gifts might mean. Or more likely, they knew exactly what it all meant and wished to distance from it. They would not have wanted to actively encourage too much spinning of the wheel. Sarah did not understand why they did not believe her about the number five thing. The fact that she just "knew" it would hit. Their response may well have been sceptical pragmatism speaking rather than overt concern. Quite possibly, it was simply disbelief that such predicting is even possible.

On the night of Simon's party, only a few days after a momentous intimate slow dance with Paul in the night club, Sarah finally got her lift home. Two years too late? Perhaps. Flood, the producer, had asked Paul if he and Sarah could get a ride home at about seven in the morning. As dawn was breaking, Sarah was driven through the hazy, lazy streets of Dublin by Hugh, Paul's driver, and permanent bodyguard. Hugh was a personable, handsome, ex-army martial artist type, who also must have had the patience of a saint. Night after night he had to wait on the whims of his sociable, fun-loving master. Hugh never knew what time he would get home. But he could be sure it would be in the small hours of the morning, if not at daybreak.

Sarah thought it was hilarious that as they left the party, Paul said "well, phew, nothing too much went amiss there then!" She looked back over her shoulder at the sight of Michael flailing all over the floor with Antoinette, and mused to herself

Well not so sure Paula would agree with you. Perhaps we can and should turn a blind eye to that at least!

Sarah did not like to think that "trouble" was going to go down once we had gone, as she did not really think it was madly fair on pregnant Paula who had retired early to her hotel room. Anyhow, as

Paul took her arm as they walked down the dark stairway to the car, and then stroked her back affectionately as she got into the car with a "come along, Sarah darling!" You can imagine that she thought she might be getting into a bit of trouble herself.

Paul helped Sarah into the car, all the while savouring the texture of her soft, long, furry, brown coat. Sensual Taurus. His resistance seemed to be at a low ebb. He then sat in the front seat of the brown Bristol car beside Hugh his driver, and Flood sat in the back beside Sarah. This surprised Sarah after his affectionate gestures But, what then amused Flood greatly was that Paul somehow managed to twist and contort his hand behind him to stroke Sarah's knee and hold her hand throughout the entire journey. Flood was intermittently chuckling under his breath as he witnessed this.

Shut up please! Sarah thought, casting him a perfunctory glare, and confused smile now and again.

Paul seemed to need physical contact, and the intimacy of that kind of reassurance and connection. He really should have sat in the back of the car with her. It would have been much cosier. Flood could have giggled to himself on the front seat then; no harm done.

On the way home, Paul asked Hugh to take a slightly irrelevant, less than direct route, and gave Sarah a guided tour of St Patrick's area of Dublin where he had gone to school. Psychically Sarah could pick up a sad loss in his energy field from so many years ago. He was speaking with warmth and regret, as if explaining himself somehow. It was shortly after this, that she gathered Paul had been working on a song about his mother Iris around this time. He must have been feeling nostalgic and reflective still at the echoes stirred from times past.

Paul was a patient, kind, and tolerant man, loved by many. Sarah could see was also misunderstood by many too. When she had first arrived in Dublin, he talked to her about how he felt much maligned, even mocked in his own country. She could not quite believe it and could tell it weighed heavy on his heart. She loved the ease between

218

them with these early conversations. Paul felt energetically like her home from home. He was the one very warm and welcoming person, who actively supported her at a deeper level.

Sarah found that Paul displayed an endearing social gaucheness, which was somewhat surprising. He wore his heart on his sleeve and responded instinctively to what was kicking off around him. She observed he lived through his senses, as she did. He could smell what to steer clear of and what to embrace. He was also intelligent, interested, and loved to meet and understand a broad spectrum of people. What was not to love?

As Sarah tried to emerge from the depth of feeling she had for Paul, it really was an uphill task. She began to apply some logic to the situation and began to ponder what she thought might work. How about manifesting a hunky rugby player, who was gorgeous, intelligent and a little bit dangerous to know? She had noticed that rugby players tend to be health conscious, attractive, sober and hot-to-trot, but also inclined to commit and *marry* their partners. So yes, Sarah proceeded to find herself one such "player." Was he anything like the prerequisite list? No, of course he was not. But I had to try to get over Paul. Sarah had to try to forget the electricity that surged when he kissed her on the lips or hugged her or held her hand in the corner of the nightclub. Somehow, she had to move beyond the man who had shown her the most romance and soul depth she had yet experienced. She could not afford to get *Stuck in a Moment* for very much longer if she were going to have any kind of successful life herself.

CHAPTER TWENTY-SEVEN

The Waiting Room

One of the perks of working in the nightclub were the amazing experiences socially. Sarah met most of the significant Hollywood players, and many famous musicians. Not many people can say they sat at tables with Dennis Hopper and his wife, with her magnificent pearl necklace; or that they sat chatting to Mathew Modine until the early hours about Tijuana, constructing a road trip down to Mexico in his soft top sports car. Or that Michael Stipe of R.E.M. demanded their huge lemon shaped candle for his hotel room. Or that Robbie Williams bounded across the night club to sit beside them, and that he was duly dismissed in their head as a "chump." Probably, a mistake, ladies, Yes? Or that Michael Douglas, and his huge aura, made a beeline for them tripping over feet in the process, and then followed them to the rest rooms deliberately bumping into them to garner attention. Pre-Zeta Jones, and yes, probably another mistake.

Any VIP nightclub hostess would be able to regale you with such tales. Even though she did not drink or party herself, Sarah kept elite company, and met some interesting people. She remained grateful for these memories and good times for many years. Yes, she occasionally did wonder what would have happened if she had responded more favourably to Michael Douglas or Robbie Williams. Her attentions were obviously focused elsewhere. She was not the smartest when it came to "gold-digging," simply because she did not do it. It was not her style. She must authentically feel a connection, or she was not interested. The man could be rich or poor, his status mattered not. For her it had to be "Soul thing," or deep emotional connection. Sarah would not even entertain the richest man on earth if their energies were not correctly aligned.

When Sarah first met Paul, it was at his best friend's autumn wedding. His special request that night was for Sarah to keep him plied with wine as someone kept running off with his bottle. Sarah thought it was an ingenious, novel suggestion, to keep them interconnected and she duly complied, keeping him topped out throughout the night. Paul's dear old dad did not look too impressed with their arrangement. But she felt an attraction growing as they shared humorous asides. Throughout the night, as the drink flowed, he seemed to warm to her too. It could have been the wine of course, but Sarah flattered herself that it felt like a familial soul connection.

Sarah was not in the least fazed by Paul's rock star status. She connected directly with the man himself. The flow was easy between them, and when she finally moved over the following spring, the chats and vibes were greatly inspiring whenever their paths crossed. Once the feelings began to get more complex, it was never awkward; but Sarah and Paul tended to just greet each other with a kiss and then moved on. It was as if deep chats could not be risked, indulged, or entertained. It seemed very odd to greet each other so intimately and then walk on by without any social niceties at all. Perhaps it was just his way of keeping me sweet. It worked. Many a time Sarah tried to handle a slightly different approach to the situation that was difficult for her. She even attempted to ignore him once or twice. A bit juvenile perhaps, but sometimes she really did want to try to move on with her life. She felt held in place by it all. Stuck in a moment. She could not be with anyone else, as she loved him.

One time, at an Enrique gig, Sarah was ignoring him studiously. He was having none of it, and seductively stroked her belly through her semi see-through dress, to get her attention. She melted of course. She was a bit lost by it all. She knew nothing could happen. She was not going to be the pushy girl and had no intention of trying to seduce him. She did not really have that level of confidence. Besides, she was used to being taken by a man who had full passion for her. She could feel this from another deep distant past. It was confusing things that this moment of "seizure" and claiming was not happening.

The first years after Sarah met Paul were tricky for her emotionally. She tried to do the right thing. She deeply fell for this man, even though she tried to stay cool about it. She noticed that at least one of his songs described the scenario and depth of emotion to a tee. Paul would doubtless say they were about something completely different. Of course, it would be daft to assume it was about his perceptions of Sarah. But equally they could have been, even if unconsciously. There was raw emotion and longing as an underlying theme. Sarah would not assume any of it was about her, nor even loosely inspired by her. But she did resonate with the sentiments. She was not interested in sounding crazy to the world or to herself. But it was difficult not to speculate considering what was happening.

Whether intentional or not a specific song seems to be about someone who "sees" things the writer cannot see. Sarah had no doubt that Paul would claim that this was about his wife, and perhaps it was. But she could not get beyond some of the words in the song which put the lie to that. There is clear mention of the night belonging to "someone else." It is *not* about the writer's current partner. It is about an unrequited longing, and the pain of feeling disconnected. There is a phrase which mentions not being able to see through the smoke. This obviously evokes the atmosphere of a night club. The writer talks about feeling they are stuck in a waiting room, which totally describes that feeling of stasis Sarah had lived with for years. Was Paul living it too? And there is clear reference of the protagonist's Bible, or Holy Book, in a line which implies the formidability of this person's faith, as all those around them flail and suffer. This could well allude to his wide as her serenity is undeniably impressive in the eye of a storm. But it also evokes a similar line in another song which mentions a girl "with crimson nails," and Jesus around her neck. This girl is in that night club again dancing to the music. Sarah used to wear a distinctive turquoise cross around her neck to work in the nightclub, painted her nails red, and certainly swayed to the music in her fish tale skirt. She knew she should not flatter herself. But all the same, the lines have resonance to what happened, if not direct reference to an identifiable emotional landscape.

The White Witch of Wicklow, who had by this time become a good friend, jokingly called her a "cruel woman," when she read the lyrics of the song. She felt the pain of it. Sarah was not sure what to think. She was a bit horrified and upset when she saw it, and realised if this was about her, she had been spectacularly standoffish, and it had pained Paul. She felt awful and needed a rewind. The psychic's comment made her reaction and perception of events even more complex. She had not meant to be in any way aloof or cruel. But what more could she have done? The other possibility is of course that the "wisewoman" was retrofitting things to suit her theories. Not something she was in the habit of doing admittedly. But always possible.

There was one time where Sarah had driven down to the studio down on Hanover Quay to find Paul late at night. He was there, his Bristol Car parked outside. She waited only a couple of minutes, and then baulked, driving off around the block. It was a big block and one-way system, but she came back around to try once more, and he was already gone. She had had the intention to finally try and sort it all out. For some reason, this night stuck in my head as the night something might have happened. It felt significant, and psychically she had been meant to resolve things, now or never. She would have at least got the closure she really needed. Or something might finally have gelled. Clarity would have been had. This was the energy of life's crossroads; and Sarah chose the wrong road. She dithered and hesitated. She telepathically felt something happened within him that night too, but there was no knowing as she did not even remember the date. Only the feeling.

Thereafter Sarah distanced herself from Paul quite considerably. The dynamic with William and Paul had stressed her for years. She fell between two stools emotionally. She probably would have responded whole heartedly to Paul if he had made a concerted move. But he did not, and it robbed her of a chance to be with someone who wanted to be with her completely. There were a few times She tried to ignore Paul, or play it cooler, in a bid to play down the link. But he seemed to sense this withdrawal and always pulled her back into his heart with a well-timed intimate gesture. She speculated he could have been messing, or indeed just being kind. But it really did feel like he meant it. From Sarah's point of view, the connection dominated much of her young adult life. It felt significant indeed. She did not feel he was a rock star doing his "thing."

Paul, was in no way a "player." He was a man deeply loyal to his wife, family, and friends. A sensitive, deeply feeling man who makes soulful connections. His affection was intense and genuine, and Sarah did not conclude he had led her on for a second. More likely he was being generous hearted trying to support her, knowing how she felt. His wife's own behaviour also indicated that she sensed something between us. She possibly had to deal with this with other women too, sarah did not know. She very adeptly intercepted an intense farewell

224

smooch Paul gave Sarah in the nightclub, with a kiss on the cheek. She leapt across the VIP bar to get involved when she saw her husband locked in quite a significant smooch with Sarah. His wife was a lovely woman, and Sarah did not think Paul should have left her for a second. But she was also a clever woman who was not quite as cool about her husband as he thought.

A specific day in March still haunted Sarah many years later. Paul was standing expectantly in front of her in Finnegan's Pub in Dalkey with no one else around. Sarah was already so hurt by the situation that after an intimate embrace she energetically pushed him away with a flippant comment. She just did not know how to behave in this situation. She knew what she wanted to do. But was it acceptable? No.

Well, they do say in Ireland that "everyone has a Paul story." Sarah could amuse herself with that thought but only for so long. It was frustrating and all very unsatisfactory. She was if he had not been "who he was," something more could have happened. But that is like saying night should be day, and day should be night. He was who he was. Sarah had not particularly wished for or looked for a connection. It was what it was. It just happened. Out of time. An echo from another time. Sometimes you walk into something that is the exact opposite of what you want or need. You get embroiled in an emotion from which it is difficult to retreat. A masterful web is spun, and you wait for an answer. But none is forthcoming. It is the magic of a compelling and powerful love thing that causes you to hang on for dear life. Such is the charisma of the man on a good day that you are happy to oblige.

Shortly after Sarah arrived in Dublin, in alignment with their growing friendship, she got especially commissioned by Paul to keep an eye on things in the nightclub. It was completely unofficial, and She was certainly not a spy. Paul would get his assistant Marc to see or phone her for the latest updates; and she would let Marc know if anything untoward was going down. Not that there ever was. She wrote up regular reports on club nights for him and generally tried to be helpful. She had lots of ideas about club nights etc but became a hostess at the nightclub rather than a manager or promoter. Generally outside promoters ran the club nights, which is probably the main reason why the club eventually closed. There was perhaps not enough in-house effort towards the end. That and the fact that Tuesday nights were a messy accident waiting to happen. The five-star hotel above clearly objected to the incongruous riff raff tumbling out of the basement in the early hours of the morning. Many young people used to come along off-their-heads, and even though the club never condoned drug taking in any form, there were some near misses regarding safety. The last thing "The Band!" needed was a scandal or drug related death on their doorstep. It is also perfectly understandable that the hotel did not like having such a noisy riot to cope with every night. The boom of the bass notes certainly did vibrate up into the floors of the posh hotel above.

Towards the end, Sarah hardly worked at the nightclub. Her own work as a professional healer and psychic had taken off, and she only worked as a hostess or on the box office occasionally. The energies at the nightclub had changed and it had become very run down and dowdy. She liked the club best when it was quiet and empty. It was tranquil and could even be quite crypt-like with its underground stream, nooks, and crannies. She knew something was wrong when it was not even pleasant to be in when empty. Energetically it needed a big clearing. It really was time to. Close. Down. A. Chapter.

Things were reaching a crescendo, and new pastures for all were beckoning. Sarah sensed this and gave Paul a letter on Paddy's Day. The club closed very quickly after that in April. Paul was in Finnegans sitting all by himself. Sarah had just penned her dilemmas for him to read. No, it was not another declaration. But She *did* need to make some practical moves. She wanted to leave Ireland. Even though her work had taken off, she was finding it stressful and hurtful to be stuck in Dalkey without the means to leave. She loved him still but expected nothing. It was just painful for her and she did not know what to do or how to handle it. Mr passive Taurus was unlikely to make any bold moves beyond the accustomed gestures of warmth and affection. These were delicious and precious to Sarah. But would not sustain her for a lifetime. Not this time anyway. Perhaps she was wrong about that. Part of her was *sure* these attentions were way better than nothing. She was just hopeful there might be something more for her somewhere. Anywhere. In these moments she was NO-where. For complex reasons she was stuck.

Sarah took a different tack and sounded Paul out about sponsorship for her work, explaining again how difficult the whole emotional journey had been. Largely all-in-her-head, she was sure. Sarah left the note with him, and he agreed to read it. Shortly afterwards there was a buzz at her door, which was literally just around the corner from Finnegans. In her embarrassment she ignored it. Probably yet another chance missed. She would never know. But this awkwardness and non-resolution was becoming a habit.

Sarah gathered there had been plans to run the club right through that summer, even though they all knew it was going to close at some point. She felt perhaps Paul wanted to distance himself, and quite rightly so. She was ready for that. She knew there was not the ease between them that there might have been in other situations or even other lifetimes. Sarah knew she had messed up. Perhaps she should have been bolder and daring. Others might have said she was too bold and daring. On balance she tried to do the right thing by respecting his marriage and wonderful family. She simply loved him. It may well have been an echo of another time and another place. But love him she did.

Another Time Another Place...

227

CHAPTER TWENTY-EIGHT
Funny-Shaped-Balls

O n the back of a lot of heartache over Paul and William, The Irish Rugby Team reawakened Sarah's interest in life, love, and everything else pertaining to a good time. She had been isolated and working hard and solidly since the closure of the nightclub. The Hotel had been a home from home for Sarah since her arrival in Dublin, and the team of staff, and Paul himself, had been like her extended family. The real inner magic kicked in way before the rugby interludes when she first fell completely for Paul.

Sarah was not sure where the intuition about the rugby team came from. But it was not in the least bit contrived. Over the years she would occasionally catch sight of a team photo and get a sense of "something." It was just a vague impression and she did not even study the faces. The feeling was very fleeting and intangible. Something and nothing. She started to take a bit more notice when the White Witch of Wicklow read for her. She saw a rugby ball in her crystal ball, for which Sarah had no explanation. She did not watch rugby, nor was she interested in any of the players. It did not make any sense to me that a rugby ball would suddenly appear in her energy field, even as a predictive measure.

Sarah had been going to readings with The White Witch for some time for support with the Paul and William situation. But when she mentioned the rugby ball, Sarah really did question her judgement. She was not a rugby fan, and she had never been to a live professional match in her life. But, as always, the White Witch's readings had a habit of being uncanny; and before Sarah knew it, she was linked to the rugby lads in many and various ways.

Sarah used to like the rugby physique when she was younger, and her first "proper" boyfriend used to play a bit. But when she moved up to study at the Scottish universities, Stirling, and Edinburgh, she developed a taste for the bohemian groove. Musicians, writers, and artists hit the spot, not macho, alpha rugby players. Even though she got on well with Paul O'Connell, Donncha O' Callaghan, and Ronan O'Gara in particular, none of them seemed to be drawn to her in *that* way. Intuitively, though they were all undoubtedly attractive, Sarah did not feel her link with them was meant to be of an intimate nature. Equally, having been celibate for a few years, she was sure she would not have said "no" if any of them had made a move.

Sarah felt linked to O'Connell for a time. But that is because he was such a lovely upstanding guy. Donncha's humour always made her giggle, as did the twinkle in Ronan's eye. O'Connell was a little too close to her ginger brother Simon in colouring and appearance for that connection to have clicked in any major way. The White Witch had confirmed it was a "just mates" scenario when Sarah asked her about Paul and Donncha. She had helped Paul speed heal a significant shoulder injury. It was not going to count for any more than that. She knew this.

The healing for Paul O' Connell was a profound experience.

Without sounding too dramatic he gave her an awakening with his own talismanic healing energy. When she was healing Paul, the first place she put her hand was on his back behind his heart. His energy was really grounding and powerful. She could really feel the life force of the man. After she had experienced such psychic bombardment on the ethers, Paul's energy rescued her. There was certainly a fair exchange of mutual help, though perhaps he was not aware of this. O'Connell was pure of heart, bravery, and focus as many Irish rugby fans will tell you. This simple fact really helped Sarah in a very unanticipated way. She wondered if she was going to fall in love with him at one point. But the White Witch put her off that path saying he was not husband material; well not for her anyway.

One thing she did know is that she felt safe with him, and that his energy grounded and connected her to a vital male life force. O'Connell's strong presence allowed her to feel protected and affirmed once again. This had not been the plan from her point of view. Sarah did not know this was going to be the upshot of her first meeting with him. She had simply offered to help him in his predicament. She did not anticipate he would help her equally in return.

Not ever having even watched a game of rugby from start to finish, Sarah had been originally bemused to encounter the odd member of the Irish Rugby Team in the corridors of their team hotel. The Fitzpatrick's Hotel in Killiney. She had been getting those psychic flashes about a "Mr Rugby" on and off for months; and here they all were suddenly in the hotel where she had lunch and did her on-line work. The impressions were not anything she could strongly pin down. She had never even met any of them formally, and from what she could see she did not actually fancy any of them either. When she saw them intermittently on their rounds at the hotel, Sarah just assumed she had been picking up that The Irish Rugby Team would be staying and training nearby. A visually pleasing backdrop to her daily life perhaps. Something persistently niggled her though, and she got increasing impressions that she was going to have something more to do with "the team."

Sarah had first made a prediction on television about The Six Nations in advance of the French v Ireland game. Sarah felt that Ireland should not be written off, and that they could indeed go onto win *The Triple Crown*. Rugby fans will remember that this was at a time when the team and Eddie O' Sullivan were subject to major flack in the media and from the Irish Nation in general. She felt strongly that the tables were going to turn very rapidly, and that The Golden Age of Irish Rugby would dawn. She was able to say with confidence that everyone would be celebrating in grand style before too long.

One Tuesday during The Six Nations campaign, Sarah was watching the news. Paul O'Connell, who she personally had not heard of before, was on television, saying that he was only fifty percent likely to be able to play the important game against Scotland on Saturday. She picked up that he had an acromioclavicular joint injury, and that he was troubled with residue pain that would affect his chances of playing. She had one of her "ding" moments, and knew she was meant to help. She knew from her days of running the healing practice that she had the ability to lift pain. AC shoulder joint injuries can heal if minor in two to three weeks, but sometimes if more serious they need surgery. Paul's issue was clearly not going to go away quickly. She felt strongly that she should at least offer her services. Of course, it would have been a bit odd to go up to the hotel and make a song and dance about it. So, she figured if she were meant to help, she would meet the right people when she went up on spec.

Sarah always listened to her guidance and intuition with this kind of thing, even at the risk of looking crazy. It was her calling to respond when so prompted, and she always listened to those promptings and whispers when they happened. She could not ignore what she was being guided to do, and she had to go up to the hotel for a work reason that evening anyway. She thought that she would make herself available simply by being there, and that the spirit would move if it were all meant to be.

Believe it or not. The only people Sarah saw that night were Paul, the team doctor, and the physiotherapist. The hotel was totally quiet, but these three characters were in situ. The first guy she bumped into in the computer room was the physiotherapist, who did not seem too impressed at her suggestion and self-introduction. She thought that was going to be as far as she got. But suspending judgement, he conceded and went to get the team doctor, Gary O' Driscoll, who asked if she knew how important Paul was to the team. She responded, "honestly? No. But she was guided to offer and see if she could help him." Gary then went to get Paul who was up for "giving it a go," as all other the options for getting him match fit had failed.

Sarah had explained to Gary who she was, and that both her brother and father were doctors, so she fully understood medical pragmatism regarding such things. She told the team Doctor that her father had to attend the Bristol student rugby sessions as part of his work remit for Bristol University. He seemed to like this story, and interestingly he was refreshingly open to an alternative approach, so long as she was not going to stick any needles in Paul. Sarah had not realised that Paul O'Connell was such a key player. Clearly, they were so keen for him to play Saturday that they would have tried anything. They did. What is more it *worked!*

Sarah was very matter of fact about hands-on healing and figured that if it worked. So be it. She was aware that many sceptics found it impossible to believe in the power of healing. But she found through many experiences that it was effective, and not simply a matter of auto suggestion. The results of her work were tangible and surprisingly quick with animals and humans alike. When guided to reach out and help people, she did not question it. She was open to helping those she was *guided to* help, no questions asked. God healed through her. She was just a vessel to connect with the chosen person who needed the

232

blessing.

On the upside, Sarah's life as a tipster also flourished. She seemed to have a ministry to sportsmen in particular, tipping the Rugby lads handsomely one lunch time up at Fitzpatrick's Hotel, just before they headed off to win the 2009 Championship. Sarah had briefed Ronan O'Gara that the result was going to be down to him. It was. Ronan's drop goal, right at the close of the match, left Ireland the winners seventeen to fifteen against Wales in Cardiff. If Ronan's steely nerve had failed in the dying seconds of that match, Ireland would have floundered and not won the championship.

Sarah knew they were going to do it, and through the posts that ball did go. Ronan did not like to think it was all down to him, because of course any match is a team effort. But Sarah knew it was important to prime him with a warning this time. It literally was going to be *him* who had to clinch the result, and she knew it. She knew she was meant to tell him this too, and as usual when she knew something like this, the relevant person crossed her path. Right. On Time.

Literally the Irish Team were about to get on the coach to go begin the journey to Cardiff for the final show down against Wales. A few of the lads and Sarah were in the computer room talking horses; not a word to the IRFU. She tipped them a fourteen-to-one horse for the race at four thirty. O' Driscoll wanted a demonstration and set me a challenge. He did not believe it possible to psychically pick out horses or winning teams etc. She had already relayed the most important message of the day to Ronan, that he was going to clinch The Championship for the team. But Ronan was at that point primed to back the horse too it seemed. He scuttled down the corridor on his phone, possibly to catch the tip. Equally he may of course have been chatting to his lovely wife Jessica.

Ronan by his own admission loved the horses, and even owned a couple. Of course, the tipped horse ran in a winner right on cue. But Sarah did not get so much as lunch that time by way of thanks. Any guy who had overheard that tip could have made thousands from the information. At least it all showed that Sarah was becoming quite a useful tipster and it gave her something to keep up her sleeve for a rainy day.

Sarah was jaded with love and romance by this point. All the men she was stumbling across, seemed to be sexually interested, for a time, but long-term commitment phobic. Time was indeed running out for her to have a child. She had spent her life avoiding the challenges of single parenthood, and she was not going to fall into that trap now. She did not want a child enough to subject them to life without a stable father figure. She also wanted a loving partner for herself. Indeed, she knew she wanted this more than she wanted a child. So, she was not going to compromise on these points any time soon. It looked like she was going to end up single and lonely. She had found out she liked funny shaped balls. But the experience of encountering various members of The Irish Rugby Team had not helped her much. It had turned out to be a lot of echoes from other lifetimes. Lots of "contracts" to balance and lots of "karma" to clear. She wondered if she had not made enough of the link with Ronan. Of all of them he had an ease of self-assurance and kept himself to himself. Nothing could happen. But was there a vague resonance and familiarity there? She barely dared consider it. She therefore did not.

Once again it was Paul the Rockstar who brought a bit of levity back into her life. His timing was good throughout the years, and their paths tended to cross when she really needed a lift and a soul connection. Sarah had not had much contact with Paul throughout the rugby shenanigans. It had been her way to try to forget him. It failed miserably.

Sarah bumped into Paul and Simon randomly in Dalkey car park, no doubt on their way into Finnegans for a pint. As usual Paul was charming and sweet and being spontaneously serenaded by him cheered Sarah immensely. She was not sure the little ditty he sang her as they waltzed around the carpark would hit the top ten any time soon. Anyone in the environs of Dalkey station car park could have watched with wry amusement, as Paul gallantly swept her off her feet, dancing her around and singing.

"Her name is Sarah
and she drives a blue car
You'd like to get to know her
'cos she is a Star!"

Thank you, Paul, I needed that. She mused. Sarah also knew by now, that this was just Paul being Paul. She must not attach too much importance to it.

CHAPTER TWENTY-NINE
Exile

Throughout a very isolating stretch, Sarah attempted to make ends meet. She had lost a couple of writing jobs, had no live-in partner, and debts were mounting fast, coming out of her ears in fact. She had carried the burden of providing for William for many years, paying most of his rent and bills, as well as her own, and technically some of the debts were his also. They were all in her name, and she had set up the business, so she did not make him feel guilty or demand help. She just shouldered the situation and sorted it. Her only light relief during this time, was the company of her little dog Harley. She really had no idea how she was going to get through it all, but she knew that she would. She had faith, that it had all happened for a reason, and that even during these horrendous challenges, she would be delivered, and things would work out in the best way possible. Naive she probably was, but it was this thought and approach that kept her sane.

Initially her approach was to knuckle down and stay put in Ireland. She began to see that until she accepted Dalkey as her real home once again, things were not going to shift. She was supposed to stick with the trials and tribulations, get through them, and come out the other side intact. Somehow. During this time, Sarah could not actually get a clear definitive answer on what she should do. Strong intuitions eluded her for the first time in her life, and she was at times in fear of her life. The reasons for this are complex and she cannot safely go into them. But suffice to say it was a hairy experience. She could not actually work out what God wanted her to do either. There seemed to be strong arguments to both stay and go. All her family, and most of her loved ones were in the United Kingdom. Yet here she was, on her own having to stay put in Ireland, to work and make ends meet. She could not even work out the responsible, logical decision. So, she stuck with that old maxim. If in doubt: do nothing.

At the most challenging times there were some peculiar spiritual agendas that seemed to want her out of the picture. There seemed to be some funky energies directed at her from so called colleagues, and others in the esoteric fields. She had naively verbalized a business plan to a colleague who acted quickly to open the "spiritual shop in Dalkey" idea she had outlined. Very promptly she organized her minions to help her set it up. The same girl also poached the house Sarah had wanted to live in on Sorrento Terrace. She was clearly unwittingly engaged with a kind of cosmic, karmic rival. Sarah was advised that to heal what was going on with this person, that she needed to visit Glastonbury. In a lifetime that needed to be dealt with, she had apparently been ostracized by this group of cult-like addicts clucking around "Madam," as we called this poacher of ideas. As always, Sarah sat reflectively loose to the past life theories which came her way. These people had allegedly drained her energies in some magic ritual and had left her to die in a Somerset ditch. Sarah really was not sure this past life account resonated. But she did observe that her father gave Glastonbury a wide berth when they were younger. Saturday jaunts were all over the West Country. But Glastonbury was studiously avoided. Sarah thought this was more to do with crowds, Christian leanings, and not wanting to corrupt his children with thoughts of wizards and warlocks, than any past life issue. However, when she did finally get to Glastonbury with a colleague to carry out some healing work for clients, she found that a lot of energy cleared off, up, and away. She found the gardens of The Chalice Well particularly refreshing and healing. She knew then she had to visit in a similar vein at least three times to clear the relevant karma. Three is a charm after all.

In the thick of this energy, apparently linked to a Glastonbury lifetime, the manifestations, and issues Sarah was dealing with got very funky indeed. She set off for the Lake District to attend her brother's second wedding to the controversial vicar's ex-wife. She did not make it further than the ferry. Once she had driven onto the busy, overladen boat, she inexplicably panicked. She had a compulsion to abort the journey and stay in Ireland. She absolutely could not go.

The ferry security men allowed her to get off the ferry, but only if she left her car on board. It was far too late to unload everyone. Having checked she was not planting a bomb and then scarpering, they allowed her to disembark and return to the safety of shore, with William and her little dog. She was advised to come and collect the car later that evening. As she had watched the ferry leave, with her silver puma and possessions on board, she wondered what on earth was happening to her. She felt persecuted, stuck and in danger of something intangible she did not fully understand. Occult forces beyond her experience were starting to cause very real chaos in her life.

In her sensitivity, the energies Sarah had been bombarded with throughout this time, suddenly got a grip of her. Her exile in Ireland was well and truly official until such a time as she could sort this out. Her parents had been over to see her in the previous couple of years. They had walked around Dalkey, went to the magnificent Kish Fish Restaurant, looking out onto Dalkey Island, and braved the walk to

Powerscourt Waterfall. Sarah's father was quite physically impaired with heart trouble, but they managed walks in Killiney, and it was a special catch-up time. Her parents stayed at the Killiney Hotel situated on the magnificent beach, just down from Paul's house, which Sarah paid for as a treat. She admitted to herself reluctantly that when she kissed her father goodbye at Coliemore Harbour, she did wonder fleetingly if it would be the last time, she would see him.

The simple reality is that at times during this whole adventure, Sarah got very challenged, and even at points *very* frightened. Her process, and evolution as an effective mystic was not easy. The Irish phase was important indeed. She knew she would not have become a professional psychic and healer had she remained in the United Kingdom. It was part of her "contract" and Irish karma to be feted, accepted, and looked to for answers and healing by the Irish nation. She did not plan it. It had its own organic life, and her destiny was apparently dictated by forces greater than her own will or intentions. This really was a case of "God laughs at our best-laid plans."

Sarah had to cope without much support. She was simply listening and following guidance. The revelations, challenges, and lessons were intense and immense; and probably reflected the extent of her calling. She found that one of the biggest lessons in the exploration of all things mystical, was to learn to listen to her own inner voice. It was an apprenticeship. A baptism of fire. A remembrance which forced her to draw on knowledge from another time. She was Daniella in the Lion's Den, and only by the Grace of God did she work her way through the purging, and the persecution.

CHAPTER THIRTY

Ca-nine

The practical difficulties had begun for Sarah when she had to leave the wonderful apartment in Dalkey, where she had lived for nine years. Harley, the sausage dog, did not want to leave the apartment. All her things had been cleared out and brought across to the mouldy, haunted Laragh Mews, set in a cul-de-sac off the long impersonal Ulverton Road, which ran alongside the rail track.

The energy in the Mews was uneasy. The previous owner had died of cancer in the house, and it had kept the resonance of suffering and unease. Sarah ended up sleeping outside the main building in the glass conservatory when William was not around. As soon as night fell, the air felt thick and heavy and "active." It was cold in the conservatory which jutted out into the small split-level garden. But at least she could see the stars and hear the wind in the trees, instead of the elements creeping up and down the strange stairs which were spiraled in the shape of DNA strands.

Harley must have sensed what was coming and sat tight in the middle of the large wooden-floored living space which had been Railway Road. Sarah literally had to drag him out of their home. They say listen to your animals. She probably should have sat tight in the apartment. She had tenant's rights having lived there for nine years. But Sarah played ball, and relinquished these, so that the landlord could do the place up to sell or re-let at a higher fee. To give him credit he had kept the rent stable for years. He was also commendably distressed when asking her to leave. His wife was the main instigator it seemed. Their wedding had sealed the deal on her rights to cross boundaries she previously could not. Hence, she was deprived of the apartment she loved: "home."

As she crossed the threshold for the final time, Sarah got the inner knowing that she would have to move "three to four times in the next eighteen months."

Great.

Sarah was extremely upset to leave her home, and this was hardly a comforting message to receive. But it was at least a preparation for what was to come. She knew such messages when she got them were accurate. They were from a Divine Source that she could trust. She was always cautious about receiving messages and intuitions from others, as she knew hers were always spot on and correct. It is not true that a psychic cannot read themselves. Sarah could. Most of the time.

She began to conclude she had put way too much trust and faith in The White Witch of Wicklow. It was not her fault. She had become a good friend, and was good company, with a wonderful wicked sense of humour and irreverent turn of phrase. They got on very well indeed. Sarah knew she cared about her. Well she thought she did. But there were a couple of random fall outs, which made her question exactly what the relationship was. The first was when Anke phoned to tell her that Donncha O' Callaghan was in the papers looking fine in his wedding regalia. This was one Christmas, when once again Sarah was facing the festive season alone. She felt this phone call was quite

241

insensitive considering. Anke knew what she had come to naively hope for regarding Donncha. Sarah had been badly treated by "Player," another of The Irish Rugby team, and subsequently, she held onto a fantasy that something might still be possible with Donncha. She knew it was *not* possible. But a girl can dream.

She had really been hoping that something would happen between her and Donnacha. But it was not based on a hunch or prediction. Just a vague diffuse "hope" that he might make a move. There was no evidence any reciprocal feeling existed. Much more energy had been generated in previous connections. Sarah had gone down all the wrong roads, and did not connect with the correct "Mr Rugby," in the first place. "Player" had tried to fob her off with Tommy Bowe, who did not have a girlfriend at that point. He was much younger, and undoubtedly cute. But he never signaled anything beyond friendly "hellos." Player was just stirring the pot after an intense fling with Sarah. He had no intention of making a commitment. He passed the buck. Well, the ball!

The whole "Mr Rugby" notion had gone horribly wrong. Part of it had stemmed from a friend seeing a vision of Sarah's wedding, and the specific hat and dress she was wearing. Sarah had been fed up at William's refusal to commit, despite many years together, and she really was hoping to find a life partner for marriage, babies, and family. It was of course just an idea, certainly not based on any reality thus far. Donncha had a long-term girlfriend, and here they were getting married, and The White Witch was going out of her way to point it out to Sarah.

Congrats to them! Happy Christmas to me!

Sarah came to realize that "Spirit" was shifting energy every time she moved, and she grew to see it as a cleansing and clearing process. Her premonition of having to move three or four times in eighteenth months certainly proved to be correct. Every six months, some issue

242

arose, such as a landlord selling, or a rent increase, or a need to make a quick exit. Sarah felt the whole environs of Dalkey and Killiney were "home," and did not get too hooked up on the bricks and mortar aspect. If she was in the correct area, it worked for her.

What was interesting was that every move she made progressed her further. She had six months in a moldy mews after the Railway Road apartment. Then came the Bedroom Studio Apartment in Castle Street Dalkey. Harley the dog got sick and died in this one. Her Christmas present that year, was a taxi driver bringing her dead dog home from University College Dublin hospital, all wrapped up in his blanket. "Player" was being a jerk just to top it all off nicely.

Merry Christmas!

She then headed up to Killiney and was ensconced right next to The Fitzpatrick's Hotel, occasional residency of the rugby team. She could swim at night, and the hotel was an extension of her apartment next door. This situation ended badly. Her lovely Black Ford coupe was reacquired by the bank, and she was six weeks without any money for rent. Oddly, this was all coordinated by the universe. It was a testing time though. Sarah maintained her faith that things would work out. She knew they always did, but sometimes the protracted vacuums where she had to await the will of God were beyond spectacular.

Mollie the dog was brought in the new year to fill the void left by Harley. Shortly after that Sarah also got Jake, a partner and company for Mollie. Mollie now had her life companion at least, and the family unit all needed a bigger place. Suddenly, Sarah was down to the last week in the Killiney apartment with no more wriggle room. She saw Beacon Hill advertised on the property web site on Daft.ie and took the plunge. It was more rent still, but suddenly, she had both rent and deposit, and was able to do the move.

The dogs and Sarah loved this place. Beacon Hill, which runs parallel to the far end of Sorrento Road towards the sea, houses the old customs houses. Situated on the small hill above Coliemore harbor in Dalkey, the grounds of the four or five slate grey houses are set up in commune style. Accessed by a magical, charming, private steep laneway off Nerano Road, this is a hidden oasis. Her neighbours were wonderful, friendly Russians, and kind Irish families. She was in heaven. It literally felt very heavenly. She was awoken by the most spectacular sunrises, and the bathtub was big enough for about three people. Not that she tried that. But it was Mermaid heaven, nonetheless. It was her ultimate place in Ireland. All the coming days spent between number one, Beacon Hill and Killiney Beach were wonderfully therapeutic. In a couple of weeks, she had been transported from destitution to a safe magical haven.

Sarah spent an idyllic couple of years in her bedroom overlooking the Nerano statue of the sailor looking out to sea. Erected in memory of a son who never came home, it became somewhat symbolic of her never getting home to see her family. She did not know if she would ever see them again. She had to knuckle down and sort her situation.

Beacon Hill was her final home in Ireland, before leaving to do bankruptcy in Cornwall. A route she had tried for so long to avoid, chasing lottery wins and rock stars. Sarah absolutely loved this magical setting. Even when it snowed, Beacon Hill was charming. She got stranded up there a few times, and it was treacherous attempting the descent into Dalkey village. It really was the best place She had ever lived. She was sad when it came to a very abrupt untimely end. She was literally propelled out of there with immaculate timing. It was all her choice, all her own doing. As usual when a move was needed, the rent was not there for the last month. The deposit covered that, and Sarah took it as always to the last possible moment.

Sarah had never fully unpacked into Beacon Hill. Her boxes were already in storage, the dogs, and the effects she would need for Cornwall were jammed in the car. Sarah left the keys in an envelope on the door and departed. She gathered the landlady showed up twenty minutes later. She just missed her. It was time to go to Cornwall, to the house on the cliff she had been paying for since the previous October. Even though Sarah did not want to leave Ireland, she had Cornwall lined up as a safe house. It was her official home for a few months before she even arrived there. How ironic that someone on the brink of choosing bankruptcy had the use of two beautiful houses by the sea.

As usual, God, Spirit, and her intuition timed Sarah's exit to perfection. Her things were put into storage ready to do the move, and she had to bundle herself and five dogs into the car and get the hell out of there. She was not thrown out. But she needed to get away from what had become a scary toxic situation with the landlord.

Sarah had been living at Beacon Hill with seven little dogs. They loved the house and the communal gardens, and the neighbors all enjoyed the puppies as they were born and grew. Mollie and Jake had made five puppies. Sarah knew this was on the cards after Jake arrived. As soon as he met Mollie, she then got the name of a third dog "Charlie." Sarah had no intention of buying any more dogs, so she then knew it was inevitable that Mollie would have Jake's pups. One thing was clear, Charlie was going to be important.

Sure enough, nature took its course. Mollie and Jake were both young, and really, they were at the youngest they should be to have puppies. It was dangerous enough for Mollie, and she did have a few problems with feeding the dogs afterwards. Sarah had to wean them under the vet's guidance, as Mollie very quickly got a calcium deficiency which threatened her life. She went off to the UCD training hospital for the night, and thankfully did not return wrapped up in a package by taxi as Harley had done. Sarah was able to go and collect her still living, though wobbly and weak, dog, the next morning.

While pregnant, Mollie was like a football as she was carrying five pups. Sarah loved the experience of looking after her through pregnancy, and then helping her birth the five puppies was amazing. She was so glad she had had this experience with her dogs. It was a real blessing and healing thing. There was an indescribable feeling of joy when all the pups arrived. Sarah felt a hole in her heart had been plugged. She received an incredible emotional repair from the whole thing. She was not quite sure why, but she knew she finally had her own family.

This may all seem a bit strange, obviously dogs are not a human family. But after everything Sarah had been through. All the disappointments, let-downs and betrayals, this unforeseen development was totally beneficial. She loved every minute of the process, helping Mollie with her birthing plan, as she rested on Sarah's on the floor between puppies.

Mollie pushed out a puppy every twenty to thirty minutes, so there was quite a gap between them. Out they all came one by one: Ralphie Boy, Charlie, Accrington Stanley, Lottie, and Penny. Sarah saved Penny as she was born. She was tiny and lifeless covered in film. She gently washed that off and rubbed her into life, Jake also helped and licked all the puppies for Mollie. He was every bit as caring as Mollie was. It is not true that the adult male dog gets jealous. Jake was a loving partner to Mollie, and a caring dad to his pups. He looked just as shell shocked as any new father when all the puppies arrived.

CHAPTER THIRTY-ONE

Escape

The White Witch of Wicklow had told Sarah that she would be with Paul ultimately and that she would hit big on the lottery. Neither of these things happened in the many years Sarah was going to her for readings. A lot happened that she predicted; but not these two main things. Sarah was okay with this. Well sort of. She went through what she went through with it all. She was not about to blame someone else for her failings and life choices. But she was not sure she was right to say what she did. The odd thing is Sarah still had a deep knowing that The White Witch was probably correct on some things. *Not* the Paul thing. Time had really marched on with that. But Sarah did concede that she could potentially win money. She had proven to herself that she had a propensity with numbers and horses. She could literally pluck winners out of the air.

The White Witch had been nothing if not consistent on this point of winning money. Money was her thing, her level of expertise. She knew how to work with it, and sniff it out, and she readily tells clients when she sees finances, pertaining to issues and resolutions in their readings. She told Sarah, she was so captivated by the amount she saw in her reading, that she used to lie awake in the morning wondering how much it was. It felt so very substantial.

In her crystal ball readings, The White Witch used to scribble the shape of the Euro sign on the table, before the Euro was even introduced into Ireland. She saw the exact Euro symbol in the crystal ball, and said it was linked to the big win. Sarah wobbled a bit on this symbolism when the Euro Millions draw was introduced. Had she just been predicting its arrival in Ireland? Sarah asked The White Witch on what day of the week was she going to win, and she described the evening before the weekend. Of course, there was no such draw when she said this. But the Friday Euro Millions draw was introduced not long after. Sarah's active concern was that she had simply been psychically picking up on the introduction of the Euro Millions draw to Ireland. Was she sure Sarah was going to win it, or was she simply seeing the draw come into existence?

Sarah left Ireland under a cloud. She was literally propelled and ejected from the Emerald Isle because she needed to go and bring some order to her financial and emotional situation. The universe knew what needed to be done, so that she could regain her equilibrium and a sense of personal freedom, that she had not felt for a long time. Sarah enjoyed a short time in Cornwall, and then a longer stretch in Porlock.

Up until the beginning of 2012, Dalkey had been Sarah's home for many years. It is where she set up her adult life, and she had come to love its people, village, and environment. She had not wanted to leave the wonderful house on Beacon Hill. But her exit from Ireland, via Carrie's house, Grainne's house, and then onto the Irish Ferry at six o' clock in the morning, was all divinely timed. Her Aunt came to "rescue" her and they drove down through Wales as dusk fell, landing back at her parent's house Conifers, for the first time in many years.

Sarah kissed the Welsh soil once she got out of the car on the first leg of the journey to walk the dogs. She was not Welsh, but she was back in the United Kingdom. A place she frequently felt she may never see again. Sarah loved Ireland, but she had been living with the thought that she was never going to be able to leave. She had made her bed, and it looked like she was going to have to lie in it. Sometimes in that moment of surrender, a path then presents itself. It can be unexpected. But it usually turns out to be just the ticket.

Sarah slept *very* well that first night back at Conifers. To be back in her underground childhood bedroom, now the guest room, was a treat. She was allowed two nights, because her parents really did not want the dogs in the house. They conceded she could stay a couple of nights on the way down to Cornwall to do the bankruptcy, "the deed," she had come to call it. On the second morning, Sarah's mother gave her the money for the legal fee, gifted by her Uncle Michael; and within a couple of days she was on the road again convoying with her aunt all the way to the end of the world. Land's End in Cornwall.

The view as they approached Hendra Cottage was spectacular. What greeted them was a huge converted barn, which looked undoubtedly spooky, and huge rolling green cliffs populated with rabbits, and not a tree in sight. Set on a hill, Hendra Cottage sat snug and proud, shielded by the small series of mounds behind it. The view from the yard out the back displayed ploughed fields, stone walls and a couple of dusty tracks, which merged with boggy land at the lowest point between the cottage and the sea. The land dipped severely by the marsh, flattened out for a few hundred squelchy yards, and then elevated sharply the other side, gearing up speed until it reached the "nobbly" terrain of the grassy cliff tops, beyond which shone The Atlantic.

The Atlantic Sea over the crest of the cliff looked elemental and formidable. Cornwall was a world apart and seemed like a different country. The energy felt disconnected from the rest of the United

Kingdom. Here was a land, that had its own flavor, history, and tastes. It literally was the end of the line. There were two similar sized houses to the right of Hendra Cottage. But nothing much by way of accommodation between this spot, and the spectacular sands of Sennen Beach miles away. Only Land's End Airport held the promise of an escape route, should this be required.

The place Sarah had chosen to do "the deed," was so far off the beaten track that when Mollie needed a vet for an adrenaline shot to cope with a bee sting in her mouth, she had to drive to the end of her road, a three-mile-long cul-de-sac, to wait by the stipulated farm gate, for a vet who then administered the drugs on the road side. It was like something out of a movie. The easy friendliness and warmth of Ireland felt a long way away. Had she failed? It did not feel like it. But all this was certainly not predicted or bargained for. The high lights of the week were the sugar frosted buns from the bakery - if they had not sold out by the time she got there - and the church service in Latin at Saint Just parish church, on a Sunday.

In lonely moments, Sarah consoled herself that she had dealt with a huge financial debt and burden in taking this path. That surely in itself should be sufficient justification for now living in the middle of nowhere with five dogs for company. Sarah had literally chosen splendid isolation. The days of smooching Paul in nightclubs were long gone. Perhaps she would meet Poldark on the next cliff walk? It helped Sarah to keep some such fantastical thought active in her mind, especially in such stark conditions.

In retrospect, Sarah did not know how she managed this phase. She would never have chosen this location second time around. But oddly, it worked for a short time. It was certainly rugged and beautiful. She must have been deeply afraid to have put herself so out of reach. Yet she had the inner strength to make it work. As usual, Sarah took the positive from the position she found herself in. One amazingly liberating thing had happened, and it was legitimate and allowed. She was finally free from the burden of debt, and the legacy of all those years of trying to build a business and look after William. Whatever The White Witch had predicted could now happen or not. It did not really matter either way anymore. Sarah was FREE!

CHAPTER THIRTY-TWO
Por-locked

Sarah started to panic as she was trying to sleep in the barn on the final night before the journey to Ireland. She was surprised. Obviously, she had grown comfortable settling back into the land of her roots. Sarah's ancestors were from Somerset and Dorset, and much of her childhood had been spent in the West Country. She loved Ireland as her home, yet there was a deep connection to the place where she had spent summer camps as a child. She enjoyed wandering the moors of Exmoor after a few weeks in Cornwall. It had become her safe-haven, and the place she could expand her soul and her vision. Here, she was at one with nature. Here energies and fitness had never been better.

Benny had made it clear he had come to the end of the road regarding the barn. For someone with OCD, a penchant for hygiene and a need for meticulous order, he had done very well with his visits to the ancient dusty, musty barn covered in ivy and imbued with mildew. He had recently told Sarah he would never be able to live full-time in the barn, and that he needed a place to call home. Sarah took this as an encouraging comment of his future intentions. She wanted a place to call home too after all the years of unsettlement. They wanted the same thing, so that was a start. But location was going to be an issue.

Benny had no intention of moving to Europe; and even though Sarah had been accepted for a National Trust cottage, *Sea View* in Bossington, it had fallen through. So too did the dream of Benny's immigration to the United Kingdom. He had too many commitments back home in America and was *so* American that living elsewhere would not work for him. Ireland started to feel like a possible alternative. But Sarah never would have been able to face a return there if not for Benny.

They had already done so much travelling on their pilgrimages throughout the United Kingdom, that they had in a way exhausted the best of what Britain had to offer. Considering his partial Irish ancestry Sarah strongly felt that Benny should experience Ireland also. But he never seemed to know when he would be able to visit again. He was starting to get weary of all the to-and-fro travel. Jet lag was an issue, and a big adjustment for him each time he made a visit. It felt like he was not sure how much longer he could sustain and justify regular transatlantic trips. The notion of moving onto Ireland injected some new energy into the proceedings, and he was enlivened by the thought of experiencing a new environment, and country.

As they were deciding to exit the barn, the eco-friendly, non-flushable, toilet in the outhouse was literally on the point of exploding. Winter was fast descending in Exmoor, and it looked like it was going to be a long, cold, few months. The barn no longer felt like a fit or safe place to stay. On top of that all the signs and synchronicities were aligned for a smooth return to Dalkey, in Southern Ireland. Sarah's friend Grainne had viewed a wonderful property for her, rented by another Grainne, and all seemed fine. It looked like Ireland was welcoming her home with open arms. There had been minimal referencing required, (they knew who she was), and she was allotted number three, Tubbermore Avenue, Dalkey, as her new place of residence for the foreseeable future.

Landing back in Ireland for the second time was a time warp experience. It felt to Sarah like she had never left. She swore there were locals who had not even noticed her absence for a couple of years. Her doctor greeted her in the supermarket, as if he had only seen her yesterday. If I had remained in Dalkey in January 2012 that probably would have been true. Dr Lavelle guided Sarah through a whole lot during her times of stress. During the psychic attack she experienced many odd conditions, and funky events. Her blood pressure at points was nudging dangerously into hypertension. She had random histamine reactions, infected bug bites, and the most obscure recurring chest infection. She had to be very alert with what was happening with her body. She swore he saved her life, certainly her equilibrium, several times. Bless him.

Exmoor was been a resting place; a place to recuperate and wait for whatever was to come next for Sarah. At times it felt like nothing new was looming on the horizon. This was *it*. A long walk into oblivion is what it felt like at times. Sarah wandering the fields or the moors with a bunch of dogs forever. She had reached her destiny. A destiny to wander "fields?"

It felt odd that this might be the case considering what she knew to be her "contract" to help and heal. But logically speaking it certainly could have been the end of the road. Not exactly a fail. People would pay good money to live in such surroundings. They *did* in fact. Sarah was after all semi-retired and had all the hours of the day pretty much to herself. Her obligations and responsibilities pertained to looking after her beloved sausage dog squad. She had a couple of radio shows a month to plan and prepare. These shows were broadcast live from her mid fifteenth-century barn in Porlock; sometimes literally from the eco loo room out the back, with the computer perching on the toilet, thereby avoiding avoid the interruption of a barking dog, who might spy a stray sheep out of the window. Sarah still wrote her string of articles for the Irish Newspapers and magazines who employed her services. Her clients were an on-going commitment. But she was able to plan and live her day in the flow she chose. She could eat when she liked, sleep when she liked, work when she liked. She was on no one's schedule but her own. Quite possibly she was on the fast track to being, that strange old lady aged eighty, living in a barn by herself with a myriad of creatures for company. Was this really, what she had signed up for?

Sarah loved the surroundings, atmosphere, and natural lifestyle, the sojourn at Doverhay Farm provided. Life had a natural mellow rhythm, her dogs protected her and kept her warm at night, and she was able to finally process all the years of disappointment, stress, and heartache. She was not sure if anything came next after this. Perhaps it did not have to. This was more than okay really. A little sedentary and repetitive; but she could not ask for a better backdrop and context. Nature was her healer, and her soul was inspired every time she walked out the door. There are not many places in the world that are capable of that kind of elevation. The microclimate found in "The Vale of Honey" was one of them.

Porlock was prolific when it came to rain, and mist because of the bleak moors situated upon the hills behind the village. The famous, insurmountable on an icy day, Porlock Hill was legendary. This road leads the motorist up onto the eastern fringes of Exmoor, and is the steepest minor road in the country, climbing over seven-hundred feet in less than a mile. With a gradient of 1-in-4, you did not attempt this climb if your vehicle's accelerator and clutch were not up to the task. Nor did you descend into the village down the hill, if your brakes were in any way impaired.

It was easy to lose your bearings in these parts if you were not local. The windy narrow road system across the moors led cars astray easily enough as there were various tracks navigating the barren wilderness. For walkers and drivers alike, it was a case of "pot-luck" in finding the quickest way from a to b.

Sarah had many arguments with Siri on the finer points of crossing Exmoor. But usually she did know what she was talking about.

"Hey Siri!"

#nevermind.

Thankfully, there were alternative routes in and out of Porlock. Sarah nearly crashed on one of the other descents into the village above Doverhay. She was trying to get back to the barn in time for a remote healing. Returning from Minehead through the back roads bypassing Luccombe and Horner, Sarah could smell that smell of rotten eggs an old car exudes when its catalytic converter is about to implode. She was a mile from home. Sarah stopped the car and asked for a farmer's help, and he suggested freewheeling along the road as much as possible before hitting the windy, steep descent into Porlock.

The approach went to plan, but "Duh." When Sarah got to top of the hill above the farm, she decided to turn off the engine. Of course, the wheel locked, and she nearly lost control of the car; thankfully managing to bump start it just before she needed to turn into the hair-pin bend. She turned the key in the lock, and thankfully the car started up just in time, averting a sharp descent into the hedge on the corner of the bend. Had it failed to do so, She, would have had a nasty accident, as she would not have been able to avoid swerving into the jeep ascending rather too quickly on the other side of the road. Well, the *same* side of the road, since all the roads around Porlock were pretty much only one lane.

With the wheel unlocked Sarah was able to pull in and let the jeep pass. She could have been forgiven that some entity or agenda was trying to prevent her receiving the healing that was due to start within the next five minutes. The car, although a battered go-cart, had given her no mechanical trouble up until that point. Then again it would be paranoid to conclude that she was being in any way energetically targeted.

The Porlock routine certainly gave the sensation of a Groundhog Day, but it was pleasurable, nonetheless. In bleak moments Sarah would wonder how she had ended up in this obscure part of Britain after all her previous opportunities. But Sarah put on a brave face. She would talk to friends online, or on the phone, and there was always something intriguing going on, in social media land which demanded her attention. Most importantly, she was able to help many people with the clarity and background support afforded by mother nature. There was no better backdrop than the barn which merged with the surrounding landscape as part of its organic manifestation.

The barn was a time warp. A time machine to another dimension. Strange things would happen in this creative space. The phrase "Barn Time" was coined as the barn had its own inner clock and throbbing heartbeat. The difference in the passing of time within and without the barn was tangible. She could hear ghosts at night, the wind in the trees, owls hooting, bats flapping, and strange sounds coming up through the floorboards. Anything could happen through the ethers in this place as it was built on one of the powerful lay lines linking the west country energetically with London via Glastonbury, Salisbury Plain, and Stonehenge.

The barn was never locked, and any passing stranger could have walked through the door had they known. But it was secure, in this twilight setting, which had me living off the land, in tune with nature and my own rhythm. Sarah could have stepped back in time, down through the centuries, and life would not have been much different. This lifestyle was organic and wholesome. Lonely but therapeutic if you could abide the isolation.

It really was lonely. Sarah would be lying if she said she was full of the joys of spring. But she did not feel empty or desolate. She was alone, not lonely if truth be told. She had grown to like my own company at last. She did not really need company. In fact, she was becoming positively reclusive, and perhaps even standoffish where her fellow humans were concerned. She had been given such short shrift in many situations, that she gave up on the thought of finding a soul mate, having a family, making her millions. She did not really need any of it. Nature was enough, and the soulful grounded feeling the land gave her was everything.

It would have been nice to have some reassurance that there were some more interesting chapters ahead. But stuck in her routine of wandering the moors or the woods daily, she drew a blank much of the time. She sensed America on the horizon. In what shape or form, she did not know. She was not sure she even wanted this. Sarah had retreated from the world really, and America was a vast energy beckoning which she was not sure she could handle. If the New World was going to feature in her future, she had to make ready and make the most of this time-out chapter.

Sarah needed to just "be." To "let the dust settle" and allow the new phase of life to come in organically. She knew it paid to be accepting of a vacuum and a transition time. This stopgap was allowing the universe to breathe in her favour and line up those new adventures. She was allowing the energies to flux and flow. Ebb and flow. She knew that sometimes the down time could be the best gift of all. A luxury that many never received or were lucky enough to experience. At this stage of life, Sarah could have been enjoying a hectic family life, or a high demanding career in the city, or a nine-to-five in some office, or classroom. She knew her destiny was none of those things. The predictable routes were not for her. As a healer and psychic worker, she *needed* this time in nature, to clear, cleanse, shake all the trauma down, and come back fighting; for the sake of her clients as well as for herself. Sarah did not know what would come next in her life, though she knew America would play a part. She used to look up at the track across the mountainous hill at Hurlstone Point, and *knew* she would walk that walk with a visiting American. She was saving that excursion for whoever this would be. She was determined not to walk it until that person arrived. She had no idea who that American was going to be. It turned out to be Benny, a fellow psychic and healer from the USA.

Snake Woods, as Benny called it, was a circular walk which began in Bossington, looped up to Hurlstone Point, across this ridge path Sarah was keeping sacred, and then through the spooky woods which then dipped back down to the tiny village of West Lynch. Snake Woods was a journey in stages. The walk was a meditation in ways, and it allowed for the processing of the latest drama, or for deep thought about a client's situation, or the planning of the next trip or work project. Having broken-the-duck with Benny on his first visit with the circular trek, Sarah walked Snake Woods pretty much daily with the dogs, whatever the weather. She got super fit, and simply loved the wilderness life.

Sarah got very used to her own company. It was just her and the dogs, for many months, interspersed with visits from Benny when he could manage them. Sarah healed, and assimilated her thoughts, finances, and emotions. The whole thing was a process of inner strengthening and catharsis. She could now do things on her own terms. Empowered.

PART THREE

1243 - 44

CHAPTER THIRTY-THREE

Handfasting

S ari awoke lying in Ronan's arms. Their union in the stable had been beyond expectations. Together they had flown the world. The consummation took them all the way to the stars. Their love was complete, encompassing. All embracing. Surely their purpose and destiny must be great indeed. She knew her "contract" as a vessel, for The Divine had also been fulfilled.

A baby was on the way. She *knew*.

She had sensed the moment his seed forcefully penetrated one of her eggs.

This was a viable union.

The legacy was ensured.

Sari was excited but also nervous about the demanding role of motherhood. She had thought about it often. She did not know what her timing would be, as she thought she would have to undertake the French pilgrimage first. At one point she became convinced that the bearer of the magical seed was in France anyway. She would not meet the baby's father until she did the journey. Or so she suspected. Little did she know that Ronan, who was right under her nose, would be the one to do the honours. She knew how she was feeling towards him and she could see a flickering of interest from him. But she tended to use too much logic about her own life. She could access the truth with her intuition for others. But she often avoided its use for herself. Of course, the messages came into her being despite herself. She was certainly surprised when the energy started to build with Ronan. But the logic dictated that this connection was a false flag. His father would never allow it. Her duty and legacy would never allow it. Only their journeys in opposite directions sealed the deal. Both knew at their reunion that they would act on the feeling. Sari also sensed that this might be the time for the baby to come through.

Motherhood would be a challenge. But she could rely on relatives and there was plenty of support from the community with the young ones and in their extended families. Despite her conviction that she was indeed pregnant, she knew she still had to get to France. Ronan would surely accompany her now. That was something at least. They now had a lot to think about. The most pressing question being should they get back on the road right away leaving Frederick to recover or die in her absence.

Sari knew she probably would not see her father again if she left now. She also knew he would therefore never see his granddaughter. He would be such a doting wonderful grandpa. She knew this too. Ronan was now willing to accompany her to France. He made that clear quickly. She heard all about Reginald's machinations and the futile trip north to *Eilean Donan*. She also gathered that they could both thank Reginald for his agendas, for these had confirmed to Ronan his heart and his true feelings. Sari was grateful for that journey which had brought Ronan to her with such force and commitment. She would not have been able to abide any further dithering or dancing around the issue. Just as her swift outward journey with Frederick her father had led to a quick resolved return for her. So, Ronan came back with love in his heart and the full recognition of what he now needed to do.

Take her!

That was *all* he needed to do. Not in a lustful heat-of-the-moment way, though that would surely be part of it. But with his whole being. With his full intention that he was all-in and fully hers, and that she was fully his. They would both have to know this required action and surrender and blissful response. There was no need for a deep conversation. This all had to be telepathically resolved. The decision had already been made on a soul level. The physical union was just the expression of this, acutely enjoyable though they both knew it would be. They had to be completely in the moment. With no thoughts of journeys, fathers, obligations or even what they were going to do the following morning. With their passions ignited and their power together consumed within their hearts, the rest would follow naturally. Their union would then dictate in the most wonderful ways their assigned destiny with each other. For her part, Sari simply had to "abandon" herself to him, with no questions or doubts. A full surrender that would be quite unusual for a virgin to make. But do it she must.

Ronan only hoped Sari had come to the same conclusions as he had. He was aware of her contract to The Divine Lineage that she embodied. But this had to be about *them*. Even if there happened to be no baby from this consummation, she had to do this for her *own* heart and soul. If it also led to the fulfillment of her role and contract, all to the good. But *she* came first in this moment. That itself would probably assure the bigger result anyway. Ronan did not want to interfere with her process, nor talk this through. It had to be mutually and implicitly understood. Right there and then. On the first instance of their reconnection.

One thing was for sure, neither Ronan nor Sari were thinking of a third element 'a baby' when they ravaged each other with a consummate passion in the stable. They married themselves to each other in that moment. A sacred act of commitment as their bodies intertwined and their souls conjoined.

No postmortem discussion was necessary. No need to analyze "what just happened?" They both just knew. Here was the future. Here was everything. With each other they could face all life's challenges. Their paternal influences would just have to acknowledge this change in the balance of power. It was now Sari and Ronan against the world. They were invincible. Together they could conquer all that came their way. There and then when they awoke, they conducted a simple handfasting ceremony. They decided to make this unbreakable and impervious to outside interferences. Again, almost without words they resolved their future together.

In an impromptu gesture Ronan took the vivid blue ribbon from Sari's hair. Her hair had been loosely plaited to one side when they met. Much of it had come undone as they undressed every aspect of each other. The blue ribbon held on to her undone mane of luscious blonde hair by a thread.

"Be mine?" Ronan said. He got down on one knee before her gesturing with the silk ribbon.

One of Sari's clients had gifted her the material after a reading which had given them all the answers they needed, about their love life, and prospective marriage. Ronan did not know this. But Sari took it as a highly appropriate use of the twine. The energy would be a match for what they were about to do.

Sari knew exactly what he meant. It was a common gesture for lovers who did not want to wait, or who did not want a church wedding, to handfast their commitment. The couple could do it themselves by mutual agreement, either as a form of betrothal or instead of getting married on consecrated ground. For Sari, the whole of nature was sacred. Ronan knew that she did not require a Catholic priest to decree their nuptials. The agreement and words between them were the ritual that would unite them for eternity.

Handfasting was as binding as marriage "Till death do us part." Yet a priest was not essential. Nor was a witness. Though Merlin and Delphine would act as very worthy witnesses in this instance. They had seen everything else after all!

"Marry Me Sari!" Ronan repeated his gesture with more words this time. As if they were really needed.

Oh Ronan! Yes! Yes! Yes!!!!" They both laughed at her mischievous reference to the heated antics that had taken place the night before.

Ronan took the ribbon and started winding it around their hands as they held each other tightly clasped.

"With the fashioning of this knot do we tie all our desires, dreams, love, and happiness wished here in this place to our lives for as long as we both shall live. In the joining of our hands and the fashioning of this knot, so are our lives now bound, one to another. By this cord we are thus bound to our vows and intentions for eternity."

Sari let Ronan lead and sanctioned the vows with a simple "Amen!" She might have said, "So Mote it be." But she felt at least a nod to Ronan's Catholic faith and upbringing would be appropriate and appreciated. Pagans though they were, they also held many of the beliefs of ecclesiastical religion, or at least felt the value of those rituals, which were in many ways a kind of magic. The bells, the chimes, the incense of the monastic churches in The Highlands, evoked the senses and suited the Celtic peoples in some ways, in others not so much.

She knew they were bound fast with this simple ceremony and its expression of love. It was just as powerful as it would have been if witnessed by their families and conducted by a cleric.

Probably more so, Sari mused to herself. She loved the purity of

Ronan's words and intentions. The authenticity of what they shared was completely theirs. Theirs alone. Most of all she loved the privacy. This was between them. A meeting of minds, hearts, and Spirit.

"Let no man put asunder."

They were "one."

So, Mote it be…

Ronan pulled Sari towards him when the vows were complete. In a warm embrace they kissed. Relaxed and confident in each other's arms. Assured of their future together and full of excitement about the destiny they now shared.

Man and wife.

CHAPTER THIRTY-FOUR

Gestation

S ari and Ronan returned to Sheena's house full of the joy of newly expressed love. Their profound love and commitment assured the future. The stable had been the scene of their union. The horses the witnesses. They had come a long way through the night, and the witching hours had irrevocably changed their lives. Sari wore the countenance of a new bride. Even though she emerged ruffled and disheveled from the stable with little sleep, she looked luminous and beautiful.

Such elegance and radiance never, before, seen, thought Ronan as he gazed on his comely bride taking her by the hand to lead her home.

It did not take much intelligence to work out what they had been up to.

Perhaps they could have walked all night, Sheena amused herself with the thought.

But she doubted it.

She also intuited she would have to play a crucial role in the fates of the resulting child.

Oh, that would be good. Always wanted a girl! Sheena mused, without stopping to think why this responsibility might fall upon her shoulders. She reprimanded herself.

Such premature thoughts and predictive flashes were truly the scourge of the Grail line!

The fate of the seer.

Serena was born on 10th May 1243, close in month and day to Sari's own birthday of 16th May 1221. The union between Ronan and Sari in the stable had been late summer which perfectly aligned the gestation period with the winter months. Sari had indeed found her man "before the winter."

Ronan and Sari decided to wait out the winter before setting off for France. This would give Frederick a chance to recover by spring if he were going to. Regardless, the two of them would be departing Scotland by the summer of 1243 at the latest. Sari had a strong pull that she needed to be fully present in *Montségur* by early 1244. She would have a major role to play in some crisis she sensed was building.

The infamous massacre of *Béziers* had occurred a decade or so before Sari's birth. But stories of the slaughter of twenty thousand innocents in a Cathar stronghold haunted her from an early age. The papal edicts against The Cathars seemed indiscriminate and unjustifiable. These were a peace-loving people who dared to think and believe differently. The Catholic Church found them a subversive threat and were ill-at-ease about what they perceived as a potential for revolution if their numbers continued to profligate. Europe remained paranoid and twitchy about The Cathars way beyond the 1209 massacre and the extensive Alibigensian Crusades.

"Kill them all!" had been the command of the Pope, and this remained in the consciousness of The Crusaders. It seemed to be ingrained in their psyche like a mantra. The search for The Holy Grail

268

ironically got diverted into the persecution of the very people who probably knew where it was, and *what i*t was.

There had been some reprieve with the death of Simon De Montfort in June 1219. This man of extreme catholic orthodoxy had been crusading against what he believed to be heresy under church orders. There was no justification for his brutality. But he had a reputation for strategy and military brilliance as well as brutality and mercilessness. His life ended at the hands of a bunch of women wielding a large stone projectile missile launched from a mangonel which crushed his head.

The Cathars were the victims of major genocide throughout the Medieval Times. Of all The Cathar strongholds *Montségur* was the best defended and the best known. At the end of the twelfth century a community of Cathar women sheltered in the community set up within the walls of *Montségur* Castle. They established a way of living peaceably and the practice of their faith was secretive and mysterious. It caught the imagination as well as aroused a lot of suspicion. Men were involved in the sect as well. There were spiritual leaders, rituals and beliefs that did not accommodate the usual mainstream catholic tenets. This group felt significant to Sari and captured her loyalty. From what she heard of them, and how they had been treated, she knew instinctively something was amiss. These people held ancient secrets and probably had more understanding of the truth than the greedy men who went abroad in the name of religion from The Vatican. Their actions were murderous and lethal and all in the name of politics and power. A faith that conducted itself peaceably yet secretively and was persecuted for it, had the hallmarks of 'Truth.' Sari *knew* that they *knew*.

The Cathars were kindred souls. A group family she felt compelled to help. She knew she was something to do with preserving their legacy. She knew about her own contract to The Divine, and she suspected it was in some way linked to the esoteric gnostic knowledge of The Cathars. She felt they might be able to teach her more about

269

herself and her legacy, whether by default or demonstration she was not yet sure.

Coming into the Thirteenth century it became more and more apparent the faith was under siege. Despite De Montfort's death the persecutions continued randomly and indiscriminately. It was the mission of the Catholic Church to stamp out this heresy completely. This was the destiny of The Cathars. To be pilloried and murdered for knowing something that The Church could not contain or understand. *Ramon de Pereille* the chatelain was ordered to render *Montségur* defensible. To make it as fortified and secure as possible. It was anticipated this would be the last shelter and stand for The Cathars should the genocide reach prolific proportions. Indeed, it had already done so in a couple of instances. The sect was under an edict which put them in prescient danger. The intention was to kill them off. They needed one place where they could perhaps hold out and live uninterrupted. A Castle in the air. Well on the top of a mountain. Difficult to scale, and impossible to attack. A final protection site for the fast dwindling Cathar concern.

Sari knew immediately that she was with child by Ronan, but she kept it to herself for a little while. She wanted to enjoy the feeling of being united to him. Just him. Even though she knew another important ingredient was already cooking within her. She could smile to herself knowingly at her good fortune. Ronan did not need to know quite yet. Sari wanted to delay the journey to France in the light of recent developments. She was not anxious to ride into danger with the new life growing inside her. She knew the journey would be treacherous, even if they managed to charter a boat right to the South of France. This would admittedly be safer than the original plan to travel to Bruges and then ride down through France. But it was still fraught with danger from the unpredictable seas and weather. The route from Saint Andrews to Biarritz would be lengthy and involved stopping at many trade ports along the way.

Journeys by land were much more dangerous than journeys by sea. At sea there were just the elements to contend with, and perhaps some pirate boats if they were very unlucky. If they proceeded right down through France on horseback, the challenges would be numerous. The legacy De Montfort had left in his wake meant turbulence and chaos in many regions throughout France. Deep-seated resentments and political and religious dissension were not healed. Robbery, murder, and kidnappings were ever-present dangers. Not only that, the main questions would be targeted at Sari if they were stopped by authorities patrolling the riding paths.

Who was she?

What was she doing here in France?

Where was she heading?

Sari did not really feel she could face this stress and trauma whilst pregnant. If they set off now, she would be probably four months into the gestation by the time they arrived. So much riding would also take its toll. It was far too risky. Even by sea, they may take a month of two to complete the journey and there were too many variables about which boats they would be able to charter. Some days would be spent in ports wondering if the next phase of the trip was even possible. The grief of leaving her father behind too, would have been too much to bear. She knew if she set off now without him, he would not live to see her return. He would never see his granddaughter. There were so many convincing reasons to stay in Scotland for the winter.

Ronan was keen to help Sari in whatever she decided, and he did not need to pressure her to go immediately to France. Even though part of him wanted to defy his father as soon as possible, he could wait before they departed. This was her journey. To be her gallant protector was his main aim. Besides, he was not stupid. The quality of their physical union was tangible. He knew that her being with child would likely be immanent, if not already present. He half suspected that Sari

271

'knew' she was already with child. He was okay with this and he did not pry. These aspects of womankind were not his level of expertise. Besides, they seemed to cope with it all very well amongst themselves he thought.

Ronan was considerate to Sari and attentive to her needs in case she was in a "delicate way." But this was proper behaviour for a husband anyway. It would always the way he treated her. He had pledged this to himself from the start. Sari would be the center of his world. He was not going to dictate to her or push her around. Watching her work all those months had taught him a lot. She thrived and achieved things by tuning in, taking her time, and announcing advisories when she was ready. She had to be left to flourish, to fulfill her destiny, and to be all that she was meant to be.

CHAPTER THIRTY-FIVE

The Birth

S ari screamed into the cold air as she clenched his hand. "Ronan!" Her breathing was shallow and rapid. The contractions were coming thick and fast. Sari was in the throes of a difficult birthing experience. Sheena was clucking around her instructing her boys to get hot cloths, water, dry cloths, wet cloths, heat, cold, water, sheets. Ronan tried to be as calm as he possibly could be. But he was not cut out for this. He wanted to run as fast as possible in the opposite direction. Their mighty passion in the stable had led to this moment. He was very afraid that having gained the world, he would now lose everything.

Ronan had not seen Sari so panicked or out of control. His role must be to calm and placate and soothe her. His strength must guide her through this. She needed his light and incentive. If he left the room she would possibly flip and die. This was down to him. He could not leave. Sheena and the boys were doing all they could. But he knew Sari needed him in this moment. He had to tune in and *be* her. *One* with her

273

in this moment. They had done this together. Somehow, he needed to take on some of the pain and guide her through.

They had not planned this. He could have waited several years before starting a family. Ronan was keen for them to have as much time as they could as a young vibrant couple, without the responsibilities of parenthood. He was nervous about diving into everything too quickly. He still had his father to placate, and once that hurdle was dealt with, there would doubtless be a clan wedding to plan and celebrate. Even though they were handfasted, Ronan knew his father would see this as a betrothal only. For the sake of the legacy of *Clann Ruaidhri* Reginald would need to see a full highland wedding and lengthy feasted celebration.

Ronan had not yet dared share this with Sari. Just as she had her legacy to honour, he would also have to show some willingness to comply, especially since he had already defied his father's choice of bride. There was nothing Reginald could do now to rend them asunder. That much placated him at least. But the bigger issues would have to be faced at some point, probably in the spring - sooner if Sari were with child quickly.

The clan would insist on the wedding before the birth of any child. Steeped as they were in some of the Catholic beliefs, they would all have to make things legitimate in the eyes of the church or his father's relationship with his clerical friends would be compromised. In their eyes at least. Of course, this could all be remedied if Sari and Ronan left immediately for France. But this was looking less and less likely. They were enjoying their special secret and their frolics in the heather too much to ponder the arduous journey in the depths of winter. France could wait. They could all wait. For the moment it was Ronan and Sari on their own terms, celebrating their mutual love and its marvelous expression.

Sari had hinted that she had to go through with any gestation they might be blessed with. Ronan was not about to take precautions with

274

their intimacy. They were both all in, so it was natural to joke about a "happy accident." The thought of a child always made them smile, and Sari could not express a wish for any delay. She already sensed it was so. Even though there were herbs she could take to end a baby's viability. She could not possibly contemplate this. She knew that she had to drop stronger hints to Ronan about what he had signed up for. At whatever time they were blessed with a child, she *had* to see it through. Ronan understood this much when they talked in general terms about their future together.

About three months into the pregnancy she started to show. So slight was her frame that her thick wool clothes could only conceal the truth for so long. Besides her levels of intimacy with Ronan had not abated. He would soon notice. She decided to wait for that moment. Most days they celebrated their union. On the moors. On the beach amongst the dunes. In the cold sea. In the slightly warmer lake. At the top of a hillock. In the arms of the heather. There were no limits to their backdrop. Sheep often came upon them bodies intertwined. Their bemused looks were not enough to stop the sideways munching of their grazing.

All part of nature's rich cycle would doubtless have been the thoughts in their heads, if only they had them. Their nonchalance and non-action said the same thing anyway.

Sari and Ronan were happy amongst the animals, exploring their creative inclinations and the surging passion between them. The shared energy was empowering them both in different ways. Ronan had never felt so vital and alive. He received a huge healing every time they touched and kissed.

A doctor should probably prescribe this treatment, he smiled to himself.

He would not have dreamt of sharing such a thought with his wife. She doubtless would have laughed. But he did not want to offend her sensibilities. He did not yet know the great extent of her humour and guttural bawdiness. She had a wicked twisted thought process at times.

Ronan had only glimpsed this and did not quite believe his ears. He decided to give it the benefit of the doubt, but he suspected it was in there somewhere. He just was not going to test it in intimate conflagrations.

Sari for her part felt loved, nurtured, protected, grounded and secure. She could lie back in Ronan's arms and feel invincible. Nothing could touch her while he was there for her. Independent though she was, she loved having Ronan as an energy buffer. There was something amazing about his energy that served her in so many ways. Their intimacy she craved. She could not get enough of him. Even though she knew she was already with child she did not have a problem with their physicality. She knew it was safe. This was their time. She did not want to faze Ronan by pointing out her small rising swelling bump too quickly. It was only a matter of time before he noticed anyway, so attentive was he to her every curve and flow.

Their honeymoon phase was rigorous and adventurous. So glad were they to have this time. A horseback ride down through France or a turbulent sea voyage seemed to be a world away from their reality for the time being.

"Sari?" Ronan gestured to the gentle swell in her belly as they lay in the stable once again. A man of few words in slightly awkward situations, Ronan looked a strange mixture of delighted and scared.

"AH!"

"Yes! It seems to be the case. I was waiting for you to notice as I was not sure if the seed would stay growing. I did not want to excite then disappoint!"

"Ah!" Said Ronan in a strange limp echo of her feigned surprise. If he were being honest to himself and to her, he had also known. Or at least suspected. Now there was no denying it to each other, nor to themselves. They both knew they had to see it through. This commitment was underlying and certain. It did not need to be discussed.

"There is something else I need to tell you. Something complicated and mysterious!"

"Of course!" Ronan already knew she held secrets and seems pleased she was eager to share some of it with her at last. He had seen her magic and her work. He knew there was more. That there much be some explanation for it all.

"Yes. This is difficult because we do not know everything. Only small parts of the truth. One part of the secret is that I am a descendent of Mary Magdalene!"

Ronan took a moment to take this in. The Catholic sentiments and leaning within the clan would have fun with this if it ever came out.

It must not! He thought to himself. They would either dismiss her as delusional or a heretic or both. It did not bode well.

Sari read the concern in his furrowed brow. She reassured him.

"Yes. Well you have seen me work. This mystical legacy is what bestows these gifts upon me. It is both a dangerous and blessed position to be in."

"I understand. I have seen the mysteries of your work and the miraculous results. If the Catholic Church were to embrace you, you would doubtless be sainted."

"Perhaps! But the problem is, these truths go against the grain of what the church believes is possible. You must keep all of this to yourself Ronan! I have never spoken of it before. Not with anyone, except of course those in the mother line. Sheena knows. My mother Magda knew, and told me all that she could."

"Yes, as father of this baby, I do need to understand. As your husband, I would like to know everything you are can tell me. I want to help and support you"

"There is a lot to this Ronan!" Sari said somewhat gravely. "A heavy burden to bear at times. I also think it is why we need to go to France. There is some link between my lineage and The Cathars of *Montségur*. They are in danger and hold manifestations of the secrets, possibly Christ's Chalice, as well as some other important artefacts from The Holy Land. The Templars have infiltrated the ranks of The Catholic Church. Some are dedicating themselves to finding and destroying The Truth. While others are keen to preserve it. These bear a hidden loyalty to the lineage. They are the true warriors of Christ. We probably must help them. The trouble will be in knowing whom we can trust when we get there."

"Our child will be born into this lineage. It usually runs through the mother lines, though sometimes the energy can infiltrate through a male also. I have often suspected that Frederick is also linked. He and Magda seemed to carry equally matched energy. As do you and I."

In the run up to the birthing time, Sari had assured him all should be well. Yes, she had seen some difficult births. But Sheena was very experienced too. They would get through it fine. Famous. Last. Words.

Sari kept working up a sweat, and as soon as they sponged her down, the chills descended. Her temperature gauge was all over the place. She drifted in and out of a reverie. One minute, she was laughing hysterically to herself. In the next she was writhing and screaming in pain. A potent herb concoction mixed by Sheena sedated her and took the edge of most of it. But the waves came in surges. The pain increasing with each flow. As the peaks intensified, Sheena administered more drops into her mouth, looking increasingly concerned.

I really must get that recipe! Sari had thought as she sunk into the next pleasant stupor. But each time it wore off quickly. This was far worse than she had anticipated. Having witnessed and attend a few births on her rounds, Sari thought she had the measure of what was required. She thought she could handle it effortlessly, and rather wanted Ronan to *not* be there, so that she could present his newly bathed daughter, looking sublime and radiant leaning back in the bed with a smile on her face.

The best intentions indeed!

Serena was coming into the world with a big loud bang.

Quite a force of nature! Sari concluded as she braced herself for another contraction. She was struggling to contain this primal energy. Serena must be powerful indeed. If she could thus incapacitate her mother, she would be formidable in her mission also.

Sari was strong. But the birthing experience was not agreeing with her. She began to fear it could go horribly wrong. An inner panic surged as her temperature soared and her contractions gained momentum. She gasped for air. She could not breathe properly.

Just like her grandmother who had died birthing Magda.

Sari did not feel she would have the same fate. But she had written her daughter a letter, as had all their mothers before them. The secrets of the lineage had to be handed down, and death in childbirth was common. All precautions were always adhered to. There was usually a stray aunt or two, sisters of the deceased who would come forward with the letters should they be required. Sheena had her letter set aside. There was also the letter that her grandmother had left Magda. Tradition allowed that the letters be passed down at the discretion of the keepers. A comprehensive catalogue of experience grew, recorded for posterity and the benefit of *The Sangreal*. Presuming the papers did not disintegrate there should be in time quite a record of what it was like to be indoctrinated in the Magdalene lineage.

Sari sometimes wondered how many such letters were out there. Were the secrets passed down orally? She knew that they were. But the written track meant that at some point one of these tomes would fall into the wrong hands. This made her nervous, especially for those in France. She prayed it would not be needed. Ronan did not know about this custom. He would have baulked even more if he had.

Famous. Last. Thoughts?

It is not supposed to end like this!

I must get to France!

All the things she had not done but felt she needed to do suddenly surged through her system. She had only just started on her life with Ronan. Surely this baby was not going to take her out in her prime. She had saved many a life where women were on the brink in childbirth. But she could not intervene on her own behalf here. She had to trust Sheena to deliver her as well as the baby.

CHAPTER THIRTY-SIX
The Letter

ear Serena, If you are reading this letter or having it read to you, I am in the other world. I am your mother Sari. Your earthly mother, my Aunt Sheena, will likely be reading this to you if you are still young. She will know the right time to share it with you. I am going to allow your father Ronan to read it first. Within a few days of my passing Sheena will show it to him. I only just began to explain to him what I now explain to you. So, he will also need to understand more about his wife and his daughter.

These words will still not be enough Dear Ronan I know. But I hope they will enable you to fully understand your daughter and the importance of her lineage. Know that I am with you both daily. You will feel me close by. I will send you signs. There will be no doubt for you that I am always by your side and in your heart. I love both of you with all my heart.

Serena will tell you more about your gifts and your blood line as you grow. Your father too will school you in the virtues of his clan. Clann Ruaidhri will welcome you into the bosom of the family and you will always be safe under the guidance of your father and his ancestors. They will school you in the matters of the world, with so much wisdom that I do not possess.

On your mother's side there is much to know. A different kind of wisdom runs in our veins. You are of the Mary Magdalene lineage. Your skills and healing abilities have been passed down from generation to generation. You can embrace these as quickly or as slowly as you like. You will find they are second nature to you anyway. I really did not have to be taught much. Mother Nature herself taught me just about everything I needed to know. I do believe that you will naturally evolve and find your own way of working with it all.

Please call Sheena "Grand Mamma!" You will largely live with her and your older brothers. Your father may remarry with my complete blessing and if he does, you will then spend more time with him and his new wife at The Castle. You can expect to spend time in both families. There is a lot you will learn. Sheena will know best how to guide you and at what pace to unfold the skills of working with herbs and reading the weather patterns. There is so much excitement in working with Mother Nature, but it all comes at a price. Please never take it lightly or abuse it in anyway. I know you will not. But as you can imagine there are temptations that come along with being powerful. It is important to keep a measure of humility. No one likes an all-knowing wise woman. You may find that you do know everything, or many things. The mistakes come where you tell everyone that you do. They come to have high expectations and then will look to trip you up. It is much better to keep your mouth shut. Let it all come to you. The Spirit people will clearly show you those you can help. The last thing you should ever do is go looking for work. Never impose your energy on anyone. It is helpful to have a certain reluctance to use the skills. Then you will know when they are really needed.

There are some difficulties that come along with our lineage. The mention of The Mary Line evokes powerful reaction, especially in ecclesiastical peoples, or those with a strong Catholic faith. You will find that people treat you with suspicion until you proof your worth. You will be watched and monitored. It is important to keep things simple. Know who you are and what you can do and never inflict it on anyone. This is not a performance art. It is gravely serious. It comes at a price. There are lessons, reprimands, and tests along the way. You will be shown these things when the time comes. You will know. Keep some detachment and breathe your way through the

282

difficulties. This is not something to be afraid of. But it is something to be careful of.

Remember you do not have to prove anything, only to yourself and to God, and probably sometimes to your father!

Learn and grow at your own pace. You will start to know what your own unique mission is. It may be that you remain in Moidart and treat the community with your healing skills as I did. You will be kept by the community and never want for anything if this is what you choose. You may want to live with your father at Castle Tioram. There is much of an earthly nature that you will see there. Your father will school you in it all.

Let me explain The Mary Magdalene Lineage to you very simply. There is a suppressed school of thought which believes our Saviour Jesus Christ married and loved a lady called Mary Magdalene. She was in fact one of his best loved disciples. Her closeness to Christ made the other disciples a little jealous. In the Gospels of Mary, it is claimed that Christ "kissed her" and "favoured her." It is said that they had a child together and that she was called Sarah.

We know that Mary Magdalene was his beloved wife. She probably had at least one child with him before his death. Along with the other disciples, she was assigned the task of continuing Jesus' church on earth after his crucifixion.

It was the three Mary's who found Christ to be missing from his tomb on the third day after his murder on The Cross. The early Christians were persecuted much like the modern day Cathars. You will hear more about The Cathars from your father, all being well.

Your father and I were planning a journey to France to help the cause of The Cathars. If you are reading this to yourself at an older age it means at least one of us survived, and that I survived birthing you.

You will at some point read this letter. I just hope it is not too quickly. I would love to explain all of this to you myself. But please if something happens to me in childbirth, do not feel guilty. My beloved grandmother passed giving birth to Magda my mother, your grandmother. Women have many burdens to bear and childbirth is not an easy thing to achieve without mishap.

You will hopefully know your grandfather Frederick, at least in your early years.

He may not have much time left. But if you did not talk to him or understand him, know that he loved you and held you as often as he could when you were a baby. He will also look after you on the earthly plane and then on the other side when his time comes. Which I fear it will soon.

I did not expect to pass before Frederick. But sometimes childbirth can be so hazardous and unexpected even for young healthy women. Things happen which we do not anticipate. So please do not feel sad if this has happened to your mother. I have achieved a big part of my obligation by bringing you into the world. Sometimes us women are vessels for a grander task, and although I would have loved more time with your father and Frederick, I would have to accept my fate. Everything happens for a reason. Do remember this always. You are a much-loved daughter and I will always be your mother, and your father's beloved wife. We loved each other with a passion. We will always have this love between us. May you find such a love. For this is what makes life truly joyous and worthwhile. Some personal happiness is a true treasure. I pray you find your heart as well as complete your contracts and missions.

More on the legacy - During the persecutions of the early Christians, the three Marys escaped by boat to Gaul (France) with Lazarus and Sarah. Mary Salome was the mother of the Apostles John and James. Mary Jacobe tended to The Christ at his funeral, as did Joseph of Arimathea.

The Mary's were the first three people to see the risen Christ, who assigned them with the task of spreading the word.

He is risen!

Their boat washed ashore at Saintes-Maries-de-la-Mer. Saint Sarah who, some believe travelled with them was a servant of Mary Jacobe. Others thought she was of noble birth and was on the shore guiding them to safety. What we know about 'Black Sarah' as she was known is that she held secrets. She knew things, just as you will know things. Just as I know things.

Patron saint of gypsies Sarah was a seer of extraordinary ability. In a vision, she was shown that the Saints who had been present at the death of Jesus would come, and that she had a mission to help them. She saw rough seas and a boat floundering in the waves. She had to be alert and watch for this moment.

284

Legend has it that Mary Salome's cloak was strong enough to be used as a raft. Sarah was there waiting to help them all ashore with prayer and her special ability to calm the seas. When I first heard these legends, I was confused. I did not understand where The Lineage came from.

Was it to do with the Gypsy Sarah? Black Sarah? She had our skills of seership, healing ability, and a strong connection to nature. But we were not sure how she could be connected to Christ's Lineage. She could not have been. It was another Sarah, birthed by Mary Magdalene who became the first of The Grail Sisters. The first of Christ's children. The only one we think.

Mary Magdalene was The Holy Grail. The one who contained the power and secrets of the early church, powered by her connection to Christ our Saviour.

You will learn that The Catholic Church has spent hundreds of years trying to destroy all the evidence and accounts of these legends. It has only very recently been persecuting The Cathars, who they suspect still hold some of the secrets. It was these I believe I was meant to retrieve and hide in France. This was a dangerous mission your father and I planned. He does not yet know what I knew I had to do. I did not manage to share that with him yet. I was going to share it all with him on our journey over there.

When we married, we wanted to enjoy each other, and we were looking forward to enjoying you together very much. It would have been such a joy to nurture and hold you when young, and to teach and encourage you as you grew and blossomed. Your father and I decided to concentrate on what was important to us for a time. To savour the joy in finding each other and to look forward to the birth of our child. I did not forget the mission I had felt coming for a long time. But your conception meant that once again the journey to France was delayed. We tried to halt it altogether. But I could not deny that it was something I still had to do. Obviously if you are reading this at an early age, I never got to France. Perhaps your father managed to. He and Frederick will have much to discuss on all of this. They will also have this letter and I give them permission to read it before you do. It will enable them to help you more, and to understand me more.

If I am now in the other world, I do not know what will have become of the treasures I felt compelled to retrieve. There is an onslaught planned on Montségur, your father and Frederick will hear of it very soon I believe. The Church and The Crusades have been hunting treasure whilst murdering mangy hundreds and thousands of innocents. They especially want to get their hands on all the copies of Mary's Gospel. The Vatican is nervous of these heresies. The male dominated church will not acknowledge powerful women, women like us who heal and know and see.

You will have to be very secretive about your skills Serena and about your true nature. It is better not to tell anybody at all. Hold it in your heart and go out into the world doing as best you can. People will still find something intriguing about you. You will strike them as different. Like you are aloof and know something they do not. Well that is because you DO!

The Magdalene Line is of course the blood line of the ancestors of Christ. Legend has it that some of them married into the French Royal family, and that The Lineage is now spread out across Europe. This may indeed be true. We only know about our part in the story. Potentially there could be a few lines expanding outwards into obscurity. Interbreeding will have thinned the more tenuous ancestral links. But there is a core lineage which we believe we are part of. We at least are conscious of it.

Mary Magdalene remarried with Jesus' brother whom he had asked to care for her. More children came and they spread their energy through the South of France down through various generations. Some of these ancestors came to Britain. One branch of the family came up to Scotland. The lines we are linked to landed first in Somerset England in a place called Glastonbury. The Vale of Avalon is steeped in the legends of The Grail. The resting place of King Arthur and his wife Guinevere is in The Abbey, a place run by monks who are keen to hype the associations with Kind Arthur. A large coffin was found containing a giant of a man and his beloved wife, and a third relative of Arthur's called Mordred. Some people doubt the legitimacy of this discovery. Personally, I sense that it is true. This is where Arthur resides. It is quite possible The Holy Chalice is hidden somewhere in the environs of The Abbey. I suspect that it is.

We are the embodiment of The Holy Grail line. The Sangreal, the royal blood line. But the original vessel also did exist. The goblet which Christ held at The Last

286

supper, if it has not disintegrated by now, is an important artefact. What people do not understand is that this is a relic. Joseph of Arimathea caught the drops of Christs' blood from the cross in this chalice, and it is said he brought it with him on the boat., I am quite sure that he did, and that he quite possibly offloaded it in the sacred place which is Avalon. This physical vessel is not as important as the blood line itself. But it is the false treasure all The Crusaders seek. A church relic that would have importance if found. But in the meantime, they are missing the point entirely. They miss what is hidden in plain sight. The True Holy Grail is you! It is me! It was Magda. This is the blessed burden with which you are now laden – The Holy Sacred blood line of Mary Magdalene.

Your Loving Mother, Sari...

CHAPTER THIRTY-SEVEN
The Wedding

S ari could see the tears pricking behind Ronan's eyes as he read the letter intended for their daughter. She was exhausted after the delivery and did not feel able to explain all that she had started to explain to him about their daughter's legacy. She figured he could ask her questions when they were both ready, so long as he understood the fundamental truths. She knew he already understood a lot. But felt it was right that he had more detail of the background, and some indication of why they all believed these things to be true. He also knew he was in a privileged position. The Sisters of The Grail did not usually share as much with their menfolk, preferring to let them witness and wonder.

Ronan looked up at them both when he had finished. The scene warmed his heart. There was Sari nursing the baby by the hearth. Sheena had been baking bread and a wonderful smell pervaded her humble dwelling. Serena had been sleeping soundly but had awoken for a feed whilst he was reading. He loved to gaze on the two closest to his heart. He felt complete. But also worried.

"I hope we can raise her to bear all this as well as you have done Sari!" he said with a sigh.

"We surely will. So much of it comes naturally. This has always been the way."

"I had no idea you could write so eloquently. There is some skill in the way you tell a story."

"Why thank you darling!" Sari retorted with a wry smile. "I guess I am still full of surprises. That can only be a good thing I think!"

"What are we going to do about my father now? I mean it worked to keep you in hiding for a while. But perhaps it would have been easier to show him while you were still with child? Now he is a grandfather and does not even know. Probably he would have insisted you move into Tioram. He will just assume you are lost in France unless word already got to him."

"I had to be with Sheena for the birth though darling. I think he would have insisted on the local doctor and I would not have born that well. In fact, he may have killed me. Look how close it went. Only Sheena could have pulled me back from the brink like that and delivered Serena safely."

"Right as usual I concede! But you know he will organize quite the wedding once he knows and we visit him to show him his grandchild. Which I think we should do soon. I do not want to risk more of his wrath than we already have. I was able to keep him happy and distracted by doing his assigned tasks through the winter. But I could see at times he wondered why I was being so compliant. He smells some trickery I swear!"

"Well, that is all as it should be. It was important to not stress everyone. To deliver Serena safely and to then rest up and plan France!"

Ronan looked at Sari incredulously. "You are still thinking of

289

France? With all you say in this letter and the dangers involved?"

"You have just given birth. You nearly died! We will have to work it out. But I do not think we can justify leaving before the end of the summer. Serena will need you for at least that long and we cannot just leave her."

"Well the sooner we go. The sooner we will return. I do still have an obligation to fulfill. But I will see what the inner guidance is. I need to hear the right messages about this, and it will take a few weeks especially as I am so tired now."

Ronan knew he was going to have to get used to these announcements. He now had the responsibility for two females of this sacred line. He would always have to "wait on the messages!" he figured.

That may take some adjustment!

Reginald had certainly been suspicious of his son's compliance on his return from Eilean Donan. He had noted that he immediately rode out to see Sari after their awkward debrief. Everyone had heard of the return of Sari and Frederick, so he suspected Ronan had been told when he saw him jump on his horse and flee The Castle without even stopping for sustenance.

Only love has that lure! Reginald smiled to himself. For all his devious intentions, he did have a heart. He that figured if something was meant to be the obstacles and challenges only served to fuel the passion and determination. But he also assumed that Sari and Frederick would be on their way again soon enough. From Ronan's original pleas to accompany her, Reginald had gathered that she had to get there and was committed to doing so. Admittedly he was worried that his son Ronan would be gallant and accompany her with a view to making a point. But he decided not to broach the subject. For weeks and months, he observed Ronan's comings and goings and said nothing more. He knew something must be consolidating but seeing as it was not right under his nose, he let it be.

Out of sight out of mind.

Despite Ronan's secretive behaviour, Reginald could see not real cause for concern. He knew that if any matter needed to be dealt with, it would raise its head soon enough. He did not need to go fishing for problems that were not even presenting. He was returning to The Castle some nights. The other nights he concluded he could be with Sari. But he was always vague when questioned about his plans, about her plans. At least he was doing his work during the day, and he was okay with him slipping out at night, even if he had announced he would stay.

So be it, he concluded.

After the obvious manipulation and the retrieval of his precious "goblets," Reginald knew he was on thin ice with his son. He figured that at least he had not gone immediately to France with Sari. He justified his going to see her right away as rightful response to the ordeal he had just completed. He knew that Ronan was angry with him and he decided to accept it and give him some extra freedoms. But he was also not stupid, and he knew logically that Ronan and Sari could be hatching a plan for the following spring. For the moment, the winter was fast descending and Ronan's chores and business were being done with more ease than usual.

What was not to like?

Sari buttoned up her wool coat securely at her neck. She looked fulsome in the wool outfit, as if she had sprouted extra curves at her bosom. Ronan smiled at her concealment of the baby for the journey to Castle Tioram.

"Well as long as she can breathe in there. It is more than I can do!" Ronan quipped.

Sari blushed. He could still make her colour-up with his intense gaze and attentions.

"Ronan! Really. She is safe and snug. That is what matters. We can see how you get on in there later!"

Sari was not one to let a witty retort pass her by. She liked to keep Ronan interested. They had the baby now. But she was still determined to prioritize their love and passion whenever she could. In some ways she saw Serena as a duty. She loved and adored her as her own. She *was* her own of course. But in another way, she was not. Serena had been gifted to them for a Divine purpose. She was their responsibility, and they had to ensure her safety and correct development in line with her heritage. Sari was aware this was a potential burden for Ronan, much as he adored his daughter. It was a lot to ask of him. He would now have to listen attentively to the whims of two females who at times may threaten to overrule his masculinity. The final word in this home came from the heavens not the "man of the house."

Sari was nervous heading up to Castle Tioram with Ronan unannounced. She knew they may have to stay a night or two, so brought extra provisions with her. But equally she could not be assured they would be welcome either. Reginald could be quite unpredictable she knew. She did not find him easy to read or predict. So, she was not going to assume that their news would be welcomed. Serena was a delight to behold and Sari had intuited that they should wait until she was a few weeks old before broaching the subject of Tioram. It was their final hurdle. How this went could shape their future together. There would either be a wedding, a banishment or some odious stasis between Ronan and his father that could simmer on for years. She did not want to be the cause of resentment between them. Reginald may well blame her for the current "situation."

How could he not be delighted with Serena? She reflected. She was also sure that if he had a reason to "not be," he would find it and nurture it and make their lives difficult indeed.

"Let me do all the talking and explaining Sari." Ronan explained as they neared the gates. Sari had found a way to comfortably ride

Delphine whilst cradling her baby under her coats. This was so doable she wondered if they could reach France this way. But she kept that thought to herself for the moment.

Ronan and Sari had concluded that it was best to just present Reginald with his grandchild and take it from there. They were announcing that they had done the handfasting ceremony very soon after Ronan's return from the north. They did not want him passing judgement on their morals or decisions. So, needed him to know that they had approached the whole thing with a modicum of responsibility. They were man and wife in God's eyes already. But with no rings. Just a ribbon.

This handsome trio were a walking fait accompli and there was not much Reginald could do about it. Ronan knew his father well. He knew he did not like sneaky dishonourable behaviour. The handfasting went very much in their favour. He would just be annoyed at having been excluded. He also knew that Reginald would take this on the chin as due punishment for the farcical trip to *Eilean Donan* that he had made his son endure. The wheel had come full circle. The karma was complete. There was not much more he could do than *be* delighted in Serena!

Sari and Ronan were asked to wait outside Reginald's meeting room. His "throne room" as Ronan and his siblings jokingly called it. Reginald really was "King of his castle," and literally did have a chair resembling a throne. All clan meetings took place in this room, and when guests were announced Reginald would make them wait outside a while before inviting them in for a formal audience. He would "hold court" just like a king. Well he was a Highland Chieftain and King of sorts. His ego demanded this bit of respect.

"Hello father!" Ronan announced as the three of them were shuffled into the room. Reginald had been expecting his son, but not Sari. They had asked for her presence to be kept as a surprise motioning to the baby. The doorman had been so intrigued and delighted that he agreed. Probably he would be reprimanded later. But it was worth it to see the look on his master's face.

Sari said nothing immediately. She was rather overwhelmed at the grandeur of the clan room. The wood panelling, the shields, swords, and chainmail armoury on the walls. She had not been aware the clans had such weaponry. There were also two helmets mounted in pride of place which she knew must be from the French who were more advanced with their protections.

Probably acquired on some raid, she mused. The items seemed to be displayed as proud trophies rather than intended for practical use.

Would make a refreshing change from the yellow horse urine-stained tunics the warriors usually wore!

It all smelt musty and dusty in what passed as Tioram's "Great Hall." But it was undeniably a grand setting for their momentous meeting with the chief of *Clann Ruaidhri!*

Sari and Ronan stopped midway between the door and Reginald's special chair so that he could not quite see who she was. Though he would doubtless make an intelligent guess, there were also plenty of fair Highland lasses she could have been. Reginald's eyesight was failing in recent years, and he would have to gesture them to come forward. That put the power in his hands in at least in one respect. Ronan had briefed her on this, and she was rather impressed with his psychology.

Sure enough, Reginald gestured Sari to come forward. He knew who the woman must be, but he did want to gaze on her fair countenance, and she needed to take that hood off her face too. Ronan could smell that his father was in a congenial mood which would help. Sari was able to work out much the same thing with her honed intuition. She responded to Reginald's beckoning gesture and moved confidently forward, boldly but respectfully, motioning for him to look at the "gift" she brought.

"May I present you with your grandchild, Sire!" She knelt before him holding Serena, as she was not going to put the baby onto his lap without first seeing his response.

That is my love, thought Ronan. *She always knows what to do.*

Reginald's face was a picture. The whole range of emotions seemed to flash through his energy field as if he were deciding which one to present first. Sari scanned them all, seeing initial anger, quickly followed by bewilderment, confusion, interest, amusement and finally delight! It was quite an amazing feat to display the whole range of human emotion thus within a minute.

Surely, he would have made a good actor! thought Sari.

"AH!" said Reginald, much as Ronan had done on hearing the same news.

Truly he was in some ways his father's son! Observed Sari.

"We thought it best to wait father." Ronan began what Sari thought might be a lengthy process of "conditioning."

"Sari's mother had such trouble with birthing her family, that we did not want to raise hopes only to have them dashed. As it was, Sari nearly died during the ordeal. It was only Sheena's timely interventions which saved her."

Sari marvelled at the utter brilliance of Ronan's sentence. It was all in there. There was no need to explain further.

Reginald must surely be a monster if he reacted badly to this. If he were, she did not want to know him anyway, and he certainly would not be part of her daughter's life if he were to show even a hint of resentment towards her.

As it was Reginald's face softened, and Sari swore she saw a tear pricking behind his eyes. He clearly was emotional and stirred in a positive way by Serena's lovely disposition. She looked much like Sari had as a baby. The blue eyes, the fulsome lips, and the delicious engaging smile. They had studiously waited for her eyes to fully open before showing Reginald, so that she could engage him in that way too. She needed to make her own connection with her grandfather.

Sari was relieved and so glad at how this was going. With minimal words and gestures, Reginald seem to have pieced the puzzle together. She was sure there would be questions and concerns. But she did not quite expect what blurted out of his mouth first.

"Why there must be a wedding! A Christening and a wedding! Let us plan it immediately!"

Ronan took a breath.

"Yes father. I anticipated that if you favoured the child you might say this. But you know we are already handfasted. We *are* married in the eyes of God. This is a legitimate child. We pledged to each other fully on the morning after my return from *Eilean Donan."*

"Ah!" said Reginald again as the more awkward pieces of the puzzle started registering with his consciousness. He knew what that all meant, but there was not much he could now do.

Onwards and upwards! Truly, he *was* filled with joy at his bonnie grandchild.

"Yes! Yes! But there must still be a clan wedding. This is a grand cause for celebration for us all! Share your happiness with The Clann Ronan!" Reginald exclaimed giving his son a rather too rigorous slap on the back.

Okay if that is the worst he can come up with - then we are resolved on this. Accepted! All good!

Sari read his mind, the glanced at each other and smiled. It was obvious this would now be the way of it. Sari dared flicker a thought that they could probably even leave promptly for France if they wanted to.

They decided to indulge Reginald's inclinations. They were also quite keen to officially announce themselves to the community and The Castle after months of hiding and being secretive.

"So be it!" said Ronan.

"We would be honoured to marry again for the sake of the clan and to formally celebrate our love!"

"Absolutely!" Declared Sari, as she moved forward to kiss Reginald on the cheek and he bashfully accepted the gesture.

So as the May blossom filled the air with what would become an evocative scent thereafter, Ronan and Sari were married from Castle Tioram. In her hair Sari wore their handfasted ribbon, as she had always done. Her gown was amongst the dusty dresses left by Reginald's mother. She found a lengthy cream-coloured tunic dress that fulfilled her desire for modesty and elegance. Its high neck and sensuously wasted flow draped into a beautiful train in the shape of a mermaid's tail. There was exquisite rare Belgique lace work around the wrists and along the bodice lines. Sari loved the association with the sea. The gown was more than adequate for a girl of modest means. Ronan matched her well with a pale blue tunic gown worn by his grandfather that covered him from head to toe. Sari smiled quizzically when she saw him, whilst he was too mesmerized by his translucent bride to catch her mischief.

"You bewitch me Sari!" He whispered to her as he took her hand.

Sari twinkled her eyes in response as she was not quite sure she could say "likewise" with Ronan in that outfit.

The simple sturdy gold rings were organized for them by Reginald. The two bands of generous width inscribed with the words *Ava Maria Gracia Plena (hail Mary Full of Grace),* were duly placed on each other's right hand.

Bonded.

Handfasted.

Now bedecked with gold and the blessings of The Clann and all the Holy Mary's.

I will be creative with the Mary's! mused Sari. She was grateful for the generous gestures from her newly acquired father-in-law. The rings had been in the family for a couple of generations and his own grandmother used them for her wedding nuptials. Sari was joyful that Ronan's childhood faith and heritage were thus honoured. Somehow without much planning the wedding paraphernalia matched and merged their energies. The dress, the ceremony, the rings, and Ronan's intriguing robe symbolized their union. "Mary" was highly relevant to both. Just for different reasons.

It could not be more perfect really. Sari graciously gave over their day and allowed it all. It was not as unbearable or overwhelming as she had feared.

The wedding fayre was simple yet sumptuous. Spring lamb, highland deer caught by Ronan in the previous hunting season, fresh salmon from the nearby rivers, and wild Scottish raspberries from the hills behind The Castle. They had not wanted much fuss. But Reginald insisted on a banquet as well as a small private ceremony in The Castle's chapel. Serena was baptized at the same time. Sari had thought long and hard about this, but she did not want to broach awkward theologies or impose any pagan perspectives, on what should be a joyous day. They had done this their way for the important part. It was now their turn to be gracious.

Serena's ceremony was a simple blessing with her parents standing by as both Reginald and Frederick signed their granddaughter with the cross on her forehead. The Holy Water had made her gurgle just a little, and Sari was just thankful she did not cry. Thus, they were all unified in the sight of God with both The Clann and The Mary Line. Not so long ago, Sari would have thought this impossible. But there is was. It happened. All in accord. All at peace.

Sari was indeed content. She now had a grand home secured for herself and Serena, a handsome, wise husband, who had artfully mastered his father and shown his credentials as a future clan leader. It was apparent that Reginald had a new-found pride and respect for his son. Ronan had followed his heart and done things in the right way - *for him*. He had been effective in using his father's agendas against him, and that inspired Reginald's approval.

Leadership qualities at last! He thought as Ronan paraded his bride out of the small exquisite chapel to the dining hall. Sari was less intimidated by The Castle now and she was happy to be welcomed into the fold. She had been impressed with Reginald's behaviour in the end. He was almost gracious in defeat. It seemed that he would indeed make a doting grandfather for Serena. Sari was flattered and honoured by his quick acceptance of her. It was as if a part of him recognized that they were all connected. He perhaps sensed that the inevitable was always going to happen. There were only so many roadblocks and obstacles he could use to test his son's intentions, and he had clearly used up his full quotient.

Frail though Frederick was, he had been able to muster enough energy to hobble Sari up the aisle to Ronan. He handed his daughter to the handsome groom with supreme pride, knowing that is final task was accomplished.

Will not be long now Magda! Frederick sent a telepathic note to his deceased wife, as he found the task enormous and truly beyond his capabilities. Lately he had been almost *asking* The Lord to take him in sleep, so world weary was he. He really wanted to see Magda again and experience eternal rest. He had rallied for as long as possible knowing of Sari's condition. Seeing his first grandchild was important to him. He wanted to hold Serena and know that all was well before he shook off this mortal coil. Borrowed time had been his for so long now, that he was almost taking it for granted. Odds had been defied by sheer will power and magical healings from Sheena and Sari. But his time was nigh.

Sure enough, he drifted off peacefully that night in one of the tower rooms of Tioram. He never saw the sun arise from behind the mainland mountains. Cast adrift with the hightide, The Castle was his last stand. No need to be washed ashore again. By the time the tide was low enough for them all to leave, he would be in the other world with his darling wife. Frederick was happy not to awake from that comfortable bed and he fell asleep with the serenest smile upon his face. His family had arrived. They would be happy and secure. His work was done.

Rest in Peace Frederick.

CHAPTER THIRTY-EIGHT

The Burial

Sari was consumed with grief at her father's passing. The day had been so long coming that they had all started to take it for granted that it might never happen. Perhaps he was eternal. She had pondered this possibility many times. He defied the odds so long and so consistently, that it really looked like he would never leave them. In one way he never would – she knew that. She could see how Frederick had struggled since their aborted journey to France. On their return he had languished for many days in a stupor, barely registering the joy of Sari and Ronan. It already looked as if he were between the worlds. But as always, he rallied in a random moment and was ready for some hearty stew and some of Sheena's freshly baked bread. His rosy cheeks and twinkly eyes had returned, and that belly laugh she loved so much was performing at full volume.

He had rallied for her sake she felt. He took delight in the union of her and Ronan once he had processed and registered what had been going on. He had given his paternal blessing long before Reginald and approved the plan to delay telling the community at Tioram. He remembered only too well the struggles Magda had had with the birthing of her son.

While they knew that Sari's first born was likely to be a girl, one could never quite be sure until the baby arrived. Even "seers" have an intermittent problem with the genders of children, especially their own. Sometimes the energy of a child on the ethers showed as the opposite of their human form. It was a curious phenomenon Sari had noted a few times. Frederick also remembered his own conviction that Sari had been a boy whilst in her mother's womb. Projection yes, but he had sensed the strong energy and was quite sure she *was* a boy. Pure projection as it turned out.

His delight was complete at Sari's news, and he could witness Ronan proving to be a loving husband and great support to his daughter. Their union was everything he had hoped for. But his huge incentive now was to hang on to meet his grandchild. Nothing would bring him greater joy.

Frederick was buried from Tioram. A simple service was held in the chapel which only a week previously witnessed the celebratory nuptials of Sari and Ronan. The stout but ornate coffin which had in fact been designed for Reginald, gave Frederick the grand recognition he truly deserved. Again, The Clann excelled itself in its attentive generosity.

"Are you sure Sir?" Sari had queried Reginald's decision when Ronan told her the origin of the coffin.

"Absolutely. I can get another one made. This was made for a grand leader. Your father earned this in many ways," Reginald reassured her, not realizing that his comment might be construed to be less than modest, as well as magnanimous. The point was the gesture.

Very generous, pondered Sari.

Reginald was honoured to look after a man he had really liked, who was now also family, if only by a day or two.

Well longer if you count the "Handfasting." He recalled.

Not that this provision for the extension of his family needed any justification, Reginald was only too pleased to do the honours. He was finding solace in being the great provider. It felt better to him these days. It was also clear that Ronan needed to see demonstrations of trust and acceptance of his new bride and child. The sad passing of Frederick enabled him to compensate for at least some of their past tensions. What is more, he very much liked Sari, and wished to make her feel welcome. Her father had died on his watch and he felt duty bound to do the right thing,

Reginald had already decided not to pry too much into Sari's work, reasoning that as a young mother she may not have much time for it anyway. A healer living within The Castle walls could not be a bad thing and he knew she would be discrete in the company of clerics. He had seen her handle them before. Reginald was satisfied that his dignity was not going to be compromised any more than it had been, so he saw the christening, wedding, and burial as a chance to make amends.

Stricken with grief at her beloved father's passing as she was. Sari did manage to also feel gratitude at the way they were all being provided for. She knew Frederick had been ready to depart the world for a long time. She would not dream of holding it against him that he chose her wedding night as an opportunity for a swift exit. She understood his reasoning. As usual Frederick's timing was designed to make a point. She trusted his vision and could see in his peaceful countenance that it made complete sense to him.

Probably his way of softening the blow, Sari thought. Frederick knew his passing would hit her hard, and even though it had been a long time coming, he knew the reality would still be traumatic, such was their bond. He always knew what to do and when to do it. Obviously, he felt complete and content that she was now secure and provided for.

"His work is done!" She sighed to herself and to Ronan who stood supportively by her side, one arm low slung around her hip so as not to be too intrusive.

"Yes love," whispered Ronan gently by way of reply. He did not really have the words for this. His mind was already starting to anticipate its implications, especially regarding France.

As she lovingly closed her father's eyes and felt the contours of his dear face one last time, she shed soft gentle tears.

"Go safely on your journey Pappa!"

"Amen," agreed Ronan.

Frederick was left to rest easy, lying in state in his turret room for a few days while the preparations for his burial were made. The air was cool enough that elaborate perfumes and embalming measures were not needed. He was swaddled and firmly wrapped with cloths that Sari enhanced with lavender. She considered this a protection and its properties would assist any lingering trauma to melt into the ethers bringing peaceful rest. He did not really need it. But it was part of her routine of preparing the dead and it allowed her to commune with his spirit and attend to him as they said their goodbyes. Frederick would stay close, he assured her.

The somber procession to a burial ground newly established on the Island of Saint Finnan (*Eilean Fhionnan*) would take a few hours ride by horse and boat. They would move slowly and reverently through the landscape guiding Frederick to his resting place. Serena would stay with Sheena and the boys who had come to Tiroam to tend to Sari and the baby as the final details were arranged.

Reginald had offered a burial in the grounds of The Castle. But it was decided that Frederick would be taken to a place he loved. The small Isle on Loch Shiel, also known as The Green Isle, had been inhabited by Saint Finan as base for his missionary work to the Islands in the seventh century. It was a pilgrimage site of penitence and repentance for disciples of the Columban-trained monk, and in the days before Christendom, it served as a burial ground for the Celts. Various clans and the Chiefs of Moidart were using the sacred space of the isle to bury their dead. There was a tendency to bury those of a catholic persuasion in the south part of the Isle. While those of "looser" beliefs who communed with the ancestors were buried in the north. Sari wondered which plot Frederick would be allotted to. In keeping with the *Clann Ruaidhri* loyalties she suspected it would be southward facing.

"All the better to see the sun Pappa!" She whispered to him, knowing he could still hear her.

The whole journey could have been done by the waterways, leaving Tioram at high tide, via the River Shiel to Loch Shiel where the Green Isle could be found close to Glenfinnan. But it was decided the convoy would travel to Acharacle with horses and cart first. There were a several suitable boats moored on the banks of the west side where the loch joined the river tributary, and they were counting on the help of a local fisherman.

The boat trip was choppy, and Sari became increasingly anxious as she saw the storm clouds gathering on the horizon. They needed to get back as quickly as possible, but it was looking as if a night away once the boat had moored back on the mainland might be called for. The horses would have rested enough. But they would not choose to do the ride back to Tioram in a storm with night falling fast..

Sari was worried about Serena and had not really wanted to leave her for so long. But she knew she was in capable hands, and of course this wrench was nothing compared to the one that was coming. Preparation had to be her motive. She could not possibly bring her young baby to France. Even this short journey from Tioram was taxing enough. If they chartered a boat all the way to France the journey could take them weeks. It was too much to subject Serena to.

Sari knew ominous decisions were looming as she committed her father to the dust. A grave digger had made swift work of the burial site in the previous days, and the interment was quick enough, though not rushed. She and Ronan, the fisherman and a couple of Ronan's strapping cousins had undertaken the task of Frederick's burial. Reginald had decided not to make the journey as his gout was playing up following the wedding banquet. He had been so kind, there was no resentment felt at his decision.

Part of Sari wished they were doing a funeral pyre burial for her father. Like the Vikings did. So that his spirit could soar on the ethers and his body could fly free. She did not like the idea of him rotting in the ground, especially ground she would not be able to visit readily. His body was a vessel, now an empty one. But it was impossible not to feel a pang of longing as they pushed away from the shore of the Isle to journey home.

"Rest easy Pappa!" She teared up as she sat to face the ever-retreating small island.

There he would be, for an eternity.

CHAPTER THIRTY-NINE
Montségur

S ari and Ronan had travelled for weeks to get to France. They concluded they must do as much of the journey as possible by waterways for speed and ease. They were initially unsure whether to bring their horses Merlin and Delphine. But figured that if the journey were largely by *Taride* they would manage. This vessel was sturdy on the seas and could carry up to twenty horses. It certainly would be good to have their trusty steeds with them for the ensuing difficulties they would surely face. The horses could read their masters telepathically and would more likely be able to lead them out of danger than a borrowed or hired stranger's horse that did not even speak English. Sari and Ronan suspected Merlin could be multi-lingual, but they did not want to assume this. The point was the magic of the horses would surely save them once their own ideas had burned through.

The logistics of their travel route turned out to be complex. They had to get to Southampton and board one of the wine trade vessels heading to Bordeaux. From there they could use the river Garonne which ran upstream to Toulouse. The final miles would be on horseback and could take up to a week depending on the terrain and weather. To begin the journey, they must travel to Ayr in the south by horse or sea from Moidart. They would then board a boat for Ireland which would finally end its journey in Southampton. The alternative was a long ride to The Lothians, where they would have to board a trade boat bound for Bruges, and then another bound for Southampton. Either way, the key objective was to reach Southampton which was the main port and trade route serving Bordeaux. It was quite a marathon undertaking.

Once Reginald knew of their resolve to leave, he made enquiries. Some of his summer visitors landed in Moidart in boats from the north. It was quite possible that if they waited for one of these, they could bypass most of the land travel. Reginald did not recommend the long ride to The Lothians. It was arduous and lengthy without spare horses. They might as well wait for one of the seasonal ships that stopped by on the wool trade runs. Boats travelled down from the Nordic regions quite regularly, and when not accompanied by a host of marauding Vikings they could be relied upon to be peaceable traders.

Sari and Ronan concluded that Reginald's advice was sound. They would have to be on standby for the trade boats that landed throughout July and August in the hope that they could be accommodated. Reginald was willing to pay a handsome fee for the right voyager, as he wanted his son and daughter-in-law back as soon as possible. One of these timely rides would bypass the need for lengthy land travel which was full of dangers and would be exceedingly tiresome for the horses. The greatest ease and comfort would surely be by boat. It was worth waiting for.

Their best chance was apparently a fearsome warrior trader who acted like he owned the high seas. A Captain Abjorn was the owner of an impressive Nordic Nava ship, called *The Njal,* and he still owed Reginald a favour from a previous season. Due in Moidart in mid-July, Reginald was optimistic he could secure Sari, Ronan and their horses safe passage direct to Bordeaux. Abjorn had absconded with a large portion of Tioram's wool production from the previous spring. It was an agreed advance on grain that would be harvested at the end of the summer and brought to Moidart in exchange. The grain never appeared. Reginald was convinced this was a strong bargaining chip. He knew he would get his grain this year. But he was sure the delay and inconvenience would be enough to secure the favour of a big diversion to The South of France. He had heard that Abjorn was trying to increase his acquisition of spices, silver, and pottery. So was going to suggest he extend his trip to Morocco to further enhance the plan. It looked like this would be their ticket to France.

"How are your sea-legs Sari?" Ronan quipped.

"Well I am "The Sea Priestess" you know and rumour has it I was once a Mermaid. Perhaps I still *am!*"

Ronan laughed. "Well I am the lover of seals apparently. Mother started to use my middle name "lover of seals" for convenience when she saw me running after the baby seals on the beach."

"Well we could revert to calling you *Dubhghall mac Ruaidhrí* if you please Ronan!" Reginald intercepted their interchange, joking across the dining table, as supper was served.

The conversation was all about the developing plans for France. Sheena had agreed to over-see Serena's health and development for the months that they were away and would bring her to Tioram for overnight stays at her grandfather's pleasure. Reginald was rather looking forward to his alone time with his granddaughter. But he was concerned about Ronan and Sari and their jaunt to France.

"Well the sooner you get this all out of the way. The sooner you can return." He said. "This has been a long time coming and if you do not achieve it during the summer while Serena is young, you probably never will. She will not notice you are gone now as much as she would if she were a year or two older. I want more grandchildren too Sari, so I would like to see your mission accomplished as soon as possible. Whatever it may be!"

Sari and Ronan smiled at his boldness and presumption. He was clearly trying to illicit information from the mysterious duo. But he also had a point. It really was a case of now or never. If they went by the end of June, or midway through July at the latest they could be back well in time for winter.

1243 was turning out to be quite the year! Sari thought to herself.

"Ah. Yes!" Sari proceeded, after a slightly awkward silence.

There were certain things they could not discuss with Reginald, so she steered the conversation back to her husband. "I had meant to ask you: 'why, the name Ronan?'" after the wedding. "I knew it was your mother's preferred name, but your signature name was unpronounceable. I forgot to double check with your father I was marrying the right man!"

They all laughed with due amusement, at Sari's wry comments.

"Have some more wine Sari!" Reginald motioned to the servant boy to attend to her goblet, one of the goblets dutifully retrieved by Ronan from *Eilean Donan*.

"You are going to have to acquire a taste for the fine wines of Bordeaux on the voyage Sari! You have to get through it somehow."

Ah. The goblet that brought us together, Ronan smirked ironically as he noticed its use at the dinner table. His father's ironic gestures and twisted humour never ceased to amaze him.

"Oh, we will find plenty to amuse us I am sure father. The seals, and the mermaids, and each other by the sound of it.

"We are all set for the rough seas Sari!"

Little did he know that this would turn out to be quite the prophesy. One worthy of The Grail line seers. Clearly, he had married into the right family.

Sari and Ronan looked astounded as they approached the environs of *Montségur* and glimpsed its prominent *Château* on the cliff in the distance. The terrain was mountainous, lush, and green, but highly inaccessible. There in the distance the Cathar stronghold nested, snugly merged with the clifftop mound it inhabited. It was part of the organic presentation of the mountain, almost indistinguishable from the limestone rock which supported it. The climb up to its gates was steep and arduous for man and beast alike. You would have to be sure of a good reception at the summit to guarantee water and replenishment. This obvious detail made Sari nervous as they began their descent into the valley below. The ascent awaiting them on the other side would have to be negotiated artfully.

Their road thus far had been treacherous. They had navigated rough seas and Ronan, who clearly did not have *his* "sea-legs" suffered unrelenting seasickness. Sari was able to nurse him effectively with a concoction made of anise and chervil, which he had to sip regularly on an empty stomach. She encouraged him to fast as much as possible and eat only when the seas were calm. It seemed to work for as long as he followed the procedure. But as soon as he lapsed, thinking he was better, back the malady came more intensely than before.

As always. It pays to listen to my wife! He found himself saying repeatedly. Every time he did not, he lived to "rue the day." This was difficult for a man's pride. But he was learning to accommodate the reality.

Travelling together had shown a different side to Sari's resilience. He was impressed. Her intuition was invaluable when dealing with the characters they met on the road. He would be briefed when to pass quietly in silence. She knew when they might gain some useful information, and when it was important not to say a word. She could ascertain when and where they could best stay for the night, and whom they could trust. He doubted he could have done this without her, and in the same breath he was totally convinced she could have done this without him!

Sari for her part gained strength from Ronan and knew she could not have performed to her best without him by her side. Whatever he might think. She needed him. He was the foil she needed.

Together they could achieve their mission and conquer the world, she found herself thinking many times. This journey was proving their commitment and mettle to each other. It was a novel honeymoon if not a safe one. At least it was bonding them very effectively.

Their agreed story line was that she was a travelling healer who was distantly related to Eleanor of Aquitaine, under a command to help who she could. Her mother had been a distant cousin of Eleanor's, and her dying wish had been that she must help as many French people as she possibly could. The Queen of the Languedoc surely supported and blessed her gifts from the other side! Ronan her companion, was her husband and protector. He was obviously required to keep her safe along the way. One look at Sari's comely appearance and luminous countenance and this was all easily justified. It did not need to be further explained. Any of the King's soldiers questioning their identities only had to gaze on Sari's face. She would transfix them with a distant smile and intense twinkle of the eye, and very quickly they were waved upon their way. It was as if they could not stand to be close to such luminosity for too long. Sari blinded them with her light. Besides, even if they were imposters, there did not seem too much harm that they could do. Thus, with an intriguing mixture of coquetry, flippancy, and imagination Sari and Ronan had made their way through potential danger to the foothills of *Montségur.*

Nothing could have prepared them for the sight of the magnificent fortress on the cliff. Looming through the morning mist, it was suspended in cloud. The modest but strong turrets peeping through the top of the thickening clumps of mist. The sun came out from behind a dark cloud directly overhead, brightening and sharpening the vista. It was an inspiring vision. Everything that Sari had anticipated. It stirred her to the core. Her very soul soared at the prospect of meeting with the *Perfecti* inside. But there was a problem. They had learned in Toulouse that the castellations were being relentlessly bombarded by the authorities. The Cathars were being contained at *Montségur* by an aggressive siege. Down in the valley below, their would-be captors were camped out watching their every turn. No one could easily leave or return.

Thousands of troops led by Hugues des Arcis had pitched their force against *Montségur* precisely at the time Serena was entering the world. The authorities were on a final mission to quell The Cathars in the region. In what was turning into a lengthy campaign, the attack was showing no signs of abating. For months now the *Château* had been subjected to unjustified bombardment, and it looked like this insidious strategy would continue throughout the wintertime. The whole thing had become a battle of wills, with a spectacular irony at its core. The Cathars could walk free at any time of their own volition. The conditions being that they renounce their faith and acquiesce to wear the "yellow cross" as an identifier.

Sari and Ronan gathered all this information at the end of their six-week journey in Toulouse, as they prepared their horses for the ride to *Montségur*. Their boat *The Njal* had arrived on 20th July in Moidart, in time for them to depart on Mary Magdalene's Feast Day. Now, here they were coming into September, exhausted after lengthy voyages, and faced with the reality of what appeared to be a futile mission. It did not look like they were even going to be able to get inside The Castle walls.

The camps of the opposing forces were sometimes quiet, insidiously waiting. Were they there or were they not? To the Cathar watch on the hill it was a game of cat-and-mouse. At points it looked like these passive-aggressors had gone off on other missions realizing the futility of their quest. At other times there was no doubt the aggressors were present. The imposing mangonel intermittently hurled stones into the air, its propulsion often falling short, landing with a thump at the foot of the cliff. The worrying part was that this machine was imperceptibly edging closer and closer to the ramparts, allowing the troops to do the same. It seemed impossible they would be able to breech the walls. But there was an insidious sense in the air that they might. The intimidation and determination were tangible. Meanwhile up in the *Château*, the Cathars were peaceably going about their day. Worshipping, praying, and singing with a haunting melody that would float down the valley to the troops. The war-worn warriors must have wondered what they were dealing with. An enemy that sent out light-filled melodies instead of arrows and burning flames was novel indeed.

By the time Sari and Ronan had arrived in France, the troops in the region had isolated various families, Nobel and poor alike and had given them the chance to recant. Some defected to the Dominican Church an austere Catholic faction. Others joined hermit members of the community living for a time on the surrounding hillsides. The treaty ending The Crusade proved useless ultimately. The French authorities determined to deal with the scourge of the heretics and finish what The Pope had started. The last year or so had driven The Cathars behind walls. Their castles, towers and *châteaux* fortified them against the enemy but still it was relentless.

Truly May 1243 was the beginning of the end. The Cathars' last stand. Those that were captured in the woodland searches could recant their beliefs or die on the spot. There was no reprieve. There is no doubt that some believers recanted to survive and bore the "yellow cross" of their shame. But that was not usually the way of the highly conscious, spiritually honed Cathar. The true *Perfecti* was not afraid to own their faith even unto death. They were aware that this was exactly what they were lining themselves up for, sooner than later.

CHAPTER FORTY

The Cathars

The troops had not worked it out yet but there was a secret way up into the *Château* on the far backside of the cliff through a series of caves and tunnels. Well concealed by thick foliage, not many knew of this route in and out of *Montségur* Only a select few. But in this way provisions were taken in, often provided by supportive locals and farmers. Even more importantly in the current climate, what needed to be smuggled out could be discretely attended to usually under cover of darkness. There was a well-established drill, and the few that operated through the caves could be relied upon for their discretion.

The Cathars occupied *Montségur* by choice. There was a way to safely leave if they wished to. They held the power and were determined to do things on their terms or not at all. In this respect the siege was a bit of a farce. Not everyone had to recant to find their way to safety. The committed few remaining were there by choice, not willing to permanently leave by the back door. Yes, they would avoid the notoriously shameful "yellow cross." But where would they go then?

They knew of the sacred retreat offered in Mary Magdalene's caves in the South west at Fontanet above *Usset-les-Bains*. But retreating to the caves would mean they were completely hidden, with no societal relevance at all. A life of penitence and prayer in the concealed limestone caves was an option. But most of them now remained on principle. It would be a compromise of all they had lived for to exit *Montségur*, the heart of their faith and mission. Such a recanting would cause their Soul's death its eternal loss in purgatory without reprieve. The body did not matter to the elevated *Perfecti*. Redemption of the Spirit was everything to The Cathar.

The Cathars, a community with alternative belief systems had been under siege as a minority before. In 1199 Pope Innocent III initiated a genocide of all heretics that would span decades and would single out The Cathars in particular. These ostensibly political crusades were undertaken in the name of religion. This was about power and control, not someone's personal faith. The authorities needed to witness public compliance, or no mercy was shown. It was dangerous to allow large groups of people to function under their own belief systems. It was damaging to both King and Country, as well as to the mercenary power wielded by The Pope, who generally held more sway than royalty anyway.

The Knights Templar recognized by The Vatican in 1139 were the church's bankers. They wielded the sword in pursuit of justice and peace in the name of Christ. But some of them imposed "The Law" upon the common peoples using extreme violence and intimidation. These were the feted front-line warriors who would not retreat unless outnumbered by three-to-one. There was a secret complicit understanding that they were on the lookout for, or were the keepers of, The Holy Grail. No one knew which. To preserve "The Chalice" as a relic and to return it to its rightful home in the bosom of The Church, The Holy Land, was the whispered mission of The Templars.

Little did they realize the irony of this sentiment - The Grail Line was after all privy to many a fine "bosom."

Montségur had been strengthened in 1204 and fortified in response to the relentless crusade against renegade factions that dared to believe something different. The edicts of The Catholic Church were considered sacrosanct, and beyond reproach by the military protagonists acting on behalf of The Vatican. During the Crusades commissioned by The Pope, launched to persecute all those not in compliance, it was apparent that this heretical sect needed a "bolt-hole."

Named "Mountain of Safety" *Montségur* proved to be ultimately less than secure. "*Ségur*" eluded The Cathars, even in their most sacred quarters. Here the loyal uncompromising *Perfecti* could remain if they chose to do so. Imprisoned and surrounded. Still in their stronghold. Ironical in the extreme, especially as this was potentially their last stand. Pilloried in the hideaway they thought was impenetrable. If they renounced their beliefs, they could leave on a warning and a reprieve. If they would not, they remained under siege in their home. The one place that was supposed to be impermeable to The French and The Crusaders.

In recent decades there had been lots of ransacking, searching, questions and torture throughout the South of France as the authorities sought the information they needed. They felt they were close to understanding and shutting down what had been the bane of The Languedoc for so long. But still they had not solved the main puzzle. They needed to unravel the riddles and finally abate the destructive rumours. It was imperative that they find the compromising documents and artefacts they *knew* The Cathars were hiding.

Factions of The Templars were supportive of The Cathars. Aside from a developing spiritual link, The Templars who understood the meaning of The Grail could see that The Cathars were non-violent, peace-loving people. Individual soldiers and knights horrified at the injustices they were witnessing, had begun to serve both-ends-against-the-middle. Rumours about The Holy Grail began to transmogrify into something far more sensational. The Templars had entrusted The Cathars with custody of The Grail. They no longer carried it or were looking for it. It was suspected to have been handed to The Cathars at *Montségur*. Where else could it be but hidden in the impenetrable *Château?*

The ruthless Albigensian Crusades had ended with Treaty of Paris-Meaux in 1229. But resistance continued. The Inquisition was active, and suspicion was rife. Previously, there had been some debate between The Catholic Church and The Cathars. Coming into the thirteenth century, Catholic priests with second churches were often *in absentia* from the Languedoc region. This naturally gave The Cathars a stronger voice in The South of France. Theological debates had even been hosted, generally at *Fanjeaux,* before Simon De Montfort got his hands on it. Safeguarded by a moat and fourteen towers, De Montfort coveted this stronghold of the heretics, and made sure he acquired it as his base, once The Cathars began fleeing to the woods and the mountains for greater protection.

Despite apparently civil debates between Catholic and Cathar clerics towards the end of the twelfth Century, attempts at unity abruptly ended with the merciless genocide and Inquisition. Heretics were too dangerous for The Church to entertain. Their ideology, theology and lifestyle would not be tolerated further. Gone were the days of healthy debate and attempts to find common ground. There was none.

Catholics considered The Cathars too all-embracing and all-inclusive. They gave women too much importance within the structures of their daily lives, both in ceremonies and with practical tasks. The male-orientated Catholic Church felt that women should be meek, barely seen, and certainly not heard. Whereas in Cathar

318

structures, important women were often church leaders and highly revered *Perfecti*. Even esteemed local aristocratic ladies of the region had aligned with the gentle charitable approach of The Cathars, seeing opportunity for their own growth and validation. Nine of them became Dominicans when their hand was forced. The 'Noble' *Perfecti* had questionable loyalties it seemed. This had gone beyond a group of women who wanted to be seen to be doing good. Lives were at stake. Quite often lives perished *on* the stake because of it.

The harsh Inquisitions increased division between the two camps. The Catholic Church could not accommodate this heresy, while The Cathars had started to perceive Catholicism as Satan's Church on earth. It had ordered their annihilation. Truly it resided in darkness and was an ante-force they had to defeat with love. It was do or die. They must continue secretly, or else fail and recant.

The fully committed Cathars went underground, retreated to the hills. In 1233 Bishop *Guilhabert de Castres* appealed to the owner of *Montségur* for a safe-harbour agreement for the heretics. He requested that *Montségur* be made the *domicilium et caput* of The Cathar Church.

Now here they all were ten years later, flames and stones raining down upon them randomly over the Castle walls.

The last stand.

"Ah! The lady with the yellow hair!" Said *Raymond de Pereille,* as he looked Sari up-and-down.

She felt under scrutiny as her energy field was being unceremoniously scanned. Sari allowed the examination. In faith she knew she was in the right place. They just had to trust the process and let it unfold.

Ronan had artfully cleared their way for the steep climb up to the *Château*. Guarded at the foot of the hill by two sleepy king's soldiers it was easy enough to recount their story. These two had not seen any action for months. No one was coming in or out of The Castle. This unexpected handsome couple proved to be the height of excitement for them. But still they did not make it difficult. Sari's confident countenance and royally connected family, along with Ronan's strange dialect was enough to convince them they were not Cathars.

"We are just passing through Sir!" Said Sari.

"We have travelled from Scotland and had been assured that we might secure accommodations at *Montségur*. We had no idea The Castle was under siege. But on The King's good pleasure we implore you we be allowed to stay the night at least. We are on the way to my distant relatives in Perpignan."

"Well, you are welcome to try. They have not let anyone through the gate in weeks. They must be well-stocked with provisions. We are waiting this out. Under orders. You can tell them so if you get in!" Said the overweight rough-faced soldier on the left waiving them on.

The soldiers had seemed to be drunk. Sari could smell the faint whiff of mead on their breath. Even if they had not been allowed past, Sari and Ronan figured they could access the path further up at nightfall, with a scramble and a climb. But, the direct approach worked, just as Sari had said it would. The handsome, younger soldier, lusty and lecherous, seemed to have no problem with Sari's presence or her request. Once again Ronan was relieved he was at her side. Their "conditions" on allowing the ascent might otherwise have been much more severe. He had heard about the penchant for fine wine and women prevalent throughout France.

"Thank you kind Sirs!" He interjected stamping his male authority on the proceedings. "We will relay your messages, and perhaps be able to bring this sorry state of affairs to a quicker resolution!"

"Yes indeed. On your way then. It is quite a climb. We will see you on the way back down likely!"

"No chance of that." muttered Sari under her breath. She knew very well they were expected and would get into *Montségur* even if they had to wait outside for the morning light. They had achieved the end of their journey. Both felt inner relief and pride as they slowly and silently climbed towards the castle-in-the-air.

"We have been waiting for you for some time." Raymond almost reprimanded, as they took in their surroundings. Interestingly Raymond had a similar arrangement for greeting his guests as Reginald did at Castle Tiroam. A special chair, wood-panelling, large oak table for dining, and lead-lined windows.

Not the helmets or weaponry though. She noted.

"Sir, yes. I have felt this. We came as soon as we could, and I hope we are not

too late to help you and to do what is required." Said Sari, who for some reason felt compelled to kneel before the supposedly great man. Sari knew she should like him in theory. But she was finding something amiss in his manner that she could not quite put her finger on.

"There are some sick people in the infirmary we would be grateful if you would attend them when you are rested. Your husband can meet with Pierre here in the morning and learn the layout of the *Château*." Raymond gestured to his left to a tall lean man with a grim lanky countenance. "We do encourage this especially now. As valued guests we want you to know the safe exit route also. But you must keep it to yourselves. Share it with no one. Not many know it here in *Le Château*. My daughter will explain more to you in the morning."

"Pierre will show you to your chambers now. There will be bread and water brought to you when you arise." Raymond's delivery was somewhat cold and distant. Detached from his reality it seemed.

Perhaps he was repenting at leisure having let The Cathars under his roof. Sari speculated. He seemed to be going through the motions as if his heart were not in it.

Months of being under siege had possibly robbed him of his joie de vivre, she reasoned. But she detected something else underlying that did not sit comfortably with her.

What was he hiding? She would endeavour to find out, as quickly as possible.

"Who are these people?" She said quietly to herself in her heart, suddenly disappointed that they had come all this way to a castle under duress to help people who seemed to be less than radiant and joyous in demeanour. She needed to understand more.

At least they had been expecting us, and it was not all a figment of my imagination. She tried to reassure herself.

Sari glanced across at Ronan who also seemed distracted and slightly disorientated. True it had been quite a climb for them up the footpath to the gate. It was also late, so some stress on all sides was probably justified.

They had arranged to leave their horses with a trustworthy farmer in orange groves not too far away. If they needed to make a quick escape, they would not be able to ride at breakneck speed down the high gradient cobbled ascent. Rumours of secret passages had reached them. Whispers on the wind. Sari could sense the secrets hidden here. They would have to trust for a quick exit should one be required. There is no reason why they would specifically be targeted by The French. But if the armouries of the soldiers were able to breach The Castle walls somehow, there was no guarantee for their safety in the confusion.

The Cathars were a special people who would not fight or take up arms, so this whole situation struck her as very incongruous. There was a strong agenda at play, and they needed to stay a while to fully understand what her calling could possibly be in this context. Yes, she could help with the wounded and the sick. But beyond that there was something else. Secrets needed to be revealed. She was something to do with this. She also wanted to get a sense of her destiny and connection with these people. They both hoped some more congenial faces would enlighten them in the coming days.

CHAPTER FORTY-ONE

The Holy Grail

A portal of luminous light opened above their heads. Like the heavens opening. Suddenly it all made sense. Sari was caught up in the moment. Ronan was looking on half participating, half trying to rationalize and understand what was going on.

"Release to it Ronan!" Sari gently whispered to him.

He sensed not to reply, which was probably a good thing. Simply smiling back at her transfixed at her extra radiance in this moment. He had never seen her look quite so angelic or aglow. Always beautiful as she was, he was hypnotized by the other-worldly quality she had acquired so effortlessly. She was emanating energies he had never seen before.

As Sari's higher chakras opened fully and aligned with the portal above, the golden light poured down upon her its rays intensifying. She was motionless receiving downloads of pink, gold, green and pale blue energy. Fully engaged in what looked like a divine baptism.

Ronan's own ability to see had amplified quite impressively being around Sari. He could vividly see these colours descend into her aura as they permeated her energy system. Sari had slowly been revealing herself to him in layers. He now understood much more. But no explanation or demonstration had prepared him for this moment. He sensed it was new to her as well. This felt like a fulcrum point. A pivotal moment. The very "thing" they had both been anticipating. Not knowing exactly what form it was going to take.

This was it.

After she had whispered reassurance to Ronan, Sari realized that she herself could now fully immerse in this divine energy. She felt sanctified, cleansed, energized and pure. She bathed in the warmth and radiance of the light as she began to hear the faintest humming descending from the heavens. Strange noises in her ears made her initially alarmed. But she knew this was a safe space.

Raymond and his daughter *Esclarmonde* had briefed her this would be special. That anything might happen, and that whatever *did* happen was perfect. Just as it should be. As it began she had caught the eyes of the fair *Esclarmonde* who smiled at her with a knowing conviction and a subtle nod. Sari knew then that she had to just let go and trust it all.

It was as if she was coming alive from the inside out. Her life to date had been building towards this blessing. This transcendency. It surpassed her expectations. The **Consolamentum**. The process of becoming. Of transmuting into one of the *Perfecti*.

Was she going to levitate and ascend? It felt to her as if she might. There was a sensation of rising. Of levitation. Of releasing her Soul and senses to the light. She did not think she was likely to be taken in this moment. But like Frederick before her, she would not have minded if she were. If this was what he had described to her so many times before, she now understood him completely.

As the dim light in the outer reaches of the chamber became illuminated by this heavenly visitation, Sari thought she saw her father smiling at her from amongst the *Perfecti*. So many faces. She could not be sure. Men with beards, sparkling eyes, and keen stares. So many with that same look of special grace and wisdom her father possessed.

"Pappa?" She whispered inaudibly to herself. Possibly he was using this vortex to show his face. Or at least suggest his presence. His reassurance that all was well. That he had crossed over to the light and was blessing her mission from a higher plane.

Sari's altered state continued to amplify in its intensity. This was a different consciousness. One that she had never experienced before, not even in her most aligned meditations. Suddenly three feet above her head a beautiful shining silver goblet with an emerald at its heart appeared.

The Grail!

She gasped as she absorbed its eternal radiance and rejuvenation qualities.

Eternal life!

She was not sure who saw this. Was she hallucinating? She had not sensed any strange herb in the wine they had consumed.

Perhaps they had laced it with a little something. She would have to ask later if she remembered!

The *Perfecti* started swaying, singing, chanting, raising energy. The heat and light in the room expanded. The Grail tipped towards her and by instinct she opened her mouth held upwards to receive. Sari was not sure if they all saw what she saw. If they participated in what she was doing. Was it just an etheric vision unique to her? It felt very private between her and The Divine. Suddenly it all made sense to her. She was being anointed.

She was the anointed one.

She hoped she was not deluding herself, but this was happening to her, and apparently no one else. The gathered group all clad in simple off-white trailing, draping tunics with gold embroidered belts for the men, hair pieces and bodices for the women. All singing softly. The same melodies that had been haunting the soldiers below for weeks and months filled the chamber. A hexagon-shaped chapel with a stone floor, pillars, and a central throne on which for this ceremony Sari had been motioned to sit. She was center stage, calm and grounded, but still not fully understanding. There had been hints that she had a special role. But she still had no real idea what it was. Whatever this was preparing her for, must be magnificent in the extreme.

Being flooded with this high-octane Divine energy was worth travelling to France for. It upgraded her and cleansed her of all that had gone before. She had not fully appreciated it, but she was carrying a residue of energy from previous clients and those she had helped. Although she would never forget her father, much of her grief had also been lifted. Her heart was no longer so heavy about him. He was not on The Green Isle. He was sanctified bathing in this magnificent Eternal Light alongside her. Sari's purification was obviously required for an elevated task. She was feeling primed, prepared, lighter, and brighter.

What she expected even less, was what happened next. As the light played down through her chakras and meridian lines permeating her energy system, she began talking in a strange language. The light language *Esclarmonde* had told her about. She did not think she would ever be able to do this. She had seen some of the other leaders speak in radiance in other rituals. But had been told it was quite a rare gift of 'The Spirit;' that it should not be pursued and that if it were going to happen it just would. It could also be that it happened once, and never again; or repeatedly and at random. The interpretation was also considered important and a desired gift. For what use was a language that no one could understand?

Sometimes an interpreter did not step forward, and this seemed to be the case with Sari's experience. The energy would bathe them all in its light, and their trust would be implicit that the messages were perfect. Possibly Sari would understand them later anyway. That could also happen. An uninterrupted download was optimal in moments like this one.

Sari had no clue what she was saying but the musicality and lightness of the language emanated from her lips. Her body started to sway in motion to the moving energy and so did her hands.

Was she suddenly a spiritual performance act?

Her wry humour allowed her to muse. She still had enough control and detachment to see the funny side and observe her experience. But on the serious side, she knew this was important. She had to receive the messages, channel what was coming through her, and allow the *Perfecti* to absorb the experience in their way also. She could sense that even they found this a unique event. It certainly was not typical of what she had been privy to thus far. This day being Saint Valentine's Day 1244, they were all receiving in gratitude and celebration these manifestations of Divine Love.

The appearance of The Holy Grail had happened to *Esclarmonde* at her *consolamentum*. She too spoke in the Spirit-filled languages. With a name meaning "Clarity of The World," she was a most esteemed *Perfecti*, most unusual for someone of such a tender age. The community put her on a pedestal and listened in awe to her channellings and prophesies. As she got to know her, Sari became increasingly puzzled as to why she herself was needed at all. Here right in their midst already was a youthful healer and visionary with almost the same skill set.

Sari and *Esclamonde* had become bonded in past weeks. They were soul sisters truly. Raymond's daughter was two years her junior, but she was just as conscious and a miraculous healer. As Sari observed her and got to know her, she wondered what extra she herself could bring to the community.

Why they had called her here on the ethers, when they already had such a jewel in their Crown?

Perhaps she did not need to help so much as be helped?

She had wondered this. The death of her father had hit her hard. His connection to France alongside her was for the healing and acceptance of his passing it seemed. He would never have reached France had they continued their journey. Did she need profound healing, or did her 'lineage' mean that she had something The Cathars needed from her? Probably it was a strange mixture of the two.

The strangest thing of all was that *Esclarmonde* was almost identical to her in appearance. Both Sari and Ronan had audibly gasped when she came into the room for breakfast the morning following their arrival. *Raymond de Péreille* had smiled to himself seeing them make the same parallel judgement they had all made in the great hall the previous night. Sari was confused suddenly on all sorts of levels. Firstly, she hoped Ronan would not confuse the two of them in a dark corridor of The Castle on some random night in the near future! Secondly, she wondered if they were distantly related? Perhaps this was one of the mysteries that needed to be solved. Thirdly, as she got to know *Esclarmonde* further, Sari saw that she had the same gifts of prophecy, guidance, and healing that she did. Could she also be of The Grail Line? In which case, why did they need another Priestess in their midst? Sari had decided to engage with the daily grind of life in the *Château*, to process and solve her puzzlement. She was sure it would all be revealed in the perfect timing. Spirit could not possibly have brought them all this way for nothing.

Esclarmonde and Sari worked side-by-side, bonding and sharing their knowledge in the infirmary over many weeks. They taught each other what they knew, and Sari learned how some of the French herbs differed to the Scottish. There were strengths in both approaches and the merging of the two girl's energies ensured some amazing healings at the *Château*.

She also learned that she need not have any fear of Ronan going astray. *Esclarmonde* had sworn herself to a life of celibacy during her baptism. Plus, daily he assured her of his devotion and love. There would be no mistakes in secret rooms in this lifetime. This she was thankful for, as she sensed a myriad of betrayals on her timelines from the deep distant past and the future to come. It would be more than she could bear if Ronan proved to be one of them.

He loved her.

CHAPTER FORTY-TWO

The Pyre

This baptism of The Holy Spirit was primed to prepare the *Perfecti* for Eternal Life. The ritual happened at conversion point, and again when the disciple was close to death. It was a twice in a lifetime event. For some, those who could not adhere to the conditions of vegetarianism and celibacy, it became a last rites ritual. The ceremony brought the *Perfecti* close to God, making him or her light-filled and ready to either work alongside him/her, or to go and be with him/her.

Original sin and the scourge of life lived in a fallen world inevitably made a human unclean, unfit for heaven. The Baptism of fire, and God's Holy Spirit, created the "Cathar Perfect." The *Perfecti*. One who was now fully pure, indoctrinated, and adept at being a "Cathar." It was not an automatic validation of leadership within the community. But it was a recognized and esteemed position. The adept was now the alchemist. They had "arrived!"

Purified.

Atoned.

Enlightened.

Ronan had been asking many questions of the *Perfecti* during his stay at The Castle. He helped with the horses and was allotted basic carpentry jobs in the community whilst Sari and Esclarmonde tended to the sick in the infirmary. Working for Raymond was easier than dealing with his father, though he missed Tioram and all its accompanying drama and intrigue. He found new resolve and purpose throwing himself into the hub of activities at *Montségur*. Though he knew The Cathars were a peaceable people who were not willing to take up arms against their aggressors. He assured *de Péreille* that he was willing to play a part in the defense of the *Château* should the time come.

"No son!" Raymond responded at his declared intentions. "If they breach the walls we will surrender. We will not fight. It is not our way. We will negotiate and try to come to some deal and agree terms. But the problem is we know they will insist on the recanting as they have everywhere. This we will not do. Here live The Cathars who would not recant. From the forests, the towers and *Fanjeux* These people will not compromise their salvation."

"Tell me Raymond. What is it that inspires them so? I was brought up a Catholic. But being around Sari, I see there is another way. I witness her energy and miracles daily. I am not saying she is 'The Divine.' Well she is to me! But I mean. I know that God is God, and we are sinners who cannot earn our salvation except by his grace. But how is what you believe different to this?"

"Well in a way it is not. That is the irony. The Church has been bombarding a spiritual religious people who hold beliefs quite like theirs. If only they realized it. Yes. There are some major differences. The Catholic church is very male driven. The Cathars honour the feminine. The Goddess within. We see the feminine in The Magdalene. Our teachings are derived from her Gospels in part. The Lineage Lines from which Sari is seeded. We know this about Sari, which is why we needed her to come here, especially at this time."

"Yes, we suspected this much. Sari has felt the calling since she was young. She always knew she had to come here. Visions and dreams and guidance have all brought her to this moment. Even with the delays we faced, Sari remained determined. She only just had a child Serena, whom we had to leave in Scotland."

"AH! The lineage is safe and secure. We were wondering this. *Esclarmonde* will not have children. She is sworn to the ways of the adept. We fear she will have an untimely end defending the cause, which is partly why we wanted Sari here also. Not to put her in danger. But to play a part. We feel that because the two of them are so alike. Like Soul Twins. This will somehow be important to the destiny of us all. With what we all face now."

"Why do the adepts hold so strongly to the principles. How are they different spiritually? What would make a man lie down and die for The Cathar cause? So many refuse to recant when faced with death. There seems to be no fear amongst you."

"Correct my son! You have seen the ceremonies. The energy. Heard the singing and seen the light. You have born witness to it all. This is Eternal Life itself. There is no death here. Only love. What the enemy thinks it can destroy? It is afraid of. It cannot control. It does not understand. It sees the power as 'Almighty.' This is of course exactly what it is. It is The Lord. The Almighty. The Mother God. The Magdalene. There are so many dimensions The Church does not understand. It misses the Truth at the core of everything. The dark forces attack what is good. What they cannot contain. They project evil upon us. Call us heretics. The evil is what they do."

"Yes! Yes. I see this. There are no justifications for the persecutions. No wonder The Templars refused to participate with this bombardment. I hear in the whisperings of the *Château.* that some even help you."

"Indeed. That is a story for another day. It is what we need Sari for. If harm comes to *Esclarmonde*. Sari may have to claim to *be* her. Or she may have to claim to *be* Sari. We do not yet know which. We knew their likeness would be important. On the ethers we could read the similar energy. But the physical likeness is a true miracle. Do you not get confused Ronan?" Raymond jokingly nudged him.

"No. No!!" He laughed. "I would know my Sari anywhere. My bonnie lass. No one can really compare. I would die for her."

"Now *that* my friend is love. *Le Grande Amour*. How beautiful it is to see the love between you."

"Thankyou. Yes. She is everything to me. Serena our daughter too. I miss her and wish to return soon. But I am compelled by what you teach here, and feel I am learning all the time. Being alongside Sari helps my awareness. I find my own senses sharpening. And this. Your church. I find I feel at home, even though I do not understand it all. There is much to learn. I feel like a chrysalis. In the embryonic stages of a spiritual breakthrough. I feel too my destiny is here in The Castle. Like Sari. She brought me here for a reason."

"Yes! The timing of her *Consolamentum* will be crucial to all our destinies. I would say 'I fear!' But I celebrate it. Welcome it. We Cathars believe in the process. Yes! Like the chrysalis goes through stages to become the butterfly, so we cocoon and ponder and learn. Formation transmutes into reformation. The physical human being begins to disappear. The basic wants, needs, desires become superfluous. Of course, you need to eat. But the first stage sees you looking up, away from pure survival mode, to something elevated, heavenly. Your Spirit ascends to its right place. Your 'high' self. Your 'Best' self if you like. Your Divine 'You.' The *real* you. The *consolamentum* brings this new beginning where we die to the old and become renewed by the light. Life truly begins. Your Soul is purified, liberated from its imperfections. You are *Perfecti!*"

"I start to understand it I think." Responded Ronan. "So much of it is humility and a willingness to learn and receive. A dying to the old self to embrace the Divine Soul. Frederick and Sari talked about this all the time in Scotland. They seemed to know The Cathar Way without having been here. How is that possible?"

"Ah! Well it is in Sari's very Soul. She *is* The Way. Part of the sacred lineage, who just '*know*'. As you have seen so many times. *Esclarmode* is the same. From as young as two or three years old, she radiated a light we had not really seen before."

"Yes. I gather Sari was the same. Nothing I have ever seen before. That is true."

Ronan and Raymond would talk and talk and talk. At the dinner table, late and night, over the horses, doing the rounds of the *Château*. Sari saw a true bond between them. She could see what a mentor role Raymond was playing in Ronan's development. Certainly, his demeanour during that hurried meeting on their night of arrival must have reflected a high dose of stress and worry about the soldiers in the valley.

It took a good few weeks before she discovered exactly what it *was* that ailed him that night. One of his conversations revealed the startling truth. Earlier that day they had had a meeting of the leaders and a ceremony in the octagonal chapel. During what was a lengthy discussion one of the *Perfecti* known for his impromptu visions started to speak.

Whenever Alpais spoke everyone fell silent. His accuracy and vision always astounded them. All his utterances came true within a few weeks. Sometimes he would describe people, actions, events. Usually he came up with some counter response if that were needed. If the prophesy was a warning or a challenge.

"I see all of us. Singing. Euphoric. Full of love.
Peaceful and calm and accepting.

334

In the valley below our fate awaits us. Some will run away in fear through the caves. Not many. Only five. One girl among us will be assigned the special mission. She must flee. She will escape and not die. All of us will die. We will choose to die. We will delight in doing so this time. Many of us will be weary by this time.

March.

"Beware the Ides of March."

On the full moon.

The night is crisp and clear.

The soldiers with the rock machine enter and burn all they can here. The stables ignite quickly. Arrows rain down upon us. More than we have ever seen. We retreat into the Chapel for respite knowing it will not be long. They will find us there. The few that remain.

Esclarmonde radiant.

Defiant.

The "girl with yellow hair. Gone. Her husband here among us.

Perfecti..

They see us calm and peaceful and in surrender. They do not know how to react. Two weeks of living with the soldiers as they watch us deciding what to do. They now control the running of the Château."

Raymond blanched at these words. His beloved *Montségur* under siege. In the moment of surrender.

Why can they just not leave us alone?

He now knew what he had to do. The "girl with yellow hair" must be immanent. Preparations needed to be made. If this prophecy were all true, and he knew it would be, he had to organized removal of The Grail, The Emerald, and the manuscripts to the forest. The burial site was ready. This must be done as soon as possible, and "the girl with yellow hair" must be shown the place within weeks of her arrival. She and her husband must know the caves well enough to navigate them at night. Possibly she would have to leave during February. Well in advance of "The Ides of March."

Alpais continued the magnificent but horrible account. Magnificent for the courage and resolve they would all show. Horrible for the grim ending they would all face.

"We are told we can leave after the two-week truce. We live alongside each other while terms are made. The Templars help us and work against The King. Their interests are the same as ours. We will pray and fast. We do not need to decide what to do we already know. Some of us will want the consolamentum. They will allow us to worship but will watch closely. Some of them will convert to our beliefs and die with us. Twenty-two of them, and the husband of "yellow hair" will receive the final blessings. Thirty of us will agree their terms and will have to wear the "yellow cross" as penance. We forgive them in advance. They will continue the cause in secret. But they make a grave choice.

Bishop Bertrand will lead us down. Raymond, Corba, your mother, Marquèse de Fourquevaux, your wife, Esclamonde, your daughter. All your family Raymond. Proud leaders of us all.

At the front of the procession Esclamonde!

The heat emanating from the valley is intense. No stakes. A Pyre. We have agreed to this. We will line up and jump. Some will stand around the edges. Others will jump when the flames are high. They just watch. Knowing we will do this. No force. No screams. We just quietly jump. To bear witness."

"In seven hundred years the laurel will turn green again."

PART FOUR

2022

CHAPTER FORTY-THREE
The Twining

Sarah was on stage. This was her first Ted talk. She had been booked to explain her life path and its possible connection to The Royal Blood lines. To her surprise her work had been recognised the world over. She had begun to write books, speak at events and hold workshops. She had not expected this turn of events. Really it felt like The Divine might be finished with her as she did not look likely to continue The Legacy Line. Pregnancy eluded her. Her relationships had not taken the direction of babies or commitment. Perhaps it all stopped with her. She was not sure what it meant. But she was fast becoming too worldly wise to even think of having a child. She was not sure this was a world she wanted to bring a baby into. She recognised it was not her choice ultimately. The Divine could spark up a connection even beyond natural years if it had to. But physically it was no longer and desire within her as a woman to procreate. Sometimes she wondered about the implications of not continuing The Sangreal energy. Technically her sister would by default have the honour, and she had already had a daughter, who did resemble Sarah significantly. She wondered if the powers-that-be had organised the lineage another way this time. Increasingly it felt that this might be the case. Ciara, her sister's child was indeed showing signs of having The Gift. Perhaps Sarah had bypassed the procreation assignment as the enormity of her task in other ways had surpassed all expectations.

These thoughts flashed through her mind as she prepared to speak. She composed herself in confidence and peace, knowing in this environment she was loved and accepted. This was only a short account designed to inspire a conversation. Many students in the audience were spiritual students, seeking to know more about reincarnation and the cycles of life.

How were the repeating patterns in history, in our personal lives, and on the world stage, steering our lessons and our future?

History repeats itself
It has to.
Nobody listens.

A Steve Turner poem from the eighties, shown to her by her parents when she was a teen popped into her head. She decided to do an impromptu start with this. A moment of inspiration. She was always interested in repeating patterns and the sensations of familiarity and knowing when experiencing these. She began.

"Renowned healer and numerologist, Lila Beck once told me that I was about to enter a phase in my life, where I would sort out karmas with many of the guys I had been married to, or otherwise linked up

339

with, in other life times.

Clearly, I have mixed with many troubadours, poets, artists, and musicians, in the past, judging by the men I have attracted, and been attracted to, in this lifetime. I sit loose to the theory of past lives. I am not sure whether to fully believe it, or how much importance to give it. But there certainly seems to be a precedent for meeting up with people, we knew in other times that we all experience. A magnetic pull and resonance, which means that the same energies hone-in on each other every time we incarnate.

On a soul level, past lives have a resonance. We can all relate to those meetings where we connect with someone, and there is so much familiarity about them, even though technically they are just strangers. These meetings have happened many times in my life. But I sit on the fence with the "past life" debacle. I believe we are meant to be present in the here and now. I think the theories can sound a bit odd, and I do understand that some people cannot get their heads around the concept. As with all things keeping an open mind is what works best. You would probably go mad if you over analysed such things. But when you develop psychically, you certainly *do* become much more aware of the energy echoes which haunt and influence us from other times.

When we pass on, I strongly believe that life goes on, and that energy cannot be extinguished. Everything is energy, so clearly, the energy is transmuted into another form. People who are deceased leave a residue energy for quite some time, and of course they live on in the hearts of loved ones. It would make complete sense that we would find the energies which resonate best with us, each time we incarnate. Whether we come back again for another round is apparently up to us. What I do keep hearing is that there are many people working through very loaded karmas in a bid not to have to return to the earth plane again. "No thank you," is the consensus.

I personally do not think there has to be a contradiction between

Christian faith and a belief in reincarnation. I am sure Christian and Buddhist philosophers have yet to reconcile the two. I believe it can be done. The disciples asked Christ if he was Elijah reincarnated, so they obviously thought it was possible.

Edward S. Casey, "the sleeping prophet," did much research on the validity of past lives, and their coherent connection with faith in Christ. Born in 1939, Casey, channelled a great many spiritual books, and worked on complex case studies, particularly medical and those involving children. He was an incredible medical intuitive and knew the exact day he was going to pass and how. He could have a patient sit down in front of him, and just know the correct diagnosis and treatment. Psychic healers like Edward Casey, give people like me validation and a historical context. Not enough is known about such healers, aside from what they write about themselves, or channel for their patients and clients. There really is a case for much more open-minded research to be done on these comprehensive Gifts, and their application. The potential is immense.

Casey did not find belief in reincarnation to be conflicted with his personal faith. He felt past life theories provided a context and setting for the current life being experienced. He did not feel it was advisable to overly focus on who an individual had once been. This philosophical view is not out there so that we can brag or speculate about who we once were. It is there to provide a framework enabling us to understand the consequences of patterns and choices. It really is all about personal responsibility in the here and now.

Only in this way, does past life theory have any relevance or valid application. We have the free will to choose how we apply the lessons. Past lives provide an indicator and framework of our potential and possibilities, should we wish to understand awareness of our psyche on these levels. What we experience in this lifetime is not dictated by inevitability. We are not obliged to repeat patterns, replay, or balance all the karma. We are best advised to be personally savvy, wise, and responsible. It is more a case of "know thyself," than a provided reason to panic or over analyse.

I was told by someone quite respected in this field that my name has always been Sarah down through all my lifetimes; and that I was something to do with the Holy Grail bloodline. This was forwarded as a way of explaining the pressure I was under regarding my public work, personal life, and all its accompanying challenges. To me it sounded like potentially loopy talk, but you never know.

Someone else, said that I had always been a woman, and had floated and wafted through all my lifetimes, like some ethereal, otherworldly goddess. I will just stay mildly amused at that theory also. Again, it could well be the case; but "how does it help me *now*," would be the main question.

A former colleague in The Psychic Society Benny, noticed during our travels in Europe, that ethereal muses in my likeness were depicted on many of the ceilings, wall hangings, and portraits of stately homes, palaces, and castles. It became an on-going joke. where would I be found next? I personally resonate with Botticelli paintings, and have always loved *The Birth of Venus* in particular. So, I will admit to *that* much.

I sit loose to all of this, as I think it could give you inflated airs and graces. But the study of past lives undoubtedly has curiosity value. Energy echoes and patterns through history make for fascinating speculation. But I believe in living in the present time, and think it is important that we focus on *now*. Giving the past too much thought can be distracting and detrimental. Leaping further back into past lives, without pointed direction can be even more seductive. But there is an opening for healing through correct recognition of the source of our pain, as it plays out in this lifetime. Past lives can be invaluable to ascertain the trigger points, and deep causes of what is playing out before us.

A friend of mine, who is an expert in karmic astrology, has

342

pinpointed links in my natal chart to Botticelli, the Pre-Raphaelites, Nostradamus, Biblical times, Tudor times, and The Cathars. I resonate with all of these, as I had psychically picked up the connections myself. It is interesting that they were then confirmed without me saying anything through a study of my natal chart. Again, at this superficial level it is observational, and curious rather than profoundly important.

I can certainly take on board the Tudor lifetime, as I was fascinated by the Tudors at school. I used to stare at a family tree history of the kings and queens of England on my bedroom wall and was particularly obsessed with the Tudors. This was a teenage girl's compulsion, which took on a new meaning when I had a hideous and inexplicable panic attack in Hampton Court aged eleven. I did not know what overwhelmed me, but I just knew she I to get out of there as quickly as possible. My parents were not amused. But my intuitive Nan understood and came to sit with me on the banks of The Thames, while the rest of the party traipsed around that "hell hole," in unnatural heat.

When I returned to Hampton Court with a colleague Benny on a spiritual pilgrimage trail, he tuned into the situation using his mediumistic abilities. He felt psychically that my energy was linked to Jane Seymour, the only wife King Henry VIII had really loved. She was the only one of Henry's wives who had a Queen's funeral and is buried beside him in Saint George's Cathedral at Windsor Castle.

Jane Seymour had died prematurely of complications giving birth to her son Edward. She went through an uncomfortable time struggling to hold onto life in Hampton Court, expiring defeated and deflated as she left behind her beloved husband and son. Benny himself felt he connected energetically to Jane's son Edward VI. So apparently, I had an energetic imprint operating as Benny's mother. Makes sense.

Such theories pertaining to past lives are complex. There are many who feel connected to John of Arc, or Mozart for example. These could be explained through a theory of soul fragments, or it could mean we are all crazy trying to pin our identities on historical figures. We will have to reserve judgement on that all this as it is not definitively provable.

There are many recorded case studies and lifetimes recounted under hypnosis. Arthur Guirdham did some comprehensive research on *The Cathars and Reincarnation*. He established through research and hypnosis that there was a substantial link between former Cathar incarnates and the West Country in the United Kingdom. He found through many recorded regression accounts that there was a pattern of those who had been around during the Cathar persecutions, reincarnating in the Bristol in particular. Such observations are anecdotal. They are indicative, but do not stand as substantiated proof. Guirdham was criticized by colleagues for his sweeping general comments, which defied science and elevated the supernatural. Does it mean he was wrong? No. Is it verifiable? Also "no."

Psychically, energetically, and spiritually this is a fascinating topic. Moira Lumberg, a respected medium from Ireland, pinpointed the Cathar lifetime as crucial to me. It is certainly interesting that I was raised in the West Country, and Bristol area. So according to Guirdham, she was onto something. In the middle of my tests and trials, I went to see her for guidance. She told me the overriding lifetime I needed to heal was the one where I had committed suicide in Paris out of loneliness. The Cathar lifetime. I have to say something resonated deep within when she said this. It was kind of shocking and I was also somewhat indignant when she said it. It also felt unreal, and not what I had signed up for. I had certainly been through stretches of extreme loneliness, not to mention disappointment. Did this automatically link me back to a Cathar lifetime which I needed to heal? I was not sure.

In the lifetime Moira identified, I had been a well-respected healer. I had escaped the horrors of the *Chateau* de Montsegur, and the Cathar

344

persecutions; only to self-destruct later in Paris from grief, desolation, and a broken heart. The Siege of *Montsegur* was a nine-month siege on the Cathars, perpetrated by the French Royal Forces. The Castle eventually surrendered in March1244, and all the remaining Cathars, who refused to renounce their Gnosticism, were burned, and murdered in a mass grave bonfire.

Many perished during these persecutions, well over two hundred souls lost their lives. I was allegedly one of only four people who escaped, carrying with them the secrets of the Holy Grail. I left behind my father, husband, and son to die in the flames. The man I loved, who also loved me, was in an arranged marriage, living locally. He was a prominent Prince, famous in the region, who could do nothing to break free from convention, and his material circumstances, despite the passion between us. I was commissioned by the Cathar community to carry and rescue *The Book of Secrets*.

The heretics of the Languedoc, the Cathars, possessed the book of love, and etheric writings which expanded the consciousness, and contained the hidden knowledge, which only the alchemical elite could handle. These secrets could not fall into the hands of the enemy who would decimate them without mercy. I fled to Paris and set up as a healer for a couple of years, before succumbing to incredible loneliness. Apparently, I hung myself out of sadness, despite being the herbalist "of some repute."

Another past life expert did not agree with the part about "hanging myself," when I ran this by him. I would like to say he is correct on that. But you never know. Again, no proofs either way. Overall, I have to say there was deep familiarity, and a resonance sparked in my soul, when Moira was recounting this lifetime.

The account had some uncanny echoes in my life since arriving in Dublin. The PhD I was signed up for in the Department of Philosophy was on Gnosticism. I was fast becoming a "healer of some repute;" and I was excruciatingly lonely; in love with an unavailable, local married man, akin to Irish royalty. Also, it always puzzled me that, despite struggling with A level French at school. I came back fluent in French after a five-day trip to Paris, just in time to get a reasonable grade in the summer. Maybe something unblocked within me. All I know is, my French teacher was incredulous.

This reading on The Cathar lifetime was incredibly powerful and has haunting echoes for me in this lifetime. I think we know the truth when we hear it. When such a crucial lifetime is pinpointed, healing is essential. Really, such information is a gift, and indicates where breakthrough opportunities might be. There is no denying that a pattern is playing out. What the outcome and resolution will be is anyone's guess. This provides the ultimate transformative opportunity.

Labyrinth by Kate Mosse, *The Da Vinci Code* by Dan Brown, and *Daughters of The Grail* by Elizabeth Chadwick, are books which speak to my soul. These books demonstrate the truth of The Holy Grail. It is not a cup, but a process. It could indeed be a "Sangreal Liineage" also. In pursuit of the Holy Grail, we are perfected. The alchemy hones our consciousness, and our souls, so that we step out of the purging fire, ascended and radiant.

I have seen much evidence that past lives are relevant to what happens to us in this lifetime. It is a concept difficult to prove, and yet energetically it makes so much sense. I find in client readings that past life impressions filter through, and that these are often responsible for the dynamics which make people feel stuck. The deepest healing takes place, when these lifetimes are exposed, and transformed. A person can thereby be fundamentally redeemed, if not totally transmogrified. At the very least echoes down through our timelines offer patterns to break, karmas to balance, and connections to heal.

Where you feel an immediate inexplicable resonance with someone pay special attention. It could be your Ronan or Sarah come to find you!"

Let go, and let God...

ABOUT THE AUTHOR

SARAH DELAMERE HURDING IS ONE OF IRELAND'S AND AMERICA'S BEST-KNOWN MYSTICS. A SEER, HEALER, LIFE COACH, WRITER, AUTHOR, ACADEMIC, FORMER CBS RADIO HOST AND WORLD PUJA NETWORK PRESENTER, OM TIMES FEATURED WRITER AND CONSCIOUSNESS FACILITATOR, SARAH BRINGS A FULL RANGE OF TALENTS TO THE TABLE.

Sarah is known for her accuracy, healing and manifesting abilities. Louis Walsh and Simon Cowell were stunned into silence when Sarah predicted the full line up of Irish Popstars SIX. She read for 32 talented kids and accurately named the final six. Sarah has also have been publicly recognised as an effective healer. She can lift pain with her hands pretty much instantly, and has helped clients with all kinds of issues and conditions. Her specialities are lifting pain and depression, as well as energy boosts, major clearings and resets using distance healing techniques. Once you sign up with Sarah, her commitment to you is relentless and strong. She works with you 24/7 with advice, guidance, energy, prayer and mutually agreed intentions for days, weeks and months depending on your needs. Find Sarah at sarahdelamer.com

#mermaidmagic

Acknowledgments

Endless gratitude for my wonderful Father

Roger Frederick Hurding

www.ingramcontent.com/pod-product-compliance
Lightning Source LLC
Chambersburg PA
CBHW071519260626
47170CB00002B/432